Aphrodite's Army

Johanna Sandstrom

Paperback: 978-1-966652-80-9
Hardcover: 978-1-968667-17-7
eBook: 978-1-966652-81-6
Library of Congress Control Number: 2025906002

This is a work of fiction.

Ordering Information:

Prime Seven Media
518 Landmann St.
Tomah City, WI 54660

Printed in the United States of America

To all the women in the world,
This is my gift to you,
An offer of the key that unlocks your light
and helps you find your way home.

Table of Contents

Chapter 1: The Rose 1

Chapter 2: Ayla 16

Chapter 3: Elena 38

Chapter 4: Phoebe 60

Chapter 5: The Orchid 84

Chapter 6: The Magician 108

Chapter 7: Temperance 129

Chapter 8: The Tower...152

Chapter 9: The Lotus.. 175

Chapter 10: The Fool 195

Chapter 11: The Chariot...221

Chapter 12: The Moon 246

Chapter 13: The Anemone 271

Chapter 14: The Sun 305

Chapter 15: The Plumeria..341

Dear reader,

I am so happy that you want to hear what I have to say.

I'd like to tell you a story about three magical women. They are not the princesses from your childhood, nor are they goddesses from your prayers; they are not impossibly perfect. They are just like you. Quite normal. But how normal are you, anyway? Within each of us lives a hope, a dream, a light. In every waking moment of this life, you have dreamed that you could be brave like that warrior, beautiful like the princess, and full of love like the goddess. But maybe you are? Maybe you are everything that you dream of; you just need to open your heart and accept the key to see it.

We are not mere dwellers on this planet that we call home. We are its caretakers. We are the current in the river, the wind in the trees, the sun that kisses its surface. We are the driving force that creates change, that dares to see ourselves for what we are. The light on Gaia's skin, the love in her beating heart, and the power in her streams. When you see your inner worth, you also know that you already have everything it takes to have the life you dream of and love every aspect of it with all your heart.

I want to tell you a story. It has been building up in me over quite some time, but I needed to create changes and walk through a spiritual awakening to grow my love for the world and myself before I could muster the courage to write it down and share it with you.

I want to invite you into a world where all the goddesses, all the divine beings, all of the angels, all of you, fit together to weave a delicate golden quilt of mysteries, love, light, and sisterhood.

For what if everything you dream of could be real and you were the hero all along?

I wish you all the love in the world,

Johanna

CHAPTER 1

The Rose

In the darkness, she could sense a soft fog, so she slowly opened her eyes. She could not make out where she was. She was sitting on a marble floor. Her fingers caressed the creases in the stone to make out the space around her. She could hear water slowly dripping. Her feet were bare, and she was dressed in a silky white dress that draped her around her body. She stood up, fixed her dress, and adjusted the golden snake belt that was wrapped around her waist. She fumbled with the golden bangles around her wrist as she scanned the space around her for clues of her whereabouts. The bangles were beautifully crafted and decorated with crystals. She even had a small golden headpiece. Apparently, she was maxed out on gems.

If only she knew why. The sound of the water had come from a small stream and fountain that moved the water softly alongside a long corridor. The walls were also marbled, and the soft pink glow from the candles echoed in peach on the corridor's beige walls. She followed the direction of the water and the warmth of the light and walked slowly in still confusion until she finally reached an arched doorway. It didn't have a door, nor a knob or a handle. Instead, it was filled with a fog so thick it was impossible to make out what was on the other side. She looked at it for a brief moment, trying to envision what would be waiting on the other side of the door and if she dared enter. She glanced back at the corridor she had just walked down. 'Could it be that bad? And what was the alternative?' She gathered courage, took a breath, and walked through.

On the other side, the light was so bright she could see it through her closed eyes. As she opened them, she was astonished by the vastness of the room she was in. It took her a few seconds just to calibrate from the cool softness of the corridor to the vibrant warmth of this space. It looked like a palace, but it appeared to be outdoors. There were palm trees in big ceramic pots and flowers of every kind hanging as a draped curtain around doorways and over the railings. She noticed that she was standing on the second floor overlooking a circular open space in the middle. She walked up to the railing and looked down to see a beautiful white marble courtyard with a big fountain in the middle. It was filled with roses, but most importantly, lots and lots of women, as elegant as she. Their buzzing voices filled the air. She noticed the staircase and started walking towards it. She glanced up at the ceiling as she walked. It was constructed of white beams that made out an elegant floral artwork that framed the sky. Huge white marble pillars joined together to form a round construction that held the ceiling up. The upper floor, where she was standing, was formed like a moon shape around the space, and to her slight left, she could see what looked like a stage carved in the same marble as the rest. It was round, and from up here, she could see the rose mandala that covered the entire stage. But what was even more amazing was that there were thousands of women dressed just like her. Silky white gowns and golden embellishments. Some were chatting, others were looking just as confused and astonished as she was, wondering where they were and why. She finally noticed the staircase and walked over to it. She looked out over the crowd, feeling a smile spreading across her face. She had never seen this many women in the same place in her life. She felt her feet skipping a beat alongside her heart as she made her way down the stairs. By the last step, she felt as if she was flying, but was abruptly startled by a beautiful blonde woman in a glitter dress and a clipboard.

"Hi there, what's your name?" She said cheerfully with a big white smile while clicking her pen and glancing down at her list. "Ehm, yes hi, I'm Ayla", she felt a brief flush of blush without really knowing why, and glanced around the room while she waited for her to continue. "Ah, there you are. Found you!" She looked at Ayla, her sunny smile beaming with warmth. "You are very welcome. Here is your rose, feel free to socialise and meet the others before we start." Her blue eyes once again met Ayla's as she handed her the rose she was holding. "Em. Sorry," Ayla cleared her throat, "Where am I? And what is it that is about to start?" But the woman was silent, smiled, and moved on to the woman behind her. Ayla hadn't even noticed that there was a queue behind her; she was still bewildered in her own mind, trying to grasp what was happening. But now she was holding a rose. It was soft blue, with its brim slightly darker than the white center. Each petal was velvety soft, and the stem was smooth. Holding it helped her to balance her mind and heart. She closed her eyes for a second and took a deep breath in and out. As she looked up, she saw a woman walking towards her.

"Hi, you look a bit lost", the woman said. Ayla smiled softly and didn't have a chance to answer before she continued. "Don't worry, we all are. None of us knows what is happening. Some of us have been waiting for hours. Do you know what's going on?" "No, I don't. I only just arrived, but it's all very confusing. I mean, it's absolutely amazing, but it's a surreal experience".

"Who's to say what's real and what's surreal? I'm Elena, by the way. What's your name?" She had so much wisdom in her eyes and a radiant smile. Ayla looked up at the sky on the ceiling, chuckled in excitement, and answered.

"I'm Ayla. That is so true. You never know what is and what is not. You are so wise."

Another woman walked towards them, holding glasses. "Hi, I got us some drinks." She gave each other a glass and continued, "Hi, I'm Phoebe". She then whisked her frizzy curls off her shoulder and corrected a golden comb that kept her hair from her face. Ayla stared at her in amazement. She was so cheerful, and they were both so nice. Elena turned to both of them and held up her glass. "Cheers!" They chimed and smiled at each other as they tasted the drink.

"Mmm. Raspberry bubbly. Very nice," Ayla exclaimed while smacking her lips slightly.

It's not alcohol, is it?

"Oh, I don't think you can have alcohol in a dream," Elena said cheerfully with a small laugh, sipping through.

"We're in a dream?" Ayla looked surprised.

"Of course, we're in a dream. Look at this place, look at you!" Phoebe exclaimed with pure joy.

"Well, half-dream really, I think," Elena added.

Phoebe continued with her theory. "I've been here for hours, so I've had a chance to talk to a few other women here. Naturally, no one knows what is going on, but everyone has the same theory. Some sort of dream state, but it all seems too real to be just a dream. We're still figuring it out." Ayla looked at her with big eyes, trying to take in what she was saying. Phoebe talked with her hands and gestured in the air with her glass in one hand and her blue rose in her other. Ayla was amazed that she hadn't spilled the drink yet.

"All in good time, I think." Elena said calmly and continued, "I believe we will know more in just a few moments."

Ayla finished her drink and offered to take everyone's empty glasses and put them on a nearby table. As she did so, the lights in the room shifted. She looked around. Candles were being lit throughout the space. She hurried back to her new friends as a voice suddenly echoed through the room. A woman entered centre stage, and now they could see her glorious yellow gown and large iridescent wings resting gracefully by her sides, enhancing her crystalline aura. Her golden blonde hair was structured into a low braided bun, adorned with an extravagant white crown.

Divine feminine, High Priestesses, Lightworkers.

We waited patiently in silence for the moment when you would be ready. And now, you are finally here, ready to embark on this journey with us.

You should congratulate yourselves for having come this far.

Before you stand the Ascended Masters and Goddesses who once walked this same path. We have spent lifetimes as supervisors to offer love, light, and hope to all of humanity on Earth. You should look at us as humble guides, although I know that isn't easy at this point in your journey.

Ayla made eye contact with Elena and Phoebe to get a glimpse of their reaction. They were as astonished as she was and equally confused, but ready to hear more. "Who had they been waiting for and why?" she thought as she looked around at the rest of the women, trying to find a trace of knowledge amongst the crowd. Some were nodding as if they knew, others were showing signs of discomfort, fiddling with dresses, hair, and lips, and most had their attention locked on the stage, waiting for more context. Soon enough, the woman continued and put our questions to rest.

"We have watched you for so long struggling in your lives, trying to find meaning and courage. You have lived in the shadows for thousands of years, facing fear, anger, and grief every day."

There was a stream of noise going through the crowd as everyone confirmed and agreed.

"Well, not really thousands. I'm not that old, " Phoebe joked to the others.

Sophia looked out at the crowd and let the reaction rest before she continued. More women showed up on the stage, wearing wonderful gowns in all the colours of the rainbow. They lined up behind her and allowed her to continue her speech.

"You do not remember, but you all already know why you are here. You made that commitment long ago to join us here today in our quest to bring back the feminine light to Earth."

There was another wind of noise running through the crowd, and yet again, she let it settle before continuing. Just standing there, peacefully looking out at everyone. "After thousands of years of being pushed into shadows, never being allowed to stand in the light, receive love, and embrace life. The time has come for us to rise, redeem ourselves from the shadows, and take back what is rightfully ours". A few women at the back started giving their best feminine warrior screams, and one woman yelled something about paint and feathers. Someone got ramped up and yelled some slur about the patriarch.

But this time, Angel Sophia interrupted with an authoritarian voice.

"We are not here to cause chaos and disruption. We are here to restore order." Her tone of voice was serious but remained mild.

The confusion was hanging like a thick blanket in the air. How can we take back our power without a fight? What does it even mean to redeem ourselves from the shadows?

Angel Sophia stood graciously still in peaceful silence as Aphrodite stepped forward to speak. Dressed in a soft pink satin gown and strawberry blonde hair braided loosely and held together with a pale blue ribbon.

"You already have the wisdom that you need inside you. But I know this is not an easy journey, and you have all been chosen because of your strength. We know that you are capable. You also know that you are capable, which is why you agreed to this. But none of us can do it unless we work together. Many of us who stand before you have once been where you are standing now, facing remembrance of your divinity, power, and light."

Mary Magdalene stepped forward as well, her brown hair loosely tied to the back and held with a magnificent red rose that matched her flowy red gown.

"We believe in you, and you must believe in yourselves. But we know that you have a lot of work ahead and many challenges to overcome. The way back to love is not easy. Therefore, we will all be here as your mentors throughout this journey. We will guide you, teach you, and comfort you, so that you can eventually connect you to your highest purpose."

Elena whispered to the others: "What's the highest purpose?" But both Ayla and Phoebe just shook their shoulders with a perplexed look in their eyes.

Aphrodite added.

"There is only you. There is only us. You must find your truth, speak your truth, be your truth. You already know who you are, you just must remember, and you can only remember by being who you are."

Phoebe blurted out in a low voice, "Wow, thanks, that sure helped."

There was a murmur across the crowd. Apparently, no one had understood a word she just said. What did that even mean, and what was the goal and end result that they were supposed to do or create?

"All in good time. The information must be given at the pace at which you are able to receive. Do not rush, this is not a competition, and there is no prize for a winner. We all win together when we are all ready."

Ayla looked over at the others. "I really don't get it," she said with a slight panic in her eyes. It was mildly comforting that everyone else was just as confused. What exactly were we asked to do, and what were they supposed to achieve? What was her role? Why was she here?

Mary Magdalene spoke again: "We all are going to help you, and each of us will be assigned to different tasks. We will be with you every day, guiding you in your daily life to help you find your way".

Angel Sophia took the word again.

"You are now about to receive a cup of rose herb tea. Before you drink, we must join in the prayer of self-reflection and unconditional love. I will wait a few minutes while you receive your drinks."

A group of angels in glitter dresses spread out in the crowd with small golden trays to serve small cups of tea.

I am the golden light
I am divine, so bright
I am the love I long for
I love myself for all that I am
I forgive myself for all that I have done

I move forward in grace
I love you
I am you. You are me. We are one
And so, it is. It is done.

Now, take a sip of your tea. You have all received the same blend of tea, but the taste will be different for each of you, depending on what chakra you are called to lead. Once you have determined the taste, you can step out into the garden and look for the gazebo marked with your chakra. To help us work through our collective wounds, we all need to work together, and that is why we will place you in teams. How you proceed will be determined by the work you do and how quickly you pace, but you will have to be assigned to one team to start with, so that you know where to begin and get proper guidance as your journey commences.

She then proceeded to shout out the instructions.

If you get a lotus, you go to the crown,
If you get lavender, you go to the third eye.
If you get ginger, you go to the throat
If you get a rose, you go to the heart
If you get star anise, you go to the solar plexus
If you get cardamom, you go to the sacral
If you get cinnamon, you go to the root

Someone waved their hand in the air and interrupted in a terrified voice, "What do you do if you can't taste anything?"

If you don't taste anything or you taste them all, you come and see me. That means you got one of the outer chakras, and I will help you sort that out.

Ayla looked at her tea and tasted it. "I think I got ginger, what did you get?"

"Definitely lavender," Phoebe answered.

"And I got rose," Elena added. That means we all have different chakras.

"Throat, third eye, and heart," Ayla said, feeling slightly sad that they didn't get the same. "Shall we look for our gazebos together?

The others agreed, so they walked towards the end of the auditorium and stopped looking out over the garden. There were distant mountains and lush forests on the horizon, but the garden itself was extensive. They walked down the steps and onto a pathway paved with smooth white granite. There was a big, planted area in the middle that was divided into sections to enable crossing to both pathways. All were lined with a low buxbom hedge with big rose bushes, bougainvillea, and many other flowers. Along each side, cypress trees rose to the sky and hid all of the gazebos from their view. They walked along the pavement together, admiring the blush peonies and white lilies. Soon, they reached a corner that revealed a passage to the first gazebo. That was the stellar gateway chakra, so they kept on walking. They passed a few pink cherry trees and eventually arrived at the next gazebo, but it said "Soul star" on the sign. They looked at each other, and Ayla asked, "How many chakras are there, actually?". Elena thought, and Phoebe started counting the entrances that apparently marked each gazebo. "Apparently, there are 12," she concluded. "12? I thought there were only 7?" Elena said and looked surprised. Phoebe corrected her, "Didn't you hear Angel Sophia say that those who didn't taste anything should come with her? So there must be 5 more that we don't know about."

"Alright, why don't we walk to the other side of the courtyard and see what chakras are lined up opposite these. Maybe that way, we can figure out which direction to walk towards."

Ayla went ahead and read the sign on the opposite side. "It says Earth Star chakra here". Elena looked around, trying to make sense of the three they had already passed. "Ok, I think I got it. Let's see what the next one says." They walked a few metres down the pavement until they reached the next entrance. "This one says Root." Elena said, "Ok, I see." That must mean that the one standing alone at the far end by is heart and the two next to it are the throat and third eye." They walked over and found that to be true.

They reached the third eye. "It was so lovely to meet you both. I hope we see each other again," Phoebe said and started walking down the passage towards the gazebo. "Good luck!" Elena yelled, and Phoebe waved in response. Ayla had the one next to hers, so they, too, took their goodbyes as Elena continued to heart.

Ayla stopped in front of her passage for a few seconds. All the pathways were created like a tunnel filled with climbing roses in red, pink, and white. It wasn't a long passage, but it was enough to get enchanted by the sweet scent and vibrant colours. She reached her gazebo and walked up the steps. Five women had found their way there already and had taken their seats on the bench that clung to the walls. Ayla greeted them and found a good place to rest among the comfort of big blue velvet cushions. They all sat in silence, not knowing what to say, as they waited for others to come. Soon, the gazebo was filled with women, with the last one having to squeeze in a seat on the bench. They looked at each other awkwardly. One of the other women laughed anxiously, and another asked if anyone could guess what was going to happen. No one had any idea, so instead they just chatted while waiting for instructions. After a while, they heard someone approaching their gazebo, and they looked at the entrance in silence. A woman appeared, dressed in a silky white gown and a large golden headpiece that held back her black curls. She smiled at them all and took center stage.

"I am Athena. You all must be wondering why you're here, and more importantly, why you have gotten this chakra. While everyone needs to work through every chakra in their body, we all need to divide up for the sake of efficiency. Also, we, as Ascended Masters, need to focus on our strengths so that the combined whole becomes one strong force. You understand?" She nodded to emphasise her question.

The other mumbled together that they got it, so she continued.

"What we need to do now as a first step is to open your throat chakra." She looked around the room to determine the level of confusion.

"We open our throat chakra in three ways. Number one, we share our story. You will be guided by me and other guides to share this with your family and friends when you wake up. We will do the other two together now.

We will start by sitting down in the lotus position on the floor. The women sat down awkwardly with their dresses flowing out to the sides, making it look like they were all one big white wavy cloud. With their arms stretched out and their head tilted slightly backwards, they followed Athena's instructions to breathe in and breathe out. They then placed their hands on their hearts and continued to soak in the soft air around them, breathing in unison. After a few minutes, Athena told them to add a sound. Breathing in, breathing out - "Ha". Breathing in, breathing out "Ho". She continued giving instructions to clear the airways and gain courage for the next step.

"And now we sing. One, two, three."

But one girl objected, "Oh, I can't sing." A few others nodded while an older woman said, "Won't we disturb the others? There are no walls, so they will hear us."

But Athena just said, "So let them. Let them hear you. Who cares if you can't sing, or think you can't sing? Who cares if anyone hears you? That is actually the point here.

The only one getting in the way of you using your voice is you."

They all agreed that she was, of course, right. So, they collected themselves and tried again. This time, they all sang, but their voices were shy and kept at bay. Athena stopped them.

"Ok, good. Now let's try again, but louder."

They collected their energies again and sang. This time, it was a bit louder; it was a pure sound in one tune. Athena smiled and said, "That was very good. I am pleased with you all." Now, one last time before we are done. They repeated the exercise and took a deep breath again to sing at a higher pitch.

This time, the sound rose to the ceiling. They all continued singing. The women of the other chakras had been instructed to do the same, and soon their voices extended past the ceilings. The etheric sound rose above the courtyard and the palace and echoed through the entire valley in a mesmerising tune.

When they were done, you could hear a cheer, clapping and laughing, running through the entire palace garden. Athena's whole face was beaming with joy and gratitude.

"Oh, that was absolutely wonderful!" She said, clasping her hands. "That sounded more etheric than I ever could have imagined. Lovely!"

She was attuned to an etheric sound that came from the palace and added, "That is all we have to do for today. Very well done, I am so proud of you. I will leave you now. You have to stay rested here, waiting for your consciousness to wake up. I will see you later." She smiled and walked back through the garden. The women looked at each other and smiled softly. "Until we meet again."

CHAPTER 2

Ayla

As the alarm sang its tune, her hand crawled out from under the pillow and pressed snooze. She felt as if she had been awoken from the deepest sleep. Just ten more minutes. She dozed off again.

Ten minutes went by in a flash, so she repeated the procedure one more time. After the second attempt to prolong sleep, she finally sat up and forced her eyes to open. While squinting with one eye, the other was trying to go back to sleep. Her mind tried to convince her that she did not need to work, but eventually she did remember that she had somewhere to be. Right, time to get up. Her toes reached for her slippers that had wandered under her bed during the night, then her heavy legs rejectingly took the few steps to the bathroom.

She turned the tap to the shower and looked at herself in the mirror as she waited for the water to run warm.

Her memory flashed fractions of a sequence. Corridor, flowers, women.

"That was one weird dream. What was that?" She stepped into the hot water and as she shampooed her hair, she received another memory flash of laughing. She shook her head and closed her eyes to rinse off the cleanser and soap.

She turned off the shower, got out, and reached for a towel. As she wrapped it around her, she repeated to herself that it was just a dream, and she needed to stop thinking about it so she could quickly get ready and get going. She hurried back into her bedroom, fished her new red trousers from under a pile of clothes on the chair. Flipped through the wardrobe in search of that crisp white t-shirt blouse with the floral cutout on the arms. It was so pretty and would look so good with the trousers. She couldn't find it. "Where did I put it?" She hurried back to the bathroom in her underwear, paused for a second to put on an upbeat song that would help her get ready, and danced to that while she did her makeup and curled her brown hair.

She then remembered that she had left a pile of clothes on the sofa in the living room. She had come home from a shopping trip, tried it on again when she came home, and had just left them there. She sighed and cursed herself. Mr. Puzzle had slept on them, so there was grey cat hair all over her new white top. She fetched a lint roller from the cleaning cabinet and cleaned it off as quickly as she could.

She put it on and went to get her big golden drop earrings.

Her memory flashed a crisp white gown and more golden jewellery. She closed her eyes and shook her head slightly. "Stop thinking about that. Leave it." She put her trousers on and noticed how Mr. Puzzle was complaining that breakfast was late. So she poured kibble in his bowl and added an extra treat of soft food on top. Now that he was happy, she turned her attention to her own breakfast. She put a bagel in the toaster and went to her wardrobe to fish out a belt while she waited. The music was still playing, so she danced and hopped her way back to the kitchen and sang along as she finished the bagel and put it in a paper bag. She would eat that later at her desk. She looked at her watch and got a stroke of panic as she realized that she had lost track of time. She quickly found the red lipstick in her make-up drawer and hurried out the door with the lipstick still in one hand, and her work bag and breakfast in the other. Thankfully, she managed to remember her jacket on her way out, because although it was sunny, there was still a residue of winter in the air. She instantly regretted her leopard ballerinas, though, but it was too late to change. When she reached the streets, she looked at her phone. Good, she had five minutes to go and the metro station was just a few hundred metres away. Still, she kept up the pace so she wouldn't miss it. Today was an important day, and she could not be late. She reached the platform with a minute to spare, put some music in her ears, and began to nod along to the beat as she silently sang along with the singer. It was one of her favourite songs and she never grew tired of it.

She got on the train, stood up by one of the railings, and held her balance with her right hand while scrolling through her phone with her left. She was updating herself on today's news, but quickly got bored with that, so she put her phone in her trench coat pocket instead and watched the other commuters. Everyone else had their face in their phones, though, so no one noticed her. One middle-aged woman was reading, and another woman was focusing her attention on her nervous husky. Ayla then noticed the little girl sitting behind her, who had apparently been staring at her this entire time. Ayla said hi, but she immediately got scared and looked at her mommy. Ayla picked up her phone again and changed the song before getting off at her stop. She buttoned her navy-blue coat and fished out a sheer scarf from her bag. As she reached the top of the stairs, she was still debating with herself whether she should stop for a good coffee at the café or get a boring one at the office. The line was quite long, but she eventually decided it was worth it. She stood in line, got herself her beloved cappuccino to go, and warmed her hands on the heat of the mug as she waited for the elevator to reach her floor.

As she stepped out, she noticed her friend Cassandra getting out from the elevator on the opposite side.

"Good morning! That's funny, we were just a second apart," she said with a happy tone. She was easily amused at times. Cassandra looked at her with an odd smile and said, "At least one of us is in a good mood. What's up with you today?"

"Oh, nothing. I just had an amazing dream and a beautiful morning. I'm wearing my new outfit that I got yesterday, and life is just beautiful."

"Yes, you look beautiful! The trousers look even better in real life, and the blouse is divine. It's so pretty with the cut-outs." Ayla danced in her outfit. "Ah, you matched it with leopard shoes, too! Bravo, really pretty." Cassandra clapped inaudibly and laughed at Ayla's childish twirl. "Did you hit your head or something? Why are you so happy? Did you meet a guy?" She was genuinely excited at the possibility, but it was actually a joke.

"No, God no. I did not meet a guy. Can't a woman just get to be happy for no reason? Must there be a reason for everything?

Other than just, you know, life." Ayla was a little annoyed by the question, but still kept her cheerful tone.

"Uh, no. No one is happy for no reason." Cassandra smirked and looked at her. As they walked down the corridor of the office, she continued, "My date was fine, by the way, thanks for asking."

Ayla laughed out loud, "Oh my God, I'm so so sorry", she placed her hand on Cassandra's arm. "I completely forgot. She straightened her smile and continued in a more serious tone, "So, how was your date?"

"I don't want to talk about it," Cassandra replied in a sturdy manner. They both laughed. Ayla assured her that she would want those details at lunchtime. Then they parted ways. Cassandra headed to marketing, and Ayla took a left to project management. Alright, I will see you at lunch. We'll talk then.

Ayla finally reached her desk, hung her coat on the rack behind her, and placed her bag next to her desk. She then took out her laptop from the safe and connected it to the wires. She gave out a slight sigh and sipped her cappuccino as she waited for the system to start. She looked around her and was surprised that she was just on time, yet she was still the first one on her team to arrive. But she soon realised that it was not true. Nora had just been to the staff kitchen to get a smoothie from the fridge, and Daniel was apparently in a meeting with Gregory. She chatted a little with Nora about the project and the meeting that they were going to have later that afternoon. Daniel came out of his meeting and mentioned a report. Gregory informed everyone that Martin had just called in sick and they needed to find his numbers. "Oh, that's not good, we need his report. Do we know where he put it? Did he send it to anyone?" She started searching through the folders on her computer and eventually found it. He had, thankfully, put everything they needed in the collective folder and sent an update on the numbers just an hour ago. There was still a graph missing on one of the slides, so as soon as Daniel got back, he started working on that. The hours went by way too quickly. By the time Cassandra popped by to ask about lunch, there were still some technicalities left to finish. "Just give me ten more minutes and then we can go," Ayla said without lifting her head. She checked everything with Nora and Daniel, so everything was ready before she left for lunch. She met up with Cassandra in the reception.

"Alright, what do you wanna eat? I don't have that long, but I really want something good."

"How about that new sushi place down at the corner. It's supposed to be good." They both liked that idea, so they headed down. They took a seat indoors in one of the booths. The interior was cozy and stylish, with deep blue walls with red and black accents on the lamps and textiles.

"Alright, so sorry about this morning. Please tell me about the guy you met last night?" Ayla said as she poured some soy sauce into the small bowl.

Cassandra flicked her braids over her shoulders and gestured with her hands, "Seriously, there is not much to tell. He was really boring. I sat there the entire time, forcing the conversation while he didn't ask me an interesting question. Not one." "Well, you are quite loud. Maybe he was intimidated?" Ayla tried to help come up with reasons why he would be quiet.

"No, he was just boring. He had a boring life and a boring job, and apparently didn't do anything in his spare time. Out of all the questions I had, he didn't have one interesting answer." Cassandra continued her banter, gesturing with her hands in the air. She stopped to take a sip from her soda.

"I'm sorry to hear that. That sounds quite exhausting. Ok, so what did he do?" "Something to do with computers or money or maybe both? I didn't really get it." She shoved her mouth with a California roll and got busy trying to chew it. Ayla laughed. "So, you weren't listening to him while you're complaining that he wasn't listening to you?"

"Well, he would have been a lot more interesting to listen to if he had had something interesting to say."

They both laughed. Cassandra flipped her black hair back and adjusted her jersey dress.

Ayla picked a nigiri and took a bite.

"But that's not really the point. If he had at least tried to keep the conversation going, like he had any questions at all for me, then it would have been a lot nicer, and I would have taken more interest than I did. I got bored halfway through because all he did was talk about things about himself that were, you know, dumb." Ayla nodded and agreed.

"What is it with men these days that makes them so incapable of having a conversation with a woman?"

"Tell me about it," Cassandra answered as she put on some new pink lipstick on her brown lips.

"It's the Food Festival this weekend. Do you want to go together?" Ayla asked. Cassandra nodded positively. "Yes! Definitely! I was going to go with my sister, but maybe we could all go together?" Ayla nodded back. That sounded like a fun evening.

On the way back to the office, they stopped to get a coffee and brought that one with them to their desks, just like that morning. Ayla started preparing for the presentation that she was going to have later that afternoon. But she found it hard to concentrate as her desk was in an open landscape. She was mouthing the words to herself as she clicked through the slides, but kept getting stuck on one part. She needed to practice out loud, so she booked the nearest meeting room and gathered her things. She balanced the laptop, her notes, and her coffee and walked slowly towards the room. She put the things down on the small table and then closed the glass door behind her. As she turned around, she jumped out of her skin.

"Oh, jeez!" She screamed, putting her hand to her heart. "You scared me half to death." There was a woman sitting in one of the armchairs. Ayla started rambling, "So sorry, I didn't see you first. I thought I had booked the room for myself, but I will go and change to another room. Sorry again."

"Oh, don't you worry about it. It's not a mistake. I am here to talk to you." "Me? What did I do?" Ayla immediately thought she was being accused of something.

"What? Why do you feel scared?" the woman asked with a confused look on her face. "Just because someone wants to talk to you doesn't mean you've done something wrong."

"It doesn't. But the way you look, I feel like I'm in for a final judgment." She gesticulated towards the woman's white dress and golden headband.

"Oh, this. I always wear this."

Ayla laughed out loud, "Yeah, right. You wear that every day? What do you do around here?"

"Well, not much. I wouldn't exactly say that I do anything around here besides listening and trying to get people's attention."

"Ok, so you're in marketing, then. What's up with the costume? Do you have a fun event going on in marketing that I don't know about?"

"Nope. These are just my clothes."

Ayla felt more and more confused and tried to reach a point in the conversation where she felt that she could just leave and get on with her things. "Ok, I've never seen you before. What do you need my help with, and could it perhaps wait till after my meeting? We can schedule a meeting at 4 pm, ok?" Ayla realised that she had talked nervously non-stop and now she gestured to the door so the woman could leave.

"You don't really get it, do you? Don't you recognize who I am?"

Ayla widened her eyes as she tried to think. "Ehm, no. No I do not get who you are but right now I am preparing for a very important meeting that is in just," she looked at her watch before she continued, "just 45 minutes and I really need to prepare for that presentation, so please can I just get to focus on that for now and we can talk later." She was ashamed of herself for having to be so rude and upset with someone she didn't even know, but she had no choice. She opened the door for the woman to leave, but instead, the woman stood up and looked at Ayla with her black eyes, and instead of walking through the door, she walked through the wall. Now, every hair on Ayla's body stood right up, and she completely lost both her voice and sense of manners in her facial expression. She was just in complete shock. She stood there for a few seconds as she decided what to do, but she immediately said, "Ok, ok, you can come back." She closed the door and sat down while the other woman sat down again in the other chair. She smirked and looked awfully proud of herself. She leaned back on the armchair's back support and started spinning slowly with her arms spread across the top.

Ayla studied her, watching how the creases in her white dress effortlessly draped both her body and the chair as she spun around. She was wearing a golden bandana around her frizzy black curls, so they stood up like Cleopatra's, and she had numerous golden bangles around her wrists, and even her sandals were golden, too.

She had big blue droplets as earrings that complemented her dark skin perfectly. "Well, let me know when you're done trying to figure out who I am," the woman said as she continued to spin around in the chair.

Ayla looked at her watch again and realised that she did not have time for this game. "You look like Cleopatra, but I don't think that's right. I'm trying to think of other names, but I can honestly hardly remember anything from history class. Please just tell me who you are."

"I'm Athena," the woman said with a broad smile, gesturing a small bow in the air. "Athena. Athena, as in the goddess Athena?" "The one and only," she said cheerfully.

"But you just walked through the wall," Ayla stumbled to find her words. "What else can you do?"

"Oh, little of this, little of that. But that's not what is important right now." Athena continued teasing.

"Isn't it? Ok, well, then why are you here, then, talking to me?" Ayla was confused on so many levels. She hardly knew where to start.

"Well, I think if you search in your heart, you know exactly why."

"Has it got anything to do with my dream last night? I remember I was wearing the same dress as you."

"Wow, I'm impressed! What else do you remember?" Athena put her face in her hands and listened intently.

Ayla thought for a moment. She concentrated hard to try to remember.

"Not much, unfortunately. I remember a castle of some sort, white walls, and lots of flowers. But that is all I remember. Oh, wait, no, I remember women. Lots and lots of women. But I don't know who they are and what we were doing there. Or what was I doing?"

Athena nodded along as she talked, then looked at her. "I'm actually amazed at how much you remember. You are doing better than most."

"Oh, really?" Ayla sparked some joy inside. She was feeling ashamed for her lack of memory, but now that shifted into a proud smile.

"Yes, really. Now, I will let you in on a little secret." She leaned closer to Ayla and whispered, "I am here to help you get through the day. You have an important meeting, I know. And you want me to leave so you can practice your speech, I know. I will soon leave you alone, but I will just tell you this. What you want to say is already in your heart." She looked at Ayla with confidence, stood up, and walked off. Ayla was left alone, staring at the place on the wall where she had disappeared. She was repeating what Athena had just said over and over. She didn't quite understand what she had meant, but she did not want to forget it. She picked up a pen and wrote it down in her notebook. She then opened her laptop and managed to get through her speech at least once in the twenty minutes that remained. She took a deep breath, collected her things, and walked to the conference room.

The client was not there yet. The others on the team helped each other to set up the space for the meeting with water, coffee, and preparations for all the technology to run smoothly.

The representatives arrived. They all shook hands and sat down. The manager,

Gregory opened the meeting with a presentation that took the client through the general scope of the project, presenting the collaborating partners and coworkers on site.

Ayla took over. She presented a virtual design of the buildings, where they could walk through and get a feel of the energy of the area. She informed them that they had currently started working on the models, and various design teams were working on the structure, materials, and design. She presented the different parts, what they needed in time and budget, along with what they could expect for the whole project. The representatives from the client company asked more specifically about the energy requirements of the site, the management, as well as communication towards the public. They also raised concerns about sustainability and eco-friendly materials that were now a requirement for every new building. Everyone in the room was familiar with the new regulations, but to communicate clearly, Ayla showed them a document, and some graphs stating specifics and told them that they could get a copy of the document after the meeting. They all agreed that it looked very good and that the whole new neighbourhood looked aesthetically pleasing with its position near the waterfront and felt both modern and fresh. They were happy with what they saw, and at the end of it, they agreed that they wanted to proceed with this design and were happy to arrange for the next meeting where they would be able to see the model.

After the client left the room, the whole team screamed with joy. They could hardly believe that all their work had paid off and that the client bought the whole concept of the design so easily. Gregory praised Ayla for her hard work and congratulated the others for their contribution to the project. Ayla felt really proud of herself.

"How about we all go for a quick drink to celebrate?" Gregory said persuasively. The team was actually really tired and all of them wanted to go home, but it felt like a good end to the week to celebrate this moment together. The drink sounded nice, especially when the company was paying.

They went down to the closest lounge bar. Gregory ordered champagne for the table, and they all toasted to the hard work of the team. Then they toasted an extra time just for Ayla, as she was the project manager. Ayla felt so happy and warm to get that sort of recognition.

They all decided to get something to eat as well, so they changed tables. The place wasn't really known for its food, but they made decent burgers and other snack food. Ayla ate rather quickly because, although it was nice to be here, she craved some alone time. Afterwards, she decided to walk home. She lived on the other side of the city, but it wasn't dark yet, and she could walk part of the way through the city park without feeling scared. The air was chilly, but spring was in the air, bringing joy in its blissful wind. Ayla looked at the various flowers that had begun to bloom. Some were closing up for the day as the sun began to set, but the soft hues of whites, yellows, and pinks were still very pleasing. She stopped at a bakery that was still open, bought a pastry, and ate that as she continued walking. She was in a state of remembrance, her mind working hard in the background to recall details from last night and piecing together the events of the day and the clues that Athena had talked about. Eventually, she started recollecting the touch of the velvet carpet on her bare feet, the sound of the dripping water, the sweet perfume of roses sipping through the air. She could, however, still not remember what had happened. Nor could she recollect any faces. But she felt satisfied with what she had already. More would come, she was sure of it. She had reached the end of the park. There was still some distance left to her apartment, and she suddenly felt very tired, so she finished her pastry and got on the next bus that was heading in her direction. It was just a few minutes, and then she was finally home. It was already 9 pm, so all she did was feed Mr. Puzzle and brush her teeth. She was so tired, she didn't even bother removing her makeup but went straight to bed instead.

That night, the dream was quiet and beautiful. No big messages or meetings with angels. She slept like a baby and awoke freshly the next morning.

It was Saturday, and she wasn't meeting Cassandra and her sister until dinner, so she had the whole day to herself. So, she took a slow morning, eating breakfast on her sofa while cuddling with Mr. Puzzle and reading a good book. It was the perfect start to the day. After a while, she picked up her phone and scrolled through her social media. "Oh, there is a Yin yoga with a gong bath starting in less than an hour." She clicked on the link to check if there were any places left. "Yes! One left!" She booked and quickly got dressed and hurried to get to the yoga studio on time.

She arrived at a place where she had never been before, but it was very calm and serene. She felt at ease. She took off her shoes and got herself some chai tea as she waited for the course to start. She looked at the other women in the room. Most of them looked like her. Same type of person, they were almost wearing the same outfit, black tights, and a grey sweater. She felt right at home even though she hadn't been to a yoga session in almost a year. The host stepped out, greeted them one by one with a slight bow. He led them to a room that was filled with white water mattresses, some bolsters, sand pillows, and most importantly, a blanket. One wall was lined with gongs of different sizes. On the center stage, there were also various types of singing bowls. Ayla felt excited and picked a spot that was closest to the big gong. Might as well get the maximum effect while she was at it. But first, they did a few movements of sun salutations and yin yoga poses to stretch out the deep muscles. Apparently, that would make the vibrations of the gong penetrate more deeply into the body, mind, and soul. They completed the yoga and were instructed to lie down on the water mattresses. The instructor walked around the room, giving a quick massage around the neck and shoulders. He then filled the room with soft smoke from white sage incense before he began.

The music started as soft and still but slowly changed in tune and vibration. He played different tunes on various instruments and received help from an assistant to accompany when needed. Ayla was at first very focused on the energies and frequencies that moved through her body, but before she knew it, she was in a deep meditative state. Sound asleep. When the session was over, her body and mind slowly came back to her consciousness as the music softened, and the gong stopped. She opened her eyes. For a second, she could not remember where she was, but soon became embarrassed as she was reminded that she had fallen asleep. She was, however, still deeply affected. That truly was one of the most invigorating experiences of her life. She stepped out feeling like a whole new person.

The sun was out, but there was a slight chill in the air. She zipped up her jacket and walked back to her place.

"You must feel pretty good about yourself now, huh?" Athena was sitting on the couch as Ayla entered her apartment. Mr.

Puzzle was curled up in her lap, and she was stroking his silver mane. Mr. Puzzle was purring, completely accepting the presence of their visitor.

"That's quite interesting that Mr. Puzzle can see you," Ayla said, surprised.

"Well, of course he can. I am, in fact, - despite what you think - real."

"But…" Ayla didn't get a chance to continue before Athena answered. "Yes, I know, I know. You think only you can see me. But the truth is that anyone can see me if they are enlightened and vibrating at the right frequency. Cats are born enlightened, so they can see all deities."

"Wow, that is a lot to process." Ayla sat down in an armchair next to Athena and thought for a moment before she continued. "What is a vibration. What is frequency? I'm not sure I understand what you are saying." Athena petted Mr. Puzzled while she answered.

"You just came from the gong class, did you not? So, you already have some firsthand experience with vibration. Vibration is a sound wave on which energy travels. "Ok, I sort of understand what you mean. But what is a frequency, then?" Ayla went to get a glass of water. "Would you like some?" She asked, but Athena declined. Instead, she tried to continue explaining. "A frequency is like the radio. You tune in to find your station, and when you have the correct number, you get the music that you want. The vibration is the music. It's what you get from listening to that radio station. You get it now?"

Ayla sipped her water and answered, "I think I do." She thought for a few seconds. "Ok, then tell me this: how does one shift from one frequency to the other?" Athena became quiet for a few moments about how to phrase it in a way that would make sense to Ayla. She then said, "For every step that takes you closer to your truth, you also raise your frequency. When you stand in your absolute truth, you are also in your highest frequency." Ayla still looked confused, so she added, "That is all I can tell you for now. You have to walk your own path and learn things in your own time, and when you are ready, you will know. Right now, you are not ready for more knowledge, but what you have will take you far."

Ayla nodded and finished her water. "Thank you for sharing your wisdom," she said.

"Of course, that is what I'm here for. I will now leave you again as I have some place else, I need to be. But we will meet again soon." Athena left Ayla alone, sitting in silence on her couch. She went to get changed and came back wearing her sweats, ready to watch some TV until she had to get ready for the evening. She needed a distraction while she let the information sink in. She put on a series that she was following, and as she was watching, she felt a slight pressure on her throat chakra, and her crown chakra became warm. She understood intuitively that something was happening and watched another episode to allow that energy to pass through her effortlessly before getting ready. It was, after all, an outdoor festival, and the weather was quite cold, so she didn't have to put too much effort into her outfit. She chose a pair of blue jeans and a soft yellow sweater. She paired that with her red lightweight jacket and her regular blue sneakers. She put a polka dot scarf on and brought both a woolen hat and gloves just in case. It was always better to be overprepared at this time of the year.

She got to the festival a bit early, so she took a stroll along the stalls as she waited. It all looked very good. There were a lot of people, and she finally managed to get through the crowd to the statue, where she was supposed to meet Cassandra and her sister. Cassandra and her sister Aimee arrived after just a few minutes. They chatted a little before they spread out to get their preferred foods, then they met up again at the seating area. The decorations were really nice; they sort of looked like an open-air barn with old carriage wheels to the sides and an enchanting light bulb garland hanging across the different sections. They had even placed pretty spring flowers in tin pots on the tables. Ayla was impressed by it all. She sat down and started eating while she waited for the other two to make their way over. Cassandra and Aimee joined her soon enough.

"This all looks so nice, it was hard to choose," Aimee said with a spark in her eye. "I wish I had the room in my stomach to eat more than one thing."

"Cassandra stole a French fry from her plate. "They're gonna be here for another three days, so we have plenty of time to come back. You can try my chicken if you want."

Ayla was amused by their conversation, and a little jealous, since her own sister was so far away.

"It must be so nice to have someone you can always do stuff with," she said.

"Yeah, you'd think," Cassandra teased and laughed as she looked at Aimee and stole another French fry.

"Hey, cut it out. Get your own." Aimee said angrily.

Ayla watched their banter, now even more amused. She tried to lighten the mood by changing the topic.

"I just must tell you about my morning. I had one of the most incredible experiences of my life!"

"Wow, what happened? What did you do?" Cassandra looked amazed, and Aimee listened politely but was multitasking, trying to get her fish burger to stay in one piece as she ate. Ayla chuckled slightly at her attempt to get the lettuce to stay inside the bun.

She continued with her exciting story and asked, "Have you ever been to gong yoga?".

"What's that?" Cassandra picked up a chicken wing from her plate before she added, "I have never even tried normal yoga. It seems so hard, and I can't handle such calm exercise; my mind goes crazy."

"Well, Gong yoga is not like regular yoga. You just stretch your body and lie on a mattress while some guy hits a big gong and plays some singing bowls."

"Wow, that sounds easy. I can see how nice that feels." Cassandra continued eating and was about to change the subject when she remembered that Ayla had pointed out the importance of the experience. "Hang on, wait a minute. Why would it be so life-changing to have some guy play you music while you sleep?" Ayla was happy to get to continue with her story.

"Well, it's not just some guy. He's like a guru or something. He looked very important. Anyway, the instruments create sound waves that make your body relax more deeply than any deep sleep that you've ever had. I'm telling you; I can't even describe it correctly. But it is magical, you must try it. I awoke feeling like a whole new person." Aimee nodded along to the conversation, "I definitely want to try that, it sounds so nice. It must be a great way to release stress, for sure."

Ayla was happy that she got to share her story. She took a sip from her beer and sat in silence for a few minutes while she pondered whether she should mention her dream or anything else that had happened. But she quickly decided that they were not the right audience. The other two had jumped into a new topic. Aimee had apparently started seeing some guy who was both tall and handsome. How thrilling. Apparently nice and very successful, too. Ayla tried to act like she was interested, but eventually zoned out. She felt a bit overwhelmed with the space and all the people, and the shallow conversation. She suddenly felt dizzy and asked the others if they wanted another beer so she could be excused to walk a little.

She went to the bar and got three beers, came back to the table, and delivered as she sat down, deep in thoughts and not paying attention to their conversation.

"Hello! Hellooo. Ayla to Earth." Cassandra laughed. "Wow, you really disappeared.

What were you thinking of?"

She shook her head to snap out of her brain fog as she sat back down. "Sorry, what were you talking about?"

"I just applied for a job at this design company. They haven't had an ad out in ages, so I really hope to at least get an interview."

"Oh, that's great," Ayla said excitedly. "I hope you get it." She smiled and invited them all to toast with their plastic beer glasses.

Aimee looked at her phone and suddenly said, "The Silent Echoes are playing in just thirty minutes. Let's get our desserts and head over to the stage."

Ayla quickly went to get a crêpe, and they met up at a bar table in the same area as the stage. They thought of going closer so they could see better, but soon decided that they were happy where they were for now. Cassandra finished her brownie and went to get them some more beer. The band started playing, and they all stood next to their table and danced politely for a few minutes, but soon joined the sea of people and danced for all they had.

After they parted ways, Ayla lined up for the taxi. She felt so happy. Ayla had not had fun like that in a long, long time. Everything that had happened these past few days felt so surreal. It felt like something was changing inside her, and she felt eager to find out what it was.

CHAPTER 3

Elena

As soon as she opened her eyes, she knew that it was still night. Her eyes slowly traced the shadows of the ceiling to the window and studied the light breeze that was playing with the silk curtain. A slight light outside gossiped that morning was not too far off, but the stars were still basking in the stillness of the moon. The sky was a dark blue saturated with a soft cyan. She picked up her phone. 3:33. She sighed and turned around towards her husband, who was snoring comfortably next to her, sound asleep. She closed her eyes and tried to force herself to go back to sleep. She then spent another hour tossing and turning, trying to find a position that would put her back into a slumber. Her body and mind would not obey, and at 5 am, she finally gave up. She put on her slippers, reached for her soft yellow kimono that was hanging on the wall next to the bed, and went down to the kitchen. Everything was so still. She opened the terrace doors so the moon could shower the living room with silver light. She filled a kettle and made herself some green tea. The living room was beautifully tinted in blue hues and glimmering hints of the streetlights outside. It was so calm and peaceful. She sat in silence for a while, embracing the unexpected luxury of a few hours to herself. Eventually, she got bored and picked up her book that was resting on the side table. She read as she slowly sipped her tea. Suddenly, a distant memory flashed by in her mind. A line in her book triggered a déjà vu. A flash of white and gold. A pink rose. She paused her reading and sighed. "That was a beautiful dream," she thought to herself, suddenly remembering a white palace filled with gold and roses. It was so tranquil and joyful. Why did I have to wake up?" She looked down at her wrist and remembered the golden bracelet that embellished it a few moments before. It felt so real, like she was still wearing the jewellery and the white gown. She sipped some more tea. Her belly rumbled, reminding her that she was not, in fact, dreaming right now but very much in her hungry body. She went back to the kitchen and got out some yoghurt and muesli. As she sat back down, she savoured the bliss of eating alone in peace. "I should really do this more often", she thought to herself as she stared at the shadows on the floor.

"Yes, you deserve to treat yourself more. You have been hungry for far too long." The voice startled Elena, she had been so deep in her own head. She nipped her arm quickly. She thought she had fallen asleep, but she was apparently awake. "Who is there?" She felt her heart throb out of fear, and her head got a little dizzy as she tried to stand up, so she sat back down and instead hugged a cushion as an imaginary armour over her chest.

"Oh, no, no, there is nothing to be afraid of. You can put down the cushion." The voice exclaimed as a woman suddenly appeared next to her on the sofa. The woman softly put her hand on Elena's trenched arm to reassure her not to get startled. She proceeded to look deep into Elena's blue eyes with a calm, gentle aura. "Now, take a few breaths." Elena's eyes were stiff with fear, but softened as she breathed deeply in, deeply out, deeply in, deeply out. All while looking into the woman's mesmerizing brown eyes.

She placed the orange velvet cushion next to her and picked up her cup of tea instead, which she cupped her hands around and sipped in silence as she quietly studied the woman. She was wearing a beautiful rose-coloured satin dress. Her chocolate brown hair had been neatly curled and put up with a big red rose, and small golden drops dangled from her ears. Her hands were resting in her lap. She was serene and beautiful, nothing to be afraid of. In the back of her head, Elena managed to recollect the image of a woman she had seen before.

"You're Mary Magdalene," she eventually managed to say in a squeaky whisper. "Why are you here?"

The woman looked at her in silence, albeit disappointed, but she was not surprised. "So, you don't remember, then? It sounded like you remembered so much, but you seem to have forgotten the most important part." Mary Magdalene stood up and walked to the patio door and watched the palm trees whisk in the wind. "Remember what?" Elena asked with a surprised expression as she watched the movement of her garments and the expressions on her face. But Mary Magdalene was so poised that Elena could not make out her true thoughts. Her own head, however, was slightly spinning, and she went back to her initial thought that the woman was just a product of her hallucination caused by tiredness. She picked up the bowl of yoghurt and finished that as she continued to watch the red silhouette. She couldn't decide what to do or what to think.

But Mary Magdalene was one step ahead. "The dream. The dream you had last night. The one that woke you up." She glanced over at her. "How much do you remember?"

Elena looked at her with an absent mind, trying to recall anything besides the white marble and pink roses.

"I only remember a beautiful palace and the grand decor. I don't remember what happened," she said at last, feeling disappointed with herself.

"Try to think harder. It is important for you to remember what was being asked of you." Mary Magdalene took her hands and looked into her eyes again, then continued, "You have an important role, my dear." She then walked towards the patio again. "It is time for me to leave, but I will be back later to check on you. In the meantime, just try to remember."

Elena stared into nothing for a while. She was quite confused about how to react and what to think. She finished her tea quickly and went to get ready before the kids woke up. She hurried back upstairs, took a quick shower, put some argan oil in her silky blonde hair, and then dressed in a light green tunic and white slip pants. She went back downstairs and set the dining room table. She put out all the various kinds of cereal, milk, and yogurt. Then she cut up some fruits and fried a few eggs too, in case someone wanted. The coffee was brewing; the table was beautifully set for a good morning.

She went back upstairs to make sure her kids were awake. Leonie was up and almost ready, Oliver was running around trying to find his socks, and little Noah was still asleep. She told the older two to go eat their breakfast while she helped her youngest to get ready. Noah was not a morning person, he was always very difficult to wake up, so she started by gently stroking his back. She then turned on a lamp and picked out his clothes. He slowly sat up with his eyes still asleep and hair tousled. As soon as he opened them, though, he yelled "Mama!" and stood up on his bed with his arms open wide to give her a hug. She picked him up in her arms and kissed his forehead. She then helped him get dressed. He sprinted down the stairs to join the others. She sat down next to him and served him his toast. Her husband was now up and dressed. He sat down next to the elder children and asked them about their day ahead while he got himself a coffee and a bowl of musli. Elena then went over to Leonie and fixed her tangled hair as she ate, braided it neatly, and tied it with a blue bow.

"You know she'll get messy the minute we get on the school bus, anyway," Oliver said, teasing. He had one eye on his phone as he was munching on his breakfast, but he still managed to keep up with what was happening around him.

Leonie stuck her tongue out at her brother.

"Well, let's see how long your shirt is white today, then," she replied.

Ok, that's enough for now! Elena put an end to the teasing before it had a chance to start. She did not have the energy for that right now. Not after her peaceful morning. And, having woken up so early, she was already feeling tired when the day had just begun. She looked at the time.

"Quickly, we need to leave within ten minutes. Drink up your juice, finish your cereal, let's go!"

She hurried the kids to the hallway, helped them get their bags and put on their shoes, then watched them sprint out the door and down the stairs. "Leonie, not so quick, help Noah!" Her husband sprinted past them without giving her much notice and got into his car without so much as a goodbye. She paused for a second to think of what had just happened. She got her own shoes on and hurried after the kids. After such a chilly morning, it suddenly got a lot more stressful. They all walked together to the school, which was just a few blocks away, and she waved them off like she always did before turning back home. It was a warm day today, and she could sense the heat building up through the chill of the morning. She went back in, cleaned up after breakfast, finished her coffee as she did the dishes, then grabbed her bag and headed out herself. She needed to go to the market for a few errands. The market was already buzzing with life, and she had to park a few blocks away. She took a deep breath and used the memory of this morning to find inner peace. She had so much to do today and was very stressed, but she tried to remain calm. She browsed through the stalls, picking up vegetables and other produce for dinner tonight and tomorrow's lunch. Eventually, she had her arms full of bags. She had even made an impulse buy of some beautiful pink peonies, and now she was balancing it all while trying to see where she was walking. She was just about to head out when she heard someone yell her name.

"Elena! Elena!" She turned around and saw Lucy, her best friend. "Thank God!" she thought, happy to see her friend and get a distraction from her busy thoughts. "Hi, Lucy! So happy to see you! What are you doing here at this hour?" Lucy hurried up to her and automatically took some of her bags. "Why did you buy so much? Let me help you with that. Where is your car?" Lucy took three bags and the flowers.

"Actually, I'm not done. I still need to pick up Oliver's cake."

"But you can hardly carry things as it is, let's drop these off first." Her persistence won, and they walked towards the car. "You look really tired. How are you feeling?"

"Well, I woke up at 3, so yes, I am. It's going to be a long day. But I'm fine. Honest." Elena gave a smile and tried to sound cheerful. She was happy, she was just tired.

"Well, let's get some lunch then, and maybe some coffee." Lucy implied.

"Oh, I don't have time for that. I have so much to do today. Besides, don't you have to be somewhere?" She was feeling slightly embarrassed that she couldn't remember why Lucy was in this part of the city.

"I've been in a meeting with Zenith Power all morning, and I was just about to head back to the office. But I do have time to eat. Although it's a bit early." She looked at her watch. "Let's go to Laura's. I haven't been there in ages."

Elena finally gave in. "Well, ok then. I ate an early breakfast, so I'm actually quite hungry." Lunch with a friend was exactly what she needed, and Laura's was such a nice restaurant. It was such a beautiful space that had the vibes of a French bistro but with an Australian touch. It was airy and bright with one main wall that had a beautiful white tile. Blush floral wallpaper lined the other walls, but best of all were the big bouquets of flowers they had placed around the room. They got a table along the long sofa. Lucy took the armchair; Elena arranged the magenta cushions and sat down comfortably. She sighed with delight. They both skimmed the menu and ordered. Lucy got a warm Angel hair noodle salad and Elena a Caesar salad. She was normally a health freak, but today she could not resist the bacon.

"So, how was your meeting?" She asked Lucy.

"Oh, it was great! The event we are putting together is going to be amazing! I'm putting you and Stephen down for two tickets. You have to come." Lucy was bubbly and vibrant. Her cherry red blouse was moving along with her excited hands that were following the conversation.

"Oh, you don't have to do that." Elena tried to come up with an excuse, but couldn't think of any.

"Of course you do! You haven't been out in ages. Just get a sitter." She put her hands on Elena's arm. "Please come. It would mean so much to me to show you what I've been working on these past months."

"Then, of course, we will be there," Elena exclaimed cheerfully without hesitation.

She didn't want to be a nuisance, but it was more important to support her friend. The food arrived, and as they started eating, Lucy looked at her with an intense look in her eye, "So, tell me what kept you up all night?"

As Elena was focused on loading her fork with some salad, bacon, and a cherry tomato, she replied.

"It's nothing, really. I actually had the most wonderful dream that I was in a white marble palace filled with roses. And then I woke up and tried to go back to the dream for the rest of the night, but couldn't. So now I've basically been up since 3 am." She said excitedly, but trying to spare any details that would give her away. "Wow, that sounds really amazing. That sounds like a wonderful dream. I once dreamt that I was in the French countryside, and I didn't want to wake up either." Lucy started talking about her dream, too, and Elena became a bit uneasy. She wanted to talk more about the dream and what had just happened, but she didn't know how without raising suspicion. Instead, she just smiled and nodded as Lucy talked about her dream in Provence and then continued talking about other weird dreams. To stop Lucy from going off for too long about lavender fields and dream symbolism, Elena changed the subject: "So, have you got anything fun besides work planned for the coming months?"

"In fact, I was wondering if you wanted to go to this silent retreat with me? I got an ad about it online. It's supposed to be very relaxing. You go away for three days and are not allowed to speak the whole time," Lucy snort-laughed and clapped her hands together, "Wouldn't that just be the best treatment for us?" Elena laughed with her.

Lucy was famous for her chatter, and Elena was quite a talker too when she wanted.

How would they ever manage a whole weekend without talking?

"Oh, I don't know. Can you imagine us two being together and not talking for a whole weekend?" She took a bite of her salad before she arranged a proper reply in her head. "Besides, I don't think Stephen would like me to be away from the kids for that long."

"Oh, that's such a lame excuse, since when does he care about that?" Lucy called out, sounding slightly agitated.

"Since always, actually," Elena answered almost instantly, wanting to end the conversation. She finished her salad and looked at her watch.

"I need to pick up the cake and then go to Alice." She tried to hide her avoidant tone of voice, but of course, Lucy knew her too well.

She said in a more serious tone, "You do know that you can talk to me about anything, right? I will look into it. If the dates are good, I think we should go. It would be good for you, I promise." She put her bag on her shoulder. "Shall we go?" Elena looked at her with a smile that concealed the simmer of a tear. She picked up her bag, too, and followed Lucy out. They parted ways, and Elena went to pick up Oliver's cake. On the way home, however, she couldn't hold it in anymore. The tears rolled down her cheeks. First, just a small drop, then they formed a stream. She put her hand to her cheek to try to control them and make herself stop. But the more she dabbed, the more it came. By the time she got home, her shirt was drenched. The worst part was that she didn't know why. She was happy, everything was good.

Everything was good.

She dabbed her face with a tissue before getting out of the car and getting all the bags and the cake from the trunk. She went inside and put it all away. She went upstairs to change into another shirt and fixed her makeup before getting back into the car to go to Bellavie Nursing Home. It was just a

10-minute drive, and thankfully, she didn't have to stay long. Still, it was one of those things she needed to do every day. She walked towards the Sunflower wing just as usual, signed in with the residence nurses, and knocked on Alice's door.

"Good morning, Alice. How are you today?" Elena said, "I brought cookies. I thought we could have some coffee together."

Alice looked at her with a childish innocence and blank stare. "Who are you?" Elena added without skipping a beat, "Oh, you know who I am, Stephen's wife." There were the same questions every day, and the same answers.

"Who is Stephen?" she asked.

"Stephen is your son, my dear. Don't you remember?" Elena said. Alice could never remember, but she always pretended that she did.

"Oh, yes, of course." With a short expression of embarrassment, she stared at Elena.

"So how about that coffee?" Elena said compassionately.

"Yes, lovely," Alice said with a smile. She had on her favourite red cardigan today and the blue velvet slippers with the embroidered anchor. She had gotten the boat slippers as a present from her late husband, Stephen's father, some 20 years ago. It was the only thing that put her mind at ease. Elena smiled back and steered her towards the sunlit lounge next to the common room that was in service when residents had visitors. The nurse came by with the coffee and some cookies. It was the same cookies every day, Scottish shortbread. Elena had bought a big box and stored it here so they would be able to have the same cookies and coffee together every day. While Elena's whole family was born and raised in Australia, Alice had an interesting past. She was born in Scotland, fell in love with an Italian man whom she emigrated to Australia with him some 50 years ago. Gino died of a heart attack five years ago, and Alice was diagnosed with dementia around the same time. She had been living here ever since. At this point, she didn't remember anything, but it was clear that she still enjoyed the visits. So, Elena kept coming. It made her happy, too, on some level, even though it was tough to see such a strong woman perish into a shell of her former self, right before her eyes. "But that's life," she thought; "You have to be there for the good and the bad". After about thirty minutes, Alice grew tired and said she needed to rest. So, the nurse took her back to her room.

When Elena got back home, it was nearly 3 pm. The kids would be home soon. She swore a little that she had taken such a long lunch, hurried up to their rooms to quickly tidy, make the beds, and throw dirty clothes in the hamper. Then ran back downstairs and prepared their afternoon snacks while she got the meat out to defrost. They all walked through the door at four o'clock on the dot. All of them threw their school bags on the floor, and their shoes flew in every direction. Elena yelled from the kitchen to put their stuff in order, and they obeyed before they sat down at the kitchen island and ate some pieces of apple and some biscuits. Oliver and Leonie were staring at their phones as they ate, and Noah was having trouble with his shoes, so Elena helped him get them off. She helped him up on the bar stool and gave him his snack. As the three of them ate in silence, Elena turned her attention to dinner. She chopped vegetables and prepared potatoes and meat. She left it to marinate as she steered the older kids from the counter to do their homework in their rooms instead. She needed some alone time, and she still hadn't created any content for today, so she still needed to do that.

She turned on the TV for Noah to watch one of his shows. Then she closed the door to the kitchen, set up her recording equipment, and pressed on.

She did live streams every day when she cooked dinner, and it didn't matter how tired she was, she still had to put out the content to satisfy her followers. She did, however, always practice honesty, and today was no different, so she told them all about her state of mind and was quick to connect that with the different parts of the cooking process. Half an hour later, the food was ready, and they could all eat. She set the table, purple placemats, and today she chose the floral plates. The kids came down to eat, and they all talked about the day, homework, and upcoming activities. Stephen came home at eight. They were all done already. The kids were outside playing. Elena picked up her book and went to read in the living room while Stephen warmed his food and ate by himself in the dining room. Elena asked about his day, and it was good, apparently. He asked about his mom, it was the usual. She told him that she needed to go to bed early today and that he had to help her get the kids to bed. He agreed without complaint. She was happy about that. At this point, she was so tired that she was starting to feel dizzy. Tomorrow was Saturday, but it was also Oliver's birthday, so she set the alarm and then made herself comfortable. She wondered what she would be dreaming about this time. She slipped into a deep sleep. First, it felt like she was dancing on some rainbow clouds, and then everything just went dark.

She woke up the next morning just a few minutes before the alarm. She turned it off, then suddenly had a combined feeling of disappointment and relief. She hadn't dreamt of anything. It had been a deep, dreamless sleep without castles, flowers, or goddesses. She smiled to herself, trying to feel content.

Stephen woke up, and they went downstairs to prepare the birthday breakfast. As they were done, she went to wake up Noah and Leonie so that they could all gather before Oliver's door to light the candle and sing as they cheerfully entered to begin celebrating his day.

Oliver sat up in his bed, his hair in disarray, and with tired eyes, he tried to make out the presents that they had brought with them and the cupcake with the candle in it. He was finally turning 10, so it was a big deal. He opened his presents while eating the cupcake and joyfully screaming at things that were on his wish list. Breakfast was already waiting for them downstairs, so as soon as he was done, they hurried down. They all sat down and chatted happily. The whole family was together, and that made Elena very happy. She looked around her and counted her blessings. She was grateful for the life she had. "Why did she cry yesterday? That was so ridiculous, let's not do that again." She held her coffee in her hands while she followed the conversation between the others. Soon, they were all done and rushed up to change so they could go to the games with their dad. Stephen helped Noah with his shoes, after which he went back to the kitchen and gave Elena a kiss. She was surprised and hardly had time to react; that kiss made her feel both happy and strange at the same time. She touched her lips slightly. He hadn't kissed her in a really long time. He went off with the kids while she stayed behind to get all the food ready for the birthday party. But she would not be entirely alone. Her mom was coming in just half an hour, and Lucy would be there soon, too.

"I thought I would never get you alone again. Do you ever have time to breathe?" Mary Magdalene came into the kitchen and sat down at one of the bar stools. "No, not right now, I don't. There is a lot going on today." Elena looked at her with an irritated look. "It's my son's birthday, what do you want me to do?"

Mary Magdalene looked at her, "Just because it's your son's birthday doesn't mean that you should miss out on all the fun."

"I am not. There is a party later. I have to cook the food, I love to do that for my son. I don't have time for you right now. Please leave." Elena took out a pie dough from the fridge and started working it with the rolling pin.

"But I'm here because you called on me. I cannot leave." Mary Magdalene was stunned.

"Did I? When did I do that, and why would I do that?" Elena tried to recollect her thoughts. She kept turning the dough around and flattening it in a stressful manner.

"What did I say?"

"Oh, it is never a conscious thought. You have to want me to come. You have to need me." Mary Magdalene came back in from the living room, holding a bowl of dry honey hoops.

Elena sighed, "Would you like some milk with that?"

Magdalene picked one up, looked at Elena through the hole, then said, "No, I'm good. I prefer them to dry. Thanks." She ate a few of them as she studied Elena's movement with the rolling pin. "Remember you cried yesterday, and this morning you were near tears again." Elena stopped and looked at her in awe. "How do you know that?"

"I am always with you, remember? I am your guide. You think you are alone, but I am always there. Not all of me, of course, I have other things to do as well, but I always listen." Mary Magdalene was eating the honey hoops like chips, munching away as she talked.

Elena was stunned. She stood in silence for a few seconds as she watched her eat. Mary Magdalene, however, continued before she had a chance to say anything. "The more you think about it, the more your head hurts. I got it. I think that's not only true in this case but for the other things, too." Mary Magdalene flicked her brown curls and continued. "Only you can do your inner work. I am only here to offer help, but I cannot give it if you are not willing to receive it. I will let you stay in your bubble of denial for now and will leave you to it. Thanks for the snacks. She did a thumbs up, and the bangles on her wrist made a delightful chiming sound. She pushed out her chair and left the room for another dimension.

Elena continued to look at the chair she had been sitting on and the bowl of cereal she had eaten from. She thought about what she had said, then shook her head. It was her oldest son's birthday. She was so happy and so grateful for everything she had.

There was a brief knock, and her mother came in, carrying a bowl of potato salad. "Oh, I told you that you didn't have to do that," Elena said straight away. "I made plenty of food."

"Oh, you can never have too much food. Besides, you were only going to serve salad with the meat, I know you. But not everyone wants to be healthy all the time," she said, putting the bowl down on the dining room table.

"I am not always a health freak. I have already peeled potatoes, and I am baking a pie. But thank you, anyway." She looked back at the front door. "Where is Dad?" "He is coming, he is just outside talking to your lovely neighbour. You know what he is like, always likes to talk to everyone." She filled up a glass of ice water and then went to sit down in the living room, where she picked up a magazine and sat in silence. "Oh, you mean Tina? Yeah, she always has news." Elena followed her with a coaster and gave it to her to put under her drink. Her mom sighed in an amused tone, thinking it funny that her daughter never changed. She took the coaster and placed it under her drink. Elena glanced out at the front door that had been left ajar. "What are they talking about?" Elena said and went to have a look.

"Hi, what's the matter?" Elena asked as she approached her dad and chatty neighbour.

"Hi, sweetie! Oh, it's nothing. I'm just giving Tina here some advice on how to get rid of a family of crows in her garden. Nasty birds, they wake them up at 4 in the morning."

"Really? I never heard anything." Elena said in surprise.

"Oh, they are nesting on the other side of the garden. I doubt the sound reaches your bedroom."

"Ok, well, let me know how that goes." Elena quickly regretted her own curiosity and went back inside to finish the cooking. About an hour later, Lucy walked through the open front door with her husband, Ned, behind her.

"Hi! You're early! Stephen isn't back yet with the kids."

"Oh, we came to help." She put her present on the counter and picked up an apron. "What can I do?" she said and went straight to the mountain of vegetables. Ned got out his glasses and a bottle of wine, which he opened as he glanced out to the living room and noticed Elena's mother. "Would you like a glass?" He held up an empty wine glass. "Yes, please! And can you help me get another glass of water as well?" she yelled from the living room.

Lucy looked at Elena and chuckled. Ned poured four glasses of wine, took one glass and some water to Elena's mother, and came back with a smile. He was always happy to be of service.

A short while later, Stephen came back with the kids. They all seemed very happy.

Ned poured another glass of wine while Elena took the kids upstairs to get changed into nicer clothes. She helped Leonie with a purple flower dress and did two baked braided pig tails with a lilac bow on each. Leonie looked adorable. Noah got a light blue shirt and marine shorts. The rest was unimportant at his age, as long as he was present. Oliver put on the new dark green shirt that he had gotten as a present this morning and khaki trousers. He looked so smart, and so old. Elena combed his dark brown waves to the side and poked his nose in affection before he turned around and hurried outside to his siblings. Guests were arriving. Some kids from school, a friend from class. Her brother, Mathew, walked in with his wife and their kids. They ran out to the garden and joined their cousins in play. More guests arrived. Most of them were family friends, but there were a few who were just Oliver's friends. They seemed to blend nicely on their own. As the garden filled up with children at play, the patio and inside filled up with adults who were chatting along in a joyful tune and filling up on refreshments. Soon, all the guests had arrived. Elena went outside onto the patio, clapped her hands, and told everyone that lunch was ready.

Stephan had pushed together some tables and decorated the patio nicely so that many kids could eat together. There were green and blue garlands everywhere. And behind Oliver's chair were two tinfoil balloons 1-0. The adults helped them get their food and drinks, especially the younger ones who couldn't balance a plate. Then, as soon as the kids were seated, they served themselves but stood up to eat. It was a beautiful spring party, and Elena was so happy how it had turned out. They had some games that the adults had to join in on. Some refused, but most were happy to make a fool of themselves and contribute to the fun of the party. Elena went inside to get the cake out and put the coffee on. Stephen helped her. He got some candles out from a cupboard and put them on the cake along with a sparkler. They went back outside and joined together to sing and cheer for Oliver. Now followed the same procedure as before, with parents running around helping the kids to take some cake and soft drinks. Stephen was in charge of cutting, so the plates travelled the room back and forth until everyone had a piece.

After the cake, most guests started to leave. Only the best friends were still there. Stephen was talking to Ned and another guy. Elena sat in the living room with Lucy and her parents. For once, everyone was too tired to talk, so they drank their coffee to some unsynced small talk. After the last friends had gone, Elena wrapped up the cake and put it in the fridge. She looked around the kitchen and felt grateful that she had so many friends who had already helped clean it up. Then she noticed Stephen looking at her all the way from the patio. He made his way over. "You were marvellous today, well done, you!" He hugged her and kissed her. Then she gave her a little bit of a squeeze on the bum. "Do you want to, later?" he said, trying to sound sexy. "Oh, God, no." She said a bit too quickly and then continued. "Sorry, it's just I've been running around all day today and yesterday. I am still sleep-deprived from the other night. All I need to do is to lie down.

"Well, good thing that is what I was asking, then." He added, trying again to sound funny and sexy, which did not make her feel any better about herself.

Now she was feeling ashamed for saying no. She shouldn't say no; they haven't done it in ages. In fact, it must be weeks since the last time. "Maybe tomorrow, she compromised. I'm just so tired."

He turned notably angry, picked up a chip from one of the bowls, and walked off. "Oh, come on." She protested, "Now you're being totally selfish."

Noah had fallen asleep on one of the lounge chairs. He picked him up and carried him up the stairs to his room. Leonie and Oliver were sitting on the hanging sofa hovering above ground as they played on their screens. Elena uncovered their ears from headphones off and told them to finish their games and go to bed. It was late, and she herself went up to get ready. She made sure the older kids were getting ready, then she too changed into pyjamas. Stephen was still downstairs, sulking on the patio with a beer. Elena sighed at his childish reaction. She had every right to just want to sleep after the day and the week she had. Besides, it wasn't fair of him to hardly notice her all week and then suddenly expect her to change mood. She got increasingly irritated the more she thought about it, so she walked up to her bathroom instead to do a skincare routine before bed. She walked into the bathroom, surprised to see Mary Magdalene sitting on the edge of the bathtub.

"Yeah, yeah. I know why you came this time."

"I'm not sure you are correct, but go on," Mary Magdalene raised her eyebrow and rested her chin on the tip of her fingers as she waited for Elena to continue with her theory.

"Well, I'm a bad wife for rejecting my husband who is suddenly affectionate, for the first time in forever. Shouldn't I want that? What is wrong with me?"

"Why are you feeling guilty?" Mary Magdalene asked.

"I don't know. I feel like I'm putting my ego before our marriage, and that's wrong." Elena continued.

Mary Magdalene looked at her with a big question mark on her face.

"You are a strong woman. You have done everything for this party. You do everything for this family while he does nothing."

"That's not true. Stephen took the kids to the trampoline park today, and he helped decorate the patio - and he even got the candles I asked him for."

Mary Magdalene rolled her eyes. "Sure, most attractive feature in a man to help bring the candles. "

Elena gave out an anxious chuckle. She heard how silly that sounded. She had literally done everything and is doing everything all day, every day. All he needs to do is show up. And then he has the audacity to keep on asking for more, like her to-do list never stops growing.

Mary Magdalene looked at her with compassion. "Maybe you should give yourself a break. It is not your ego that wants to rest, it is you. You have worked hard, and you need it. You do not need to convince yourself that you have earned the right to self-love. If that really makes him upset, then let him be. You do not need to fix everything."

Elena looked at her in awe. "Not even my therapist has been that blunt with me before. Thank you!"

"Well, that is what I'm here for. Now, go to sleep. You have a long night ahead."

Elena looked at her with a slight panic on her face. "What do you mean by that?" "Don't you worry. It's not as bad as it sounds. And I will be right there with you. See you soon." Mary Magdalene left, and Elena lay there in the dark for a while, too scared to close her eyes. But eventually, she could not fight it and dozed off into a slumber.

CHAPTER 4

Phoebe

*B*efore she even opened her eyes, she knew she was late. She could feel it in her whole body. One second, she was deep asleep, and the next, she flung herself out of bed. Late, very late. She thought she had set an alarm, but this was not what she needed today. She looked at her phone. She had set an alarm but had turned it off in her sleep. She hurriedly sprang to the bathroom, quickly brushed her teeth, put some deodorant on, and some oil to tame her curls. She threw some blush, mascara, and eyeshadow in her bag so she would finish that later if she got time. Threw on a pair of navy shorts and the sky-blue pike that was the company's uniform. Quickly picked out a t-shirt to put in her bag for later, got dressed while putting on her shoes. Earrings! She almost forgot. She quickly grabbed her hoops and ran out the door. She hurried down the street and only stopped when she reached the square. She took a minute to catch her breath, looked at her phone, and continued running towards the other end. She ran past the cart of a sweet elder man named Alfonso, who only served espresso and pastel de Nata. "Are you not going to have breakfast today?" he yelled to her.

"Not today, I'm terribly late. I don't have time," she waved and hurried along. He waved for her to come back and quickly put two pastries in a paper bag. "Here, here. You can't go hungry. You pay me later, ok." She hurried back to get the bag, thanked him, and then continued running. After a few blocks, she reached the tourist office. "I'm here, I'm so sorry. It won't happen again." She was grasping a stitch in her stomach and catching her breath as she leaned over the counter.

Rosaline looked up from the other side. She was unpleased and said in an irritated tone.

"We have already had today's briefing. Group 1 has already left. Zorina took care of them since you weren't here. But good for you that we had a lot of tourists coming in today, so we have another group that will start in exactly 16 minutes." She looked at Phoebe with an irritated stare and a serious face. "Next time, come on time." She continued and shook her head when she saw the paper bag in Phoebe's hand, added in a judgmental tone, "You can eat outside.".

Phoebe scolded herself for not hearing the alarm, for stopping to accept the pastries, and for being too slow a runner. She sat down on the bench outside and fished out the pastries from the paper bag. She took a deep breath, closed her eyes, and bathed her face in the morning sun as she ate her breakfast.

Somebody sat down beside her, so she opened them again. "Ah, Gabriel! So good to see you!" She looked at him with one eye; he was a bit blurry in the yellow light, but she soon made out what he was holding in his hand. "Oh my God, thank you! You are a lifesaver!" She exclaimed and accepted the coffee. He laughed, gave her the coffee mug, stole a small piece of pastry, and sat with her in silence for a few minutes as they both soaked in the sun. "Do you want to grab some lunch later?" He asked with a hint of shyness in his voice.

She opened one eye and glanced at him. "I'm sorry, I have a full-day group today. I have to eat together with them. I can text you when I'm done, ok? Thanks for the coffee." He left to get to his work while she finished drinking her coffee. Soon, the 16 minutes were up, she threw everything in the nearby bin and headed over to the group of people that was waiting for her by the stairs at the far end of the square.

"Good morning! You must be in Group 2. I will be your guide today. We will be spending the next few hours together. Does everyone here understand English?" Everyone nodded, an elder man double-checked his ticket and mumbled something to his wife, then gestured in the air that they were, in fact, in the correct group. She continued with a polite smile. "Great! My name is Phoebe. I have lived in Porto most of my life, so you're in good hands. I'm going to show you all the famous sights in Porto and will include a few of my favourite places as well to show you the different sides of this beautiful city. We are starting where we are right now, at Sé Cathedral, the famous cathedral. I'm sure you all know why." She laughed politely and waited patiently as everyone made their way from the heat of the sun to the cool stillness inside the Cathedral's stone walls. She took them through the building, giving them plenty of time to admire the blue tiles as they walked.

She noticed that the elder man was struggling to keep up.

"Are you alright, sir?" Phoebe was concerned that he would suffer through what was mostly a walking tour.

"Yes, I'm fine, thank you. I'm just slow, pardon me." The wife looked Phoebe in the eye and let a laugh slip through as she complained about how they were not in their youth anymore. Phoebe noticed an accent but couldn't figure out where they were from. "If you want, I can ask one of our chauffeurs to join us with a cart. He can drive you between the places, so you don't have to walk so long?"

"No, no, we do not want to be of inconvenience, and I am quite keen to see the city the right way. Walking is good for me, anyway." He looked straight into her eyes with big blue puppy eyes and a friendly smile. His left hand was holding on to his walking cane, and his right hand was gesturing in the air to reassure her that he was fine. Phoebe nodded, "Ok, then. It's all fairly close anyway, and we will take the tram for parts of the distance." She took out her phone and sent a quick text to the office, giving them a heads up that there might be a need for a cart later. Then she looked at the group and continued talking about the history of these marvellous blue tiles. She herself never grew tired of looking at them. In the midst of everyday life, one got used to them, but as a tour guide, she got to marvel at them every day. A true masterpiece. They walked around the cathedral for about half an hour, gasping at images and admiring the architecture and greenery of the courtyards. The elder man and his wife sat down on a bench while the others walked up the stairs to explore the space on the top floor. Soon, they were all done and ready to move on to the next site. They walked after each other on the narrow sidewalk connecting the Cathedral to Palacio da Bolsa.

After coming from the busy streets, the palace was a quiet retreat. Even with the large number of tourists at this popular site, there was still plenty of space to find stillness. This building was just as astonishing as the cathedral, but with its own merit. The decorated silver walls in the vast ballroom were shimmering in the morning sun. It was a remarkable building. She took them through the embellished rooms, talking about architecture, historic people, culture, and heritage. They all got plenty of beautiful shots on their phones and cameras.

A middle-aged lady was there with her daughter, and they stopped everywhere to take selfies. When they arrived at the courtyard, they asked Phoebe to take a picture of them both, which she happily did. The old man sat down on one of the sofas and looked up at the ceiling. He looked happy and amazed to be in this place. Phoebe glanced over at some of the single men on the tour. One of them had stayed too long reading a sign with historic information. He looked up and searched for the room for the rest of the group. As usual, Phoebe was one step ahead and waved at him to get his attention. When the group was completed again and no one was missing, they left for the next part of the tour, which was to take the tram to Capela das Almas. It was always an interesting part of the tour to get on the tram. There were always one or two who had never been on one before, and certainly never on an iconic cart in Porto. It bridged history and culture into modern everyday life in a beautiful way, and it was always fun to share that experience with the tourists.

The chapel was only a few stops away, so all of them stood up, except for the elder couple who had managed to get a seat. She had learned that their names were Hans and Marie. They were in their late 70s and had travelled to Portugal for the first time from Denmark. Then we had Louise and her daughter Amanda, from Switzerland.

She tried to recall the country of origin of the man standing next to her. "Where are you from?" She figured it's better to ask than to guess. "The Netherlands," he said, beaming a friendly smile. His height actually gave him away, she almost felt embarrassed that she asked, but then remembered there are plenty of other countries in Europe with tall people. She glanced over at another man who was also travelling alone. He was looking out the window, though, with his thoughts elsewhere, so she would have to talk to him later. The two older British women suddenly got pleased about getting seats and sat down. They continued to chat as they changed position in the cart and laughed in between every other word, utterly pleased with life. Phoebe found joy in watching them in their merriment. One was correcting her sunglasses on her head and nodded as the other one went on about a story from home.

Soon, the cart reached its destination, so she alerted everyone to get off. The chauffeur stopped a few extra minutes to allow the old man to get off without stress. They walked the few metres from the tram stop to the chapel. There were a few tourist groups there already, so they had to wait for their turn to go inside. When she walked through the doors, Phoebe could sense a small tickle on her throat and let out a cough to try to get rid of it. It did not. She also felt a slight pressure on her shoulders that creeped her out. She straightened her back, put her hand on her lower back, and whispered some information to her group before they all began walking down the narrow rows. There were people there for their morning prayer, and she didn't want them to disturb them. She glanced at the various sculptures and paintings. She glanced up at Mother Mary, and for a second, it appeared as if Mother Mary moved her fingers slightly in an attempt to wave. Phoebe blinked, looked away, and continued walking. They were out again in just 30 minutes, and now they started walking back to the center via the beautiful streets of the old town. Phoebe wanted to show them different sides of the city, so first they walked along narrow streets with cobblestones and then they reached the grand avenues and park, where they could stroll together as a group and she could gather them for historic stories and useful information for their trip. They also passed a market where some of them wanted to stop. Amanda, the young girl, saw some earrings that she liked, and one of the British ladies saw a funny t-shirt that she wanted to get for her husband. Phoebe waited as the tourists took ten minutes to shop before they resumed the walk. They crossed the streets and went through a small but quaint park. As the sun had reached an upright position, they were all happy with the shade from the trees in the park. Although the weather was pleasant, there was a slight breeze coming through from the sea that reminded them that spring had only just begun. Some of them joked that they were happy it was not the heat of summer. This early in the spring, the sun was happily welcomed by everyone. Most of them still had their jackets on because the morning had been chilly, but they were all coming off now. Everyone looked happy. Phoebe steered them through the city and talked as they walked. Eventually, they made it to Livraria Lello, the famous bookstore that is always crowded with visitors. She wanted to do this stop before lunch, because after lunch, the queue would be even longer. They stood in line and patiently waited for their turn. One of the British ladies complained. Amanda looked bored, but generally, there was a good tone due to the happy fact that they could already get a glimpse of the library. Eventually, they made it through the doors and got a chance to follow the stream of the crowd along the narrow passageways of the architectural gem. Everyone gasped, as they always did. They touched the wood and ran their hands over the railings.

They walked over the bridge, took what looked like a thousand photos from various angles, amazed at the construction. Soon enough, however, the tour ended in the bookstore. That was, after all, the purpose of this building. Most people in the group wanted to buy a souvenir or a book. Phoebe stepped to the side to wait for everyone to make their purchases. At this point, they were all hungry. Phoebe took them to one of the tourist company's alliance restaurants. It was big, but not as touristy as other places, and the food was authentic and good. Phoebe knew the waitress, so as the group sat down at their table, she chatted a little bit with her. They were a friendly group and tried to get to know each other a bit better while they skimmed through the menu. The other man was apparently from Finland. He had a travel partner who, for some reason, didn't feel like sightseeing and had gone shopping instead, which was why he had to go on the tour by himself. They all ordered a variety of local dishes and some wine, and continued their friendly chat as they ate. It was a lovely group, and Phoebe finally had the chance to sit down, calm herself a little, and join in the conversation. After her hectic morning, it was a warm welcome to sit down, and she loved getting to know everyone. But they were also on a schedule, so soon enough they had to pay and keep going.

They continued walking, now as a tighter group, and they chatted about their travels and home countries as they walked towards their next stop, which was Igreja do Carmo.

As they all went inside, the vast golden altar left no one unaffected. The elder woman, Marie, wiped a tear from the corner of her eye. The elder man held himself up with the cane and studied the space with his mouth open. She had understood that out of the whole group, the elder couple were the only ones who were actually religious. And now, they were visually affected. Phoebe smiled, seeing their expressions touched her heart. She began talking about the different features, the symbols, and various statues that were placed in high places around the church. It was a beautiful space but also intimidating. The architecture of the building left most feeling small, which was probably the point of it all. The whole church was rather heavy in its aesthetic with dark wood and golden features, while religious figures looked down on them from their pillars. After she had done her speech, she let the others explore on their own while she herself walked around in silence. She had been working as a tourist guide for over a year and had been here more times than she could remember. She both loved the protective atmosphere but always felt a sense of unease when looking at the painted figures. Today was not different. She suddenly felt a slight dizziness, so she sat down on a bench.

She looked up on Mother Mary. Her eyes traced the drapes of the robes, up to the script in her hands, and stalled a little at the cute depiction of little Jesus. Her crown was also very beautiful, and the carved gemstones actually looked real. Her feet were really tired, she took out her water bottle from her bag and had a sip, then continued to stare at Mary in a half-dreamy state. All of a sudden, Mary winked. Phoebe looked away. "Ok, she was really tired," she thought. She looked somewhere else instead, studying golden flowers that embellished the walls. But her curiosity took over, so she looked again. She winked again. Phoebe felt a shiver creep up on her arms and back. Her uneasiness made her get up and walk to another part of the church. She passed a few other figures, looked them in the face. They did not wink. She shook her head. Why was she checking wooden figures to see if they moved? Just a slight case of delusional senses. She must be going mad, maybe she was getting sick. She put her hand on her stomach and did a quick check with her internal world. Nope, no fever, nothing wrong with her stomach, just a slight sweat. She walked across the church to join the group. She briefly looked up at Mary holding her scroll and noticed her eyes were following her. She felt a shiver down her spine. This was not normal, she needed to get out of the church. "Are you ready to leave?" She asked the others.

"No, not yet. We haven't gotten to the living quarters yet. We have been studying artwork." The group agreed they wanted to stay another 20 minutes to see everything properly.

"Ok, I will go outside for some fresh air." Phoebe started walking towards the entrance. She needed to leave before she completely lost her mind.

"Are you planning to ignore me all day?"

Phoebe stopped in her tracks. She looked up at Mother Mary with a serious face. "That's right. I'm not going to entertain the idea that you're actually winking and waving and trying to talk to me. That's crazy." She turned to continue walking.

"Fine, suit yourself." Mary looked up again but continued to glance at her through the corner of her eye.

Phoebe started walking but stopped in her tracks. "Wait, what do you mean all day?" she continued.

Mary let out an audible puff as an attempt to conceal a laugh. "I have been trying to get your attention since this morning, haven't you noticed?" Mary answered with a serious but ever-so-peaceful expression of wonder on her face.

Phoebe suddenly remembered she was standing in a big room, and there were people at the other end. She looked around to make sure no one was paying attention to her before she answered.

"Why would you want to talk to me?"

"I am your guide after all. I have to help you process the events from last night. But I cannot help you until you accept my presence." "Last night?" Phoebe asked, surprised.

"Well, during your dream. Where were you? Do you remember?"

Phoebe thought for a second. She didn't remember anything. It was all just black.

She hardly ever remembered her dreams, though.

"Sorry, I don't remember anything. All I know is that I was in such a deep sleep that I slept through my alarm and got late for work."

She sat down and took out her water bottle to drink a few drops while searching for her memory.

"No, nothing. It's all just blank. You must have the wrong person." She continued, "I would never approach the wrong person. Only those who ask for me will be able to talk to me. But I understand that it is a lot to process. I will let it all sink in for now. But I will be back later." She looked at her with a soft smile.

"Why can't you just tell me what happened?" Phoebe asked

"Because that is not how this works. All I can do is guide you, you must do the work yourself. And you must make haste. We have a lot to do in a very short time. Your training starts tomorrow."

"Training, what training? I didn't sign up for training." Phoebe protested

Mary opened her scroll and looked at it as a mere gesture before she continued, "Actually, it says right here that you did. Training starts at midnight tomorrow night."

"What's that?" Phoebe was frightened but curious.

"Oh, nothing much, just your soul contract." She looked at Phoebe. She let out a laugh. "Oh, silly. Don't look so frightened. That's not your soul contract. Why would I carry that one around? Only you have your contract. Now, whether you want to remember it or not is up to you." She suddenly went stiff but continued talking: "The others are coming. I will see you later."

Phoebe felt uneasy. That was one intense minute. She had bitten off all of her nails in one emotional effort to smother her anxiety. Three deep breaths. One. Two. Three.

She put on a smile and approached her group, which was, indeed, done exploring and heading towards the exit. They had not noticed that she was still inside the church, but now, they all left together. They chatted in a merry tune while Phoebe tried to stay afloat with her cloudy head. The streets were busy with an afternoon jam outside. Suddenly, the bright light and the sounds were not as welcome to her. She felt a slight migraine taking a firm grip on her head. But at least the warmth of the sun felt nice. She took another deep breath.

"Who wants to get ice cream before our last stop?" She called out.

They all did, so they took a slight detour to a popular place, they waited, and got their scoops of gelato. As they reached the Crystal Garden, they were all very happy to be at the last stop. The elder couple had kept up despite all, but now their legs were tired. Amanda was complaining about a blister. Louise took out a band-aid from her purse and tended to her daughter's wound. They decided to take a stop at a corner of the garden. Phoebe said a few words about the place, but she was bad at remembering plants, so she kept it to a minimum. There were plenty of signs everywhere anyway, so they could gain more knowledge from those if they wanted.

They finished their ice-creams, and then the tour was finally over. Phoebe was exhausted and happy to be able to relax at last. Her encounter with Mother Mary had left a deep mark, and now she was not as enthusiastic as she was before. She had tried to hide it, of course, and the ice cream sure had helped with that mission. But now that everyone had said their farewells and left to explore the garden by themselves, she felt relieved.

She left the garden and started walking back towards the cathedral and was about to text Gabriel to get some coffee, but changed her mind midway. She needed to be alone. She sent him a text that she would go home and rest instead.

She took the tram home, felt very relieved when the cool stairwell greeted her, and was finally at ease as she opened her apartment door. What a day. A siesta was more than well deserved. She was quick to take off her shoes and get under the covers. She needed a power nap. Now.

This time, she set two alarms to be sure she would wake up in no later than one hour.

An hour's power nap felt like 5 minutes. She woke up in disarray. She had been in such deep REM sleep when the first alarm went off. She had still heard it and managed to press the snooze button. But that hardly helped. The next time it rang, she felt even worse. She snoozed again and again. The fourth time it rang, she finally sat up. She rubbed her eyes and tried to get the energy up in her body. She looked around the room. She suddenly remembered that she still hadn't showered today, so she got undressed and jumped in the shower. She stood underneath the warm water for a bit too long. She put her face directly into the harder stream of pressure closest to the showerhead. That felt so nice and really soothed the headache.

She took out the skirt and top that she had packed in her bag this morning. They were all wrinkled, so she threw them on a chair and picked out a soft citrus yellow dress instead. She did her makeup, fizzied up her curls into a fashionable afro, and tried out the new glitter oil on her light brown skin. She loved getting dressed up. She chose another pair of earrings that were more decorated than the simple hoop she had worn all day, put her sneakers back on, picked out a smaller shoulder bag, and put a light blue sweater around her shoulders before she headed out the door. By now, the air had become lighter, and as the sun was making its way across the horizon, the streets filled with a soft glow from the streetlights. Walking down the street, she felt increasingly energized and happy.

The restaurant was just a few blocks away, but the short walk really made a difference to her mood. She got in and was immediately greeted by her friends. They had taken a table by the window, so they had seen her as if she had skipped across the square.

"You're in an awfully good mood," Jacqueline exclaimed, cheering her on as she made her way towards them. Phoebe twirled.

"Yes! I've had a wonderful day at my job, and I have just taken a 1.5-hour power nap. I feel fantastic." She replied cheerfully, then she stopped herself slightly and added,

"I mean, I was awfully late for work this morning, stressed through most of the day, got an awful headache, so I had to go home and rest. But I feel fabulous now! She smiled brightly.

She sat down and looked at Gabriel across the table and added, "Thank you so much for saving me this morning, you are such a good friend." "Any time," Gabriel said, giving her a wink.

Bernie was sitting next to him and looking at both of them, trying to piece together what had happened, but soon he just asked.

"I didn't do anything; I just got her coffee". Gabriel answered with a chuckle while he shook his shoulders and gestured with his hands.

Phoebe watched them talk and tried to think of something to add, but couldn't.

Instead, she just picked up one of the menus and said, "Have you guys ordered already? Jacqueline looked at Phoebe and said, "Come on, let's order at the bar. "I know what others want."

They walked up to the bar in the middle of the room and got the waiter's attention.

Jacqueline turned to Phoebe as they waited and said, "I'm sure you must have realized by now?" "Realized what?" Phoebe looked confused.

"That Gabriel likes you? That can hardly come as a surprise."

"What? No. That's not true. He's my best friend."

"I'm not your best friend?" Jacqueline pretended to look hurt, and then she added, "Come on, he is always looking at you like some puppy dog, and he does everything for you at the wink of an eye. Haven't you noticed?"

The waiter arrived and they ordered the food and some beer for the table. They added two mojitos to that for themselves.

Phoebe felt annoyed, and as soon as the waiter had gone, she added to their conversation,

"Listen, Gabriel and I have been friends for a long time. If he had wanted anything more, he would have said something by now."

"Oh, come on. That's not fair for you to put it all on him. You know it isn't easy for guys to break the barrier once they've been put in the friend zone. You need to give him a lifeline." Jacqueline snorted and accepted her mojito from the waiter. Phoebe accepted hers and continued, "If I throw him that line and he doesn't take the bait, then I will have lost my great friend. Things will be awkward forever."

"Well, admitting you like him too is the first step. That's good," Jacqueline put up her glass in a half-hearted cheer.

Phoebe blushed and sipped her drink to distract herself. "Well, of course I like him.

I've liked him for a long time, but I would never act on it. It's not worth the risk." Jacqueline squinted into her eyes, trying to follow that train of thought, and finally just shook her head and said, "Well, the risk is not losing a friend, the risk is losing love." Phoebe stared at her. The food arrived, so they went back to join the others at the table. Phoebe glanced at Gabriel as he picked up a fajita and watched the others as they ate their food. She picked up her fish taco and ate in silence for a few moments before snapping out of it and joining in the conversation. Apparently, the others wanted to go clubbing afterwards and were discussing where to go. But Phoebe still had a headache, so she declined, causing a stir, but she was persistent. After dinner, the others went their way while she started walking back home.

She hadn't walked far when she heard some footsteps behind her and turned around in fright, but quickly got relieved when she saw it was Gabriel.

"I thought you were going clubbing with the others?"

"I couldn't let you walk home at night. What kind of friend would I be if I let anything happen to you?"

She was touched but added jokingly, "A very bad one, that's for sure."

The two of them started walking. They took a little detour down to the pier, talking about the day and various other unimportant things.

She looked up at his face as she continued walking. The glimmer of the street lights reflected in his blonde hair and bathed his shoulders in a soft glow.

He noticed her looking at him and said jokingly, "How will I face your father if you take a fall?"

She laughed and said, "Extra points for that," as she looked down towards her feet and the cobblestone.

"Extra points for what?" He said, thinking he knew the answer but was too afraid to ask.

She felt her cheeks blush, and she stared down at the ground to avoid his gaze.

As they continued walking, he accidentally grazed her hand a few times to check if his gut feeling was correct about the shift in energy.

When they reached the corner of the street, he instead took her hand. She looked at it and then looked up into his blue eyes. For a second, they locked gazes before he leaned forward and kissed her lips softly.

He stopped and apologised for his blunt behaviour. She looked at him with her big, brown eyes. She didn't know what to say, so she just put her hand on his neck and pulled him closer again. He kissed her again, intensely and passionately. She succumbed to the moment and lost track of both space and time. Her head was spinning, and she couldn't believe it had finally happened.

When they eventually stopped, his smile was the biggest she had ever seen on him. She was glowing herself, her heart pounding, and her hand slightly shaking. She looked at him in the eye again and said, "Never in a million years did I think that would ever happen." He laughed and hugged her and just agreed, "Me neither." They continued walking, and he added, "You know, I've wanted to do that so many times, but my nerves always stopped me."

She hugged him and said, "Me, too. I have dreamt of it for a long time, but I was afraid of what would happen to our friendship."

"The eternal fear of losing something good in the attempt to grasp for something great."

They strolled the streets, stopped here and there to smother each other with romance. Eventually, they arrived at her apartment.

He pulled her closer, kissed her, and bid good goodnight. But she stopped his movement with a quick tug on his arm. He looked deep into her eyes to try to read her thoughts. But she said in half a whisper, "Don't leave."

He took her in his arms again, and they kissed passionately in the dim light of the streetlight. She took out her key and opened the entrance door, and as they made their way up the staircase, they stopped at every flight to kiss intensely. As soon as they set foot in the apartment, things heated up instantly.

As he kissed her, she moved backwards until her back touched the wall. He leaned towards her and put his hand on her back to pull her closer, gently caressing her breast through her clothes. She let her hand reach up to his chest underneath his T-shirt as his right hand reached for the zipper on the back of her dress. She gently tugged at his belt, and they both stumbled into a passionate dance of undressing on their way to bed. Everything blended together into a heated bliss, and as their bodies landed on the bed in synchronized union, it almost felt like the two of them had become one. She could hardly feel where she ended and he began, but she could feel his heavy breathing on his chest and his hands caressing her body. His devotion to her in his lovemaking was amorous magic that breathed fire into her very being as if it had been the elixir she had been yearning for her entire life. Her mind disappeared into a blissful fog, and she gasped for air as she caressed him back and embraced his very being.

After they were finished, she curled up in his arms, pressed her cheek to his chest so she could listen to his heartbeat. He stroked her arm, giggled to himself, and said, "Never in my wildest dreams would I have dared to imagine, when I woke up this morning, that the day would end like this." He kissed her hair, and she just added, "I just can't believe that it finally happened. You make me so happy."

They both dozed off and slept through the night in each other's arms.

The next morning, as they woke up, they both giggled. She looked up towards him and said, "I can't believe it really happened. I thought it was just a dream. A beautiful dream". She kissed him tenderly. "Do you want breakfast in bed?" he asked and sat up to put his boxers on and go to the kitchen. She thought for a moment, then replied, "I'm afraid that's not really possible. All I have is some eggs and yoghurt. There might be some coffee in the cupboard, but that's it."

"Ok, no problem. I'll go get something. I'll be back in a few minutes." He started getting dressed. She added, "Let's just go to the Caramel Café. They have a beautiful breakfast and a romantic little courtyard in the back."

She quickly threw on a pair of jeans and a T-shirt, and they walked down together, holding hands. She was suddenly smitten by every word he said, high on her feelings for him. She wasn't used to feeling like this, and she didn't know how to contain herself, so she just let herself savour the moment. They ordered and found a spot in the sun. He looked at her with a sweet tenderness in his eyes. She stroked his hand, focused her attention on that to avoid his gaze as she was feeling awkward getting so much attention. She leaned over and kissed him, and said, "Now, will you please stop looking at me, you're making me uncomfortable."

"Only if you stop looking at me first." He answered, flushing his eyebrows. She leaned her chin to her hand and fluttered her eyelashes towards him and laughed in a flirtatious manner. She was over the moon, but she had never been in this kind of situation before, and she didn't really know how to act. He was a person she had known for so long that she knew him, but still didn't. Everything was new and odd all of a sudden, yet it felt familiar and safe.

He said what she was thinking. "We have known each other for so long that this feels a bit strange. We normally talk about everything, and suddenly I don't want to talk at all, just stare at you." He laughed awkwardly and took a sip from his coffee. They sat at the café for a while, basking in the glory of the moment. Phoebe didn't want it to end, but soon enough, reality caught up. She looked at her watch and saw a text from her boss, asking her to fill in later that afternoon. So, she said goodbye to Gabriel and went back home to change into her work clothes.

As she came through the door, however, she noticed that someone was there. She didn't get scared, though, because she immediately saw who it was.

"Oh, my. I forgot about you," she said.

"Yes, I can see that. I believe you forgot about anything other than your new love." Mother Mary said in a rather harsh tone.

"He is not just my new love, he is Gabriel." Phoebe corrected her.

"Well. Naturally, I am very happy for you. I know you have been pining over him for quite some time. But you have work to do, and now you must also focus on your work." She said.

"I am. I am going to work right now," Phoebe stated irritably.

"My dear, not that work. That is completely irrelevant. I am referring to your soul work." Mother Mary said in a surprised manner as she adjusted her blue mantle. She looked calm and poised, and her voice was filled with compassion as she continued.

"You still have a lot of ground left to cover in a very short time."

Phoebe got annoyed, "But I don't have time for this right now."

Mother Mary walked up to her and looked at her with a serious expression. "You cannot run away from this like you run away from everything else." "I don't do that," Phoebe sighed and discreetly rolled her eyes.

Mother Mary straightened her white gown as a means of entertaining herself as she waited for Phoebe to change.

"I believe that love has gotten to your brain, and I'm willing to overlook it, for now. " She said, "But let me just say this. Love is beautiful, my dear."

Phoebe interrupted dreamily and sat down on the couch to put on her socks. "Love is amazing!" She said with a big smile.

Mother Mary got a little frustrated and closed her eyes to think.

"Do you have any recollection at all from your dream the other night?"

"Nope, still nothing. I'm telling you you've got the wrong girl." Phoebe answered in a rebellious manner, sounding like a teenager.

"My dear, you are the one who has called me to you. Can you phantom why you would do that at this hour?"

Phoebe stopped her track abruptly and looked at her. She thought of something to say and suddenly felt a slight embarrassment. "I am sorry, but I really don't. Before yesterday, I never even thought of you as being real. I have never been to church other than for my job. I'm not even sure I believe so, I really don't get why you would want to talk to me out of all people. I have not done anything to deserve your visit."

Mother Mary looked at her in silence first. Then she said peacefully,

"I chose to be your guide because you needed me most. You are so lost, my child, and you don't even see it."

Phoebe tried to object, but instead she asked, "If I am lost when I am feeling this happy, then tell me what it is I am doing wrong." Mother Mary looked deep into her eyes and said,

"You can love another as much as you want, just don't forget to love yourself." She left before Phoebe got a chance to answer.

CHAPTER 5

The Orchid

The first sound she heard before opening her eyes was the dripping of water from the small fountain next to her. The water was sipping through a rock, bouncing down walls of stone and green moss as it made its way down into a golden basin. She was seated in the lotus position with her hands in her lap. Four pillars surrounded the circle she was sitting in, holding up a stone circle high above her head. A beautiful purple wisteria climbed up the pillars and peeked through above her. Elena noticed she was holding a white rose. She held it up to her nose and breathed in the sweet aroma, then she looked around to understand what kind of place she was in. It seemed like a beautiful garden. Behind her, flower bushes competed for space and framed a stone wall. The path leading away from her was lined with planted flowers in pink, peach, and violet. She finally noticed that the stone she was sitting on was cold, so she stood up. She traced the flowers with her eyes but could not see the end of the path. There was a whole forest to the left, filled with oak, ash, and birch. Lanterns were placed on their branches and offered some light in the night. She stepped onto the path and noticed how it lit up under her feet. She held the hem of her lilac dress so that she could see better. There was a magic glow in yellow and pink as she put her weight on her foot, which disappeared when she removed it. She was rather amused. Her feet were bare, so she could see the light echoing through the soles of her feet as she touched it. For a few moments, she played with that back and forth until she eventually collected herself and continued her walk. She reached a slight turn, where the forest opened up to a small meadow filled with cosmos, daisies, and poppies. The path took her through the meadow, and she noticed how large gemstones were placed amongst the grass like small, enchanted castles. The lights were now not only in the trees but filled the meadow with a glorious glow in pinks, yellows, and blues. She was bewildered with childish amusement and danced around the fields with the blue trees as her only witness. She eventually had enough and continued the path at the other end. She walked amongst the dark trees. A few minutes later, she reached a small wooden bridge painted red. It was tiny, really, but it helped her cross the stream. The water was dark, but she could still make out the three koi fish swimming in the ripples. One was bright red, one was white with golden spots, and the last one was almost black. She crossed to the other side and noticed that the landscape had changed. Instead of the enchanted forest, she was now standing in front of a tunnel shaped by tall bamboo trees. She buried her bare feet in the cold sand. For a moment, she was too scared to enter. "What was waiting on the other side?" But she could see a dim light at the end of it. There were also a few lanterns placed on the ground that helped her gather courage. She began moving towards the light, and soon, she noticed how all sound completely disappeared. In the cool air and stillness of the trees, it was almost as if time stood still. She was just there, touching the leaves as she walked, enjoying the softness of the white sand under her feet. A dragonfly flew up to her, hovering in mid-air, and disappeared again. Soon, she had walked so far that she could neither see the beginning nor the end. She felt scared as she realized that the light was neither getting bigger nor brighter. But her only choice was to continue. Eventually, the light got brighter and she found herself on the other side.

She peeked out from the tunnel and was met by sunshine. After having come from a serene nighttime walk in the forest, then through the dark tunnel, this light was quite a contrast. As her eyes adjusted, she noticed that she was standing on the edge of a circle, and she was not alone. There were eleven more openings to bamboo tunnels, and in each stood another woman, dressed just like her. They could, however, only see each other and wave. It was too far to talk, and they were separated by a maze of boxwood that reached up to their waist, creating edges to an intricate garden of Mediterranean bushes, tropical flowers, and palm trees. The passage was an easy stroll on grained granite, but what first seemed like a fun challenge soon turned into a frustrating menace. It was maddening to be able to see each other, and the end destination, yet not figured out how to get there. Elena started by taking a right, but that led to a dead end, so she walked back and took the left instead and continued in that lane until that one too led to another dead end. She had apparently missed a small hole in the wall, so she traced her steps and walked through the hole to the next section. Everyone was having the same issues, and the tension rose to their heads. Their only comfort was knowing that they were not alone. After what felt like forever, they finally reached the other side. They all looked at each other and smiled proudly. One girl, however, was still struggling, so they all tried their best to help her find her way out. Elena noticed Phoebe first and waved. Ayla stepped out into the light, too, and the three of them were delighted to be in the same group. They soon learned that the struggling woman's name was Danica. She finally made it out with the help of the others. They greeted the other women too, and then silenced themselves and turned towards a woman standing in front of a small Chinese garden house. She was standing in the center of a large donut-shaped jade stone. She had watched their defeat in the maze in silence and stillness. Although her face appeared serious, she soon revealed a subtle smile as she began to speak.

"I have only admiration and compassion for you. I once stood in your place and remembered the struggle. I know that it is a difficult challenge when you are caught up in it, but it is also difficult to watch and not be able to help. It is only when you reach the end that you can look back and see your own progress and purpose with a clear mind and bright vision."

She straightened out her light green kimono and smoothed the pink satin belt wrapped around her waist. Her dress was beautiful in hues of jade green, sky blue, and light pink. Embroideries of peonies, roses, and cherry blossoms decorated the whole front. She began speaking with a soft but firm voice.

"I am Kuan Yin. I am one of your guides. Some of you have met me already, and the others will get to know me soon enough. Be assured that I know you and more of you than you think." Elena was astonished by the seriousness in her tone. "Kuan Yin is the goddess of love and compassion", she thought, "Why is she so serious?"

Kuan Yin looked at her, and she felt a sudden shame as she remembered that Kuan Yin could hear her thoughts, including the one she had just thought. So, best to stop thinking. Altogether. Like now."

Kuan Yin let out a laugh. "This is not military school, and I am not some commander-in-chief. All of you seem to be scared of me." She paused briefly before she continued, "I get it. You are in a place you do not recognise and are being exposed to various types of tests. You feel unsafe and alone. I once stood where you stand now, although it was a different time and the path was different. Together with many others, I paved the way during my journey so that I could stand here today. We are now at a place in human history that is challenging, scary, but critical. The time is now, and it is only you who has the power to make the change. You are the chosen ones for this mission. I can guide you, but I cannot do it for you." The women sighed loudly at the same time and looked around with uneasy expressions in their eyes. Kuan Yin witnessed their silent processing of uncomfortable emotions and continued.

"You have already walked through an enchanted garden, a bamboo tunnel, and a triggering maze. But I am afraid the night is not over. You are about to embark on a ride over Lake Tamara to the Mirror Palace. There, we will join the other groups for a collective ceremony and three more activities that we will do together. You will stay with me and in this group the entire time. It is critical that you do not wander off on your own or dawdle. We have a lot to cover in a short time." "Yes, ma'am." They all instinctively said the same thing.

Kuan Yin instantly corrected them calmly. "I am not your superior. I am your equal." She swished her dress and started walking towards the shoreline.

Phoebe raised her hand and asked bluntly. "How come we are divided into groups of twelve?" She looked around the room to make sure she had counted that correctly. Danica answered, "Because we each represent a chakra, right?"

Elena added, "That makes sense. Because the three of us stood together during the ceremony in Rose Temple, and we all got different tea. Which chakras do you all have? I have a heart."

Ayla nodded to what she said and confirmed the theory by stating that they indeed must have different chakras, since she had the throat and Phoebe had the third eye. Danica added, "Ok, so we solved that mystery, but why do we have different chakras, and why are we all in the same group and not with someone else?"

They were discussing various theories among themselves to try to figure it out.

Kuan Yin had stopped in her tracks and stood in silence to listen to their dialogue.

"These are all excellent questions.

You all have a chakra each because it was necessary to divide up the work as such, so that one person in each group could take the lead. The reason for the chakra that you have got is based on your placement in the world, your soul contract, and your karma. You will stay with each other for the rest of your journey."

"Ok, then can we get five minutes to get to know each other?"
"Yes, of course. Let's do a quick introduction:

Nora from Sweden has the Stellar gateway,
Danica from has the Soul star,
Akira from Japan has the Causal chakra.
Ming from China has Crown,
Phoebe from Portugal has a Third Eye,
Ayla from Canada has the Throat chakra,
Elena from Australia has the Heart,
Jiya from India has Solar Plexus,
Meira from Lithuania has Naval,
Esther from Poland has Sacral,
Evelyn from the UK has Root
Hanwi from the US has the Earth star.

They all looked at each other, waving as they said their names and trying to process all the other information.

Kuan Yin then proceeded to walk towards the shoreline where a boat was waiting. They all followed her and got aboard and sat down on a cushioned bench. The boat looked like a low canal boat, and it was lined with silver. They all paired together two by two while Kuan Yin sat alone at the back. As soon as everyone was seated, the boat started moving without any apparent motor. "How is it moving without any help?" Ayla asked curiously.

"We are thirteen powerful women. We are moving it with our mind." Kuan Yin answered.

"But only you know where we are going," Ayla added.

"Your souls know too. You have been there before, you just don't remember." Kuan Yin turned silent and rested her gaze on the horizon.

Elena watched as the waves of the water splashed towards the boat. She studied the different shades of blue and teal, foretelling the movement of the water. She first followed the shoreline, but it became more and more distant as they approached the open lake. The light blue and pink sky, mirrored the surface. A few white clouds were also visible in the reflection. They travelled for a while, the wind swirling in their hair. No one was wearing chunky golden jewellery today. They were all in the same lilac midi dress with some simple white florals in their hair and a pink bracelet in rhodonite. All of them were still holding the white rose. The vastness of the open lake made Elena a bit uneasy, so she began studying the boat instead. Something was inscribed in the silver metal. She could not make out what it was. Even the benches they were sitting on had some sort of writing on them. It looked like scribbles. She studied the lines and the dots. The other women were also getting uneasy as they made their way across the waters. Soon, however, they approached the shoreline again on the other side of the lake. She had seen the mountainous outline in the distance and only realized once they got close that it reached the sky and even had some snow at the top. But the place they were moving towards looked like a palace at the foot of the mountains. It was perfectly symmetrical with two towers on either end, and a long white wall between them. At the center, she could make out the tip of a pyramid, but she could not imagine what it was exactly.

As their boat approached the shoreline, she noticed the stone staircase that was lodged into the steep shoreline, connecting the palace to the docks. It was over three stories tall. Elena glanced over at Phoebe, who was sitting next to her. Phoebe had noticed it too and nudged her in the side as she said, "Those look like the workout of a lifetime. I'm glad I'm asleep." She laughed at herself. Jiya, who was sitting behind her, said with widened eyes and a quiet voice, "That will probably not help you. I think we will all wake up with sore legs tomorrow." The boat arrived at the dock. They all stood up to get ready to disembark. Many more boats arrived at about the same time, and all the women got out of their boats but seemed to stop in their steps to stare at the monstrosity of the staircase. There were actually two staircases that meandered like two snakes in mirrored synchronicity up to the top of the rock. But the sacred symbolism didn't help this time. It must have been five stories tall, at least.

Kuan Yin stepped out of the boat. From the other boats stepped Mother Mary, Isis, Mary Magdalene, Athena, Portia, Lady Nada, Tara, and many more Ascended Masters.

They all looked at the woman who seemed to have frozen in their steps. "Well, there is only one way up!" Athena proclaimed, urging the others on. The women started climbing, holding their dresses up as they walked. The steps leading up to the first resting point were fairly easy. Some stopped there to rest for a little. Elena moved on, she was finally happy about her good fitness routine. She cheered the others on as she passed by them. She reached the next resting point but kept going. Both Ayla and Phoebe had to stop to breathe. But even Elena lost her breath by the third resting point. She stopped to take in the view. The lake was much bigger than it had felt in the boat. It spread out so far and wide that she could not see the end of it and nestled among treetops and hillsides. She turned around and looked up. Only two more flights to go. She continued to climb and soon, she finally reached the top. Most women in the entourage were leaning over the railing, while others were lying flat on the ground. Elena saw a couple of benches in the middle of the square and walked over to sit down. Having lost muscle power in her legs for a few moments, Meira was struggling to get up the steps, but soon her head bobbed up over the top staircase. Elena watched her struggle, keeping a straight face although it looked rather amusing. As she was waiting for the others to regain their strength, Elena looked around in an attempt to understand where she was. It was a beautiful square lined with large quartz crystals and a few olive trees. It looked like an auditorium of some sort with all the benches lined up towards the palace entrance. They were all carved in the same stone as the ground, which is why at first, she didn't see them all. Apart from the olive trees, she couldn't see a trace of greenery on the grounds. Not like the last palace that had flowers and bushes everywhere. She interrupted herself as she noticed that the rest of her group had made it up the stairs. They were catching their breath, and some of them were even stretching. They argued that it was better to be safe than sorry and took precautions in case it actually was true that the sore muscles would be felt when they woke up.

After a while, the Ascended Masters joined the crowd of women. They marched through the auditorium and took their positions in front of the entrance. The others in the group quickly joined Elena on the bench, seated in the centre left. The heavy glass doors opened, and Angel Sophia stepped out with a radiant glow. She was wearing a magnificent white mermaid gown that had a pearlescent shimmer in gold and white. When she first entered, her aura was so strong that her wings stretched out and shone brightly. But as soon as she reached the center of the stage, the wings became translucent and folded to her back like a glowing mantle. She looked around.

Both at the Ascended Masters and then towards the women in the audience.

"My children. Thank you for your courage to be here today. I praise you for the work you have done to get you to this point. You are brave souls with strong hearts. I know that the last few days have stirred up unprocessed emotions and insecurities. You have all been assigned help from our dear guides and mentors. They will continue to guide you, so feel safe to lean on them.

Every one of you has walked many miles to get to where you are today, in this life and the lifetimes before. You have prepared for this, and you have already trained for this without your conscious knowledge. But it will still not be easy. Today, you have already passed through a variety of tests, and there are a few yet to come. You must now stay in your groups so that you do not get lost. Technically, you are in a dream while your physical body is asleep, but the effect of getting lost here can cause trauma in your heart that is challenging to heal. I wish you luck as you enter this sacred building and bid that you take with you the wisdom as you continue on your journey. I love you, I see you, I am always with you. And so, it is."

They all stood up to meet with their guide. The glass doors opened to reveal more entrances so that all of them could enter seamlessly and without delay. Elena touched the palace wall as she entered. From a distance, the building had appeared an angelic white stone, but now that she was next to it, she noticed that it was built with selenite. The facade glowed in a protective white light. She looked up at the archways and the magnificent pillars in labradorite. She touched that one too, for healing light and protection. When she went inside, however, the energy shifted. They arrived in a vast hallway where the royal blue walls in sanded stone arched up towards a tall ceiling that was entirely covered in big mirrors.

At every two to three meters, there was a ceiling rose from which star-shaped chandeliers pierced down a few metres, offering a soft, pristine white light. The brisk air from the lake mixed with the warmer air of the palace, which felt nice on the skin. Their group stopped for a second to adorn the features before continuing. Neither one of them could contain their inner child and started making faces towards the mirrors in the ceiling as they walked underneath them.

Ayla mentioned the beauty of the star-shaped lamps. Meira pointed out that they were, in fact, not stars but shaped as merkabas, one of the most sacred symbols of divine light. Elena looked at her in awe, "That was impressive. How did you know that?" Meira glanced at the others and answered, "I actually don't know, I just knew it. Maybe I have read it somewhere. I'm a university professor in real life, but in a completely different field."

Kuan Yin had stopped further down the hallway to wait for them. The women hurried along so as not to keep her waiting. They entered another part of the building, where the features changed. Now they had reached a long white corridor. The tiles on the floor in the entrance changed to smooth white concrete, and the aesthetic turned a lot more minimalistic.

The corridor was open towards the right with archways that displayed a glow of different colours. The women peeked through each archway as they passed. The sun was shining through, so they thought that they were leading to a courtyard or something, but they were wrong. In the middle of the palace was a conservatory with a glass ceiling in the shape of a pyramid. That was the pointy part of the building that Elena had seen from the boat. The archways were actually not doorways; they were windows, each framing a different coloured stained glass. The wall to their left was smooth and white, just like the ground. As the coloured glass reflected onto the wall, the light formed a row of consecutive colours, just like a rainbow. They got a chance to look through the windows and take in the beauty of the conservatory. It was very large with rainbow windows covering all four sides of the square. The sun shimmered through the glass ceiling and as its light reached the colourful archways, it bounced in synchronicity, creating a magical rainbow ray.

"That is one of the most amazing things I have ever seen". The testament came from the group's oldest member, Evelyn, who had been quite quiet up until now. But now, she was awestruck with her mouth open as she peeked through the window and up to the peak of the pyramid.

Everyone agreed, Kuan Yin too. She smiled and said, "There are many beautiful places on this and other realms, but this room is one of my personal favourites." "Are we allowed to go in there?" Akira said with hope in her voice.

"The purpose of the room is to receive rainbow light through its reflections so that you can absorb the amount that you are able to handle. But stepping into the rainbow light is quite different. You will get to do that at a later stage, but in a different place.

Now let's go to our wing."

They arrived at a double door in heavy wood. It was painted dark green with a golden handle. She waited for a second so that all the women would be gathered before she opened the doors.

Kuan Yin told them to close their eyes as they entered the room. She closed the doors behind them before they were allowed to open them again and take in the magic. The room was dark, but there were thousands of strings of light hanging from the ceiling, and the room's four walls were lined with mirrors, creating the effect of standing in infinite space. Each string had some sort of coloured light on it, and they were all pouring down from the ceiling at different lengths. Spread out across the room, there were even more mirrors in different shapes and at different angles. They were all so affected by the beauty of this space that they were lost for words. They stayed in silence even as they stepped into the light and navigated the room. They soon found out that some of the lights were anchored onto the floor, providing them with a pathway that helped them walk through space. It twirled and curled its way forth like a serpent. Each time they approached the wall, they were greeted by their own reflection in the mirror. Some of the mirrors were distorted just like in a fun house, and made them laugh and stop in their tracks to play with their reflection. But no one said a word or reacted fully until they reached the end. They were immediately taken into a lounge that formed a link between the star room and the next section. The lounge was not big, but it was big enough to seat them comfortably. The same tone of dark violet covered the floor, walls, and ceiling, and two magenta sofas were attached to either side of the room, forming mirroring waves. Velvet cushions in yellow and teal were spread out on the sofas, and live candles were burning in the grand chandelier that hung from the ceiling, offering a dim light to the whole space. Once everyone was seated, Kuan Yin spoke. "The space that we just went through is truly mesmerizing, but it also has a subtle challenge that will present itself in your physical lives. We will now do a meditation together to anchor the energy that we have just received and open our hearts to compassion and forgiveness. Place your hands in an outward position and face your palms upwards. Put your white rose in your lap for now and close your eyes."

I accept all fragments of me, all that I am afraid of, all that I love. I henceforth allow myself to love myself unconditionally and release me from the separation of my wholeness. I witness my strength, I witness my sorrow, I witness my fears and free myself for the light of tomorrow. I give space to my heart in all its glory and embrace all parts of me and all of my story. This is just the beginning, not the end. So as a first step on my journey, with myself I make amends.

"You are now ready for the next part.

While the purpose of the last room was to reflect, the purpose of the next room is to trust. You will know why in just a few seconds."

"How many more rooms are there?" asked Akira.

But Kuan Yin did not answer directly. She just said.

"Each section of this palace is designed to open your eyes to the parts of your heart and soul that need healing. It is easy to get lost in the process of healing one's heart. The number of rooms is finite, but the number of lessons is infinite. Therefore, I will not tell you how much is left. You must trust the process."

The doors at the end of the lounge opened, creating a stream of white light. After having just been in the dark mirror room and then the dark purple lounge, the brightness overwhelmed them. They picked up their roses and walked towards it. They first walked confidently, but as soon as they stepped into the light, they gasped. Once everyone had passed through to the next room, Kuan Yin closed the doors behind them so that the bright light and the golden railing were all that they could see. They were standing on a white marble platform, the same white colour on the walls. So, for a second, it looked like they were floating in nothingness. But some of the women had already peeked at the task ahead, and they knew that was not the case.

Danica was the first to walk up to the railing, and she quickly took a step back. The elder woman, Evelyn, had followed her and was now holding the railing firmly with her arms stretched out. The panic was slowly consuming her.

Elena leaned over the golden railing to understand what she was looking at. It was a spiral staircase unlike any other she had seen. The steps were in a colourful glass mosaic, but each step seemed to be disconnected from the other. It almost looked like they were hovering in mid-air. Elena loved adventure and was never afraid of anything, so she was more excited than anything. But she could understand why Evelyn and a few others were so scared. She looked around the space. It became clear to her that they were standing in one of the towers because the room was shaped like a cylinder. The staircase began as attached to the walls but soon detached to descend into a central point. From where they were standing, it looked like a spiralling fossil.

Elena turned to Evelyn and put her hand on her arm. "There is no need to panic. We are all here, and we will get through this together." Evelyn looked at her in silence, her blue eyes widened, and her mind disconnected.

Elena noticed the white marble bench, got Evelyn's attention, and steered her so that she could sit down. Some of the other women were already sitting down, waiting for instructions.

Kuan Yin was standing a few metres away, holding the railing with her right hand.

She looked down, and then she looked at the women.

"I was once in a physical body on Earth as well. I understand that the fear of heights is rational. However, remember that your physical body is safe in your bed at home. So, nothing would happen to you if you were to fall. I know it does not feel like that right now, though." She paused and looked at them all compassionately before she continued, "Before we begin, I want to let you in on a little secret: there are railings in glass that will support you all the way down. But the steps are, in fact, not connected so you need to tread carefully. For those who are particularly afraid, I suggest that you walk in the middle." She looked at Evelyn and added. "I will walk after you to ease your discomfort."

Elena volunteered to walk first. She was so excited that she could hardly contain herself. She did feel bad for a second about leaving Evelyn's side, but she knew she was going to be alright walking in the middle of Akira and Kuan Yin. She started walking, holding on to the railing with her right hand and slightly holding on to the wall with her left. After one turn around the cylinder, the staircase separated from the safety of the wall, and instead, a second railing appeared. She had at this point been able to keep a good pace so that all 12 women who were behind her would have room to control their steps without having to pause on a hovering plate. As the conversation was going behind her, it soon became clear from everyone's complaints and shrieks that it was much scarier to stop than to keep going. But now she suddenly felt how fear flickered at the back of her throat, and her heart started pounding. Once the stairs were free from the wall, it got a lot more frightening. The adrenaline pumped in her ears. The others could understand her fear and stood still in their place, patiently waiting so as not to rush her. Evelyn, Akira, and Kuan Yin were far behind, so they were not affected by this momentary pause. Elena breathed and continued. After a few more turns, they reached a point where they had approached so closely to the center point to the extent that the right railings disappeared and were replaced with a white center column. At this point, however, they were only a few meters above ground, so Elena just let go of safety and skipped down the remaining steps. When her feet finally touched solid ground, though, she felt relieved. She turned and watched the others. Phoebe, Hanwi, and Jiya had been right behind her, but Ayla and Meira had not come midway yet. So, while Akira and Kuan Yin were assisting Evelyn at the point where the staircase detached from the walls, the remaining six were hovering at the midpoint, trying to cope with the feeling of insecurity on each step. Elena sat down on one of the gigantic white pillows that were strategically placed as a resting place after finishing this defeat. She noticed the glasses of water, picked one up and drank gratefully. They were all emotionally and mentally exhausted. The stirring of emotions from the floating staircase, the feeling of unease, but also the adrenaline that was still pounding in her heart and head. She thought about the stillness of the Mirror room, where she had laughed at the reflection of herself in every turn and treasured the enchanting space of magical lights. As her bare feet had touched the cool metal floor, it had bestowed a cool serenity inside. She felt peaceful and powerful. She turned towards the other girls.

"What do you suppose the symbolic meaning of this exercise was?"

Jiya was quick to answer, "To trust divine."

Hanwi added: "And to trust each other."

Phoebe sat down with her glass of water, looked at the others, listened to the conversation, and nodded in agreement. "I think courage is a big part of it," she said.

"Yeah, that too," Hanwi said, and everyone nodded.

Anya, who had overheard their conversation as she was approaching the ground, said.

"I think we need to be reminded that we can trust ourselves in every step." "Without laughing at ourselves like we did in the other room," Jiya added. It seemed all fun and games at first, but now that I think of it, it feels so wrong that I laughed at a big bum or spaghetti arm. But it also feels wrong that I judged my own fear coming down the stairs."

"Wow, I didn't even think of that." Elena was amazed by Jiya's insight. "But come to think of it, my biggest fear was not walking down the stairs. Obviously, as you saw, I thought it was rather fun. My biggest fear was your judgment of my pace, my fear of how I shared information about the staircase with the rest of you. I bet you could sense that when I got scared in the middle and paused. I hope I didn't cause you distress." Elena said.

Meira tilted her head in surprise; "I didn't even notice that you paused or that you were scared. You seemed so confident."

Hanwi agreed and said, "Oh, that's another lesson then. How we see each other at the moment of fear and trust."

"This was all very intense," Phoebe said at last as she scratched the back of her head, "I wonder what is next."

Soon, Evelyn had made it all the way down to the safe ground. You could tell that she was completely exhausted in every possible way and grateful that it was finally over. She got offered a pillow chair, and she threw herself in it, cheering in relief. "I just cannot believe I just survived that!" She stuck her tongue out in exhaustion and reminded herself of where she was, so she quickly added, "Oh, you know what I mean!" Everyone laughed. They completely knew what she meant. Even though they were here in a mental state, it did not mean that the experience was any less real.

After they all had rested and felt ready, Kuan Yin spoke again: "That was a challenging test. I am proud of you, and you should be proud of yourself. I believe the next part will be a lot more welcome and less scary." She said with a trace of excitement on her face.

She opened the doors behind them to reveal the next room.

Akira immediately screamed in excitement, and Phoebe yelled, "I can't believe this was waiting for us this whole time, and just a minute ago, we were in survival mode!" She laughed and clasped her hands. The others stood in awe. Elena was busy taking everything in before she added, "This looks like my childhood dream, like a dream within a dream."

It was a really big space. At first glance, it looked like a fun and crazy garden, with green grass, palm trees, a fountain, and some sun chairs. But as they studied the different sections, it became clear that the only things that were real were the green grass and the palm trees.

At the far-right corner was a colourful castle that was raised to look like it was sitting on a cloud. It had a cerise roof and yellow-coloured walls that glittered in the lights. A brightly coloured steep staircase led up to a small window, and off to the left side of it was nothing other than a bright pink slide. A slide big enough to fit an adult. It led to the section in the left corner, which had a fake beach that covered nearly all the back and left wall. The beach itself was made of sand that glittered in different soft pastels. But the best part was the slide from the castle ended in fake water. Which, of course, wasn't even water at all. It was a giant ball pit, filled with translucent balls in light metallic hues of blue, turquoise, purple, and white. The entire surface shimmered like the sea as the ceiling lights bounced off them. Four sun beds shaped like oyster shells were placed in the colourful shimmering sand, completing the whole mermaid experience with mermaid tail blankets and pearlescent round pillows.

"This is quite childish, isn't it?" Edith said in a judgmental tone, "Why would you set up a children's playground in a retreat? What is the point of this?" But Kuan Yin ignored Edith's cynicism and just said.

"This is the most important room of them all. Of course, there are some hidden elements here. It is designed to unleash your dormant inner child. I will leave you alone to explore on your own. I will be back in two hours. Enjoy!"

Edith said something else about not being serious enough, but no one listened to her. As soon as Kuan Yin had left, they all started running. Phoebe and Hanwi were the first to run up to the castle tree house and ride the slide to the ball pit, laughing with laughter. Ayla and Meira went towards the sun chairs and sat down.

"This is so soft," Meira was delightfully playing with her chair as she got comfortable with the blanket and pillow. Ayla did the same, pressing the buttons on the side to see what they did. Suddenly, one of the buttons caused a serenade of soap bubbles to shoot out all around them. Meira laughed in excitement and pressed the same button on hers, and they both cheered and stretched their arms out into the air in a childish manner to touch them as they rose to the ceiling.

Akira noticed a big swing in the other corner. It was big enough to lie down on. There was more than one of them, so Jiya joined her. This was nice. They were lined with white linen, and as soon as they put their heads to one of the many pillows, they unleashed a surround system that both blew wind and let out a sound into the entire room of crashing waves and singing dolphins.

Edith shook her head. She was still grumpy with the idea of something so childish after the defeat of the staircase. Healing was meant to be serious. She looked around the room and noticed a tipi tent to the right. She walked through the soft grass to get there. She popped her head in and saw that it was the perfect spot to relax and meditate. "It's big enough for two," she said to Evelyn, "if you want to join me?" Evelyn did. She needed to rest her mind a bit after the last room. The two of them lay down in the tent and looked up at the fabric ceiling. It was sand coloured with pastel tassels hanging from every crease. The floor itself felt like a big round mattress, and there were pillows all around in lavender and soft pinks. They decided to just lay down in the middle and stare at the tassels for a while. But just as with the other stations, there was an element of surprise. Evelyn found a control panel and soon a meditative sound filled the inside of the tent. She pressed another button and a gloom of colour filled the space, shifting smoothly from red to pink to purple to blue to green to yellow to orange, and then back again. The experience was so beautiful, and they could very well stay there for the whole time.

Elena popped her head through the tent door. "This looks cozy. Room for one more?" She had already played at the other stations, and this looked comforting. Evelyn said she wanted some help to try the slide first. Jiya and Hanwi said she could join them. Edith was persuaded to try one of the swings, and Elena got to try the tent together with Ayla.

After having explored the space like a couple of kids for a while, Kuan Yin came back. They all immediately sounded like a group of kids, too, even Edith, when they tried to persuade her to give them five more minutes.

Kuan Yin laughed out loud. If you knew where we were going now, you wouldn't be so sad.

They followed her through some patio doors to an outside area that was beautifully framed by a low marble wall. The floor was filled with an extensive geometric pattern of the flower of life. They gazed up at the enchanting stars as an etheric sound slowly started to fill the space with a transitioning beat. Some women from the other groups were already there, and soon enough, the space was filled with women who were swaying their hips to the music and taking in the etheric atmosphere.

CHAPTER 6

The Magician

Grinning from ear to ear, Phoebe woke up as if in a trance. She had just had the most wonderful dream, and she actually remembered parts of it this time. She turned around to try to wake Gabriel up with a kiss. But he just made a grunt and continued sleeping. She gave him a couple more kisses, on his arm, on his cheek, on his forehead. But all her attempts failed, and he continued to snore. So, she got up instead.

She made herself an espresso and sat in the kitchen, wearing his T-shirt. After a while, he came in, wearing only boxers. He walked straight over and gave her a kiss. "Good morning, you're up early."

"It's not that early. I tried to wake you, but you wouldn't budge", she said with a slight giggle. He walked back towards the bedroom and said over his shoulder, "Nice shirt, by the way, is it new?" She chuckled but didn't reply, just continued to soak in the morning sun shining through the window while sipping her coffee and reading the newspaper. He came back with clothes on, except for his missing T-shirt, made himself an espresso too, and opened a few cabinets before looking over at her. "Do you have anything edible, or is coffee your only stream of life?"

She pointed to the big free-standing cupboard by the window. "I don't eat very much in the morning, but there are cereals in the cupboard and milk in the fridge. Actually, pour some for me, too." As he sat down, he kept looking at her complexion in the light, and he then followed her movement with his gaze and stared at her face. It was cute, but also kind of annoying. She put her newspaper down, folded it, and teased him by mirroring his movement and staring back. They managed to keep it up for a few minutes until he eventually folded.

"Alright, you got me. Cut it out," he said, his face glowing with joy, "So what do you want to do today?". He munched on some cereal as he waited for her response. "It's Sunday. So, I'm going to Peniche to have lunch with my dad, like I always do." "Oh, cool, can I come?" He said briskly, shoving his mouth with another spoon.

She looked at him in surprise with her eyebrows pressed together in an effort to think quickly. "Isn't that a little early? We only just started going out."

"Come on, I've met your dad before." He said and directed his attention to catching all the last cereal on one spoon.

She watched his play. "Em, yeah, you have. But that was just briefly, a few months ago, and we were just friends then. Are you sure you're ready for that? You know he can be intense."

He looked at her, crunching as he pondered the question.

Then he grinned, held his spoon up in his hand, and gestured with it to help make his point, "You know I'm always at my best behaviour. I can handle your dad, don't worry." He then proceeded to fill the spoon with the last of the milk and lick the residue off his spoon. She stared at his movement for a few seconds and quickly shook her head and blinked with a slight blush on her cheeks.

"Well, ok then. If you really want to, then that's fine with me. So, let's catch the train in an hour?"

"Let's take my car instead. It's much more convenient." He picked up more drops of milk and continued his innocent quest to eat his milk to the last drop. She stared at him for a few minutes and caught herself zoning in on his hand. Then she stood up without a word, walked over to him seductively, and sat down in his lap. In a slight whisper, she said. "Well, there is only one way I'm going to be ok with taking the car instead of the train. And that is if you do that to me first." She smirked at her own dirty comment; he laughed and licked the milk off the corner of his lip as he put the spoon down on the table. Then he stood up, lifting her in his arms, and carried her to the sheets.

They got dressed, she put on a blue cotton dress, he went home to change into something more representative for lunch with dad, and came back twenty minutes later looking fresh in his little car.

She commented on their matching outfits, felt a bit unsure if it looked weird or not, but eventually decided that she liked her dress and did not want to change. She got in and changed the music to something a bit more upbeat. He looked at her and protested, but was eventually forced to surrender. They drove through the countryside with the windows down to get some wind in their hair as they sang loudly and badly.

After about two hours, they reached an intersection. And just as Gabriel was about to turn right towards Peniche, Phoebe read the other sign showing an image of Mother Mary, and "Shrine of Fatima" was written in big letters on the road sign next to it. "Oh, please, can we just stop there before lunch?" Phoebe said persistently. She had a weird sensation in her gut telling her that she needed to go there. He objected, "It's like an extra 30 minutes. Can't we do it on the way back?"

"I feel like I need to go there now. Please. I promise I'll be quick. I just need to check something. I'll write to my dad that we will be late."

"Ok, as long as I don't get the blame, then it's fine by me." He changed lanes and turned left instead. "What could be so important there, anyway?"

"I don't know, actually, I just had a weird sensation that I needed to go there. I've had these weird dreams these past few days with Mother Mary showing up. I don't know, It feels like she is trying to tell me something, and I thought maybe this could help me figure out what it is."

"Oh, ok. I didn't know you were religious."

"Neither did I. But maybe I am, after all."

He parked the car, and they walked together up the steps leading to the passageways and made their way up the slope towards the entrance. As they were about to go inside, he stalled a little to read a text, while she continued into the church. It was grand and all white. She first looked around at the sculptures by the entrance. Then, she walked straight to the altar, looked up at Mother Mary, and greeted her with a nod and discreet smile.

Gabriel joined Phoebe and stood next to her, looking up at the sculptures and other decorations of the church. They proceeded to walk around the complex, viewing the artwork of the fifteen mysteries of the Rosary, and taking in the magnitude of the building, its energies, and the significance of the texts and symbols. Phoebe was first considerate to keep his pace. But when she stepped out into the gardens, she wandered off, caught in her own head. She followed the stone path to look at the various sculptures and statues. Phoebe was silently reciting a prayer she had memorized, as she looked up at the faces of the saints. She eventually reached Mother Mary's sculpture again. Phoebe smiled at her. Her heart filled with warmth. She started a conversation with Mother Mary in her head, asking for guidance and knowledge. She was hoping that her silent conversation would be enough and that Mother Mary would be able to respond in some way or answer her later. She finally felt like she was able to accept the fact that she was talking to Mother Mary for real, and not in her imagination. She looked to see where Gabriel had gone and saw that he had walked ahead and was now looking at a statue of Jesus.

She looked back at Mary and said, "Thank you for your guidance. I love you. Please let me know how best I can serve". She made a shy bow, feeling slightly uncomfortable as she was not used to anything religious. She then turned to continue walking but stopped as she noticed something shimmering in blue by Mary's robe. She reached through the fence and picked it up. It was a glass rose in a wonderful azure blue colour. It was lodged in a triangular-shaped silver cup with a braided pattern on its sides. The flat underside was plain except for an engraving of the trinity knot. She couldn't quite remember what it stood for but admired the beauty of it. The glass appeared to have small bubbles inside that looked like glitter when the sun's light touched them.

"Are you ready?" Gabriel startled her.

She looked up and started walking towards him. "Yes, ready as can be."

She put the glass figure in her purse for now to keep it safe until she got home. They got in the car and continued their drive to her father in Peniche. Their lunch had now become dinner, but no one seemed to mind. They met up at the town square, where her father was already waiting. She walked up to him and kissed him on his cheeks as she apologized for being late.

"Hi, Gabriel. Nice to meet you again." He put his hand forth to shake Gabriel's hand. It was happily accepted at the receiving end. Phoebe's father was wearing a striped linen shirt in yellow and green, and blue pressed trousers with leather sandals. His brown moustache was neatly combed, and he wore a typical white straw hat. He was one of a kind, but she loved him for it. She squinted her eyes and looked at him, then she squinted her eyes some more to look at Gabriel. She suddenly realized how short she was compared to them and begged to start walking to spare her eyes from the sun. They found a nice place in the shade. As they sat down and looked at the menu, they kept on chatting about their jobs and other adventures. They all ordered the same steak and a bottle of red for the table.

Phoebe's dad was curious about how they finally ended up together, after all this time. They told him the story about their mutual longing and waited for something more, and the eventual courage to finally act on it.

Gabriel told him about himself and his family in the South. Phoebe's mind kept wandering off to her conversation with Mother Mary yesterday, and to the rose that Mother Mary had given her that afternoon, but most importantly, she tried to process it all while slowly being reminded of the absence of her mother. She usually managed to push those feelings away. She missed her. She would have liked Gabriel. She felt her emotions get to her throat, so she quickly redirected her thoughts. She joined the conversation again, albeit within a certain distance.

As the food came, Phoebe said, "I think it's time for me to travel back to Mexico, to visit Mom's side of the family."

Her dad looked at her, "Sweetie, do you think you're ready for that?"

"As ready as I'll ever be, I think." She nodded slowly. Gabriel took her hand and looked at her, reassuring her that all was ok. "I will go with you, honey. If you want." She looked at her dad. "You still keep in touch with them, right? So, do you have their contact information?"

"Only your abuela. He picked up his phone and searched through some emails. "Here you go. That's her number and e-mail address. I can send you a tag with the contact info, if you'd like?"

"Thank you, but that's ok. I'm already writing them down."

The deserts came. Phoebe had ordered a caramel flan, Gabriel a Leite creme, and her father got the Toucinho do Céu. Gabriel got himself a double espresso since he was driving back, while the other two got to enjoy some port wine. He was a bit jealous, though, so Phoebe offered him a taste of hers.

Gabriel turned to Phoebe and asked, "So when do you think you will want to go to Mexico? I have some vacation days saved, so we can go whenever you want."

"I actually think I want to go as soon as possible. Maybe in a few weeks?" She said. "You can't do that! What about your job? The season is just beginning, and you need to be on it if you want to become a regular." Her father objected.

"Well, some things are more important than work. Besides, I'm actually really good at my job. They would never fire me." She looked at him and gestured with her hand as she continued," It's just that something inside me is itching to go, and I think I just must follow it." I don't want to disrupt my life, I just want to see where it takes me.

She looked at Gabriel, who was surprisingly supportive.

Her father tried to come up with excuses but eventually realised that he had already lost the discussion and changed the subject. To his pleasant surprise, Gabriel apparently liked jazz. Phoebe let the two of them talk about their mutual musical interest as she pondered what she had just said. The idea had actually come out of nowhere, and she had just blurted it out, but it was actually a really good idea. The evening light was slowly slipping away, and they still had to drive back, so Phoebe's father went inside to take care of the bill. Gabriel leaned over to her and whispered softly, "Your mocha skin is shining like pure gold in the evening light." Then he kissed her shoulder

She blushed and looked him deep into his eyes.

"Had I known you were such a smooth talker, I would have snatched you up a long time ago. Where have you been hiding that?" She gave him a shove on his shoulder. He blushed and added, "I've been hiding it deep in my heart, saving it for when you were ready to hear it."

Now she blushed even more and hid her face in her hands. She didn't know how to reply. She was stunned and smitten. She thought of how silly it was that both of them hid their feelings from each other for so long. All the way home, she couldn't think of anything else besides Gabriel's words. Nobody had ever said anything, even remotely as romantic as that, to her. She felt like the luckiest girl in the world.

They both had work the next day, so he just dropped her off at her place while he went home to his.

She went up to her apartment. She walked through her entrance and saw that Mother Mary was already there.

"Wow, that was quick."

"I know it's late, and you have a lot going on in your mind. I just wanted to follow up as soon as I could."

Phoebe took out the blue rose and placed it on the table.

"What is this that you gave me? It is absolutely beautiful, but I can't figure out what to do with it."

"It's a blue rose." Mother Mary answered simply.

"Yes, I can see that. But what does it mean?"

"It has many meanings, most of which are too hard for me to explain. You will not understand me anyway. But as a whole, it stands for the purity of the feminine heart." "Ok?" She looked at Mother Mary in confusion. "So, I must purify my heart? Have I done something wrong?"

"No, no. That is not what I said. You must open your mind to the purity of your heart. The blue rose is already inside you. This one will help you to find it."

"Ok?" Phoebe looked even more confused. "How do I do that?"

"That is something I cannot help you with. Only you know the answer to that question."

Phoebe picked up the rose and looked at it. Then she sat down on the couch, holding the rose in her hands. "Find the purity in my heart".

Mother Mary added, "I fear you are taking that too literally. Your heart is not impure. But you overthink everything, my dear. You are not ready for all the wisdom that is available to you. But I will tell you this: Just follow your heart." Phoebe sat down on the couch and looked at the blue rose in her hands. "Isn't that what I've just done? I followed my heart to Gabriel."

"Yes, so far so good. I am proud of you for finally listening to your heart. But there is one more person who needs your heart."

"Who? My dad? We just came from him. " Her mind was racing, trying to think of other people she might need to give more to, but Mother Mary interrupted her train of thought.

"You," she said with a prominent voice. Mother Mary then went up to Phoebe and put her hand on her heart. "You need your heart."

Phoebe teared up and put the rose back on the table in order to wipe her cheeks. She thought of her mom again. Mother Mary looked at her with great compassion. "I have given you all that you need for now. I will allow it all to sink in and will be back tomorrow."

Phoebe kept sobbing for a while. She kept staring at the rose back on the table and took out the contact information for her abuela. She looked at it, trying to think of what to say.

She made herself some tea to calm her senses and sat down on her couch, sipping the hot herbs.

She tried to make sense of what Mother Mary had just said and what she was supposed to do now. Maybe she should just go to Mexico, find her roots again. She hadn't been back since her mother died, and that was ten years ago. While she had never lived in Mexico, they had always gone there for long periods when she was little. Now, the only family she had met was her father's family in Portugal. She needed to experience her heritage through her own lens and get her connection to her mother's side. While still sobbing through her teeth, she sent her abuela a text and an e-mail asking if she could come visit.

Then she went to get ready and go to bed. She had a full day tour again tomorrow, and with everything that had happened over the weekend, she needed a full night's sleep.

She couldn't, though. Sleep. She had to sleep, but she couldn't. She was so tired, but she still couldn't sleep. She tossed and turned, getting more and more upset with herself. Her mind kept repeating what Mother Mary had said. But her mind also kept repeating the wonderful things that Gabriel had said to her. She felt lost and couldn't calm down her thoughts. She eventually went up and took a sleeping pill. It was something she hated doing, but now it was needed if she were to survive tomorrow. She made sure that her two alarms were still active and dozed off.

The next day, she woke up feeling rested. Gabriel had already sent her a sweet text, which started off her day in a great mood. She had heard both her alarms and now had plenty of time to walk down to the tourist office and enjoy a peaceful breakfast before the tour started. Gabriel had to get to work early today, so she wouldn't meet him until later. But she enjoyed her time alone. She did the tour. There were many Danish people today, a few British people as usual, and a German. Everything ran smoothly, and there were no odd interactions with Mother Mary this time. She took them through the city, enjoyed lunch, and savoured her ice cream. By 4 pm, her work was done, and she went to meet up with Gabriel close to his office. They walked along the beach leading up to a secluded part of town, where they found a spot in the shade in the park and shared a picnic. She soaked in the romance and accepted her luck. Laughing, teasing, and loving. As the evening fell and they had to part, he managed to convince her to sleep at his place, even if it meant that she would have to commute to work the next day. She still thought it was worth it, though. He made her happy. Besides, his place was nicer and bigger.

The next day repeated the same pattern. In the evening, they went home to his place, and he cooked for her. It was nothing fancy, but she loved the heartfelt sentiment. After dinner, though, she received the message that she had been waiting for. Phoebe opened it without a word and read it in silence with both anxiety and happiness portraying on her nerves at the same time. It was an email from one of her aunts. She had seen her message to her Abuela. They were all so happy that she contacted them and would love for her to visit any time she liked. Their door is always open to family. When could she come?

Phoebe got excited and opened an app immediately to look at flights.

"What are you doing?" Gabriel asked, looking over her shoulder.

"My aunt just wrote saying that I can come at any time, so I'm just looking for flights, why?"

"Ok. I thought you wanted to go together. Or at least it sounded like you wanted me to come on the trip. Can you wait until I've checked with my boss?"

"Sure, of course. I do want to go with you. I'm just checking what's available." She put her phone down but fidgeted nervously on its case as she tried to put a dimmer on her excitement.

He noticed her anxiety and added, "You're still allowed to look."

She felt unsure, but she picked up her phone again and scrolled through the search results. "Oh, there is a good one on Friday!" She said out loud, without thinking.

He looked at her in disappointment.

"So, you do want to go without me, then? You know I can't get off work that quickly."

"Right, right. When do you think you can go?" She put her phone down and looked at him intently.

He continued, "My boss needs a heads up of at least two weeks. But he can't approve longer vacations on such short notice, especially when we are in a hectic period right now. So, I think we will have to wait until next month."

"Next month?!" She yelled in surprise, "But that's too late. I need to go now."

"Why? What's so important is that you can't wait one month?"

Phoebe looked at him and didn't know what to say. She didn't know how to explain the blue rose and everything else that had been going on.

"There is some stuff going on in my life right now, and Mother Mary told me to go follow my heart, and I feel deeply that my heart wants me to find my roots." "Mother Mary told you to follow your heart?" he said in an annoyed voice. "Do you hear yourself?" If you want to go, just admit that you want to go. There is no need to drag her into it. I just thought I was important enough to you that you would want to wait for me to join you."

"Well, you are important to me. We are. I mean, I love us and what we have started." She looked down at the floor and felt so lost. She didn't even understand where her impulse had come from or how to deal with this mess. "It is just that I feel that this is something that I have got to do right now, ok? It can't wait a month. I have to do it now. I don't know how to explain it better than that for now."

"Ok, then fine," he said, looking sad. "Go without me. In fact, you can leave right now." He took the kitchen towel off his shoulder and threw it in the sink.

"Oh, come on, Gabriel. You know I didn't mean it like that. You mean the world to me. And being with you is the best thing that has ever happened to me. But it's just that I cannot wait another month to go. You must understand that." He looked at her with sadness in his eyes and sighed.

"You do what you have to do, then."

She picked up her bag and left, sobbing as she rushed down the street. She couldn't really get her head around what had just happened. Like her little world of paradise had just collapsed, and she had no idea what she was doing and why. As she waited for the tram, she picked up her phone again and looked for flights. But tears were streaming down her face, so she stopped and focused on her emotions instead. She put the phone away and waited with that until she was home and could open her laptop. As soon as she was home, she found a good flight and checked her savings. She had enough money for the trip. She paced back and forth, thinking of what to do. She didn't want to sabotage her relationship with Gabriel by going, but she also couldn't not go. She didn't know how she was supposed to act. She was hoping that Mother Mary would show up and tell her what to do, but she didn't. She picked up the rose, instead, looked deep into it, and decided to meditate to receive clarity. She closed her eyes and sat in stillness for a while. The meditation helped a little. She had received a call to follow her heart. Her heart told her to find her roots. But her heart also told her to love Gabriel. How could it be so conflicted and ask her to both go and stay at the same time? Mother Mary still didn't show up. But she came to the conclusion that if he really loved her and had waited for her for all this time, then that meant that they were meant to be. And if they were meant to be, then that meant that their love would survive her going away on a trip. If it could not survive her trip, then it was not meant to be. Simple as that. She could hardly keep track of her own thoughts but had finally made a decision. She booked the flight.

The next morning, she woke up to a text from Gabriel saying that he was sorry for overreacting. It made her heart happy. She knew the problem would solve itself. She got ready and headed to work. When she reached the office, he was sitting on the bench outside with a red rose in his hand.

"I'm sorry," he said as he gave her the flower.

She accepted the rose and gave him a shy smile as she smelled it. "I'm sorry too, for the bad timing. I did not mean to hurt you. "Thank you for this," she said and held up the rose. "I love it. Unfortunately, it can't come with me on the tour, though. I will place it here at the office for now. " He offered to take it instead and to meet up later. She smiled and gave it back to him as she gave him a kiss. She said goodbye and crossed the sea of people on the square to reach the group of tourists, yet again. She led them into the cathedral to commence the daily trip around Porto. As she walked up the steps, she looked over her shoulder at him to find him still standing there, still looking at her. She smiled and waved at him before she went inside.

Later that evening, Phoebe met up with Gabriel at a small restaurant close to her home. He gave her the rose again, and she smiled.

They ordered two pizzas, and as the food arrived, he said,

"So, I talked to my boss. He will allow me some vacation days so I can go in two weeks. But unfortunately, I am only allowed to go away for a week, since it's our busiest time."

"Oh. That's a shame," Phoebe cleared her throat and felt her anxiety rise as she tried to find the words for what she was about to say. "Actually, I already booked. I leave on Friday morning."

"Friday morning, as in two days? Actually, less than that, it's Wednesday evening now." He looked bewildered and confused. "Why would you book a ticket without even telling me?"

"Honestly, I thought you would say no. And a part of me did not want to give you the opportunity to make me stay."

"Babe, you need to stop being afraid that I will control you. I just want to be a part of your world. That you include me and consider my feelings, too." She looked away, not knowing what to say.

"I'm sorry. I guess I'm not very good at relationships. I thought you would make me stay."

He looked at her, " Well, the sad part is that now I can't go with you. I really wanted to see that part of you, but you were so afraid that I would say no that you didn't even give me the opportunity to say yes."

She felt like a fool. Embarrassed that she had rushed in without thinking.

"Well, I will be gone for three weeks. You can still join me."

"Three weeks?!" He said loudly in utter surprise, "Three weeks?!" After having waited for each other for so long, we finally get together, and the first thing you do is to go away for three weeks. How do you think that makes me feel?"

"I don't know. You tell me. It's not like I'm breaking up with you or anything. I just found myself in a place where I need to do this for myself. And we have already waited for each other for so long, what difference does three weeks do?" "Well, you make me feel like insignificant shit, that's what." He looked away, feeling both sad and angry at the same time, not knowing what to say next. He chewed on a slice of pizza and sat in silence for a few minutes while she looked at him, then looked away instead to concentrate on her own pizza. She really didn't know what to say. It's not like she chose this. She was chosen. And this was apparently what she needed to do. Or maybe she did choose it, on some level. Besides, she was so happy to go back and see her family, and although she wished she hadn't hurt him, she was also kind of happy to get to explore by herself. Even though she wished she could somehow find a way to also show him how she felt, so he wouldn't feel hurt. But she didn't know how. So, she just ate her food instead.

But after a while, she found her voice again. She put her hand on his and looked deep into his eyes.

"I love you."

His eyes softened, and this time he was the one with blushed cheeks.

"I can't believe you said that after just one week."

"Well, we've known each other for three years, so I felt it was overdue." She continued, "You mean the world to me, but I mean the world to me, too. This is just something I have to do. You have not lost me, and I am not running away from you. I cherish every moment we are together, because I love you. I do want you to join me, if you still want to."

He picked up her hands and added, "I love you, too. If this is what you need to do, then I understand. I will wait, and I will give you some distance to sort out whatever it is that is going on inside of you. Let me know once you get there how you feel. If you say ok, then I will join you in two weeks."

She leaned over to give him a kiss and got some tomato sauce on her white sweater. She laughed and put some water on it with a napkin. She then said, flashing her eyebrows, "I leave in just two nights, so let's make the most of it until then." He smirked. "You think I'm such a smooth talker, you should hear yourself."

To make the most of their time, they both called in sick the next day. Phoebe had already informed her boss about her leaving, something that had not been happily received. Her boss was not at all happy about the sudden changes to the plans, but there was not much she could do as Phoebe was not a full-time employee. She was also one of the most skilled guides among the staff and would be back just in time for the hectic tourist season to start, so firing her would not be a smart option. But she did receive a warning, which she accepted with grace.

Instead of going to work, she and Gabriel spent the day in each other's company, hiking outside of town. They walked through a natural reserve, in a dense forest on the hillside overlooking the city. It was the perfect place for a romantic hideout to absorb their new romance before being separated. Gabriel had arranged for yet another picnic at a perfect lookout spot with the whole city at their feet. He looked at her with those dreamy blue eyes of his, smiling like a child at the things he had brought. He unpacked all sorts of foods, including wine. They sat down on the quilt and enjoyed a moment of romance where time could stand still, and their love surrounded them with joy and peace as they relished nature and the beautiful scenery. They continued walking their route, and when they hadn't seen or passed anyone in a while, he pulled her close, kissed her, then passionately. She whispered something into his ear. He just chuckled a little bit and answered with a spark in his eye "I can arrange that". They walked off track into the woods for a few meters and finally found a big rock out of view. He kissed her intensely, and although they both felt like they wanted to stay in that innocent moment forever, their lust for each other was getting to every part of them except their heads. They succumbed to their passion and let their feelings guide them through a few minutes of amorous bliss. But once their heads had buzzed their way out of the heat of the moment, they felt glad that they had not been caught, fixed their clothes, and picked up their bags to walk back to the tracks.

To their relief, no one had passed by or noticed. They were still alone as they walked back to the tracks, which made them both a bit pleased with themselves, having gotten away with a moment of disorderly behaviour. They continued their walk for the rest of the day in a more conducted manner, enjoying the scenery and the scents of the forest as well as each other's company. Laughing and joking in youthful bliss and sipping from their cup of love, creating memories that could linger while they were apart.

CHAPTER 7

Temperance

Ayla regretted waking up even before she opened her eyes. She shut them again and put her cover over her head. "Ooooh." She screamed, but her mouth was so dry that almost no sound came out. She sat up and took a sip from the glass on her nightstand. "Why on Earth did I have to drink that much?" she lay back down and closed her eyes to fall back to sleep. Her head was spinning, and her eyes were hurting for some reason. She went through her mind to try to count how much she drank last night. But her mind couldn't grasp it. She remembered a beer with dinner and then another beer when they danced. But that was it. Did she get this hungover from two beers? She whined again, "Wow, I am such a loser, I need to get out more often if I get drunk from two beers. Maybe it was three actually. Cassandra did get her one more while they were dancing. Three beers. But still, that is nothing."

An hour later, she woke up again feeling more refreshed. She sat up and walked to the bathroom. Her legs were so sore she halted and tilted. "What did I do yesterday? Why am I so sore? I must be getting old. It is not ok to get this sort of thing just from a night of dancing. Why do I go to the gym only to wake up to this?" She put on her bathrobe and walked in pain to the kitchen and threw herself on her couch with the breakfast tray next to her. Mr. Puzzle came up and snuggled up in her lap, manipulatively praying for any opportunity to steal her ham and cheese. Of course, she gave him a piece.

She called her mom, who lived on the other end of town, and arranged for a late lunch. She felt she needed to see her and talk to her. As Ayla sat in silence with her morning coffee, she stared out the window and suddenly remembered why she had such a headache. The dream from last night was becoming painfully clear. She massaged her calves as she remembered the stairs. So many stairs. First up, then down, not to mention all the other walking. She remembered the lights and the laughter. She put her hand to her head. "This is not a hangover after all, then. Good to know. "

She went to get ready. She did a light makeup with just some powder, blush, and a natural eye shadow. She sat on her bed to put on her jeans, laughing at herself as her sore muscles made an impossible feat out of an ordinary task. She eventually got the jeans on. They were the type with holes that she knew her mother would comment on. She did not care. She thought they looked cool. She put a blue striped sweater over her white t-shirt, then a pair of sneakers, and headed out.

She was obviously not going to walk. Not with these sore legs and the pain-stricken headache. She took the tram, so she got there early. She had planned for extra time to run a few errands before her mom would get there, but as she noticed that their favourite restaurant was filling up for a crowded lunch, she changed her plans and went to get a table. Its popularity on this Sunday afternoon was not surprising as it was the city's best fish restaurant, and the sun was beautifully highlighting the outside seating area overlooking the harbour. She put a blanket over her legs and waited as she tried to heal her migraine in the cold spring air. She was glad she had brought her lightweight jacket. She did not, in any case, want to move inside, but it was a bit more chilly than she thought it would be. Thankfully, the waiter read her mind and came over to turn on the heater next to her. Her mom peeked around the corner, throwing her hand in the air as she saw Ayla.

"Hi! Are you fine sitting out here?" she said as she tightened her red scarf. "I'm fine if you're ok with it. I mean, it's nice to take advantage of the spring sun while it's out. Besides, the waiter just turned the heater on. Unless you want to sit inside?" But her mom just brushed that idea off the table. She agreed. "That's true. Have you ordered already?" she asked. "No, not yet. I was waiting for you," Ayla replied.

They called on the waiter and ordered two pan-fried halibuts with lots of brown butter and boiled potatoes. They always got the same order, and there was a reason for it. It was the best. And especially on a day like this, it could cure anything.

The food came, and they dug in.

"So, how did your presentation go?" Her mom asked as she began eating.

"I actually completely aced it! We got them in on the whole project. So we can finally start the next phase. Everyone was so happy and proud of me. We had a small after-work on Friday to celebrate."

Her mom brimmed with excitement, "Oh, I'm so proud of you! I knew you would do it. That must mean you will get that promotion, then? Have you talked to Greg already?"

"No, no I haven't. I didn't get the chance to. The meeting was on Friday afternoon. I'll talk to him next week, but it's pretty much a done deal. It will probably be fine." Ayla said as she pulled out a hair tie out of her pocket to tie her brown curls into a messy ponytail.

"Of course it will all work out well for you, sweetie, I mean, I've been working so hard these past years, he must have noticed your efforts." Her mom looked at her intensely and continued eating.

Ayla looked at her with a smile and agreed. But she also had an odd feeling about it that she couldn't quite explain.

They finished their food and ordered dessert and coffee. She had been able to hide it up until now but had to at last mention her headache to her mother.

"Oh, no. My dear. It's important to stay hydrated, especially when you're stressed." She said, looking intensely at her again with her green eyes.

"I don't think it's from lack of water, I'm pretty good at drinking," Ayla responded.

"Ok, so you drank too much, then, when you were out with Cassie last night?" "I thought so too first, but I actually only had three beers last night. It's not even close enough to get drunk on."

"Well, maybe you've gotten pollen allergies. I mean it's common to get those later in life." You could see her mind turning to figure out more plausible explanations. But, instead, Ayla begged her to stop with the guessing game. She took a spoon with ice cream and a brownie and ate in silence while she pondered her options. Should she dare tell her or not? She looked at her mother and followed her movements as her mother corrected her brown bob that kept slipping over her ears and had another spoonful of Crème Brulée. Finally, Ayla mustered the courage to say:

"Actually, I had a few weird dreams this past week. And some weird things have happened too."

"Oh, ok." Her mother didn't really know what to say, so she just took a sip from her coffee and sat in silence for a second as she pondered her response. "What was the dream about then?"

"Well, both dreams took place in some sort of palace or temple or something. I was together with some other women doing some trauma healing. Mother Mary was there too, and Isis, and Mary Magdalene. It was quite beautiful. I don't know if you know who Kuan Yin is?" She started feeling excited about sharing this information and the possibility of being able to talk about it.

But her mother just laughed, ignoring the question. "That sounds like a fun dream. I can understand why you are tired if you can remember all that. You can't get enough REM sleep, though. Take one of those pills I gave you, it will really help. I promise."

Ayla got a little annoyed that her mother didn't take it seriously. BuAt she also understood why. She stared down at her coffee and looked back up. "Yes, I will try that pill tonight. Thank you for the tip. Maybe it will help." They smiled awkwardly at each other and sat in silence for a few moments. Then they continued chatting about various other things that were unimportant in nature but entertaining in their simplicity. As the sun was turning the afternoon into evening, they said goodbye, and Ayla went back home. She got ready for an early night's sleep. She burned a stick of lavender incense to make her sleepy and laid out her clothes for the next day at work. A blue shirt this time and pressed white trousers with a ballerina ballet shoe. She felt pleased. She loved dressing up for work, and she was going to talk to Gregory tomorrow, so she chose colours that she knew he liked. He was a boat person, just like her, so he would appreciate her shoes. That might give her some extra points in her favour when bringing up the promotion.

The next day, however, her head was feeling much worse. She picked up her phone and sent a quick e-mail to HR to request a sick day. She tried to go back to sleep, but her pounding head was making it hard to even do that. She went to get some aspirin from the medicine drawer in the kitchen, poured a glass of water, and swallowed. But instead of going back to the bedroom, she went to her living room to stream something that was easily digestible. She watched for a while and noticed that those pills had not done their thing. Her head was still throbbing, and her throat felt sore as well. She got up again and made herself some ginger tea with honey in it. By the time she got back to the living room, Athena was sitting in one of the armchairs.

This time, she was not surprised. She just mumbled, " Oh, good. I was wondering when you would turn up."

"I just thought I would check in on you. How are you feeling?" She didn't sound worried, though, and her voice was surprisingly upbeat. Ayla glanced over at her with an annoyed look on her face.

"How does it look like I'm feeling? I'm sick." She snuggled up on the couch again, balancing her tea as she adjusted her seat. What are you so cheerful about? "Oh, I'm just excited." She joyfully clasped her hands to the side. "It is just so beautiful to witness your process. You have come a long way in such a short time." "What?!" Ayla said surprised, "It's been like three days. What have I done these few days? Oh, like except for partying and having lunch with my mom." Her snarky comment made Athena roll her eyes.

"Well, for your information, you have done excellent work. You went to that Gong meditation that you liked. And you actually told your mom about us. Bravo!" She clapped in the air and added, "Not many people dare to do that so soon. You've got something extra."

"Well, I don't feel extra right now," Ayla said and coughed.

"Don't you worry about that. We will have you back on your feet in no time. Besides, you're not actually sick."

"I'm not? Then what would you call this?"

"It's just ascension symptoms, honey. Your chakras are clearing. I'm happy for you. But I'll tell you, no amount of pills and tea will help you with that. What you need is some fresh air and maybe a change of scenery." She nodded her head like a prudent mother.

"I don't think they would let me travel like this. "Ayla said and put her tea down to rest her head on the pillow.

"Don't you worry about that. Just think of where you want to go and we'll make sure that it happens." Athena looked at her with compassion and added,"

"Remember, you are a fighter, like me. You have got a long road ahead of you. You're just getting started. I know it doesn't feel so good right now, but it will." Athena leaned over to stroke Ayla's hair away from her face. Think about it, at least. She took her farewell and left.

Ayla continued watching the movie, and she paused and sipped her tea. She paused again and went to get some toast. Then continued watching the movie with a distracted mind. She tried not to think of what Athena had said about going away. She was already freaking out about missing one day of work as it was. But her head was also so tired that she almost couldn't follow the plot of the movie. By the end of it, she had come to realize that she hadn't taken a day off at all in nearly a year. No sick days, no holidays, nothing. She had just been working so hard on this project. So, if she took some sick days to clear her head, then it wouldn't be the end of the world. Besides, there were three other people on the team, not just her. They would manage fine without her for a few days.

But where could she go feeling like this? She could only think of one place. Home. She picked up her phone and called her dad. He answered the call fairly quickly, and although he was concerned about her being sick, he was happy about her coming home. She checked the flights right away. Fortunately, there was one seat left in just a few hours. She mustered her strength to go pack and get ready. Then she went over to her neighbor to ask for help with Mr. Puzzle and picked the cat up in her arms for a snuggle before she left.

The weather outside had gone back to winter, and the warm spring sun of yesterday had been replaced with a grey sheet of clouds. She had treated herself to a taxi to save her energy, and she was happy about that decision right now. Standing out in the cold waiting for an airport shuttle with her head and sore throat would not have been fun. She reached the airport in a swift. As she was just getting on a short domestic flight, she had already checked in and could head directly to the gate. She bought a smoothie and managed to get into her own zone as she waited for boarding by listening to some music. She had loaded up on cough drops in an attempt to avoid having anyone uncomfortable about her condition while onboard. She didn't need them, though, because she fell asleep on the plane and woke up just minutes before they landed in Halifax. She had, however, drooled all over her sweater, and she quickly dabbed it and looked around to see if anyone had noticed. If they had, she wouldn't have known anyway, so it actually didn't matter. She cleared her throat in embarrassment and noticed how much better it already felt. She went straight to the bus terminal to catch the next bus to Lunenburg. She was still tired but didn't fall asleep this time. Instead, she just looked out the window and enjoyed her music as her gaze traced the passing of the hills and the ocean. By the time she had arrived, her head was feeling lighter, too. Maybe this was exactly what she needed, just as Athena had said.

Her dad was waiting for her in the parking lot to pick her up. She was happy to see him and gave him a big hug as he took her bag. His house was just a short drive away. She walked through the front door into the hallway and took a deep breath to breathe in her childhood memories as she looked around.

"Oh, you've redecorated. It looks nice!"

"Yes, well. When I redid the kitchen, everything else looked kind of dull, so I gave it a lick of paint. Your room is now a guest room. Sorry about that. But it's nice and comfortable." She gave him a smile. "That's completely fine, Dad. I know I haven't been home in a while. You can't keep a room just for me."

He looked at her with his blue eyes and smiled awkwardly, straightened his flannel shirt, and scratched his grey beard. He went to get towels for her, and as he came back, he said. "Are you hungry? I made some soup."

"Yes, please. Soup is exactly what I need." She said and thanked him as he handed her the fresh towels. She put her bag on the floor and eventually found her sheepskin slippers in the wardrobe.

"Wow, I love the kitchen island. It all looks really nice and modern. Lovely blue colour on the cabinets. I like how you mixed dark blue and light blue like that. Or perhaps it's white?"

"According to the designer, it's called 'crisp blue', so both are correct, I guess." He chuckled and turned to stir the soup that was heating up. He then took out a beer from the fridge.

"I assume you don't want a beer with your headache. What do you want to drink?" "I'll just have an orange soda, thanks."

She helped herself to the soda, then figured out the orientation of the kitchen so that she could set the table.

The warm food brought comfort exactly when she needed it. They chatted politely as they ate, and she kept looking around the room to comment on the new interior. An interior designer had apparently taken care of most of it, but it was nice how his British heritage was showing through in the patterns of the heavy fabrics. It was a nice touch and an interesting contrast to the otherwise light colour palette. After dinner, he went upstairs to his study while she watched some TV in the living room. To her surprise, he didn't have any streaming services, so she had to watch regular TV. One of the channels was showing an old 90s movie, so in a half-bored state of mind, she watched that until it was finally late enough to go to bed.

The next day, both her head and throat were feeling a lot better. The sun was out, and she wanted to sit in the light on the terrace, but it was a lot colder than it looked. She sat down by the kitchen island instead. His dad eventually came down, poured some coffee, and sat down at the other end of it.

"Have you decided what you're going to do today?" he asked. "I don't suppose you have any friends left here, do you?"

"No, most of them have moved to the big cities. I think I'll just walk around. Maybe take a boat ride or something. When will you be home from work?"

"I'll just work from home today. I have a meeting at 2 pm that I need to attend at the office, but we can have dinner together at 5 pm, if that works for you. I thought I would make that roast chicken that you like."

Her heart filled with joy at his hospitality. At the same time, she felt a slight shame for not having been home for such a long time.

"That sounds lovely, Dad. Thank you." She went to get ready and left him to his work.

She walked down to the waterfront. It was cold and the wind was icy, but the sun was glittering beautifully on the waves. She looked out on the horizon and took a deep breath. This was exactly what she needed. Some fresh air and a change of scenery, just as Athena had ordered. She followed the walkway down to the harbour, stopping along the way to peek through the windows of some of the new shops. The streets hadn't changed, though, so she knew her way around. She found a nice-looking bakery and stopped to get coffee and a croissant. She had already had breakfast, but one could never have too many croissants. She got her take-away mug and little paper bag and went to sit on a bench by the fishing shacks. There was a soft breeze carrying a whiff of fish that might have been off-putting to some, but to her, it was home. She leaned her head on the wooden facade and breathed slowly. She felt safe and complete. Her head was pounding slightly, and she felt a tingle in her shoulders. She tried to come up with a plan. She had come all the way out here on a spontaneous whim, but it was too far off to go back straight away. She decided that she would spend a few days curating her bliss and go back to reality when she was feeling better, possibly on Thursday. She needed two whole days at least.

She finished her coffee and saw that a tour boat was leaving for Peggy's Cove. She had herself been a guide on that tour during her late teens. She knew it by heart, but it was nice to be able to just tag along and take in some nostalgia. There were not many tourists this time of year, but there was a family of five from Germany and an adventurous Italian couple. She introduced herself properly to the guide, so he knew that she was local. They went around the bay and started at the Bluenose Ship. She admired the craftsmanship like she always had and smelled the wood for a few minutes. While the others explored the ship further and took a trip to the museum, she took a short walk and found the big stones by the shore that she used to play a balancing game on when she was little.

Her mind revisited the boat ride in her dream. She thought of the exquisite silver metal that covered the boat, and then she remembered the unusual writing that decorated everything. Her curiosity made her take out her phone and search for ancient writings. She looked through images of writings from the old Egyptian, Mesopotamian, and rune stones. She found a few others, too, but after looking at them, she realized that she couldn't remember the ones in her dream well enough to know if it was any of these. "Maybe it's a combination of them all," she thought, and closed her phone when she noticed that the others were done at the museum. They all got on the boat again. They had one stop in another village before they reached the final stop, Peggy's Cove. Ayla felt a childish joy of being back here. She wandered off to one of her favourite places almost immediately while the others explored the lighthouse. She walked the shoreline, climbed a steep stonewall, and eventually got to a tiny beach. She sat down on the rocks and looked out over the ocean. Watching the vast blues always made her feel small and insignificant. Today was no different, although it started to sink in that maybe she was a little bit special to be singled out like this by Athena and the other goddesses, like she had. Hopefully, it all was real and not something she had just made up. Probably it was all real.

Almost certain that it was. Real.

She started playing with the rocks. Picking them up, creating small piles, and throwing a few in the water. No matter how hard she had practiced as a young girl, she still couldn't throw a sandwich. But it was fun to try either way. As she was scanning the rocks, a small piece of metal gave off a spark in the light of the sun. She tried to make out where exactly it had come from and eventually shoved some rocks to the side to pick it up. She looked at it, bewildered. It was a delicate piece of metal that was formed as a square, the size of her palm. Floral markings framed a circular white face that was protected by an iridescent glass. The white face shimmered like a pearl. It was decorated with a floral web that, together, created a five-petal flower. She had never seen anything like it before and couldn't make out what it was. It almost looked like a watch, but it had neither numbers nor arms. Then she thought it was a compass, but there were no markings to suggest that either. She flipped it around. The backside was smooth except for a small carving of a dolphin. She flipped it back and saw something move. A little ball in gold followed the lines of the flower. She noticed that there was, after all, a really thin arm stretched out on top of the flower to secure the small ball as it traced the lines of the web.

She put it in her pocket so she could take it to the antique store, and maybe reunite it with its owner, if she was lucky. It must be someone's highly missed family heirloom or some other prized possession that has gone missing.

As soon as she came back to Lunenburg, she walked towards the antique shop. It was one of those places that served both as a second-hand shop and a pawn shop. They had many wonderful things of all sorts. Furniture, lamps, porcelain, and old decorations in brass and glass. She toured the aisles, scanning for gems, as she waited for her turn. The shop owner eventually looked at her, and she hurried up to the counter and pulled out her find.

"Hi! I was just over at Peggy's Cove and found this object on the beach. I thought maybe you would know what it is or if you can recognise the dolphin seal on the back, so I can return it to its owner. Thanks." She smiled an awkward smile as she waited for a response.

The shop owner took it in her hands and studied it for a little bit. Put on her magnifying monocular to examine the metal and the details. She then tilted it back and forth to study the movement of the tiny metal ball. She looked quite amused but turned to Ayla and said, "Whatever it is, it is quite a fun little invention. But unfortunately, I have no idea what it is."

"Perhaps it's a movie prop?" Ayla tried to find an explanation that seemed plausible. "It can't be a movie prop. That's 24 Karat Gold. And the white face looks like it could be made with real pearl, but I can't tell for sure. I think this could be really old actually, and suggest you bring it to an archaeologist."

"Wow. That's incredible!" She looked at it with a stunned face, then looked back at the shop owner and added, "Well, this is really exciting! I wonder how old it is. Thank you so much for your help!"

"Hang on! I know someone who works in the history department at the university in Halifax. I will try to contact him during the day and can give you a call when I've talked to him."

Ayla brimmed from ear to ear. This was turning out to be one of the most exciting days of her life. She went straight back to her dad's house. He was, thankfully, at home and sitting in his study. She told him what had happened and showed him the artifact. He looked at it with awe.

"Wow, my dear, this is a beautiful piece! I can't believe it was just lying on the rocks like that. Thank God that you were the one who found it and not someone else who would not have done it justice. I wonder who it belonged to."

She was still brimming, unable to contain her excitement. She mentioned the historian in Halifax. Her phone chimed, delivering a message from the shopkeeper telling her that her friend could meet her the next day.

"I guess I will be going to Halifax tomorrow, then."

Her dad looked happy that she was happy and went to get the dinner ready.

"Have you talked to Sandrine lately?" he asked, trying to see if she knew more than him.

Ayla answered nonchalantly, "I talked to her a few weeks ago, and she was fine then.

Why? Has something happened?"

"No, no. I just thought maybe she shares more information with you. I talked to her just the other day, so I know she is doing ok."

Ayla looked at him and said, "Well, let's just call her. It's not that late there, she's probably still up."

She started an app for international calls and pressed on her sister's name. Despite the late time, she did answer. She was surprised to see both her dad and her sister in the same video call, though. "Hi, how are you guys? I can't believe you are together, that is so wonderful! How come you are in the same room on a Tuesday?" Their dad just said, "Hi Sandie, I hope you're still doing well. I think Ayla needs to talk to you," and then he left to do the dishes.

Ayla laughed a little at his blunt comment and proceeded to tell her sister about her headache, about her coming out here for the first time in forever. But most importantly, she picked up her new precious find and showed it to her sister on the screen.

"Isn't it the most beautiful thing? Have you ever seen anything like it?"

Sandrine looked at her screen so closely that you could only see her nose. Ayla laughed a little. "Here, I can send you a picture instead." Aurelia opened another chat to look at it. "Wow, that is amazing!" she said, "And no one knows what it is?"

"Not yet at least. I have a meeting with a historian at the museum in Halifax tomorrow, so I'll see what they say then."

"Ok, well, keep me updated! I am actually really interested. I want to know what it is." Sandrine said.

The next day, she took the early bus to Halifax. She would take the opportunity to spend the entire day in the city that she had missed for so long. She had not planned to go there at all on this trip but was happy about this turn of events. She spent the day walking in the harbour and visiting a few of the shops near the center. The precious artifact that she kept in her inner pocket was influencing her mind, and she bought a pair of pearl earrings and put them on immediately. She had never worn pearls before, but it felt like a good day to start. By the early afternoon, she made her way to the Museum of National History, where she was meeting the historian. Their meeting wasn't until 3 pm, but she wanted to receive the energy of the place and try to see if there was anything in there that resembled her object. There were so many items on display from various regions in Canada. But after having gone through what she felt was the entire place, she couldn't find anything that was even half as precious. So, it was apparently the wrong place for this type of item.

A guy came towards her, and she could tell by his blue shirt and khaki trousers that he was the historian. First, she scolded herself for her stereotypical judgment of his attire, but soon after laughed at herself for being correct. They sat down at one of the tables in the cafeteria, and he inspected the golden plate and its embellishment. He made some noises revealing deep thoughts and concluded after some time that he, unfortunately, did not know what it was. He recommended her to visit another historian once she got back to Toronto. Someone at the Royal Museum who must, at the very least, be able to tell her of its origins.

The next morning, she took an early flight back to Toronto. She had already called the new contact and was going to meet with her in the afternoon.

She got home, felt awkward as she entered her apartment. She had only been gone for three days, but it felt like a lifetime ago. She had bought takeaways on her way home and placed them on a plate. But instead of eating to a series on the couch, like she normally did, she sat by the proper table in the kitchen. She took out the medallion, looked at it again, and placed it on the table. The gold had hardly touched the wood when Athena walked in.

"Boy, are you late for the party? Where have you been?"

"What do you mean, where have I been? I've been right there with you, and you know it. I just haven't been visible."

"But why not visible? I needed to talk to you."

"Oh, you didn't need me that much, honey. You were with your father, and there was never a good time to talk to you. You need to learn to be patient. You are hurrying around town trying desperately to find information on this thing you found that you think of nothing else." Athena shook her head in a displeased manner. "With that attitude, you'll never get to know what it is."

"So, you know what it is?"

"Na-uh. I did not say that. I said that you will not know what it is if you do not learn patience. The object came to you for a reason. Because you are the person who knows what it is. The answer is within, my friend."

Ayla looked at Athena in shock. "But I don't know what it is. How can I suddenly learn something new all by myself?"

"Interesting question. And the answer is the same. Patience, dear. Patience."

"Ok, should I cancel the meeting then?"

"You have many guides around you at all times. Many of them are ascended masters, some are angels, but some are just regular people, just like you. And you need to trust that what they will tell you is what you need to know."

"What they tell me is what I need to know. Ok, got it. So, I will go and hear what she says."

Ayla was confident again. She put the artifact away so that Mr. Puzzle would not be tempted to throw it off the table.

After she had finished, she went to change quickly and left for her meeting with the Royal Museum. She made her way to the other end of the city feeling both excited and nervous. But as she walked through the entrance to the vast building, she had an odd feeling. She had lived in Toronto for nearly ten years and had never been to the museum. She had never really been interested in history and museums, so she had skipped all of those attractions. Yet, this building was oddly familiar. The heavy stone staircase, the big chandeliers, the enormous paintings, and the rugs of various kinds. It all was a bit daunting. But she kept her composure. Soon, Mme. Lessard came out to greet her and signaled to Ayla to follow her through the museum to a private section away from the public. It was part of the official meeting room and looked like it was taken directly out of a history book with its golden mirrors and hand-woven silk rugs. Mme. Lessard sat down in her pencil skirt and satin blouse. The big table and velvet chairs made them both look small. Ayla took out the artifact and placed it in front of her to allow her to study it.

She looked closely at the iridescent plate and the golden web of the flower. She put on her magnifying glasses to look at the dolphin on the back. She eventually found some markings on the side of the sheet. The item was so thin that everyone else had mistaken all the carvings on the side for just being decorative. But there were lines and dots all the way around. She didn't know what it meant, but came to the conclusion that it must have some meaning. She then studied the style of the dolphin and admitted that she had never seen that style of carved golden jewellery before. Even the flowers on the frame were quite unique in their style. She then picked up her phone to ask a colleague to join them. She served Ayla some water while they waited. A new person came in, and he introduced himself as an archaeoastronomer. Ayla looked confused at his mention of his title. "That sounds like a very interesting job, please tell me more," she said instead of admitting to the fact that she had no idea what archeoastronomy was. "I study the history and archeology of astrology. So the intersection between the occurrence of historical events to the alignment of the stars." She nodded affirmatively with a highly impressed expression. "Cool," was all she could get out. It really was cool, she didn't know what else to say.

He took the piece in his hands. He looked at the five-petal flower, the floral frame, and the carvings on the side. He then turned it around and studied the dolphin emblem. His eyes lit up. He put the piece back on the table, excused himself, and ran off to get something. Ayla and the other woman sat in silence and confusion as they awaited his return. He came back with a book under his arm and opened it to page 244.

"Hereth within lies the secret. The secret that was known all along."

And under it was an image of the same dolphin.

Ayla tried to make sense of the text and the occurrence of the image. She stared at it for a while and continued reading in hopes of finding the explanation in the following line. It did not help.

"Ok, so someone made a jewellery with this adoration carved in it. That is quite odd." She looked up towards him in search of some sense in his eyes.

But instead of answering, he flipped his book to another page and said, "Not just someone, my dear."

He pointed to an image showing the webbed flower that was carved into the pearl surface. "I believe you are holding an original compass from Atlantis.

Ayla laughed out loud. "What? No, I'm not. Atlantis is not real; it's just a fairytale." She looked back and forth between Mr. Bouchard and Mme. Lessard with utter confusion and disbelief.

"No, my dear, I am quite certain," he said in a slightly condescending voice. "All the symbols are correlating to their beliefs, even the Venus flower. It could be a replica, of course, but in that case, it is very good nonetheless. I can get my team to take some tests, if you would like?"

Ayla looked at the jewellery in her hand and looked at him again.

"Ok, so if it were to be from Atlantis, how come it would wash up on the shore of

Nova Scotia, and now of all times?"

"One can never know why things happen when they do. But I do believe you are holding a highly valued artifact that many museums around the world want. Of course, we would love to have it too, but I don't think it's within our budget." Ayla thought for a moment. It did not belong to her; she just found it. Maybe she should just hand it over to the team. At least to run some tests. But something inside her would not allow her to do that. Instead, she thanked them both and put it back in her coat pocket.

"Here, please, take the book. You might need it. We would, obviously, like to brag about this to the newspaper, but I understand if you don't want to."

He was right. She didn't. Besides, if she was going to keep it, she didn't want anyone to know that she had it.

CHAPTER 8

The Tower

She started off the day in a really good mood. The sun was shining, birds were chirping, and she was singing to herself as she skipped about the bedroom to find her workout clothes without waking Stephen. She felt how the energy just kept pumping, and she needed to go for a jog. It was Sunday, and everyone else was asleep. She changed in the hallway and quickly left to avoid disturbing anyone's peace. It was still early, and there was crisp, cool air hugging the landscape. The sun's rays drenched the valley in gold. She put her headphones on, checked her running watch, and headed down the road. The pace of her feet was meditative and helped her to zone out from the outside world. Her breathing kept an even rhythm. She wasn't clear about what direction she wanted to run in, so first she took a right to head towards Lynden Park but as the sun started sipping through the crowns of the trees, she began fantasizing about breakfast at a sweet little bakery that was closer to the center. So, she stopped for a minute to send a text to Stephen, telling him to fix breakfast as she was out running. So, instead, she took a right further down Fordham Avenue so that she could cross Willison Park. She continued running through the quiet neighbourhoods. It was so early that the only other people who were out were dog owners, cyclists, and other runners. Some of them she knew, but she greeted everyone cheerfully either way, like she always did. She finally made it to Anderson Park and paused to stretch as soon as

she had passed the gates. She sat down on one of the benches to change the playlist and then continued running through the greenery of the park. The trees brushed in the soft air. She kept running all the way through the area, following the path through wavering leaves and past the small pond. Eventually, she got too tired and stopped. She clocked herself on her timer and walked the rest of the way to the café that was just a few blocks away. The aroma of coffee beans greeted her as soon as she stepped through the glass doors. The morning sun cast a warm glow on the red bricks of the back walls. The sunroom was looking particularly appealing with the light brimming through the bushes outside and bouncing off the white interior. She ordered a cappuccino, an orange juice, and the Light Sunday breakfast. She sat down in pure bliss of this new day, slowly sipping her coffee, savouring her fruit yoghurt, and meticulously tearing the croissant, making sure to pick up all the flakes that dropped onto the plate. She embraced the moment and the luxury of getting a slow morning.

Her phone chimed, and she picked it up. She had a missed call from Stephen and a text from Lucy. She tried calling Stephen back, but he didn't pick up. Then she checked Lucy's text. It was about the silent retreat. She opened the link and read the information and reviews while trying to envision what it would be like to go off for a few days and not speak the entire time. It looked so serene and pretty, though. Maybe it was exactly what she needed. She finished her breakfast and walked home. But as soon as she walked through the doors, she realized that no one was home. She found a note on the kitchen island in Leonie's handwriting saying they had gone to the Frog Reserve to play some sports and would be back later. Elena took the opportunity to clean the house. She changed all the sheets and towels, gathered everyone's laundry and put it on a machine, and was pleased with herself that she managed to clean all the bathrooms and the common areas before the laundry was done. But she then got to the kitchen and saw that everything from their breakfast was still standing on the dining table. Stephen hadn't even bothered to put away anything other than the dairy. Elena's mood instantly shifted from happy and energetic to irritated. She cleared it away, washed the dishes, then she poured up a glass of juice and went to sit in the hanging lounge chair on the patio.

She sat in peace for a few minutes, but soon enough, Noah came running through the house towards her, yelling happily that he had hit the ball. Leonie was complaining about something that Oliver had teased her about. All the kids swarmed around her.

Stephen came out and snarked,

"Here you are, resting like a champ. Well, we went to the sports center, then we met the Miller family and hung with them for a while. They got ice cream on the way home." He made a gesture in the air, implying that he was upset about something.

"For your information, I have not been 'resting'. I just spent 3 hours cleaning the house, and thanks to you, I also had to clean up the kitchen. So, excuse me for wanting to sit down for a few minutes." The kids had gone quiet while they argued, then resumed their stories as soon as their father had gone back inside.

Elena sat and listened to them, trying hard not to think of the oddly placed argument between her and her husband. After a while, however, she went back inside to look for him. She eventually found him in the laundry room, looking for a T-shirt, and quickly asked, "Why were you so angry earlier?".

He snarked but said nothing. She studied his movements and continued,

"And what are you doing?"

"I'm looking for my football shirt. I'm going to the pub with Carlos."

"What, why? I thought we were going to have Sunday dinner together?" "Yeah, well, I thought we were going to have Sunday brunch together, too. Shit happens." He rolled his eyes and passed her through the doorway as he put on his T-shirt. "Ok, so you are punishing me for wanting some time to myself. All I did was go for a run and get some coffee. How could I have known you would all leave for the day?"

"I'm not punishing you, but I called you three times, and you didn't pick up."

"Because I was running and listening to music!"

He rushed towards her and said angrily, "I have just taken care of the kids all day because you thought you would rather have breakfast by yourself than with your family. I'm exhausted. I need a beer. I need to chill." He walked towards the door, and she followed after him, continuing her argument.

"Well, how exhausted don't you think I am every day because you leave at 8 and are gone for 12 hours while I have to take care of everything alone?"

He said angrily, "Well, is it my fault that I have to work? You sound like a fricking spoiled princess."

"Wow. That was just too far. I am not a spoiled princess! I cook, I clean, I take care of the kids all day every day, and I even take care of your mother. And yesterday I cooked all day, and I fixed the cake and the drinks. I didn't even get to spend any time with the kids. Then you walk in with your fancy candles and suddenly you're the man of the hour! All I'm asking for is just a little perspective. After everything I did yesterday, how is it too much for me to just want two hours to myself on a Sunday morning?" She shouted at him, and he stood by the kitchen door, just staring at her with anger in his eyes. Then he turned around and left. She followed him out and added, "You know what, just go. We will do just fine without you anyway." She threw her hands in the air and stormed back inside.

She slammed the door, closed her eyes in anger, sat down on a chair, and cried discreetly. She eventually collected herself, managed to calm down, and went back outside to the kids. The four of them had a lovely evening together, eating dinner and playing a board game. Stephen still wasn't home when it was time to go to bed. She put the kids to bed and did her skin routine, praying to calm down her nerves before she went to bed. She then wrote a post-it note and put it on the bedroom door before going to bed. "Couch." That's all she needed to write. Her day, which had started in such a good mood, had ended in tragedy. She didn't really understand what had just happened. She knew that things hadn't been great for a while, but not like this. She snuggled up in her cover and fell asleep.

The next two days, he had gone to work before anyone had woken up. She pretended that she didn't care and went on with her thing. She made breakfast, walked the kids to school, went to the nursing home to check on Alice, made dinner, and helped with homework. He came home after everyone else had gone to sleep. The pattern repeated itself the next day. He didn't say a word to her, he didn't text, just assumed she would fix everything at home while he sulked.

The second evening, she decided to wait up for him. She sat in the living room, waiting for him to come home. He walked through the door at 9 pm and looked at her with disappointment as he walked through the door.

"Sit down." He sat down at the edge of the couch and looked at her irritably. "I will not allow this to go on for another day. You get angry with me for leaving you alone with the kids for a few hours, meanwhile, you somehow think it's ok to just deal with it and leave us all wondering where you are for two full days?" He looked down at the floor, still in an angry manner, before he said anything. "You never have time for me." He looked at her with stiffness in his eyes. "I am mad at you because you make sure that everyone else is ok. But you never check with me." She was shocked and sat in silence as she collected her rage to give a somewhat composed response.

"All you do every day is go to work and come home, while I cook, clean, take care of the kids, and make sure everything is flawless, and somehow you have the audacity to accuse me of not giving you enough love? Where is my love?" She began crying, but repeated the question, "Where is my love? You never have time for me, but somehow, I should go out of my way to feed your ego. But where is my love?" Her eyes filled with tears. She collected her thoughts and just said, "Tomorrow is Lucy's event, she was counting on your appearance. But I guess you're not coming to that?" He shook his head.

"And this weekend, I was planning to go away on a silent retreat with Lucy." "Cancel it," he said immediately.

"Well, I thought since I have taken care of the kids alone for the past few days that it would be nice for you to take over?"

"No, I will not do that," he just said, maintaining a cold look on his face. "I also need some alone time."

"But you've already had alone time all week. Ok, fine, I'll just ask my parents to take them."

He said with a disgusted tone, "Why would you leave the kids alone in the middle of our fight? They need their mother."

She looked at him again, hardly believing what he had just said.

"They need their father, too. Why is it ok for you to take a whole week off but not for me to take a weekend myself? Or even breakfast? And you wonder why I don't have enough time for you. You are unbelievable." She stood up and looked at him in anger before storming up to the bedroom and closing the door.

The next day went by rather quickly. Elena just had a few errands, went to see Alice, and came home just in time for dinner. Her mom was there to help out. Elena was happy but tired from all the drama. Stephen could have just stayed home to watch the kids since he wasn't going to the party, but instead he decided to continue being moody and was eating out with a friend. Elena had bought take-out on the way home and was handing out burgers and fries to everyone. She sat down and ate her chicken burger while chatting calmly with her kids and her mom. She was feeling somewhat empty inside and didn't know how to resolve the argument with Stephen. She wasn't sure she understood what had caused it in the first place. All she felt she could do was wait for him to calm down about whatever he was upset about, so they could talk. Maybe she should book a meeting with a couple's therapist. She watched the kids eat and chat amongst themselves and generally being in a good mood. She was glad that they were not affected by their parents' fighting. Eventually, she left to get ready. She put on an aquamarine dress with thin straps. The sleek silk dress was very fitting and reached her calves. She chose a pearlescent sling heel to go with it and white pearl dangler earrings. Her makeup was ready, and she had straightened her blonde hair and worn it out. She looked at herself in the mirror and smiled at what she saw. But it also saddened her that the person she wanted to share this night with was not here. And she didn't even know what she had done wrong. She shrugged and picked her mood up, forced another smile, and walked back downstairs. The kids had put on a movie that they wanted to show Grandma. She gave Noah a peck on his cheek and the other two a small pat on the head before she walked out to the taxi.

She got out by the harbour. The wind was a bit strong, and she held onto her dress and bag as she walked up the steps to the entrance. The streetlamps lit up the concrete in front of her. The big windows of the building shimmered in various gloomy lights and revealed her reflection as she approached them. A portman opened the door for her to the big entrance hall. There were lots of people there. Some were checking in their jackets, others had already settled in at the bar upstairs. All she could see was the night sky through the big windows, spotlights, and even more lights from the lamps at the bar. She skimmed the room, trying to find Lucy. She didn't at first, so she decided to get something to drink at the bar. A whiskey sour would do nicely after the week she had had. Just as the bartender handed her the pink drink, Lucy finally found her. She waved and made her way over.

"Oh my God, I'm so happy you came!" She hugged Elena tightly and added, "Wow, you look gorgeous!"

Elena beamed and replied, "Well, thank you very much. You don't look bad yourself in that gorgeous burgundy dress. It complements your skin perfectly." Ned gave her a brief hug, too, and said he was happy to see her. He knew all the details already, so he kept it at that. He ordered their drinks while Lucy talked to Elena.

"So, how are things at home? Still not talking?"

"No. I just wish I knew why," Elena said, feeling choked up but working hard at holding her tears in.

"I just don't get what has gotten into him." Lucy said, "Ned, do you know? Did he say anything to you?"

Ned just put his hands up and said, "Nope, I know nothing. Don't look at me." Lucy looked at her with a concerned look, and then she changed the topic.

"Let's just forget about him for now. Have you had anything to eat?"

"Well, I had dinner before I left, so I'm not really hungry."

"Oh, come on. The appetisers that the waiters are serving are excellent. You don't want to miss them." Lucy waved at a waiter and put some shrimps, a scallop, and a bite-sized tart on her plate. Elena did the same but also saw that they also had pickles and prosciutto.

They found a rounded booth where the three of them could sit down. Elena put her silver shell purse on the table next to her plate and turned to Lucy. "Tell me about the company and this great new discovery of theirs."

Lucy had put her silky black hair up in a sleek ponytail, but now it was falling down, so she adjusted it as she spoke. The company had been her client for a year. It was her first big break after starting her own firm, and she had worked hard to make this event the success that it was. Elena was amazed and looked around the room. There were over a hundred people here, most were high-positioned managers at various big corporations.

"The company itself is actually very young." She said, "They created this high-tech innovation where they turn stones into green energy. That's why there are so many important people here tonight; they all want to be a part of it."

"Wow, that's crazy!" Elena looked amazed and tried to work that out in her head. "How do you create energy from a stone? Wouldn't someone have come up with that a long time ago?"

"Well, apparently, it's not a regular stone. It is a stone that was discovered by some researchers off the coast of Australia, and then they figured out how to grind them down to somehow get energy." She shook her shoulders, indicating that her level of information ended there. She was a business major, not an engineer.

Elena pouted her mouth and nodded her head in an attempt to look impressed. "Alright, then. I'm just happy to be here. Thank you so much for getting me out of the house! Cheers!" The three of them clinked their glasses and toasted to a wonderful evening.

After about half an hour, the light shifted in the room. A red spotlight lit up a path among the tables, people moved to make way, and the company owner stepped up. People were clapping and cheering him on as he made his way to the stage. He signaled in the air to raise the volume of the music and for people to keep on clapping. He stopped on stage for a few minutes, clapping at himself and showering in the merriment. Lucy left for a few minutes to make sure that her team was doing alright, but came back shortly after. She was so happy that everything was running so smoothly. The guys in charge of the lightning were doing a good job. She did a thumbs up in the air towards someone, Elena didn't quite catch who, but she did turn towards Lucy and said.

"Who the hell is this guy? He is so full of himself!"

"What? No, he's not! He is so charismatic and has such a brilliant mind. Everyone loves him, as you can tell."

Yes. Elena could tell. It almost resembled a church in here. She cringed. She found the atmosphere disturbing, but instead of saying anything more, she just put the straw to her mouth and continued to sip her free drink. She picked up a handful of peanuts and began eating them in silence, one by one. Focusing really hard on her nuts so she wouldn't have to listen to the big guy on stage. After he had done his thing to pump up the energy in the venue, he started talking about some amazing adventures he had been on and the amazing other men that he had met. He brought forward a flashy hologram presentation that lit up the room with a black curtain as a backdrop. He was using it to tell his story and give context to the product by showing on a map how they had travelled to the far east and then back, all the research they had done, and what they had found. He showed statistics and numbers and all sorts of other data backing up the brilliance of this new discovery.

Then, as a last stunt to his showmanship, he walked across the stage towards a podium. Elena was vaguely listening to his story, but when he started moving across the stage, she followed intently, lifting her head so she could see properly. He said something that she couldn't hear, and then he snagged the fabric.

The very second he did that, though, a high-pitched metal sound filled the room.

Elena dropped her peanuts and put her hands to her ears and shrieked in horror.

"Oh, my God, what is that?" She yelled, staring at Lucy in disbelief.

"What is what?" Asked Lucy, looking concerned but unaffected.

"The sound!" Elena was confused over why she had to explain that noise. But Ned looked normal too, holding his drink calmly in his hand while trying to get a better view of the object. "What sound?" He said, looking towards Elena and then back at the object.

The sound settled and rested in the background like an uncomfortable hovering tinnitus. Elena looked at them, trying to make out what had just happened. She decided that she needed to understand what that thing was. After the business owner had finished his speech, he gave the audience the opportunity to have a look at his emblem.

Elena stood up and asked the other two if they wanted to join her. They did so; they all gave up their good seats to go over to check it out. As they came nearer, Elena noticed it was a black stone with a slight green hue. Lucy had only heard him talk about it; she had never actually seen it, so she was excited. It was very shiny, and you could see small cracks that revealed that the center was, in fact, green. Elena approached it with a pain-struck curiosity, not knowing what to expect. Ned reached it first, looked at it, and just commented, "Nice! It's very nice! Cool that this thing could bring so much energy. Where has it been hiding all this time?" He walked on and took some seats at a bar table with highchairs.

Lucy stopped and studied it. Elena stood beside her. There were lots of people in the room and the sound was bouncing off glasses, metal pillars, and giant windows. But she could still hear a vague etheric singing. She looked around herself. Then she leaned forward next to Lucy to look at the stone more closely. The green in the stone gave out a soft glow. "Wow, amazing how it glows. That explains the powerful energy." She said with a convinced tone. "What do you mean glows?" Lucy looked at her in surprise, then looked at the stone. "It's just a black rock. Well, the black is a little shiny, but it's not glowing." Elena looked at her in wonder, leaned a little bit further, and stared at the stone. "No, no. It's definitely glowing. You need to look closer." Lucy did, but still couldn't see it.

Elena straightened her back, looked away awkwardly and said, "Anyway, cool stone. Let's not get caught up, the line is long." They walked towards another section of the venue and took a seat at the table Ned was holding for them. He immediately went to the bar to get them some more drinks. Elena kept glancing over towards the stone, trying to figure out what was going on. She glanced over at her friends.

"Are you sure all you see is a black stone?" She asked, still utterly confused.

"It's just a rock, Elena," Ned said as he placed a new drink in front of her.

Lucy agreed, "Just a black rock, nothing special." She had seen more exciting rocks, in fact.

Elena glanced over to the rock again and then back to her friends.

"And you don't hear any singing or a noise of some sort?" She continued.

"Just the music!" Lucy nodded to the beat but looked slightly concerned about her friend.

Elena eventually dropped it. She took a sip from her drink while trying to keep the conversation afloat and ignoring the etheric sound in the background, which apparently only she could hear. But, eventually, she had enough. She needed to go home and rest. She smiled at Lucy and Ned and said, "Well, thank you for a lovely evening. I think I need to go home now. See you tomorrow. Do you want to take my car or yours?"

"I don't mind driving. I'll pick you up." Lucy waved and smiled at her, and then she turned to talk to Ned.

Elena waved back and made her way out. As soon as she left the building, however, the sound disappeared, confirming to her that it was, in fact, the stone. But even though the uncomfortable sound stayed in the building, the experience echoed in her mind. The whole way home, she was trying to figure out what it was. She was recollecting the strange dreams she had had these last couple of weeks with that rose palace and then the mirror palace a few nights ago. She also thought of the conversations she had had with Mary Magdalene. Was she going mad or was she going sane? She couldn't quite tell anymore.

She watched the darkness sweep by from her taxi window as he drove her to her home. There were a few glistening lights here and there, but apart from that, the neighbourhood was asleep. She tiptoed up to her bedroom. Stephen was already asleep on the couch, and the whole house was dark with a glim silver light shining through the big window in the living room. She undressed, took her earrings off, and got under the cover without even taking her makeup off or brushing her teeth. She felt like a rebel, but her whole body was still echoing the sound wave of that stone, and she forced herself to fall asleep before she could ponder it any further.

As it turned out, it was still glued to her mind the moment she woke up. She walked down the stairs to check on Stephen. She actually wanted to share this information with him, but he had already left for work, it seemed, since his shoes weren't there.

She went back up to wake up the kids and take them to school. She took out the cereal from the cupboard and some milk from the fridge and watched from the other side of the kitchen island as they gulped down their breakfast. She was just drinking coffee. She wasn't hungry. The fight with Stephen had caused her stress, so her stomach was giving her a hard time. At the moment, the thoughts of that stone also consumed her thoughts, so feeding her system was the last thing on her mind. They all walked to school together, as they always did. She waved them off and kissed them since she wouldn't see them all weekend. "I'll see you Sunday, ok? Have fun at Grandma's!" As soon as they had gone in, she picked up her phone and called Lucy.

"Hey, I need to talk about last night."

"What about last night?"

"The stone. That sound I heard. Can I come over right now?"

"Why are you still thinking about that? I told you it was nothing. Besides, I'm on my way to the office. Can't this wait?"

"No, I'm sorry, this can't wait. The stone has been glued to my mind since last night, and I think I finally figured out why."

"Alright, we can meet at my office in 20 minutes. But I have a meeting at 9 am, so you can't stay long."

Elena went home and changed clothes quickly. She then got in her car to drive the short distance to Lucy's office.

As she got out, she realized that she didn't know what she actually wanted to say. She just knew that she had to talk to her about it.

She stood in the elevator, watching the light shift on the buttons as it went higher and higher. It eventually plunged, and she got off. The receptionist knew who she was, so she just walked straight through and down the corridor towards Lucy's office. The beige carpet removed almost all sound, but she could see a few heads pop up to look at her as she passed by the open landscape and the different glass offices until she reached Lucy's at the end.

Elena didn't even say anything when she entered the room, and she didn't need to.

Lucy noticed her anxious demeanor.

"Hey, what's up?" She asked without looking up.

"There is something about that stone. They just can't use it. They have to find something else. Is there a way that you can talk to them about it?"

"I most certainly will not. I worked very hard to get that client. They are so important that the reputation of my company lives or dies with our connection with them. I just can't. Besides, we are just a PR firm. They have no reason to listen to us."

"But my whole gut is screaming. I need to do something."

"Why would you think the stone is so bad anyway? You're not a scientist or a researcher. Everyone is applauding this product. How can you be so self-righteous as to claim that you are better than them?"

"I am not. I am not. I just have this information, and they don't. They need to hear me out."

"Why, what information do you have? Who have you talked to? What are you not telling me?"

"Well," Elena hesitated for a moment, "You know that dream I had a few nights ago?" "The one about the roses, yes." Lucy looked at her with an annoyed expression and judgmental look in her eyes.

"Well, it turns out it's real. I had a similar one a few nights after, and now I'm starting to hear things and see things that apparently no one else is seeing."

Lucy looked angry and deeply concerned at the same time, "Well, hello, you've been fighting with Stephen for days, you've hardly slept. I believe it's called a nervous breakdown. I am happy to help you in a few hours, but right now I have a very important meeting.

"I'm sorry to barge in on you like this, but it is very important that you help me get a meeting with Zenith Power.

Lucy looked up at her with an angry look.

Elena swallowed and looked away. Unsure what to do now, she simply sat down in the chair opposite Lucy and stared into space for a few moments.

"Please, Lucy. You have to believe me. I would never ask you for anything if I didn't truly believe it. I know how hard you have worked to build your company, and I do not want it to be the reason for something that causes you pain. But I just can't sit by and watch, I have to act." She kept concentrating on her mind, searching for the correct words. But Lucy was quiet and kept looking at her paper as if she were writing something. Eventually, Elena walked towards the door. Lucy made a coughing sound as she had one foot out and said,

"You can take your own car up," she said without looking up.

Elena walked towards the elevators, trying to hold back her tears. First Stephen, now Lucy. What was happening? The world was turning against her, and no one believed her. She smudged a tear before it could make an appearance and waited for the elevator with a sense of urgency to get out of the building.

As she got home, she finished packing her bags really quickly so she could get going to the retreat. She got in the car and started driving when she suddenly realized she had forgotten about Alice. She was supposed to go to her that afternoon. She pulled over at the nursery home and had a quick cup of coffee with her. When she got back, Mary Magdalene was already in the car.

"Are you coming on the trip?"

"Of course I am! A three-day silent retreat with your best friend with whom you are now arguing. That is some heavy stuff. You need me."

Elena glanced at her and sighed. "Well, I'm only arguing with her because of you." "You are very brave." Mary Magdalene looked at her, placed her hand on her arm.

"Now, let's go!" She put the sunshade down to protect her eyes from the warm rays. "Do you really need that?" Elena said, surprised as she took a turn out on the main road that would take them to the freeway out of Melbourne.

"I might be in a different dimension, but I can still get the sun in my eyes, so yes." Mary Magdalene glanced at her and added, "Besides, you are wearing the only sunglasses available, and you need those because you are driving." She then started tampering with the radio to change the channel. She eventually found something she liked. Elena looked at her in dismay. "Love songs, really?"

"Yes, really! They are the best!" She started singing along, getting on Elena's nerves slightly.

"Fine, we can listen to it for a little bit, but I am not listening to that the whole way up. I'll fall asleep at the wheel.

Mary Magdalene looked at her and laughed, then continued singing along more loudly. Elena let out an annoyed laugh and set course for the north.

It was a three-hour drive, but now that she had started driving earlier, she had time to stop for a proper lunch and take the scenic route for a part of the way. Mary Magdalene was trying to keep the energy up in the car as best she could. She looked out the window, pointing at various pretty things like the scenery, birds, and trees. Nothing worked; Elena was consumed with her own emotions. After a few hours, she said irritated, "Don't you have somewhere else to be?"

Mary Magdalene looked at her with a slightly serious face and answered simply, "Not really, no. This is where I'm needed, so this is where I am".

Elena looked at her quickly and said, "Well, you ruined my life. Everyone is mad at me, and all these things are happening, so my life is falling apart. Things were perfect and everyone was happy, and now everything is a mess instead."

Mary Magdalene picked up a piece of chocolate without saying anything. She munched on that while glancing out the window, following the hilltops and trees sweeping by. She looked back at Elena and simply said,

"Your life was not perfect. And you were not happy. You were doing everything for everyone else. Always smiling, always making sure that everyone had what they needed. All the while, you were giving nothing to yourself. Everyone was taking and expecting you to show up for all the time to do their things on their agenda. All the while, they were taking you for granted and were so busy with their own needs that they failed to see you. And you did, too. All that has happened is actually that you gave voice to your point of view, your emotions, and your boundaries. If they can't respect you for that, then maybe you need people in your life that can."

Elena was a bit taken aback at what she had just said. The words she had just spoken resonated throughout her whole body and gave her the chills. She was so right, but it was painful to hear. She had been taken for granted for so long. Her needs had been overlooked. She had been asking for the bare minimum and not even getting that.

She felt slightly ashamed about having allowed herself to be neglected for so long.

She sat in silence, not knowing what to say.

"Oh, don't be so hard on yourself." Mary Magdalene said, reminding Elena that she could read her mind.

"Well, Lucy is my oldest friend. I've known her since high school. And I can't just let a 20-year-old marriage go to ruin just because you showed up."

Mary Magdalene just looked at her, letting Elena talk things out to herself. "But I have failed myself, that's the worst part," she said at last. The tears started streaming down her face. "I have failed myself." Mary Magdalene stayed silent, allowing Elena to release the emotions at her own pace.

Then she said. "My dear Elena. You have not failed yourself. You have loved others with all of your heart, and that is beautiful. You just forgot to love yourself, that is all. But I am here now. We will get through this together. Just take a few deep breaths. You will figure it out."

Mary Magdalene continued to munch on chocolate. She opened the other bar that had pistachios in it. Elena studied her movements as she took a piece. She took one herself and tasted it, then quickly spat it out.

"Oh, my God, that's disgusting. You can have all of it." Mary Magdalene just smiled. She was quite pleased with the taste. "You know pistachios are good for you." Elena glanced at her again and added, "Well, not together with chocolate and heaps of sugar,"

"Chocolate is good for you, too," Magdalene added and looked at a piece. "It's just the sugar that's not so good, but all crises need a remedy, and it does a pretty good job at that. Here, have another try".

"Ew, no, thank you. I bought it for you; you can have it. I had some of the other bar, that's enough for me. Didn't we have some chips somewhere?"

"Nope, that's all gone. All we have now are some apples."

"Alright, then. Give me one."

Mary Magdalene handed her a red apple.

CHAPTER 9

The Lotus

Phoebe opened her eyes and quickly realized that she was in a new retreat dream. She smiled with relief. It had been an intense week filled with triggers and different types of challenges, and she was so happy to get to meet her friends again. She could feel a gentle breeze on her skin. She was, yet again, seated in a lotus position, although this time her hands were in a prayer position in front of her chest. There was no flower to hold this time. Instead, she was wearing a white lily behind her ear and also an exquisite necklace made of jasmine flowers. Her normally untamed curls were in a sleek bun at the back of her head, and holding it all together was a golden round crown. A golden bracelet decorated her upper arm.

She touched the soft petals of the lily and accidentally got some yellow powder on her index finger. She smudged it off. She checked the crown on her head to understand how it was put into place before she stood up. Barefoot again, and today she was wearing a silk saari. It was dark green with golden embroidery. The sash shifted slightly as she stood up, so she corrected it before she straightened her back to look around. All she could see was water and green, lush hills in the distance that towered like grand fortresses. She was standing in a square room with a solid roof. There actually were no windows; it was just open, which is why it had felt like she was outside. She walked towards one of them and quickly understood that she was at the top of a pagoda. Her eyes followed the horizon. She first couldn't tell if it was a sunset or a sunrise, but as she could hear birds chirping in the distance and some ducks playing in the water, it became clear that it was morning. She followed the edge of the open-air room to investigate her surroundings. She finally saw the other pagodas. Some were far in the distance, others were closer to hers. She walked over to the stairs in the middle of the room and briefly sighed. She walked down to the next level, walked around, then down to the next level, and the next, and the next. Each level became bigger in size and required more steps to take before reaching the staircase. At that moment, she felt like it would never end, and she would turn around and walk the stairs for the rest of her dream, but the pagoda was actually only 5 stories. There were still a lot of steps, though.

When she reached the ground floor, she straightened her crown and corrected her skirt. The pagodas were all placed on small islands in the lake, connected to the shoreline by a narrow wooden bridge that was so low that it almost touched the water. She crossed the bridge and when she reached solid ground, she noticed a large stone gate that rose over the landscape. She was all alone. She was expecting others to come towards her from the other pagodas, but no one showed. She waited for a few minutes, but when no one came, she started following the dirt track towards the tower gates. She soon realized that the gate was much further than she had first realized. The stone blocks that stood erected on either side of the track looked big even from a distance, but that was nothing compared to their enormous true size. They must have been over fifteen meters tall. The triangular-shaped pyramids mirrored each other perfectly, carved in stone with extravagant symbols of dragons, other etheric beings, and an ancient script. She eventually walked through, looking up as she did, and stopped when she reached the center. The ground was cold from its shadow, and she could hardly see the top from where she was standing. She gently placed her hand on the left one, then adjusted her body to touch the other as well, but it was too far. She tried touching them both at the same time, but the distance apart was too wide, so she took a step towards the other and leaned over to put her hand on that one as well. Only after she had passed through the two pyramids did she notice a vast temple in the distance. She continued walking the dirt road while allowing her gaze to explore her surroundings. Next to the narrow dirt track was a wide grass field, but beyond that, the jungle stood tall. Monkeys were watching her; there were some birds flying about. Amongst the dense trees, there were plenty of bushes, making sure that every inch of the forest floor was green. The sun was high in the sky, and before she reached the temple, the sweat had started streaming down her face. It was a long way to walk on a very hot day. But she had finally made it and was now standing in the shadow of a tall stone wall. There were no windows, just bricks of grey stone shrines layered delicately one upon the other to form a construction that was several meters tall and, well, from where she was standing, she could actually only get a glimpse of the end of the wall. It dimly went into the jungle and stopped where the jungle deepened. The same in the other direction. But the track had led her there. To the middle. Where a closed wooden door was all that foretold that this was, in fact, not a barrier wall but a fortress or temple of some kind. She waited.

Soon, the door opened, and someone stepped out.

Phoebe looked around. She was still the only one there.

A woman appeared. She was wearing a golden sarong but was bare-chested from the waist up. Only three long golden necklaces covered up her bosom, bluntly revealing the complexion of her green skin. Her shoulders danced with blue curls, and big golden hoop earrings adorned her ears. She wore a tall golden crown on top of her head and looked around with an intense look in her eyes.

Phoebe did not know what to think, but right now she felt very afraid. As she was the only one there, she didn't know how to react or what to say. Especially when she appeared to not even notice her.

"Pardon me, ma'am. I don't know if you can see me." Phoebe said bluntly. "I wish to understand what is going on. Thank you." She looked down at the ground, trying to understand what she was supposed to do. Was she even allowed to speak? Was she allowed to look at her, or what was going on?

The woman ignored her questions. Instead, she said,

"My child. I am Green Tara, and it brings me joy to have you here today. You are here because you are ready to clear your inner fears. You will be tested, and you will unlock triggers, but trust that you are not alone and that you are protected. Now follow me."

Phoebe walked towards the entrance and hurried after her. She entered and noticed that there was only one way to go, and Tara was leading the way down a sandstone corridor with carvings on the sides. Phoebe followed Tara down the path, but Tara soon disappeared, and she suddenly found herself all alone in the dark. The only source of light came from the entrance door. Her heart was beating heavily, and her breath was shallow. Despite her fear, she kept walking. Cold stone to her feet, fingers grazing the carvings on the side. She kept on walking until everything fell completely dark. She paused and looked back at the entrance door that was now a small dot. She took a deep breath. She breathed again. Although it was already dark around her, she closed her eyes and felt a tingle around her temples. She opened them again and kept going. All of a sudden, torches were lit in green along the left side of the corridor. She was thankful for the light. They revealed a text that looked like Sanskrit or something similar. There were also some people carved next to it. Women and men. Some dragons, too, and a few symbols that she could not understand. She understood the falcon, though. Come to think of it, it almost looked like an Egyptian wall. But she was not in Egypt; she was in the middle of the Asian jungle somewhere. Or probably not because this was a dream. Everything felt way too real, though. She kept on going. After walking down one side of the temple walls, she finally reached a corner.

Green Tara was there, waiting for her.

"My child. You have now managed to overcome your fears by stepping into complete darkness. I congratulate you on making it this far. However, the journey is far from over.

You are inside the Temple of Inner Peace. I know it may not feel like it right now, but it is designed for you to walk in peace as you reflect on your fears and constraints. I am sorry to tell you that it will all be in complete darkness. But don't worry. I will be waiting for you at every corner, ready to share my light." She looked at Phoebe with compassionate eyes and continued.

"The first thing I need you to do is to sit in solitude. So, get into a lotus position.

Now, close your eyes and repeat after me

"Om Tare Tuttare Ture Soha"

"Om Tare Tuttare Ture Soha"

"Very good. Now repeat that until your heart feels lighter in the dark. I will leave you now to your solitude. My voice will guide you, but you are on your own during the challenge. I will meet you at the next corner.

Phoebe did as she was told. She sat down and attempted to meditate, something she had never tried on her own before. Her mind wandered, but she eventually managed to still it and sat in silence, trying to concentrate on the beat of her heart until a voice told her to get up and keep walking into the void.

Her hand was gently touching the wall so that she would feel where she was going, now that she could no longer rely on her vision.

Soon, the air cooled. She could smell the damp stone before she felt the water with her left hand. It was running down the wall, and she wasn't sure what to think. When the ground suddenly became wet, she was struck with fear. She stood still for a moment, not knowing what to do. There was water dripping down from both walls, and the ground beneath her feet was not only becoming wet, but it was becoming deeper with each step. She took a few more steps and noticed how the water continued to rise. She heard Tara's voice whisper, "trust". Her step felt increasingly insecure, but she knew that Tara was with her. Soon, the water was so deep that it reached her knees. She continued to wade through it. Eventually, it reached her waist. At this point, she wasn't sure what to expect if she continued. Would the water devour her? She could still not see anything; there was no source of light that offered any sort of relief to her fear. Phoebe, who had always been afraid of water, was now struck with fear that it was blocking the flow of her body. She was hoping to hear some sort of word of relief coming from Tara, but the only thing she said was, "Float."

Phoebe looked up to try to make out if she had heard correctly. She took a few steps in an attempt to avoid the order, but by the third time, Tara whispered again, "Lie down in the water and float."

Phoebe's heart was throbbing, and she said out loud, "Great, I'm inside my worst nightmare. Any possibility I can wake up, like now? Please." She hesitated, but she eventually managed to gather her courage to allow herself to lie down in the water and float. She started paddling with her arms in an attempt to stay in control but was eventually able to release herself from the fear of drowning. It was, after all, not deep, and despite not seeing anything, there was only one way to go, and once she was able to relax, she noticed that the stream in the water was carrying her effortlessly. She was eventually delivered to the other side. First, she was struggling like a stranded seal to get out of the water and start walking again but was eventually able to stand up. She noticed a soft shimmer and walked towards it.

She had reached the second corner of the temple, and Tara was standing before her again, although she had changed colour from Green to Black. In the dark void of the tunnel, a Black Tara did not offer much light, but there was a small shimmering black fire that offered some sense of direction and warmth. Phoebe sat down on the stool, and Tara covered her shoulders with a blanket.

"I applaud you, my child, for coming this far. That was the most daunting test, I know."

Now close your eyes and repeat after me.

"Om Tare Tuttare Ture "

"Om Tare Tuttare Ture "

"Very good. Now, we will say it together."

After three more repetitions, Phoebe opened her eyes again and saw Black Tara holding a black egg.

She handed it to Phoebe together with a black scroll and a feather pen.

"Like they had in the good old days." The historian in Phoebe got excited about the tools but was curious about the task.

"Your task now is to write down everything anyone has ever done that hurt you." She looked at Phoebe and studied her expression.

"And all I've got is just one paper?" Phoebe tried to laugh, but it was too painful. "It's a scroll. It will add space if you need it." She stepped back into the darkness and proceeded to be a witness.

Phoebe sat down in the Lotus position again and wrote down everything that came up. The ink from the black feather pen shimmered in purple hues on the black paper.

After she was done, she looked around to find Tara. She stepped out and spoke.

"Good, now place the scroll inside the egg."

Phoebe fiddled around the egg and eventually found a cove, opened the lid, and placed her scroll inside. "Now place it in the fire." Phoebe looked around. It was pitch dark; she reminded herself that there had been a small black fire. But she couldn't see it. If there were a fire, there would be light. "Where is it?" She asked eventually.

"Take one step in the direction you are facing and put it down." Phoebe did as she was told, and suddenly a black fire devoured it, first being completely black, then transforming to purple. "Feeling lighter?" Tara asked

"Not really," Phoebe answered, feeling disappointed.

"It will come, don't worry. Now, the next part will be a little bit easier to navigate as it will not take place in total darkness."

The Phoebe was still standing in complete darkness, but now with a small flickering light in purple. She walked the few steps towards the next part.

"Ok, I'm ready," she said.

Along one side of the tunnel, a line of torches lit up in a soft blue light.

She began walking, wondering to herself what to expect.

The carvings in the sandstone on the walls had gone, and in their place were five lines. She touched the wall as she had done before. The slight touch of her finger had initiated a sound that travelled down the tunnel. She pressed again on a different line, and the same thing happened. She looked at the lines and wondered if they were a blank sheet of music. To her amusement, she was correct. She pressed two different parts at the same time, and two different sounds vibrated through the tunnel. She didn't know any music, but she played around with her different fingers and suddenly let out a laugh. It echoed. By now, she had already walked parts of the tunnel, so the sound spread in both directions. She enjoyed herself for a little while, but after having cheerfully played with the instrument for a few moments inside the tunnel of a temple she did not know the way out of, the childish tune changed. By start, the tunes she had already played echoed back to her again. They bounced off the stone walls in an enchanting way. She had played again, and the echo itself had created a mesmerizing tune. But as she reached the middle of the tunnel, the tune changed, and the echo became haunting, and whispers joined the tune in their song. First, they just sounded like an etheric whisper, and she couldn't make them out. Then they got louder, and louder and louder.

"I'm not good enough."

"Nobody cares what I say."

She searched for some clues about where the voices came from. But soon she realized that they were not Tara or anyone else. It was the echo of her inner voice. "I'm such an idiot."

"I'm not perfect enough."

I don't belong here."

All the hurtful things she said to herself every day. She looked around to make some sense of how they were echoing towards her now. Having them surround her like this made her mind spin, and her whole essence was aching in effect. It felt like her own words were zoning in on her, trapping her. She stood still, twisting and turning and feeling the anxiety rise to a point where she could no longer take it. Soon enough, she found herself curled into a ball on the floor. "Why was she so mean to herself?" she thought, covering her ears. "Please make it stop". Soon, she saw a pair of blue feet. She looked up. It was Tara, but this time her skin was blue. Phoebe looked up, unsure of what to do, and felt ashamed of herself.

"I'm sorry, I didn't pass that test."

But Blue Tara just put her hand out and helped her up.

"Nobody does," she said, and when Phoebe was standing up, she continued, "Everyone wonders why everyone else is mean to them, but they never stop to listen to their own voice. That inner voice is your worst enemy." She led Phoebe the rest of the way and sat her down on a small stool in the third corner.

Now close your eyes and repeat after me.

"Om Bhim Tare Vrim Soha"

"Om Bhim Tare Vrim Soha"

"Very good. Now, we will say it together just like we did last time."

She proceeded to give Phoebe a piece of paper and a blue feather pen.

"Now, my dear. This time, you need to write down everything about yourself that you don't like."

"Wasn't the tunnel enough?" Phoebe asked.

"I'm afraid not. You need to write down everything you can think of."

Phoebe started writing. It didn't take her long to fill the page. This time, however, it was not a magic scroll. Blue Tara handed her another piece of paper. She kept on writing. And one more. After she had filled in the third piece of paper, she felt like she was done. She looked at Tara.

"Now, tear them up and place them in the bowl in front of you." Phoebe did as instructed, and Tara observed.

"Now tear them up into smaller pieces."

Phoebe teared them all up one more time. She placed them all back into the bowl, and Tara handed her a lit match. "Go ahead". Phoebe took the match from her hand and lit the pieces of paper on fire. She sighed in relief. It felt incredibly liberating. She watched as they burned with satisfaction. As the last piece of paper had burned up, the small flame that remained changed to blue and increased in strength again.

Phoebe watched with wonder and looked at Blue Tara.

"First, you had to rid yourself of the negative voice inside. Then, your new voice needed protection." Soon, the blue flame tamed itself and formed itself into a blue lotus. Tara kneeled down and picked it up.

"May your thoughts always be pure. May you always speak your truth," she said as she placed it in Phoebe's cupped hands. "Thank you."

"We have now reached the third tunnel. As you can see, it is red."

"Yes, I can see that. Do I dare enter?"

"My dear, it's the only way out."

Phoebe felt how Tara's answer did not soothe her senses. But she was at least a bit lighter after the last exercise. It couldn't get much worse anyway. She had already been through a black pool, and the echo of her voice. What could possibly be worse than that?

She started walking, and as she wandered down the tunnel, she admired the carvings on the walls. They spoke of love, passion, and devotion. Just like in the first tunnel, there were men and women, a couple of horses, roses, and lilies.

As she was admiring one of the images, she noticed how the wall behind her moved. She turned around and noticed a metal spike coming towards her. It stopped midway. After releasing her first instinct of fear, she went over to study it. "Oh, no," she thought the second she saw what was written on it.

"I hate my thighs."

She looked down at the vastness of the tunnel, realizing what was at stake and how long she had left to walk. She took a deep breath, trying to soothe her nerves by looking at the romantic images on the walls. She gathered her courage and kept walking.

A new spike rushed at her and stopped midway, too.

"I need to lose weight."

She held herself high and kept walking. The next one rushed towards her,

"I hate my skin."

She sighed. She kept walking, but as she had walked a bit into the tunnel, the next one didn't stop midway; it only left a narrow gap where she could pass. "Ouch," apparently it was a little sharper, too, than the previous one.

"I'm not beautiful."

"I'm not perfect."

As she took another step, all the other spikes in the tunnel appeared at once, with a daunting sound of metal that echoed through the space. Some were shallow, others only allowed a narrow passage. Some, she apparently had to crawl under. They gradually became nastier, too. Just like with her own inner critical voice about her capabilities, this was her inner critic.

It suddenly became painfully clear that she lacked compassion towards herself.

She eventually made it to the next corner, where a Red Tara was waiting.

"My child, you need to be kinder to yourself," she said as she looked at the number of spikes.

"Why the spikes?"

"The spikes you put up to shield yourself from getting hurt are the very spikes that keep you from love. You cannot cause yourself to bleed and expect others to clean your wounds. Only when you love yourself will you be able to accept the love of another. That is true love."

Now, close your eyes again and repeat after me.

"Om Tare Tam Soha"

"Om Tare Tam Soha"

She handed Phoebe a new scroll and feather pen, together with a red egg.

Phoebe accepted them and looked up at her, waiting for instructions.

"This time, you write a love letter to yourself, and you list every little thing that you like about yourself, even if it's just a toenail. And as you write, you repeat the mantra I just told you."

Phoebe wrote. First, she had trouble coming up with things. Then she thought of the things that had been written on the spikes, and she decided to change the formatting. "I am beautiful."

"My skin is perfect."

"My body is the right size."

"My pinkie finger is pretty." She laughed at herself at that one as she thought about what Tara had said. Then she continued with the same endorsement for every part of her body and her face. When she was done, she felt uplifted. She continued with all her personality traits. Both the ones she liked and the ones she didn't like, changing the narrative.

She felt satisfied and proud of what she had accomplished, and when she was done, she looked up at Red Tara again.

"I am proud of you. That is not an easy task, but you understood the assignment." As she spoke, a red fire appeared on a triangular golden plate. She pointed to Phoebe to put it in, but Phoebe hesitated.

"The other times, I placed my writing in the fire to clear the lower energies from my inner world. Why would I want to get rid of the good ones?" Red Tara knew that question would come.

"The black and purple flame clears traumas and lower energies. The blue one strengthens your voice and protects your spirit. The red one ignites your divine spark. By placing your scroll in it, you cleanse your aura and open yourself to new beginnings."

Phoebe liked the sound of that, so she quickly obeyed.

"This time, you will pass through a short green tunnel to stabilize your inner compassion before the next stage of this journey. I will meet you there."

Phoebe started walking again. The soft green light from the torches was soothing, but she was also feeling a sense of anxiety, wondering what this tunnel would bring her. She walked, and walked and walked, all the while having a fear in her stomach that something bad would happen at any moment. She kept alert and looked around her with every step. But soon enough, she reached a wall. Nothing had happened, but she could not figure out how to get out.

"Over here," Tara said and peeked her head out from an opening. "You were so busy looking for danger that you did not see the way out," she said, smiling softly.

Phoebe walked back towards her.

This time, Tara was yellow, the same colour as the space behind her.

"You will now enter the last part of this temple. You are to walk in the brightness of yellow for one full circle, but before you do, we need to do one last meditation together. Repeat after me:

"Om Tare Tuttare Ture Pushtim Kuru Soha."

This one was a bit more difficult, but Phoebe finally managed to repeat the words. "Om Tare Tuttare Ture Pushtim Kuru Soha."

After repeating the mantra to herself a few times, she left Tara and walked into the next part. The first thing she noticed was that a snake was carved into the tunnel, and she was facing its head. She looked at it and saw how the curves of its body continued in the distance, beyond the curve of the yellow wall. She noticed that the snake's tail was carved into the opposite wall. She pondered if that meant that she would be going all the way around and then back again? She chose to embrace the experience instead of allowing fear to steer her mind. She looked at the snake's head carved into the wall, studying its eyes and tongue. She then put her hand on its slithering back and traced its curves with her hand as she continued walking. She couldn't find the source of this yellow light. There were no torches, no candles, no apparent light source. But it was really bright.

Her mind kept spinning. Thoughts of not being good enough rose to the surface. She paused and collected her emotions. As she did that, she felt the presence of the wind. It kissed her skin and played with her hair, whispering "you are worthy". She gathered herself and continued walking, and her mind started circling about whether she had the capacity for what was being asked of her. The wind kissed her skin again and whispered, "You are capable". She walked and walked. Now that the walls were rounded, she knew she was walking in a circle with no possible way of knowing when the circle would end. All she could do was hold onto the snake's back and follow it to the end. She did pause again, however, and the fear of failure rose inside her. Just like the last time, the wind greeted her fear and whispered, "You deserve to be happy".

Yet again, she embraced the warm sensation of the wind and basked in the yellow light as she repeated the words to herself.

She repeated the lessons to herself as she continued following the snake, as an attempt to try convincing herself that they were true.

"I am enough, I am capable, I deserve to be happy."

Soon enough, she noticed that she was closing in on the snake's tail. The light got brighter, and she suddenly realized that it was the sun's rays that were mixing with the yellow light. There was still a bit of a distance left, but she could see the opening where the sun was shining through. In pure joy and relief, she started running, first a slow jog, but eventually she sprinted to reach the sun and breathe in some fresh air. She closed her eyes and basked in the pure joy of being done with the tests. "I am worthy", she thought and stepped out.

She was now standing outside again, in a big courtyard at the center of the temple. But there was no apparent way out. It was enclosed by the outer wall of the circular snake tunnel. Tara was nowhere to be found, so she was left to explore on her own merit. The whole area was decorated with white sandstone that reflected brightness in the sun, and in the middle stood a magnificent tree. Phoebe straightened her back and walked towards the tree in wonder. She stood before its trunk and admired its golden leaves. Its bark was pure white, making it appear almost like a ghost in the white surroundings. She leaned over and touched it, and as she did it her hand received what felt like an electric shock. She stood back in wonder. Then she noticed the presence of another energy than hers behind her. Thinking that it was Tara, she turned around. It was not, but her eyes filled with tears as she saw all of her friends standing next to her. Elena, Ayla, Meira, Jiya, Evelyn,

Akira, Nora, Edith, Hanwi. They were all here. Phoebe was so happy yet so confused. Where were they this entire time?

Now, White Tara appeared next to the tree.

"Healing requires solitude. Only when you are forced to stop and listen to your own heart can you find the fears that you need to release. After going through my prominent tests, you were finally ready to lift the veil and see that you were never alone. You have been walking the same path together."

After so many trials, they were all tired, but they were happy to be together. They hugged each other and smiled.

"Now, form a circle around the tree, and we will together sing this mantra before we part

"Om Tare Tuttare Ture Mama Ayuh Punya Jñana Pustim Kuru Svaha"

The women repeated together and needed a few trials to get the words right. Eventually, Jiya took the lead in helping them with the pronunciation and remembrance of the words.

"Om Tare Tuttare Ture Mama Ayuh Punya Jñana Pustim Kuru Svaha"

CHAPTER 10

The Fool

She looked at her work clothes that were still lying on the chair from before her trip. She was astounded at how much had happened in just four days. She took out the compass and put it on the table to look at while she was eating her breakfast. She found it strange how it was supposed to be a compass, but it didn't have an arrow or orientation. She turned it back and forth to watch the little metal ball tick between its position on the carved surface and the iridescent glass. It didn't move along the lines but slightly back and forth, but she couldn't figure out what kept it from tracing the flower freely. She put the book she had been given by the museum in her work bag and thought she would read it at lunch. She got ready and headed to work. She was quite early today but hurried either way so she could get a head start on her workload before the team arrived. She walked into the almost empty office, coffee in hand as usual, and made her way through the maze of desks and chairs. She eventually got to hers and did her usual morning routine, coffee on the table and sipping slowly while waiting for everything to load and start. She looked out the window, thinking of what to do about the compass. Why had she been the one to find it, and what was it exactly? Was it an indication for her to go somewhere?

She started by checking her e-mails. In just four days, she had received about a hundred of them in her inbox. She sighed and clicked on the first one. Thankfully, that one was a reply-all thread, which was both annoying and a relief because now she could uncheck almost twenty unread messages. She read it the whole way through, but her mind kept wandering and she couldn't focus. She eventually got bored and tried to search the internet for any information about her gem. There was very little. She found some information about the Venus flower that was carved into its surface, but she didn't get a chance to finish reading it because the rest of her colleagues came in. It was apparently eight o'clock, and she had not spent her extra hour wisely.

She cleared her throat and asked them to recap the various topics of the emails.

They talked about work and other things for a while. Soon, their fourth member, Daniel, came in, beaming from ear to ear.

"Why are you so happy?" Martin asked in a voice that implied a tease. "It's nothing. I'm not supposed to say." He answered

"Oh, come on," begged Lara, "Now we really want to know. What is it?" But he waved it off a second time and just stared at his computer to escape their glares. Ayla studied him, trying to read his energy, but said nothing.

She continued working, looking at her screen in an attempt to focus and keep her mind from running off, but her gut was telling her that something wasn't right. She tried to calm it by going over to Cassandra. "Hey girl." Cassandra said, "Feeling better?"

Ayla immediately felt ashamed that she had forgotten to inform Cassandra at all about her adventures these last days. She had been so stuck in her own head. "Right, I'm fine. Thanks." She didn't know what else to say. But she brushed it off and continued, "How about you? How are you?"

"I'm good, I'm good. I'm just going through the marketing material for your project.

Do you want to see it?"

"Yes, please, show me!" Ayla was happy that her casual escape from her desk could still count as being work related. She took a chair and sat down next to Cassandra, who clicked through a document and showed her the images they had chosen. It all looked really good.

"I'm really impressed. Great job! Do you want to have lunch later? I think I need to talk to you about something." Ayla said,

Cassandra widened her eyes and replied, "Oh my God, what is it? Is something wrong?" Her black eyes pierced into Ayla's.

"What? No, not at all. I just have some information I feel like I need to share." "Ok, good. For a second there, my mind went straight to crisis mode. I'm not sure I could deal with that right now," she said, gesturing with her hands in relief. "Yeah, sure. Is noon good for you?"

Ayla nodded and left her with her work to go back to her desk. On her way over, she noticed Daniel talking with another colleague in the hallway. She asked Lara and Martin as she sat down if there was anything she had missed while she was gone.

Martin leaned over from across the table and said, "I don't know for sure yet, but I hear Daniel is up for promotion to manager." Ayla looked at him in shock, her mind started spinning, and she suddenly felt a flash of emotions that she didn't know how to control. She stood up and walked straight to Gregory's office. She managed to compose herself slightly before entering, but was rather quick at making it obvious that she was upset.

"Hey, what's up? Feeling better?" Gregory looked at her in a condescending manner. "Yeah, I'm fine. I'm just, you know, a bit confused about something. I have been working tirelessly for over a year for a promotion I had been made to believe was mine as soon as we had closed the deal. But the rumor in the hallway is that the promotion I was working towards has suddenly been given to Daniel?"

Gregory shrugged his shoulders and just said, "Well, I'm sorry you had to hear that from someone else."

Ayla shook her head. "But why? I have been working here for seven years, never missing anything, always dedicated to my work. Last week, you even gave a toast to my efforts! Daniel hasn't even been here for a year."

"Well, I see potential in him as a leader. I need people I can count on." Gregory answered assertively.

"Have I ever given you any reason to believe that I wasn't reliable?" Her blood was pounding in her ears at this point. She couldn't believe what she was hearing. All those late nights, all the missed holidays, and skipped lunches. For what?

"Well, that's the way it is now. You just have to deal with it."

"I will deal with it." She stormed out, and as soon as she was in a quiet corner, she just did a little dance with her fists to try to control her cry. She entered the elevator to go talk to Human Resources. She felt like she had suddenly been caught in a storm of discrimination, and all she wanted was someone to help her make it right. She stormed into Human Resources and managed to get a meeting with the manager straight away. She was, unfortunately, unable to do anything because no apparent law had been broken. It was just a simple case of injustice. Ayla left just minutes after, feeling completely uprooted by everything she thought her life was. She walked into the bathroom, making sure nobody was there, and screamed all she could in sheer desperation as tears streamed down her face uncontrollably. "Seven years. She had been there seven years, and her efforts had led to nothing. He had been there for only one year, and he got promoted over her.

He was younger, too. Life was so unfair." She stood in front of the mirror and tried to stop her tears from ruining her makeup, but she couldn't. She was hoping that Athena would pop up, but she didn't. She was left to cope with herself. Her mind was spinning, trying to think of her options while forcing herself to control her emotions, and making the crying stop before she left the bathroom. She couldn't let anyone see that she was sad. "Neutral face, neutral face." She managed to hold her composure all the way back to her floor, but the minute she walked into her department, the feelings of despair rose to her heart again, and it started pounding really heavily. She felt slightly dizzy but managed to get herself to her desk. She sat down, and Lara asked her immediately how she was doing and gave her some powder from her makeup bag. "I have some mascara too, if you want to fix your face."

Ayla thanked her but declined. "I'm not ashamed of my emotions. I have been hurt, and I'm allowed to be sad."

Lara gave her a shy smile and said, "Well, I knew he was up to no good the minute he started. He has been after your job for months, buttering Gregory up, but you have been too focused on the actual work to notice. I guess it's not the hard worker that gets promoted, but the one who can suck up."

Ayla smiled gently at her attempt to make her feel better. "It seems to me that the only way to get a promotion is to be a man."

Lara's smile disappeared. She tried to come up with excuses, but she knew that Ayla was right. Ayla looked at her, thanked her for her kind gesture, and tried to go back to work while calming her nerves. But her head started spinning again as she read the e-mails requesting her opinion, approval, and review. She thought about how much of her life she had sacrificed for this workplace, for these projects that she had been a part of. To her, it had essentially been a satisfaction to see the end result. But knowing that her efforts would not get rewarded put a sour twist to it all. Her mind was suddenly made up. She stood up, took a piece of paper and wrote something on it, then took it to Gregory's office, barged in through the closed door, put the paper on his desk and left without so much as looking over her shoulder. He was on the phone and just looked at her with an irritated and confused look, and at the sight of her back, he picked up the paper and read the words. "I quit". He immediately hung up and followed her to her desk. But she was already gone.

Ayla had stormed out of his office and gone straight back to her desk, left all of her work things on her desk, and just took her personal stuff and left. The second she walked through the doors and stepped outside, she felt liberated, and her tears turned into laughter. A laughter that was both a sense of relief and a release from all emotions. She started walking, jacket on her arm even though it was actually chilly, and the almost empty briefcase lightly dancing in her hands. She didn't look back, and she didn't stop until she had already walked a block and remembered her lunch with Cassandra. She took out her phone and just wrote to her quickly what had happened, and that she was not up for lunch, she needed to go. "But where?" She thought and fiddled with her phone. She had a sense that she needed to get out of town, but where was she supposed to go? She sat down briefly on a bench by the square and took out her book. She flipped through the pages, watching the images go by of symbols from astrology and human history. Her first thought was that the compass would know, so she went home to get it. All the time, she was thinking and hoping that Athena would show up this time to point her in the right direction. But as she opened the door to the apartment and peeked through the rooms, she realized that she was still on her own. She took out the compass from a kitchen drawer and petted Mr. Puzzle as she held it in her hand. She had now learned that the webbed flower was the flower of Venus. Countless civilizations had followed that planet meticulously for thousands of years. She didn't really understand why, yet. But it was clear that if the little ball was tracing the flower, then it must be linked to that. She flipped it over and looked at the dolphin on the back of it. "Where are the dolphins?" She thought but laughed at her own ignorance. The dolphin was probably just a symbol for something, not a destination. She found similar symbols in her book, but not any clear explanation.

She took out her phone and called Mr. Bouchard.

"Hello, this is Ayla Wilson from yesterday, with the compass?"

"Yes, I remember. What is your question?"

"I wonder if you have any ideas about where Atlantis would be, if it were to be real? I have searched through the book you gave me, but can't find any clear clues." "That's because no one knows. There are many theories circulating in the world, but no one knows for sure.

"Ok, so it is perhaps just a fairytale, then?"

"Who knows? But maybe it is for you to find out."

"How do I do that?"

"You are the one with the compass, not me. I think it's the only thing that can guide you to where you need to go."

"Ok, thank you, anyway, for your help," Ayla said and hung up, feeling saddened to not have received the help she felt that she desperately needed. She looked around the room. Still no sign of Athena.

"Why would she leave me alone in all this?" She thought, thinking about potential destinations. Eventually, she just stood up, took out a duffel bag, and packed her essentials. She sent a quick text to her neighbour to ask for more help with Mr. Puzzle. She kissed him on his forehead and walked out. She decided to just let her feet take her and not think too much. They took her to the train station. She allowed fate to take the wheel and just looked at the board. What was the destination of the next train leaving Toronto? "Halifax, no.

She wasn't going home this time. Montreal? No. Also wrong direction. Her gut gave her a sense that she needed to head west. Vancouver? That sounded like a good idea, going to the other side of the country. Yikes, that's a four-day train; she could just take the plane instead. She picked up her phone and started checking for flights, but something inside her made her stop. Maybe four days in silence on a train heading west was exactly what she needed right now. To clear her head and find information about her next steps. She walked up to the travel agent at the ticket office and asked about it. The man behind the counter gave her a brochure and told her about her different options. She looked at it. It was quite expensive. And if she was going to sit on a train for four days, she definitely wanted the prestige class. She thought about everything that had just happened and eventually said yes, let's do it. The next train thankfully had one cabin left.

Feeling excited, she went and got herself some snacks and magazines. A book might be a good idea to buy for a trip. She hadn't read anything in ages, but she thought that it might come in handy. She also bought a notebook and a pen that both looked like they were up for a new adventure.

She strolled the different stalls at the train station, suddenly remembering that it was actually lunchtime, so she got herself something to eat while she waited for the time to pass. An hour later, she was finally able to board the train. She found her cabin and sat down, filled with anticipation of what was in store. In all her life, she had always just kept to the East, and this was really exciting.

As the train started rolling, she unloaded her things, snacks, books, and magazines were all thrown on the bed, and she was already listening to some music. She had obviously bought a coffee and was drinking a sweetened version in pure bliss. The train was moving quite quickly, and soon, they had left the city behind, and the countryside was expanding with every minute. Her eyes were caressing the hillsides and the trees, feeling ecstatic at seeing her beloved city from this angle. Soon, the landscape shifted to welcome mountainous regions and dynamic drops. At this point, she finally got the company she was craving when Athena suddenly showed up.

"Here you are enjoying yourself. Having a good time?"

"I am now! But where have you been? You weren't there when I needed you." Ayla said in disappointment.

"I can't show up every time you feel lost. You need to trust your own voice. Plus, if I had shown up before, we wouldn't be in this lovely place heading west. Pray tell me what made you head west?" Athena said with a sarcastic voice.

"I have no idea. I let my gut take the lead. And I'm happy I did. I should do that more often."

"Good. good. I gather things went well at the office today?" Athena said with an even more sarcastic tone while sitting next to Ayla on the bed.

"Not really, no." Ayla gestured at the obvious.

"Sometimes, all we need is a nudge to get going in the right direction." She looked at Ayla, "It was something that just needed to happen for you to realize that place was not good for you."

"That was you?"

"What? Oh please, I don't have that kind of power. " She said, and took a cheese snack from the bag. "That was all you. You have been wanting to leave that place for years. I don't know why you kept convincing yourself to stay and get recognition and all that nonsense."

"For your information, I liked being recognised for my skills and knowledge. It brought me joy." Ayla said and took the bag from Athena as she was eating them all.

"You don't even need these."

"Neither do you, if I may." Athena said and took another one before Ayla put them away." She then turned to Ayla again,

"Just because your ego is happy to be fed compliments doesn't mean it's good for your soul."

Ayla thought of what she just said and answered, "Well, I had friends there, too. It wasn't just work."

Athena just looked at her for a moment, "Yes, sure. But friends are not trees. If they want to remain in your life, they will. No matter where you work." Then she stood up, "Anyway, I'll let you do it." She was about to leave, but Ayla interrupted her. "No, wait. I forgot to ask you about the thing. "What thing?" Athena looked stunned.

"The compass, or whatever."

"I can't tell you that. Not because I don't want to. The compass is designed to guide you to your own inner knowledge. If I tell you, you will miss everything that it wants to say. Just trust your instinct, honey," She winked and left.

Ayla sighed. Always the same answer. Can't tell her this, can't tell her that. She took it out from her inner pocket to look at it. The pearlescent face shimmered in the soft afternoon light. She sighed again and put it back. She looked out the window and continued to trace the landscape. They were approaching a beautiful lake. She put on her music again and let her thoughts run free as she followed the movements of the train.

She searched through videos on her phone. Maybe it would help to do a meditation, and the knowledge might come. She found one that had dolphin sounds in it, which felt soothing and appropriate considering everything. She listened to that until she fell asleep.

She woke up in the early morning by the train's glistening sound on the tracks. But at this point, her thoughts had caught up with her, and she wasn't as upbeat as she was yesterday evening. She was feeling slightly depressed because of everything that happened yesterday, overwhelmed over everything that was going on, and the fear of uncertainty was crippling up. She opened her phone. It seemed that her loved ones had the same emotions. Her mom had called her a couple of times, then sent her a text about how utterly disappointed she was with her lack of judgment. Her dad had just sent a text that he was worried, and Cassandra sent her a chat with "What just happened? Want to talk?" But the truth was that Ayla didn't want to talk to any of them. All she wanted was to just be alone and take in the presence of the landscape. She went to the restaurant cart and bought a coffee and a sandwich. She stayed there as she ate, for the sake of taking in other influences.

"Is this your first time?" The cashier asked.

"Yes, I've never been west before, and I've also never seen the mountains like this. It is stunning."

"We'll be taking a break at the next stop, so you'll be able to get off and walk around if you like." She was friendly and basked in a big smile.

"That sounds nice, I will do that. Thank you." Ayla replied in a mellow voice. The next stop was the Sioux Lookout near Winnipeg, but the train still had a few more hours to go. She took out the book she had bought and started reading. She read for about an hour but kept glancing over at her new notebook and pen. She wasn't sure what to write at first. Maybe the notebook was too pretty for her to write what she wanted to write in it. But eventually, she picked it up and began to pour her heart out onto the pages, summing up the emotions that she was holding onto inside, from yesterday to the events leading up to it. She was sad about a lot of things, it turned out. She thought about how this all came to be at this exact moment in her life. Everything was such a weird coincidence. Why was she suddenly uprooting her entire life? And why was she so sensitive? She couldn't control her emotions. Maybe that was a good thing. She kept on writing. Everything that came to her mind was allowed to leave her concerns and settle onto the pages. She suddenly realized that she actually didn't really know who Athena actually was. All she knew was that she was a Greek goddess of war or something. But why had she been appointed as her guide? She took out her phone and searched for the various links. She's a goddess of war, wisdom, and strategy, among others. She kept on reading the stories of Greek mythology, trying to memorize everything as she read.

So, the goddess of wisdom is guiding me to find my inner wisdom, got it.

"But why would the goddess of war want to impose her wisdom onto her? " She had never hurt a fly. Naturally, Athena didn't show up to answer that question herself, so Ayla had to suffice with pondering the question herself. After several attempts, however, she had to claim herself defeated. She could not wrap her head around it and left it where it was. She was sure she would get the answer at a later time.

They were slowly approaching the stop, and Ayla prepared herself for what she wanted to do in the short window of time that she had. She put the compass in her bag and hurried down to the shoreline of Pelican Lake. She placed it in the sand and sat down next to it. She closed her eyes and tried to come up with anything clever to say. She struggled but eventually remembered a phrase from her meditation video the night before.

"I am that I am." She said and simply closed her eyes. She breathed deeply and exhaled, and repeated the sentence again. "I am that I am."

She opened her eyes again, feeling happy about this idea. She stood up to collect her things and headed back to the train. But just as she was about to lean down and pick up the compass, she noticed that the whole flower lit up in magenta pink. She stared at it in awe. "What was that?" She walked to the other side, thinking it might have been the sun's rays that had created an illusion. But it remained alight. She walked around it in a circle and eventually accepted the fact that it really was true. She picked it up and looked at it in wonder.

What caused this? She had to save that thought because now it was crucial for her to get back so that the train would leave for Vancouver with all her things, but without her.

She got back on the train, and as soon as she was in her cabin, she took out the compass again. It had gone back to white, but it still had a slight glow. Her spirits were high for a while. That was one of the most extraordinary things she had ever seen. She spent almost an hour searching the internet, trying to find any clues to what could have caused it, but she eventually gave up. The train kept moving, and soon they were in Winnipeg, and she had a brief opportunity again to get out for a few minutes to buy some more snacks at the closest store. As the landscape turned dark, she sat yet again with her notebook and filled its pages with the content of her heart.

By the next morning, she had decided that she would stop in Jasper to join a guided group hike in the Rocky Mountains. She felt that she needed to experience this wondrous landscape and spent the rest of the day searching for all the information she needed and by the time her train slowly approached the station in the late afternoon, she had gathered all the essential details about her stop. She got off and was a little relieved to be on solid ground. Although it was a breathtaking experience to see the country from the rails, it was also a bit daunting to have so little freedom for so many hours. But now, her legs were rested and ready for a hike. She found the office of the tour company and talked to the woman in charge. She had already called from the train, but she just wanted to make sure that she had everything. She hadn't planned for a hike. The things in her bag were all just regular wear. She quickly oriented herself and found a store that sold the necessities.

Meanwhile, she tried to find a place to store her bag during the hike. She spent the evening getting all things sorted and found a conveniently located hotel for the night. She woke up early the next morning, feeling excited and ready to take on an adventure. She felt a rush of new energy as she approached the meeting place for the group. It was, however, quite obvious that she had bought everything she was wearing in the local store. And it was almost equally obvious that she had never been on a hike before. First, she felt the impostor syndrome creeping up; she felt out of place and quite uncomfortable. The guide came out, introduced herself, and started talking about the two-day trip. Ayla scanned the crowd and quickly realized that most were probably in the same shoes as her. Rookies. But everyone has got to start somewhere. They began the walk and followed the trail through the tall trees. For a while, all she could see was a dense forest, but soon the landscape started shifting, and she acknowledged that she had made the right choice. The nature was breathtaking, the valley and scenery left no one untouched. The others on the tour seemed to be a scattered bunch: an elder couple, two singles, two friends, and another younger couple. She exchanged a few words with all of them in the beginning but soon found herself having to focus on herself. She was getting a small pressure on her throat and shoulders, which in some areas were more intense. By the time they got to Lake Louise, they took a break for lunch. She stood in awe, overlooking the turquoise lake and drinking from her water bottle. But she had a hard time catching her breath. She sat down on a large tree stump and rested for a bit. She had picked a tour that arranged with the food, a conscious choice to assist in her spontaneity. Someone walked towards her and sat down on the tree next to her. "How are you doing? You seem a little out of breath." It was one of the men on the tour.

She looked at him, feeling touched by what he had noticed. "Thank you for checking in on me. I'm doing much better, thank you. The water helped a lot. And the view."

"Yes, the view is extraordinary. Is it your first time here?"

"Yes, I live in Toronto, this is my first time in the west, and definitely my first time in the Rockies. And also, I've never hiked before. So, lots of new experiences all at once." She laughed at her own feeling of being an outsider and added, "How about you?"

"I've come here quite a lot, but I'm also brought up in this region, so it makes more sense, I guess." He smiled at her and adjusted the cap on his head with an awkward chuckle.

"I'm sorry, I don't remember your name," Ayla said, not noticing the subtle cues. "Oh, so sorry. That was clumsy of me. I'm Samuel, nice to meet you. I thought you already knew since we talked a bit when we walked up." He gave out an awkward chuckle again and stretched out his hand. She felt embarrassed at having missed that but accepted the shake and replied, "Sorry about that, I was so caught in my own world, I didn't hear everything you said back there. I'm Ayla." She smiled back. Then they got interrupted by the guide, who needed more cooks for the food, so they joined the others and helped prepare everything. After having eaten, they proceeded with the afternoon hike. It would be a bit longer than the morning hike, but most of the track had a view over the lake, which made it all the better.

Ayla walked alone for a while. She thought about everything that Athena was standing for, and she thought about the job and the dreams she had so suddenly left behind. Why was she even in this situation? What had she not seen before? She thought about the time she left Lunenburg for university, all the sacrifices she made to study for a degree she hardly knew anything about, and then insisted on staying on the line that she had worked towards, not willing to even see the alternatives because that meant giving up everything she had worked towards. The moment she thought the last thought, she didn't only feel ridiculous, she felt like she had committed fraud against herself. Like keeping up a lie that not even she believed in. She shook her shoulders and mumbled, "Well, that makes me, and like half the country. I'm hardly alone."

She kept on walking and eventually, the breathtaking scenery made her quiet her mind. She was thinking about problems instead of admiring where she was at. So, she interrupted her thoughts and marvelled for a few moments about the view instead. They were invited to sit down as a group on a few logs and have some refreshments. Ayla took out her water but was happily ready with the cup she had brought once she heard that the guide had coffee. She had bought chocolate cookies and took one before she passed them around the group.

When they continued their walk, Samuel slowed down and walked next to her. Ayla looked at him and tried to think of something to say. "So, you said you're from here.

Are you born here or have you moved here?

"Actually, I don't live here anymore. I'm from the southern part of Alberta, but I currently live in Vancouver. I moved there for work. What about you?"

"I live in Toronto, but I'm actually from Lunenburg, south of Halifax." He looked slightly confused, so she added, "It's a small town on the Atlantic coast. He nodded and added, "That sounds like a dream."

"What? How is that a dream?"

"Isn't it everyone's dream, a small town near the ocean? That's one of the reasons why I moved to Vancouver, to be near the sea."

All she could do was to agree. He was right, it was the best part of life. And she had been missing for far too long. The river didn't even begin to make up for the breeze of the ocean.

"So, what do you do then? "If you had to move to Vancouver for it?" she asked. "I'm a lifestyle consultant," he said, so I can actually work everywhere. I travel around and give people advice on places to visit for their well-being. I also do one-on-one coaching."

"That sounds like one of the best jobs on the planet." She said, looking both impressed and sad at the same time.

"It is actually. But your expression tells me that you do something less fun." "I guess what I do sounds fun and creative on paper, but in reality, it's a lot of hierarchy, late nights, and tiresome planning. I'm an architect or aspired to be one anyway."

"Why, what happened?" He asked.

"I quit. Two days ago. Some jerk in my team stole my promotion, so I had enough and just left. Got on the first train out of there and here I am." She chuckled to herself in a slight feeling of awkwardness and squinted her eyes to look up towards him as they walked.

"Here you are. Good for you. I'm happy for you."

"You're happy for me," she said sarcastically, "Thank you. I believe you're the first person who has said that to me."

They continued the afternoon hike and chatted casually along the way. As the lights started shifting in the sky, inviting the subtle cues of the evening, they finally made it to camp. This was the lazy man's trip, so there were glamping tents at the destination, waiting patiently for their arrival. They felt thankful for that, considering how exhausted they were. In parts, it had been a challenging hike. They all got involved with cooking the food almost right away. A simple potato salad and some meat for the grill. One of the other hikers had been wise and brought marshmallows so they could make s'mores and was generously handing them out to everyone. By the time that the moon peeked over the trees, everyone had finished and was helping to clean up. Ayla was sharing a tent with another girl, so she went over to get acquainted with her and get some of her things out of her bag. Her name was Claudia, and she lived in Quebec. She had been out here hiking for a few weeks and had gotten this tour to give herself a little luxury before continuing south. She was sweet and nice, but they didn't really click, so Ayla excused herself and walked down to the lake. When she reached the shoreline, she sat down and looked up at the stars. She pondered over everything that had led her to that very place, looking up at a bright moon in a clear sky by a lake in the middle of the Rockies. She sighed gently and counted her blessings. She was grateful for having the opportunity to do this trip, and she was grateful to herself for finally having the courage to walk away from something that was apparently unhealthy. A part of her wished she had done it sooner, but she also acknowledged that she still had enjoyed the past few years and the lesson they taught her in the end. She took out the compass from her pocket and looked at it. She was about to put it on the rock when she heard footsteps and turned around. It was Samuel. She put the compass back into her pocket and greeted him.

"Is it alright if I join you?" he asked calmly.

"Yes, sure. Be my guest. I'm just admiring the clear sky and the beautiful full moon." "It is a full moon tomorrow. Although the moon is always beautiful so," he said. "Oh, is it? I feel embarrassed. I should have known that," she said, beating herself up in her mind for being slow at learning these things.

"I wouldn't exactly consider that something to be ashamed of. Why do you say that?" "It's just that lately, a lot of things are happening, so I'm trying to learn astrology and stuff so that I will stay on track with everything, but it's really hard."

He looked at her with a surprised look, "Don't beat yourself up about it. There are a lot of things to remember. I only actually know the moon's cycle and a bit about the zodiacs, but not much else."

She looked at him in amazement and said. "That is still really impressive and way ahead of me. I need to study."

He smiled and accepted the compliment.

"So, what made you choose to get off in Jasper to go on your first-ever hike in the Rockies without a plan or preparation? I get how you ended up on the train, but that's easier to just let destiny take the wheel."

"Well, the Rockies spoke to me. Like, there was something I needed to do. Or perhaps my soul was longing for a little bit of adventure." She looked at him with her hazel eyes, but as he met her gaze, her shyness took over, and she looked away. She tried to concentrate on something across the lake as an attempt to calm her mind, which was spinning around, making her feel dizzy. She cleared her throat to beat her shyness before she continued, "You know, the truth is, I have recently had many weird things happening in my life. And then last week, I found this thing. Something about it led me to here. I'm not sure what, yet." She hesitated and briefly looked at him before she took out her compass and showed it to him.

He took it in his hands and looked at it, studying the different details. "This is amazing, what a beautiful find. Have you had someone look at it?" he asked.

"I have. I went to several places, actually. One archaeoastronomist in Toronto thinks it's some old thing from Atlantis, if you believe in that sort of thing." She looked at him awkwardly, embarrassed for having shared so much. But instead of stopping herself, she continued, "I'm reading everything I can find about it and trying to figure it out, but it has proven to be very difficult. But the coolest thing happened when I stopped by Pelican Lake in Winnipeg. I placed it in the sand, and it lit up. I guess I wanted to see if it would happen again and get a longer chance to study it if it did."

"Cool," he just said and studied it a bit further before looking at her, "Do you want me to put it down so we can see if it works?"

"Yes, please, go ahead," she said and followed his movement as he placed it in the sand. They looked at it in anticipation.

"Maybe it just works in the sunlight," she said, and was about to pick it up when a vague shimmer suddenly appeared on its surface. She laughed, "Did you see that?" "Yes, I did, that's incredible," he said.

"Well, it's not the same as last time, but it's at least something. Last time the flower turned pink."

"Well, maybe it's just the difference between the two locations," he said. She chuckled slightly and paused to try to comprehend before asking, "What do you mean?"

"Well, maybe they are different points according to your compass. Like they open different doors or something." He picked it up in his hands to try to make sense of it.

"That would be incredible. Any ideas?"

"Well, for starters, Lake Louise is said to be the etheric retreat of Archangel Michael and Archangel Faith. That's why I come here every year, actually. To seek clarity and truth in my life's choices."

"I'm embarrassed to say that I don't know who they are. I've only just started reading up on these things. But that makes total sense. That's probably why I was directed to come here."

"Probably. And maybe we would meet." He said, smiling awkwardly again. "Yes, maybe." She smiled shyly. It felt nice to talk to someone about these things who not only believed her but also understood. "Thank you for listening," she said. He looked at her and paused for a brief moment as he looked into her eyes, searching for clues. He then gently stroked her cheek and kissed her softly. She looked deep into his eyes and beamed from ear to ear. That was an unexpected turn in an unexpected trip. She looked up at the stars and tried to think of something to say. "So, you come here every year? That's impressive. What else do you do?"

"I travel. Apart from my lifestyle coaching, I host retreats and staff. After this, I'm going to Hawaii."

"Hawaii? That's really cool. I've never been there. What will you do there?"

"I'm the facilitator of a spiritual retreat that attracts people from around the world.

Hawaii is pretty special with its energy."

She looked him in the eye, trying to read his mind before she spoke, "So you are also awake, then?"

He handed her the compass back as he answered, "Yes, I believe I am." He thought for a moment and continued, "Why don't you come to my retreat in Hawaii? I think it will be good for you."

"Well, to be honest, going on this trip was a spontaneous whim. Somehow, it feels like Hawaii is just a little bit too crazy for me. I'm normally, you know, all for planning and stuff. I'm already a little out of my comfort zone as it is."

"Alright. I don't leave for another three days, so you have plenty of time to get further out of your comfort zone." He looked at her with a dreamy look, but in the end he just smiled. He leaned over, stroked her hair from her face, and kissed her softly again.

"What will you do instead, then? Will you go back to Toronto?" He said as he gazed up at the stars.

"I believe so. I need to figure things out." She looked at the compass in her hands. It was still shimmering in the moonlight. She couldn't quite envision what her life would be like once she got back. She looked towards him. "Maybe Hawaii doesn't sound so bad after all." She said at last, and he smiled back at her and gave her a kiss on her head as he pulled her closer and said.

"You just made me very happy."

The next day started early. Ayla woke up to birdsong at the break of dawn. She looked over at her roommate, who was still sound asleep, and sneaked out quietly. It was a beautiful morning with crisp blue skies. The lake was a perfect vision. She made herself a cup of coffee and went down to the shore to enjoy the serene atmosphere. After having been alone with peace for about half an hour, she heard the familiar voice behind her.

"Good morning, you're up early." Samuel was walking towards her with his own cup of instant coffee.

"Good morning. The birds woke me up, but it's ok. It was a nice way to start the day."

He sat down next to her and gave her a kiss.

Today's walk was a lot easier than yesterdays. And the upbeat of their hearts made the whole journey down to the town go smoothly. Samuel was flying back to Vancouver, and Ayla had decided to take the train the rest of the way, as planned. She found it was good to get that extra time in her headspace before rushing off to Hawaii with some guy she had just met. The journaling helped and eventually made her see that she had nothing to lose.

CHAPTER 11

The Chariot

She was observing the expansive landscape below with excitement in her heart. They were landing in a few minutes, and she was over the moon with joy. She hurried off the plane and got her luggage as quickly as she could. Her uncle Miguel was picking her up from the airport and would drive her the rest of the way. He was waiting for her with a big sign so she wouldn't miss him. She greeted him and gave him a hug. He took her bag and hurried out because he had parked his car by the entrance, which wasn't actually allowed. The heat immediately issued a warm welcome as soon as they exited the cool of the airport. Phoebe sighed in relief to finally be here, stood still for a few seconds as she adjusted to the warmth, before she got in the car. Her uncle warned her about car sickness, and he wasn't wrong about that. Where they were going, the roads serpented around the hills for miles. But the scenery was beautiful, and she tried to enjoy it as best as she could while holding down her discomfort. She tried the best she could to keep the conversation going and get to know her uncle. He complied with small talk but was compassionate about her state of being. After a few hours, they finally arrived. He stopped the car next to a colourful yellow colonial townhouse with white features and a blue door. Bouganvilla was flowing over the pots from the balconies on the second floor. The whole street was lined up with brightly coloured buildings, all of them decorating the neighbourhood proudly in their own unique way. Streetlights had taken the air of lanterns and shone dimly in the evening light.

She hardly made it out of the car before three women came rushing out from the blue door to hug her and greet her. There was a man, too, who stood in the background, equally excited to see her, though. They helped her with her bags and brought her inside.

They had created a minor feast for her arrival and propped her up to sit down by the table. Phoebe looked at all the food and the decorations and felt deeply touched to her core. She was so tired from all the travelling, but she was also very hungry. "Wow, you didn't have to do this! I'm deeply touched. "Thank you," she said as she put her hand to her heart.

"Of course we did," Catalina looked at her with a spark in her eyes and continued, "You must be exhausted from your travels. Please, sit down." She pointed to the chair and urged her to sit. Phoebe happily accepted, sat down, and looked at the food and the people around her with much gratitude. She followed Catalina's movements as she hurried to get the lemonade and fill up her glass. She learned quickly that she was her aunt, her mother's baby sister. The other two women were her other aunt, Valentina, and her cousin Regina. The other man was Catalina's husband, Emiliano, and Miguel was Valentina's husband. She recited their names and relations in her head and was so happy with herself that she managed to remember them so quickly. She had, of course, already met most of them during her visits with her mom, but that was such a long time ago. "Where is Abuela?" she asked. "Oh, she is here, it is just that it was late, and she had to go to bed, sorry about that," Valentina answered as she gave her a piece of bread. "Here, eat some more." They all listened intently as she talked about life, her job, and her father.

After a while, she felt too tired to stay alert, so she had to excuse herself. Catalina immediately got up, and Emiliano helped her carry her bags to her room.

She unpacked a few things that craved the hanger and changed into her pyjamas. She carried her toiletries to the bathroom to get ready for bed. She was exhausted, but she noticed that the Wi-Fi was finally working, so she sent Gabriel a romantic text, telling him that she had made it to the destination and that she missed him. She fell asleep rather quickly but woke up at 4 am. She didn't feel rested, however, as she had revisited the dream from the night before. It made her feel uncomfortable, and now she struggled to fall back to sleep. She stared up at the ceiling, following the movements of the shadows. She tried to go back to sleep for a while, but eventually turned her lights on to do some journaling. What did she want to do while she was here? She wanted to see the city, she wanted to do sightseeing in the area, and most importantly, she wanted to visit her mother's grave. She took the blue glass rose out and placed it on her desk. The bubbles inside it glimmered in the streetlights. She looked at it for a while, joyfully allowing herself to be enchanted by its colour and energy.

After having entertained herself in her room for a while, she got dressed and went downstairs. There was a light in blue and silver that bounced off the walls of the hallways. They were arching beautifully, allowing air to flow through the house from the courtyard. She didn't have a tour yesterday, so she missed that there was a pool covering most of the courtyard. There were a few lounge chairs too, next to a large citrus tree and a small plantation of palm trees, and a big aloe vera plant. She sat down with a blanket over her and watched the moon and the stars above.

She woke up to the sound of clinking glasses. Catalina was walking towards her, holding a tray.

"Good morning! I hope you were able to sleep." She said with a radiant smile.

Phoebe sat up in the lounge chair and smiled awkwardly.

"I couldn't sleep, so I came down here. The open air made it a lot easier." She looked at the tray that had a balanced breakfast, glasses, and a carafe of orange juice on ice. "Oh, my goodness. This is so beautiful!" she said and sat up to help Catalina put it down and unload the things.

"You're welcome!" Catalina said with pure joy in her voice. She picked up a bowl and filled it with melons, oranges, and berries of different kinds. "Here you go." She gave it to Phoebe, who looked at it with delight. Then she filled a bowl for herself and sat down in the other lounge chair. Phoebe picked up a blackberry and ate it as she poured up some orange juice for both of them.

"This is pure luxury, thank you. I feel truly blessed," she said, and looked at her aunt. "Have you thought of what you want to do yet? While you're here?" She looked at Phoebe and took a sip from her juice. The sun was getting in her eyes, so she went to get her sunglasses and picked up a sunhat for Phoebe. "Here you go."

"I tried to make a list, but I realised I don't know the area well enough. I want to get to know the town, I want to explore important places, and I want to visit Mom." Phoebe said and took another blackberry.

"Ok, well. Let's begin by taking a slow day today. The rest of the family is coming over for dinner tonight, and we will have a fiesta in your honour."

Phoebe blushed, "Didn't you have that yesterday already?"

"My, dear, God no. Yesterday was just dinner, today is fiesta." She leaned over and hugged her. "I have missed you so much these past years, and I am so happy that you are here."

Emiliano walked over and handed Phoebe a cup of freshly pressed coffee.

"I thought you might be needing this," he said.

"Wow, thank you! Yes, that's exactly what I needed." Phoebe happily accepted the cup.

"Would you like some tortilla and eggs?" He continued.

"No, thank you. Not today. My stomach is already full from all the fruit." Phoebe gestured and apologised for declining his offer.

Catalina went to get some for herself and came back with a plate.

"Here, you can try if you want to." She put one on Phoebe's plate.

"Thank you." Phoebe looked awkwardly at her. Since she usually didn't have a big appetite for breakfast, she really was full, but she was so grateful for the hospitality that she picked one up and ate politely.

After breakfast, Catalina took her on a little sightseeing tour around the neighbourhood. Valentina and her other cousin, Juanita, joined, and they took a few hours to show her the market and a few shops. But soon enough, the sun had reached its upright position, and the heat was too much for Phoebe. She was used to warm weather in Portugal, but this heat was scorching, and it wasn't even the height of summer. As they got back, Phoebe headed straight for the pool to cool off. She spent the afternoon in the shade of the orange tree, reading a book and texting with Gabriel.

He was curious about everything, and she tried to fill him in as best she could.

Eventually, her abuela woke up from her afternoon nap and sat down next to her. She was a compassionate woman, and her aura was peaceful. But she didn't say much. Phoebe tried to maintain a polite conversation, but they eventually ran out of things to say, for now.

As the colours in the sky shifted, Phoebe went upstairs to change into a dress that she had bought for the trip. It was bright pink with bold red florals on it and big puff sleeves. She was so happy to finally get to wear it. She had brought a pair of white espadrilles to go with it and big earrings as bold as the dress.

She made her way down the stairs and noticed that many family members had arrived already. All of them had scattered between the kitchen and the dining room, but they all swarmed towards her as soon as they saw her and cheered and hugged her. She hugged them back, feeling both surprised and ashamed. She had no idea that her mother's side was so big, while she had been keeping to her small corner of Portugal for so long, feeling lonely and alone. She was overwhelmed with emotion, but instead of resisting, she allowed herself to get soaked up by the merriment that filled the air.

The table soon filled with tortillas, salsa, and different kinds of meat. It was all so colourful and joyful to see. She sat down on the blue chair in the middle, again. It was a big table, and it managed to fit all twenty of them when they squeezed together, but some of the others had to sit on stools. Catalina had sat down to her right, and Valentina was sitting opposite her. Her mother had an older brother who lived outside of town, and he had brought his wife. But she apparently also had altogether eight cousins, three of them lived nearby and were here tonight with spouses and children. It was a full house. Abuela sat at the head of the table and beamed proudly at the sight of all of them together.

The party continued into the late evening, but as Phoebe was still jetlagged, she eventually could not fight the pressing effects from the lack of sleep and was forced to bid goodnight.

The next day, she woke up with renewed energy. Her two cousins, Regina and Juanita, wanted to take her on some sightseeing and shopping around the city center. They picked her up directly after breakfast and took her to a local market with textiles and a variety of bright local artifacts. It was an enchanting atmosphere filled with bright colours and happy faces. Phoebe walked along the stalls and told her cousins about her tourist tours back at home and the various things she liked to do. So, as they contemplated what to do next, they considered the cultural value of the famous local bookstore. It wasn't as fancy as the one in Porto, but it was a local gem, nonetheless.

As they walked inside, Phoebe noticed a pungent smell of smoke, leather, and wood. The whole space was filled to the brim with so many local curiosities that she hardly knew where to rest her eyes. She started walking along the narrow passages, looking at the different things on the shelves. The shopkeeper said hello from the back of the shop and came to stand near the counter. Her cousin Regina picked up a wooden sculpture of a skull with a funny face. They all chuckled and kept up the game by picking up more funny items to show each other. Phoebe asked them about some of the things, realizing that her mom had only told her some of her Mexican culture, but left out a good portion of it. The storekeeper overheard their conversation and told them that if they wanted to experience Mexican culture, they had to go to the Jade Museum. That would help her learn about her heritage. They looked it up and all agreed it would be a fun trip. But they first stopped for a quick lunch at the town square before they continued on their quest for culture. Neither Regina nor Juanita had been there, either, despite having lived in the city their entire lives. As they walked towards the building, they all felt a sense of wonder that only grew as they entered and saw the creations on the inside. The elaborately decorated green structures that greeted them quickly took them to a whole other world. The magnificent space was creatively decorated to attune to its historic tale. Phoebe walked among the displays of jade and artifacts relating to its traditions, rituals, and historical richness; she felt a chill down her spine. Everything felt both scary and familiar at the same time, and her whole body tingled. Although she had been to many religious sites back at home, she had never seen anything like this before. There were so many objects of curious kinds, some scarier than the others. But all breathed history, even those who were replicas. The tour eventually came to an end, and as they browsed through the gift shop, she bought a few jade stones in different shades of green. She also bought a necklace that she put on immediately.

"That was fun! " She said, putting her purchase into her bag. "What do you want to do next?"

Regina checked her phone for places nearby. Although she had lived in this town all her life, it was the first time she had experienced it in the eyes of a tourist. She scrolled through the various places that were within walking distance and thought for a moment before she said, "I know. Let's go to the Chocolateria! That's always fun!" Everyone agreed with that. They walked across the square and continued down the narrow streets that finally led them to a small townhouse with a terrace at the front, decorated beautifully with palm trees and colourful garlands. They walked past the terrace and entered the shop. Phoebe was flabbergasted the second she stepped inside. She had never seen so much chocolate in one place in her entire life. There was chocolate everywhere, in all its forms. It was a sweet little courtyard with a fountain in the middle and a couple of simple tables on the inside. All the walls surrounding it were lined with bookshelves and tables of all kinds and packed with everything from roasted beans to delicate pralines.

"Wow, I have never seen anything like this before!" she said, as she regained her speech.

"You've actually been here before. When we were little, you don't remember?"

Phoebe shook her head and felt a slight embarrassment, "No, I don't."

Juanita added, "Oh, there's no wonder you don't remember. You were like eight.

Let's just get some chocolate. Raw, dark, or sweet?"

"Raw?" Phoebe looked confused. "I would like the regular kind."

Regina looked at her with a surprised look on her face, "Ok, I'll take it from here." She walked up to the waitress and ordered three regular cocoa drinks, some roasted cocoas, and an assortment of the sweet stuff.

They picked one of the tables on the terrace with a bench filled with colourful pillows and chairs to match. They sat down as they waited for their order, and as the waitress made her way towards their table, Phoebe looked at the brown gold with glee. She clapped her hands and picked up the hot cocoa to drink, but she immediately put it down. "Oh my god, what is that?" She drank some water and scraped her tongue. Her cousins laughed at her, and she looked at them with disappointment in her eyes.

"Drink up, it's good for you," Regina said and lifted her bowl up to cheer. Phoebe's eyes had filled with a veil of agony, but she lifted her bowl too and took another sip, despite her discomfort.

Juanita commended her efforts and said, "The sweet kind is good for your heart, and the bitter kind is good for your soul."

Phoebe listened to her talk about the traditions and rituals of the cocoa bean while she made a strong effort to consume the beverage.

Suddenly, Regina exclaimed, "Oh, I know! We should all go to one of the local shamans for a cacao ceremony."

But Phoebe objected, "Oh, I don't think I can drink any more of this stuff." "Oh, come on, it would be good for you." "I bet it would," Phoebe muttered.

She proceeded to try some of the other chocolates and was pleasantly relieved that they were more tailored to her palate.

After a day packed with culture, Phoebe felt tired and wanted to relax by the pool for the rest of the afternoon. Her cousins walked her back and then went off in their separate ways. Phoebe greeted Abuela real quick, then walked up to her room. She wanted to call Gabriel and talk about her day.

But as she walked in, Mother Mary was sitting at her desk, looking at her notes. "You are quite effective. You have written; sightseeing and seeing the town. It's only day two, and you have already done both of them! I'm impressed."

Phoebe looked at her, threw her bag, and went shopping on the bed, and said, "I've been wondering when you would show up. I was expecting to see you yesterday."

"That wouldn't be fair now, would it? I had to give you space to settle in."

Phoebe sat down on the bed, looked at her, and sighed, "What do you want?"

"Oh, nothing much. I just wanted to see how you are."

"Terrific, actually. Why shouldn't I be?"

"No, that's good. I just thought perhaps that being here without your mother might be emotional for you."

"I mean, it's not optimal and I wish I hadn't stayed away for so long, but what can one do?"

"Right, right. Perhaps tomorrow is a good day to go visit her? You know, get it over with?"

"I'm not avoiding her, if that's what you think. I was going to go there."

"Yes, well. Don't forget to bring some pink carnations. You know she liked those." "And some marigolds, I know. That much I know."

As the new day dawned, Phoebe found herself awake, yet again. She was still slightly jetlagged, but she was also contemplating the visit to the grave. It is what she came here to do, but she was dreading it, nonetheless.

She eventually got dressed and had breakfast alone in the kitchen. She was just about to go when Catalina came in, hugging her kimono, "Are you sure you want to go alone? I can come with you, if you like."

"Thank you, but I think I have to go alone. I will call you after I'm done. I will probably want some company afterwards."

Catalina just nodded and watched as Phoebe walked out the door. Phoebe had ordered a cab that would take her to a church located at the other end of town. The church and its grounds were placed on a hill, with a stunning vista from the top. Her father had gone to great lengths to get her there after she had passed, as she had been persistently asking to be laid to rest at the church with the magical view. But that currently meant that Phoebe had a lot of stairs to climb.

"This feels oddly familiar," Phoebe thought to herself as she started climbing. She had stopped along the way to buy flowers and was now holding the bouquet in her right hand as she held the railing with her left. She eventually made it all the way up and stopped to take in the view of the valley. She completely understood her mother's sentiment to this spot and marvelled herself at its beauty. It was still early, and the lights in the sky were a lovely mix of light blues and pinks. She paused for a few seconds, taking in the view while she tried to remember which direction to walk in, but eventually she figured out how to navigate the space and found her mother. She stood still with the flowers in her hands and just stared at the small opening that was made to look like a door. She fantasized that her mother would come out of it, as if nothing had happened. Her mind took her through memories from their last time together, and then she recollected the events of the past weeks and thought, "Well, at this point, anything is possible. It could happen. It could just be undone." But just as she knew, she was surrounded with silence. She sat herself down in a lotus position, flowers in her lap, and prayed and meditated on light and hope. Tears filled her eyes, and as she sat there crying, she directed a few extra words to Mother Mary, since she knew she was listening, to keep her mother safe. She then put the flowers in front of the tiny door and memorized it all before she left. She walked down the stairs again, crossed the street, and found a small café. She ordered, and as she sat down, she called her father. He answered right away, and they talked about memories for almost an hour. She cried some more, and he tried to console her over the phone. She then called Gabriel. He was equally comforting but didn't know how to handle it, being so far away. He just said that he would join her as soon as he could, if she wanted him to, and then he said some beautiful things that helped her to lift her spirit. She then took a cab back to her aunt's house, who immediately brought her a drink and gave her space to talk about it all. They were really comforting and consoling. She regretted not allowing Catalina to join, but she reminded her that some things are meant to be experienced alone. They agreed to go on a small excursion during the afternoon to a national park to help soothe her mind. Phoebe went up to change clothes. She was hoping to see Mother Mary, and got disappointed when she didn't.

Catalina had gone to fetch the car, so Phoebe hurried back down so that she wouldn't keep her waiting. They drove out to a beautiful area with a lush landscape of green hillsides and picturesque springs. Catalina had only been there once before, so she was just as thrilled as Phoebe.

They walked around amongst the trees, admiring the flowers and different textures of the landscape. They eventually made it to the tourist attraction of the park and bought tickets for a tour. This cave was one of the attractions in the area that made people travel far and wide to experience its magnificence. It was easy to see why.

When entering it, the cool rock greeted them with both serenity and awe. Phoebe admired the stone and touched a part of it on the way in. She felt a small spark on her finger and quickly removed her hand, while studying her tip to try to figure out the cause of it. Catalina looked up, feeling small as she marvelled at the height.

She adjusted the small helmet they had received for safety.

"I wonder how much this thing would actually help in the face of a crisis." She said.

"Probably not much. But I bet there must be some reason for it." Phoebe answered. "I guess it will hurt a lot less when a boulder falls on you with that small orange thing."

They laughed a little at how silly they looked but continued like two school children after the guide.

"You do stuff like this all the time?"

"Walk into caves? No, never."

"No, I mean, being a tour guide."

"Oh, that! Yes, that is generally the gist. Except my walks are through safe religious and historic buildings, not dangerous caves."

She looked up at the tall ceilings of the cave that had been lit up with various sources of light, to allow the onlooker to experience the vastness of it all. "This does sort of feel like a church, though." "A bit more natural one," Catalina added.

They were taken down a steel staircase, making them feel even smaller in this vast space. Phoebe looked up and felt a chill all over her body. It was quite cold in here, and she had not brought a sweater, but she knew that the chills came from something else as well. She breathed slowly to calibrate the energy.

"Are you scared?" Catalina asked.

"No. A little uncomfortable but not scared. Are you?"

"A little, but nothing out of the ordinary. Besides, it is not far now until we reach the end."

They were led towards a bridge on scaffolding and walked the passage as the grand space gradually reduced in size. It was still many meters wide and to the ceiling too, but the effect was felt amongst the group as people's claustrophobic tendencies got revealed. Catalina was suddenly feeling anxious, and the group paused for a minute before they continued. The guide assured her that it would be over at the next turn, and she was not wrong. Just a few minutes later, they reached the last part of the cave. Here, the ceiling was tall again, and a small lake revealed itself. It was bright turquoise in colour and almost completely round. At the very end was a small triangular opening that mirrored perfectly into the water, together creating a diamond. They all got the honor to walk in the sand and touch the water. She noticed that the couple prayed. She hadn't thought of this as being a religious site but decided to try that too. Although she couldn't think of anything to say so she just briefly put her hands together and gestured a small bow. Catalina didn't even notice; she was busy looking up towards the small hole above them and admiring the setting. "It is quite breathtaking, isn't it?" She looked over at Phoebe and sensed a tear, "Oh, my dear, what's going on?" She hugged her and kissed her forehead like a mother would, and Phoebe just hugged her back and let it out. She didn't even know why she was crying exactly; it all just came pouring out.

Once they were out again, they were one richer experience but yet happy that it was over. It had been quite a daunting walk through the cave, and although they had originally planned for a hike to the other end of the park to see the waterfall, they decided to go home instead.

Phoebe was quiet the whole way back and went straight to her room when she got back. She did a bit of journaling with reflections about the day, and then she called Gabriel. She needed to hear his voice again to soothe her crying heart. She suddenly found herself in an emotional ditch, and thankfully, he was very supportive.

"It seems like this trip is too much for you. You shouldn't be alone right now. I'll try to arrange it so I can come over in just a few days, ok?"

"You don't have to do that. I'm no fun right now. I just hit a low, that's all. Why are you forcing yourself to be alone when you're going through a hard time instead of accepting my comfort and love?"

"I don't know. It's just that I feel that I need to do this on my own." They eventually hung up, and she stared at her phone. She wasn't sure what to do now. Catelina knocked on her door and came in.

"I thought you might like some fruit," she said, and put a plate on her desk. She walked back out but stopped in the doorway and said. "I'll be downstairs if you need me."

Phoebe skimmed through her list and took out her phone to try to think of ways to get her out of this headspace and places to go. At first, she couldn't. She decided to take a power nap instead. When she woke up, it was already dark outside. She looked at her phone and saw that it was dinnertime, so she sat up and patted her face to wake herself up. She then went downstairs and found Catalina, her abuela, and Uncle Emiliano in the kitchen. Catalina lit up when she saw Phoebe.

"Oh, good. We were just about to eat. I didn't want to wake you, but I'm glad you're up. Come, sit." Phoebe took a chair and stared at her plate. Catalina picked it up before she could say anything and filled it with food. She then poured some lime water into her glass and told her to drink up. "It's important to stay hydrated, especially when you're sad. " Phoebe looked at her and the glass and drank up. Catalina filled it up again and sat down, feeling satisfied. "Now, eat," she said in a firm tone.

"Thank you," was all that Phoebe could get out. She smiled a vague smile but ate in silence. The others had a quiet conversation next to her. When she was done, she put her plate away and went back to her room. She changed into pyjamas and went back to sleep straight away. Her whole being was exhausted; body, mind, and soul were in a state of vacuum.

She woke up the next day with a headache, but apart from that, she felt better. She walked downstairs to find Catalina but couldn't, so she just made herself a coffee and picked up an orange and went to sit on a lounge chair. Catalina soon came back from a morning shopping trip and walked straight up to Phoebe when she saw her. "Hi, you slept like a baby. Are you feeling better?" She squinted her eyes as she talked. Phoebe answered politely, "I'm feeling a lot better, thanks. Still have a headache, though."

"I'm about to make lunch. Would you rather have that or breakfast?" Catalina asked. "I would just like to sit here for a while with my orange and coffee. Is that ok with you? I'll come and help you when I'm done."

"Yes, of course. Sit. You don't have to help me. It's just simple quesadillas."

Phoebe closed her eyes and enjoyed the sun in her face for a while as she let it soothe her forehead. But as soon as she had finished her orange and coffee, she stopped sulking and went to help her aunt in the kitchen. She insisted on being helpful. When they sat down to eat, they started with a gentle chat about the day. "How about we take a boat ride through the canyon tomorrow. It will be nice for you to see something more and feel the breeze of the lake."

"That sounds lovely. Good idea, thank you."

"Good. We will leave early in the morning, then. You feel free to take the rest of the day to yourself."

Phoebe thanked her for the lunch and went back up to her room. She was still feeling low, and she was actually hoping for Mother Mary to help her out right now. But she wasn't there. Phoebe sighed, picked up her journal again, and laid down on her bed with music in her ears, scribbling notes and processing emotions. Gabriel sent her a text that he missed her, and she texted him back. She said that she didn't know how much longer she wanted to stay. The trip had so far managed to put her spirits down by quite a lot, and she wasn't sure it was worth it.

"Are you sure it's the trip and not that nightmare you keep having? It sounded quite heavy to me," he wrote back as a reply.

She froze as she tried to recollect the different parts of it. "Probably both, but that must have a big part of it. Or the reason why she couldn't pick her spirits up, instead of dwelling on her fears and sadness." She answered him back, reassuring him that he had helped her and that she was thankful.

They texted each other back and forth for a while as she tried to journal and come up with a plan. By dinnertime, her aunt Valentina came along with her cousins and uncle. Phoebe felt relieved to see them. They were concerned about her well-being and came to make sure she was ok.

"How about we go to a shaman ceremony tomorrow?" Regina suggested, "That might help you relieve some of the pain you are feeling."

"Yes, why don't we make an evening of it, just the three of us?" Juanita added. "That sounds like exactly what I need, although I was hoping to avoid the bitter cacao, but I guess it's worth it," she said before pausing and collecting her energy. "Who else is coming on the boat trip tomorrow?"

"All three of us are," answered Valentina. "We heard that you were feeling down and thought it's best to go away together."

"Well, normally we would all have to work, but we will find ways to get out of it," Regina said in a convincing voice.

"Thank you, I'm touched." Phoebe said, feeling slightly puzzled, "But you didn't have to do that. I can take care of myself."

"It is an easy decision. It is what you do for family."

Phoebe teared up but quickly swallowed her emotions. She wasn't used to crying in front of others. "Let's eat," she just said, and scooped a forkful of food from her plate.

After enjoying a heartfelt dinner with her wonderful family, Phoebe was feeling a lot lighter as she went back up to her room for the night.

But Mother Mary was waiting for her, and her mere presence made it impossible to hold back the sadness. Phoebe let her tears flow, letting it all out while.

"Thank you for showing up," she uttered among her sobs.

"Of course, my child. I am always here for you. Even when you can't see me, I am always here." Mother Mary said, embracing her in her comforting arms.

"Where were you yesterday?" Phoebe asked.

"I was right there with you, but you needed to go through the experience by yourself. So that you could witness yourself as well, and you could give compassion to yourself that you felt you were lacking. But your love is always there. For your mother, for yourself, for others. But there is also so much pain in your heart. I see your pain."

"Thank you." Phoebe wiped her tears and tried to speak through a cry-ridden voice. "What do I do now? What is the next part of the journey?"

 Mother Mary looked at her compassionately and said calmly. "Most of your journey is just about being here and allowing yourself to be a witness and to witness. You have been so afraid to open the wound of your mother for so long that you have, in effect, been running from love. You have delved deep into your father's side with your historic studies and anchored your Portuguese side. But in that process, you have unknowingly rejected your mother's side. And now you have finally opened it again. That is what causes the pain."

"I see what you mean. It was just so painful that I couldn't open that wound or anything associated with it. But I am ready to do what I have to do to heal this part of me."

"That is good. I am happy to hear it."

"What do you need me to do?"

"I don't need you to do anything. You need to heal your heart and unpack the burden of this wound. You have now opened it. You are here, embracing the culture and the part of you that was missing. But to fully transmute it, you must anchor into your mother's side. Not as an outsider looking in, but by understanding that part of your roots."

Phoebe felt relieved that she was receiving powerful wisdom and love from Mother Mary in the midst of her quiet sadness. "Follow your heart. It will help you find what you are missing." She said. "Good night, I'll see you tomorrow." "No surprising dreams tonight?"

"No, you can rest peacefully. You have had enough lessons for one day. Sleep tight."

Phoebe woke up early the next day and helped her aunt to pack food for the trip. They picked up Valentina, Juanita, and Regina up on their way to join the cruise at 8 am. They had booked one of the more comfortable boats with a sunroof so they could enjoy the view without being sun kissed, but that also meant that it was slower moving and needed longer time to complete the trip. The boat began its journey over the turquoise waters. The calming waters brought peace to Phoebe's troubled spirit. She felt at ease once again. What Mother Mary had said the night before had soothed her soul, and she was relieved that she got to be present for this beautiful day with her family. She sat in front of the others around her, feeling supported and loved. The boat's motor rumbled discreetly as they made their way along the river. The way it slithered around the rocks so effortlessly was an unbelievable feat for Phoebe to wrap her head around. That this route had been made possible over thousands of years in a beautiful synchronic dance between two forces. She kept repeating herself to her family about her philosophy and emotions.

They saw her and agreed, but mostly they thought she was cute in her expression. As the tour neared its finish, Phoebe had been caught up in her head about this experience and what else she needed to feel in the area. As they drove back home, she asked them about the Mayan pyramids and which one she should go to. Valentina answered, "Actually, I'm not sure which point in Mayan culture is mostly linked to our family. We are so mixed at this point with Spanish, African, and Portuguese in your case, that I don't think it matters. But the one in Yucatan is the best preserved. That being said, since the Palenques are still raw in some areas, they could hold more of the history that you seek."

Phoebe took out her phone and researched both of them. "I might want to go to both. Is that manageable?"

"Not unless you want to spend the next few weeks on a bus," Regina said. "It takes over a day to go to Yucatan, and the roads will make you want to quit after half of the distance. The other one is just a few hours away, which is still far, but you can do stuff along the way, which makes it easier."

"Ok, I hear you," Phoebe said and scrolled through the images on her phone. They got back, and Phoebe helped the other unload the bags from the car to the curb of the street. But she hadn't even put them down when a familiar face peeked out of the blue door.

"Oh my God, Gabriel?" She ran towards him and gave him a really tight hug. He hugged her hair and kissed her tenderly. She started crying and held her hand in her heart. "I can't believe you came all the way here just for me." She looked at her aunts and cousins, "Did you guys know the entire day?"

"Yes." They said, beaming with pride and joy. "He contacted us and wanted it to be a surprise. Who can say no to that handsome face?"

"This is like the best surprise ever. Why didn't you tell me, though?"

"Because you told me not to come over and over, and I knew that it was just your pride getting in your way. And what you were actually saying was "I don't want to sound weak, but please come." He said, teasing slightly.

She hit his arm with affection, "I'm a little offended, but I also know that you're right."

Juanita cleared her throat and said, "I hate to be a ballbuster, but we did book that shaman ceremony, and if we still want to go, we sort of need to leave now."

"Right, that's true." Phoebe looked at her phone and then at Gabriel, "You're ok with going to that, right?"

"Yes, of course. It sounds fun." He answered.

They all got back in the car and drove to a small place at the edge of town and arrived at a small house completely made of smooth sandstone and wooden beams. They all stepped inside feeling unweary. It was the first time for both Phoebe and Gabriel to do anything like this, but thankfully, the other two were experienced. They sat down on a yoga mat and joined in the experience. They were instructed to lie down and allow their bodies to absorb the sound waves from the different instruments. Phoebe instantly felt that it was helping her relieve the pain that she was carrying inside her. She allowed herself to cry and to be present in her emotions. She looked over towards Gabriel and noticed that he was focusing on his own healing, which was just as it was supposed to be.

The ceremony lasted about two hours and was so intense that when they drove back to the town, everyone was quiet and completely focused on their own inner worlds. None of them knew what to say, but felt happy to not be alone. Even when they got back, everyone ate their dinner quietly with just a few words to summarize the experience and try to change the subject. Eventually, they were all tired. Catalina had made up a bed in the second guest room for Gabriel. He kissed Phoebe goodnight and went to bed after an eventful day.

CHAPTER 12

The Moon

The forest was becoming more dense the further they drove. For a moment, Elena wondered if she had entered the correct address, but soon, a small house revealed itself. Among all the greenery, a mansion was soon in full view with a picturesque garden and a big gravel parking lot with a small roundabout in the middle that boasted a big tree with gorgeous yellow flowers hanging off its thin branches. Mary Magdalene looked at Elena and said, "Alright, I'll leave you now. See you later." She left. Elena got the bags from the back seat and passed by a low stone wall to get to the entrance.

It was a glorious building in white sandstone with dark wooden frames around its big windows. The door was a heavy mahogany, but it rolled lightly to the side when she pulled the handle. She stepped into an airy reception and lounge. There were a couple of armchairs and other seating arrangements to the right, and she could see the view from where she was standing. She gasped, put her hand on her heart, and left her bags on the floor to walk over to have a quick look. There was no one there, but the veranda doors were open, letting the breeze into the room and revealing the lovely outside seating area in stone with a big table and vines climbing to one side. It was lovely, but the view over the mountains was really something else.

Someone appeared behind her. Elena turned around a saw a middle-aged woman, about her age. She was wearing beige yoga pants with a white mandala pattern on the sides and a thin sweater in white, her red curls braided loosely to the side.

"Oh, hello! I'm sorry, I was just so amazed by the scenery that I just walked right through."

"You're early, but that's alright." She gave her a big smile and walked towards Elena. "Hi, I'm Avery, nice to meet you. I'll show you to your room so you can settle in while we wait for the others." She walked back indoors, and Elena followed her. She walked by a big round table in dark wood with an enormous flower bouquet of white lilies on it and wondered how she had missed that one. Some skin care products and essential oils were neatly displayed on it. She noticed the glass cabinet displaying a variety of crystals and thought to herself that she would need to load up on those before going home. She followed Avery, who walked towards the reception and picked up a clipboard.

"What's your name?"

"I'm Elena Foselli." She followed the pencil in her hand until it stopped. She looked up and beamed, "Perfect, alright. Welcome to you.' I'm so pleased to see someone joining us all the way from Melbourne. Here is your key. Come with me, I'll show you to your room."

Elena followed her through a corridor with glass doors on both sides. The sanded walls continued in white, and the tiled floor as well. It had a cooling effect and felt really nice, especially in this humidity. Elena couldn't see what was inside the rooms as beige curtains were blocking, but she suspected those were some common rooms for yoga and meditation, perhaps other things. To be honest, she hadn't read all the details on the site that Lucy had sent her. They arrived at an archway and stepped outside. The rooms were lined up to the left, and as the tiled floor continued, the wall to the right did not. Instead, it opened up to a garden and a gorgeous view of the mountains. They stopped in room 8. The door to the room was a double-sided terrace door with windows so one could enjoy the vista. She walked inside and immediately appreciated the coolness coming from the air conditioner. The room was bright and airy with a teal throw on the bed and some linen throw pillows in light blue and turquoise. By the big terrace doors, there was a light-blue curtain that one could close if one needed privacy and there was also a lounge chair next to the window, so it was possible to enjoy the view any way one liked. Avery left her, and she unpacked her toiletries and quickly decided that the first thing she wanted to do was to take a shower. The bathroom was so luxurious with soft mosaic tiles in greys, beige, and white with sprinkles of gold in it and the big shower had a lovely shower head with a rain effect. The copper metal was a stunning detail. They even had luxurious local soaps that smelled like jasmine and lavender. After a refreshing shower, she put on the bathrobe, picked up her book, and opened the terrace doors fully. She sat down in the lounge chair and almost fell asleep. At first, she insisted on reading her book. But as she struggled with the pages, she decided to allow herself to take that power nap, after all. The others wouldn't arrive for at least half an hour, and it was still over an hour until the first meditation and dinner.

After her refreshing power nap, she got dressed and went to the reception to see if there was any activity. Some girls had arrived, so she went over to say hi. However, this was, after all, a silent retreat, and not everyone welcomed a chat. She talked to two girls, then went to look at the crystals in the glass cupboard. After a few minutes, Lucy finally walked through the door. She looked at her, gave her a vague smile, and checked into her room. She came out again after just a few minutes, but she ignored Elena and chose to stand at the other end of the room, which came as quite a shock, but Elena tried to remain focused on the teacher and the evening without analyzing too much.

They were directed into one of the rooms, which, just as guessed, was a meditation room. They all sat down in a ring on blue yoga mats that had already been laid out.

Again, Lucy decided to sit elsewhere. Avery began her speech.

"Welcome, everyone to Sunbeam Yoga Spa & Retreat. I am so pleased that you have decided to join us this weekend. My name is Avery, and this is my husband Mark, who will also be guiding some of the meditation and yoga sessions. Now, this is what we call a Silent retreat. That means that there is no talking during sessions and as little as possible during the two days that we have together. We will have three meditations and two yoga sessions every day, with time in between to either enjoy our gardens or our spa. During all sessions, we will remain in complete silence the entire time. We will be eating breakfast, lunch, and dinner together as a group. For those who want, that is the best opportunity to get a chance to get that chatty energy out.

For those who came here to be in complete silence, that is, of course, fine, as it is the aim if you are capable. Our system is that we have two stickers. If you pick the purple one, that means you want to remain silent; for those who pick the coral one, that means you are open to chat. Now, let's do a quick meditation, and then we will go for a lovely meal together, and you will have the rest of the evening to yourself. We start tomorrow at 8 am."

As the minutes went by, Elena felt anxiety building up in her throat. She opened her eyes before the meditation so she could catch Lucy on the way out. "Please, Lucy. I really need us to be friends right now. Can't we just ignore what happened this morning and have a lovely weekend together?"

Lucy looked at her with sad eyes. "Then you shouldn't have barged in on me like that this morning."

"Yes, I'm sorry. I didn't know what else to do and thought I would be able to explain everything to you. But I failed miserably at that."

"You know, you could have just called me instead of storming into my office. What is it with this stone, anyway?"

"Well, actually, I don't know. Yet." Elena replied and looked ashamed.

"You don't know? You don't know. Wow, you just decided to barge in on me like that, trying to make me give up my one important client for no reason?" She paused before she continued, "That is so typical of you. You have always been jealous of me, ever since we were kids. Always finding a way to get the spotlight in my triumphs."

"What? I don't do that. I am so very proud of you, and you know that?"

"Oh really? Like the time I announced my engagement, and you announced that you were pregnant? Or when I graduated with top grades at university and you announced your engagement? Or how about that time.."

Elena turned inwards for a few moments. Her mind flashed memories of last night, the time Lucy got a promotion at the same time as she got pregnant, and the time she accidentally got engaged when Lucy had just met Ned. She was right.

"I never meant to dim the light on your happiness. You must know that. Things must have just accidentally happened at the same time," she said. "But I didn't mean to. They just happened to coincide."

She looked into Lucy's brown eyes, trying to find a trace of resonance. But instead, Lucy just shook her shoulders and walked away. She turned towards her on her way out, "Nothing is a coincidence."

Elena went to her room and threw herself on the bed. She lay there for a minute, staring up at the ceiling. Things were getting out of hand, and she didn't know how to stop them. She suddenly realized that she hadn't told Lucy about the details in her dreams yet. Maybe that would help. She went to look for her in the lounge area, then she went to the seating area outside, but she couldn't find her. Instead, she found Avery and insisted on helping her prepare dinner and set the table. Soon enough, dinner was ready, and Avery rang the bell. Everyone emerged from their hiding places, including

Lucy. But she ignored Elena and sat down at the other end of the table. Elena tried to ignore her pain and shifted her attention to the women sitting closest to her. Two of them were open to chat, so they talked about this and that while Elena kept one stream of attention directed towards Lucy, trying to predict her thoughts. But she eventually gave up and focused on having a nice time herself. Even after dinner, she decided to just leave Lucy alone and focus on her own needs. She went to the spa and sat in the hot tub for a good hour, just staring at the view and drinking tea. It was exactly what her soul needed right now.

The next day, she woke up with peace in her heart and mind. She had decided that she did not want to disrupt her lovely weekend by being triggered by Lucy or saddened by their fight, she was also not going to place any blame on her for her reaction. She just wanted to stay in this calm state of mind until departure on Sunday. She went to change her sticker from coral to purple before joining the breakfast.

She filled a bowl with yoghurt, musli, and fruits and sat down next to some other women. They smiled. All of them were wearing purple stickers, so they ate in silence. Elena picked up her teacup and cupped her hands around it. The morning was already showing signs of heat, but it was still nice to soothe herself this way. She remained in that position until the clock struck 8 am, and it was time for the morning meditation. She drank up her tea and joined the others. They were starting in the main meditation building today. It was a beautiful construction shaped almost like a tent with strong wooden beams and big glass windows displaying the valley and the mountains in the distance. It was also almost completely round, so it had a nice flow. Elena sat down by the front, near a window, where her focus on the teacher would be undisturbed. She followed her guide in the meditation, after which she felt a lot lighter. It came to her attention that although she had been awakened over a week ago, this was her first meditation since then. She suddenly felt the benefit of it in a way that she had never done before. She felt excited about the coming days and what they might bring to her awareness. They got a quick break before the first yoga session. Avery and Mark took turns teaching yoga and meditation, guiding one each day. Mark warmed up the participants with a slow-paced restorative Yin yoga. After lunch, Avery took over and guided them through Vinyasa yoga and heart-opening meditation. Elena had followed through on every movement and direction throughout the day, but stretching the heart like that released some sadness about her problems with Stephen. She suddenly began to realize that she was done being taken advantage of, and the thought scared her of what that meant. During the afternoon, she was able to walk around the garden. She found a lovely bench next to a vibrant magenta bougainvillea. She had brought her book and sat down to read. But it wasn't long before she looked up to see Lucy walking towards her.

"I need to talk to you," she said in a demanding tone.

"Well, I'm wearing a purple sticker, see?"

She stared at her with an irritated look and looked over at the view before she continued.

"I know I got angry, but then I realized that you are already in a vulnerable place because of the fight with Stephen, you wouldn't want to start a fight with me during a time when you needed me unless it was important." She looked at her intensely and sat down next to her. "So, my curiosity eventually took over, and now I want to know. What is it about the stone that gives you reason to cause such a fuss?" Elena sighed in relief, and she paused to select her words carefully.

"To be honest, I haven't received all that information yet. But the way the stone was shrieking made it appear otherworldly to me, or like it was calling out for help." Lucy did the best she could to try to follow Elena's story as she continued.

"Well, you know that dream I had about a week ago, well, it turns out it was just a starting point to something much bigger. Something I'm a bit scared to say out loud because I'm afraid you will judge me.

Lucy looked at her and said, "I'm already judging you, so you might as well tell me the story."

Elena paused to process that comment, but decided she wanted to tell her either way.

"Well, it's a little hard to explain, actually. After that dream, I've had a few visits from Mary Magdalene, and I have had two more dreams. One, where I was in some magical castle, and the other where I was in a healing temple in Bali or something. All three of them felt more than just dreams in a way that I can't begin to describe." Lucy looked at her with harsh judgment in her eyes,

"Ok. I think either you are having a really tough week with everything that has been going on at home. Or you might need to see a shrink. I know a good one, I can give you her number later."

Elena looked away, feeling extremely hurt and lost at that comment.

"I do not need to see a shrink. And while it has been a stressful and difficult week, it is not the cause of my feelings. It is rather the other way around. You know what, forget I said anything." She picked up her book again and continued reading. Lucy tried to say something, but Elena made it clear that she did not want to be disturbed, so she eventually left.

It didn't take long after she left for Mary Magdalene to appear in the same spot where Lucy had been sitting.

Elena got annoyed at the very sight of her.

"Please go away. I do not want to look any more crazy than I already am."

"You don't want to look crazy, or you don't want to be crazy?"

Elena paused her answer to reflect on what she had just implied before she answered, "Either or."

"Well, I can tell you with confidence that you are neither." Mary Magdalene answered

"Why should I trust you with that sentiment, when you are the very person who makes me look like I'm crazy?" Elena asked

"Well, the judgment of others is a hard trauma to deal with, believe me, I know. So, I will not tease you any further. I just wanted to check that you are, ok?" Mary Magdalene asked.

"I'm terrific." Elena answered sarcastically, "Now, please go."

Mary Magdalene gave her a compassionate but mildly concerned look but did as she was told.

"Alright, I'll see you later." Then she left.

Elena sighed again and continued to read her book but quickly decided that she had had enough of this bench and went to take a few minutes in solitude in her room before dinner. She didn't speak to Lucy for the rest of the day, and even the next day, she remained scarce in her interaction with Lucy. Instead of wandering the garden, she enjoyed the spa. She got a massage and stone treatment, after which she immediately felt compelled to purchase the various crystals that had been used. She went to the cabinet and picked out citrine, amazonite, rhodonite, and a black tourmaline. She went back to her room to study her new purchase. But she quickly ducked instinctively when she saw Mary Magdalene through the window. She wasn't sure if she was ready for what she had to say. She awkwardly tried to pretend she wasn't there and attempted to sneak off without getting noticed, but Mary Magdalene just yelled through the door, "Nice try, but you do realize that I can see you at all times? So those petty little attempts to avoid me won't work."

Elena felt embarrassed when she realized what she had just attempted to do and opened the door to accept the interaction.

"You know, ignoring the problem will not make it go away." Mary Magdalene said as Elena walked in.

"Which problem are you referring to, the one where my best friend thinks I'm crazy or the one where I'm being pressured by an Ascended Master?"

"I'm referring to you running from your problems, all of them." Mary Magdalene just pressed her eyebrows together and looked at her, surprised. "I'm not running, I just need space and peace of mind," Elena said.

"That is a sweet sentiment, but we do not have time for that." Mary Magdalene answered, determined to get to the point. She sighed and looked serious. Then she changed her tone before she continued with what she had to say.

"You can hear the cries of the stone because it's the cries from Gaia, Mother Earth." Elena looked at her in disbelief.

"I'm sorry, what?"

"Your broken heart resonates with the broken heart of Mother Earth. That is why you received the heart chakra. That is why you can hear the stone cry." "I don't have a broken heart." Elena pleaded.

Mary Magdalene looked at her with a surprised look,

"No amount of denial will help you right now." She just said and continued,

Elena sat in silence and eventually shook her head, "Alright, I suppose you are right. What do I do? Should I rescue the stone?"

"No, that will not help. The stone he has found is in abundant supply, although intended for other purposes. What you need to do is to heal the stone."

"Heal the stone. How do I do that?" Elena said, looking confused and searching for Mary Magdalene for answers.

Mary Magdalene looked at her. "By healing your own heart, you can help heal Gaia too. And by helping Gaia heal, you will heal your own heart. It's interlinked."

Elena thought for a moment and said, "I'm not sure I know what it is I've done wrong?"

"For years, you have been neglecting yourself so that you can be there for everyone else. Let me ask you this. Who are you?"

"I'm a mother, a daughter, a wife, a sister, and a friend." Elena tried to think if she had forgotten one, no, that was all of them. She smiled as Mary Magdalene, who only looked at her, was displeased and crossed her arms. "I didn't ask for your titles. I asked who you are."

"I just told you. What else could you mean?"

"What makes you happy, what makes you feel free, what tickles your soul?" "Tickles my soul. I don't know." She was amused at first, but soon enough she just stared down at the floor as she thought for a moment. An intense sense of uprootedness came upon her, and she almost started crying as she answered, "I don't know. I don't know, ok?"

Mary Magdalene looked at her with compassion and put her hand on Elena's as she said, "You will when you are ready."

Elena looked at her with a simmer of tears, feeling both embarrassed and overwhelmed.

"There is nothing to be ashamed of. This is common. I will guide you through it." Mary Magdalene smiled softly, said goodbye, and left again. Elena sat alone on her bed, looking at the object, trying to figure out how it could be helpful.

As it was almost time for dinner, Elena went out to the common room again. Part of her was hoping to run into Lucy and give her an update, but part of her was still mad about her comment. She was certainly not crazy, and she knew that now. But she needed to come up with a plan or at least a sense of direction, and she needed help with that. Lucy had, however, gone to the spa and didn't show up until right before it was time to eat, so any conversation had to wait.

After dinner, they had a ceremonial meditation. Elena focused all of her attention on trying to get some answers about herself and her purpose. Although struggling to achieve peace, she eventually felt happy with her efforts. Afterwards, she went back to her room and took out her notebook to write a list. "What do I like?" she thought. She wrote down the ocean, and she wrote running. After that, her mind went blank. She felt horrified that she could only think of two things, and neither of them were actual things. In the end, she had to give up and went to bed instead, with a perplexed mind and heart.

The next day was Sunday, and the retreat would end at lunchtime. Her mind had at this point consumed her, and Elena spent most of the day just thinking about her life. She had devoted so much of it to catering to others' needs and likes that she had forgotten who she was. What did she even like when she was a child, or a teenager? She hardly remembered any of it and definitely had no recollection of what she enjoyed doing. After the closing ceremony at lunchtime, she packed and got ready straight away. She found Lucy and told her that she was heading home. They both agreed to at least text each other when they arrived home, so they would know they had made it safely. Elena got in the car and started driving. Mary

Magdalene didn't show up this time, so instead of the scenic route, she took the highway and drove the distance in solitude, muddled in her thoughts.

When she arrived home, it was already dinnertime. She walked through the door, and just as she had hoped, Leonie, Oliver, and Noah came running towards her and gave her a big hug. Her mom had cooked dinner. Elena gave her a hug. "Thank you so much for all the help". She said and gave her a souvenir from the retreat. It was a small gift set with jasmine soap and a scented candle.

"How are you holding up?" she asked.

"I'm much better, thank you," Elena answered.

Her mom went to get an envelope that was sitting on the counter. "This came on Friday," she said.

Elena looked at it, opened it briefly, and looked at the first lines without taking it out of the envelope. She already had a hunch about what it was, but now they were staring at her right in the face. And although she had dreaded the thought of a divorce, it now made her feel like she was finally free. But she tried not to reveal her emotions. She placed it back on the counter and focused her attention on her kids. "Let's eat," she said.

Her mom had already done everything, so there was nothing left for Elena to do.

They all ate, and the kids eventually left to watch some TV upstairs.

Elena turned to her mother and said, as she played with the rim of her wine glass, "You know, I got the chance to really dive deep into myself at this retreat. It was very soothing, but it also raised a lot of questions." Her mother shrugged, "Oh, really, about what?"

"Well, for starters." She said, feeling anxious, "I don't really know anything about myself."

"What do you mean?" Her mother asked in a harsh tone.

She felt her heart throbbing, not knowing how to put this delicately.

"Well, I found myself wondering who I am without you, knowing the kids and Stephen and all of the responsibilities, and I realized that I don't know. And on the drive back home, I realized that not only do I not know who I am, but I also don't know anything about my ancestors or anyone else in our family. All my grandparents died when I was young or before I was born, and you never really told me anything about it." "Well, there isn't much to tell," her mother just replied.

"So, you don't know?" Elena corrected her.

"That's right. I don't know. I don't know our story. Why don't you just focus on us being Australian?"

"Sure, but in search of my identity, I feel like I need to dig deeper. Rediscover our lineage, maybe I can do a DNA analysis?"

"My dear. You are feeling confused and sad, I get it. But there is no reason to go looking for trouble. Why don't you just focus on yourself?"

"Ok, that's the other part. I don't even remember what I used to like before I got married. she said, feeling sad but relieved to finally admit the truth.

Her mother just looked at her in silence with a serious face. She was trying to think of things but soon realized that she herself did not quite remember.

"You were all about sports and boys, but that's what it is for everyone. Is it not? There's nothing wrong with that." She noticed that she was not of any good help on the matter at this instant, so she bid goodnight instead and left Elena alone to tend to the evening.

The next morning, after she had taken the kids to school, she sat down in her kitchen with the list she had started. She had still only written two things, and she was baffled at her inability to write anything else. She put her pen down, collected her notebook and things, and headed out. She started driving without any clear view about the direction. She went towards the one thing she had written, the ocean. Eventually, she ended up at a lookout point. She stopped the car and got out. There was a bench, but she decided to sit down on the grass and take in the view and the wind. She felt lost, hoping that someone would come and save her. She decided to walk down to the beach instead. It was a windy day, so it was almost empty, but she had felt the sudden urge to lay down in the sand. She did, fully dressed. She had placed her bag beside her and was toying with the sand, covering herself and her clothes with the soothing white grains of stone. She eventually removed her shoes so she could ground herself in the sand. After nestling herself for a while, she then became still and looked up at the ceyon sky, following the clouds and making up figures as they went by. She realized that she had found something else that she had enjoyed doing as a kid. Eventually, her stomach let out a rumbling sound. She thought she had only been there for ten minutes, but she looked at her phone and saw that it was noon. 'Let's find some place to eat', she thought. She got in her car and decided to continue her search near the shore. She headed towards the pier and found a nice little restaurant with an ocean view. For once, she had no desire to eat healthy. She ordered what she wanted. She had taken a seat on the terrace and enjoyed how the wind played with her hair. She took out her sunglasses and stared out towards the horizon as she waited for her food to arrive. Some fish and chips were exactly the comfort food she needed. She ate with a happy heart and continued her dreamy quest for clues and answers. First, she had felt anxious and stressed about receiving the information she craved, but the ocean calmed her heart. Today was a day of reminiscence, tomorrow was a day for clues.

She spent most of the afternoon at the café, but eventually went home and began preparing dinner and got the snacks ready in time for when the kids arrived from school. They then enjoyed the evening together, playing a game and watching some TV. She had had one of the best days in a long time, and she felt at peace.

On the next day, she had finally figured out what she needed to explore in order to receive the information she needed. She spent the morning in two of the museums downtown, to learn a bit more about her European heritage, but while in one museum, she came to an exhibition about the history and culture of aboriginals and their relationship to the Earth. It felt much more like home than the grand paintings of sailors and aristocrats. She took a quick lunch in the museum's café, and as she did so, she searched through the city's renowned Aboriginal museums. She found one that resonated and decided to go there in the afternoon. That one was on the outskirts, so she was suddenly relieved that she had taken the car. The museum had been decorated entirely in black, which was quite the contrast coming from the sunstruck outside in broad daylight. She felt intrigued right away and entered. The black walls were a clever contrast to the colourful fabrics and artifacts, creating an impressive impact on the visitors. She walked around, looking at the various paintings, instruments and jewelry. It occurred to her that they were so down to Earth and had an inspiring way to tune into Mother Earth. She felt compelled to learn their secret. She read through the texts and eventually found a guide.

She asked her if there was any ceremony that she would be allowed to participate in to experience the energy and receive some wisdom. The guide thought for a moment before she answered,

"We do have several ceremonies a month, some are open to the public, and for others, you need to be a member. Then they are also different depending on the time of year or part of the month. Like tomorrow, since it's the full moon, we have a ceremony that spiritually cleanses you, connects you to Earth, and aligns you with your purpose."

"That is exactly what I need right now. Please tell me more." She wrote the details down and got her number before she left. All the way home, she was so thrilled with the odd coincidence that she would be stumbling onto that museum and that they would have a ceremony that was so conveniently aligned with her needs.

She got home just in time before the kids and did her usual bit to prepare dinner and snacks. Her mother called her and said she would join them. She found that odd, as she never came to her own accord.

"Is Dad coming, too?" she asked

She checked with him in the background and just replied "Yes," and hung up. Elena was a little bit curious but left it at that while she prepared the food and greeted the kids as they came home. But soon enough, her parents walked in. Her mother was carrying a box full of papers and stuff. She walked over to the kitchen counter and put it down.

"I just spent the last two days going through the photos, documents, and diaries that I had at home, and this is what I found. You're welcome!" She proceeded to go straight to the wine fridge, take out some glasses, and pour up some wine.

"Thank you, some wine would be nice," her father said as he accepted his glass.

"So, tell me, what exactly did you find, then?"

"You think I had time to read them all? I just read a few and brought the rest over to you. But this is all there is from both my side and your father's side. He had saved surprisingly little from his childhood."

"Well, my sister took most of it, but she has moved so many times and at this point she doesn't remember where it is."

Elena just followed their amicable banter and looked at them compassionately.

"Thank you, this is very thoughtful. Let's look at them together, after dinner?" After dinner, the kids hung with their grandfather while Elena and her mother went through the stuff in the box. Her mother made sure to document the different details they found, but after about two hours, they seemed to have reached the end of the box.

"It's just as I thought, then." Her mother sighed and looked at all the papers that they had spread out on the table. We are so scattered it's hard to tell. But being able to pinpoint an origin is not the most important. The stories, hopes, and dreams, that is what we need to remember."

Elena smiled. That was a nice way of putting it.

They cleaned everything up and Elena mustered the courage to ask for help again the following day, so that she could go to the full moon ceremony in the evening. "You know I love the kids as much as you do, you can ask any time," was her simple answer.

By the next day, Elena had gotten the hang of her new life. She realized it wasn't much different than before, just one less person to take care of. She still needed to sign those papers, though. After she had dropped the kids off at school, she went home and sat down with the envelope and a pen. She took out the papers and skimmed through what was written. There was nothing out of the ordinary; everything seemed in accordance with the agreement. But she would let her lawyer look them over, just in case, to make sure that she and the kids were covered. As she sat there, going through the papers, the doorbell rang. She went to the door to see who it was.

It was Lucy.

She walked in with an energy of urgency.

"So, as it turns out, you were right," she said and walked straight to the kitchen counter.

"I knew that, and please come in," Elena said sarcastically and was about to continue with her own sentiments, but Lucy interrupted her.

"So, I went to the office on Monday and started digging, since I couldn't get your words about the stone out of my head." She started taking out some things from her bag, and Elena studied her movements as she tried to take in her story. "Ok, go on," she just said.

"Well, it turns out that stone is not exactly scarce; it is abundantly available, but apparently it is a sacred stone, and he sourced it illegally without the necessary permits for the intended scale of his company. So, now the information sort of "leaked," and he is being reprimanded and his business license revoked. Thankfully, I already received the payment from the release party last week." She looked both shocked and pleased at the same time. Elena could hardly tell what was going on. "Ok, let me get this straight. You leaked the information to the press when you found out the truth about a stone that I had an odd hunch about?" Lucy put her hand to her waist, smiled, and said proudly, "That's right."

"Oh my, that makes me so happy. Thank you!" Elena said and hugged Lucy. "Now, please tell me more," she continued and glanced at the pile of papers.

"So, it turns out that the stone is not just any old rock; it's a volcanic rock from Hawaii. I managed to get my hands on one piece; in case it could help you get answers."

"Actually, Mary Magdalene told me that its cries are caused by Gaia's broken heart, and I can hear it because it resonates with mine." Elena looked down at the table as she said the last part.

Lucy looked at her and placed her hand on hers, "Aw, sweetie, I'm so sorry for you. That is awful. But it's still pretty cool." She went over to her bag and said. "Well, anyway. Here is the stone, I brought it in case it could help bring you closure about this." She took out a small gift box and placed it on the table. Elena looked at her with amazement. "That is quite impressive. Wait, I just need to cover my ears before you take it out of the box." Lucy waited and then took it out. Elena had put her hands on her ears but slowly dared to let go.

"Good, it's not that bad this time. Now it's just a slight etheric hum. Now let's look at this gorgeous gem." She picked it up and placed it in her palm, and to her surprise immediately sprang to life, giving up a shimmer of green glow." Elena looked at it with a shocked expression and said, "Do you see that?"

"This time I do, actually," Lucy said and stared at it. She leaned closer. It's quite amazing how you can make it glow like that. Let me try." She took it from Elena and placed it in her own hand. Nothing, its colour went back to a dark green somber hue. "Ok, now I really believe you." She said and put it back on the table. She picked up one of the books she had found about crystals in the Pacific and flipped through its pages, searching for answers.

Elena glanced at a brochure about Hawaii. It looked like a dream. Turquoise water, sandy beaches, and palm trees. "It would be nice to go," she said. "Maybe just being there will give the answers?" She read about the ceremonies and said, "I'm actually going to an Aboriginal Full Moon ceremony tonight. Do you want to join me?"

Lucy just looked up, thought for a second, and shrugged her shoulders as she answered, "Sure. Why not?"

Elena arrived at the same time as Lucy, and they walked into the space together. It was an open-air hut with a low white wall circling it, but without windows; the roof was held up by wooden pillars, creating a space that felt sacred. In the middle of the space was a circular fire pit lowered into the smooth stone floor. As everyone gathered, a woman started singing, and a few others began playing their instruments. Elena closed her eyes and rocked her body to the music. The experience was very soothing, and they kept singing and playing the instruments for quite some time, turning the vibe to accommodate the mysterious atmosphere. In the beginning, she and Lucy had been sitting on chairs, but they soon joined the others on the floor as it was much more grounding. Another woman began singing in a high tune, and they did a ritual with the fire itself, paying tribute to both the moon and the fire as they cheered about the new beginnings yet to come. For the first time in weeks, Elena felt safe, she felt seen, and she felt raw in a beautiful way. She was grateful that she was able to join this circle, about her reunion with her friend, and she felt curious about where life was taking her, even though sadness still dwelt within. At the beginning of the ceremony, they had all been invited to place a glass of water under the moon. Now, as it was closing, they were encouraged to drink it and fill their reserves with sacred moon water. The analogy was beautiful, and Elena really appreciated the experience. She went home feeling fresh and enlightened.

CHAPTER 13

The Anemone

Upon first look, it didn't seem like much. This time, she wasn't seated in a lotus position, but instead, she was standing up. Ayla tried to determine what she was wearing. It wasn't a dress. She wasn't barefoot either, but wearing proper boots. There were no fancy jewellery to accessorize the outfit this time, and her hair was braided into one long ponytail. She swallowed in an attempt to gather her strength. She looked around but noticed she couldn't really see anything. Everything around her was dark. She stretched her arms out and realized that she was standing inside a tree. She didn't get scared, though. The tree was her allied friend and her protector. But she searched around her for a door and opened it once she found it. Outside was a landscape of hilltops in the background and a vast meadow with wildflowers. But the sky was dark. She could catch a glimpse of the dim light of the moon, but the stars were not visible through the fog. She stepped out and fully got an idea of what she was wearing. It was a dark red jumpsuit in a thick fabric, with draped legs and a big leather belt designed like armor, black tourmaline was sewn into the fabric to create an embellished hem over her chest. Attached to the belt was a small dagger. She was also carrying a small shield on her back. Once it hit her that she was dressed as a warrior, she stopped in her tracks and looked back. She hesitated to walk any further. All she wanted was to climb back into the tree. She looked around and noticed that there were all kinds of bad omens, but above all, there were crows, many crows. She thought about her options and realized she didn't have any, so she gathered strength and courage in her heart and took a few hesitant steps out in the meadow. But she had not walked far when she saw something in the corner of her eye. She looked to her right to see what it was and instantly felt relieved to learn that she was not alone. She looked to the left and soon gathered that all the other eleven women in her team were right there with her. There was Meira and Hanwi, Akira and Phoebe, Evelyn and Edith; she couldn't see further than that, but she trusted that all twelve were right where they were supposed to be. They all smiled towards each other and waved happily, but they were too far apart to properly talk. They looked behind them and saw that their trees lined up in a straight line and understood that was how they had to continue. Straight lines across the field. They started marching with steady steps. Twelve dark figures across the dark field, filled with purple and black anemones. By the time they had reached the middle, the fog had lifted, and the silhouettes of three women emerged as they approached.

They stopped before them; it was hard to make out the details in the dark, but they all had a superior glow of divine sovereignty and power. The first one had her blonde hair loosely braided into two, a wide silver forehead headpiece embellished with symbols, and wearing a royal blue gown with a mantle lined with fur. The second had a crown made of oak leaves adorning untamed curls in bright orange, vividly dancing on her dark green velvet gown. The third wore a gown as black as the night had bewildered raven-black waves held together with a silver headpiece with a waning moon at the front, mimicking the one above. She glanced at the twelve of them with an assertive look on her face and made sure to stop at each one before she spoke.

"Greetings, everyone. I gather that your sentiments of today are not what they have been in previous dreams. We have been waiting for the right moment to unleash this transformation upon you. You have now reached the part of your healing referred to as the dark night of the soul. You are experiencing many challenges in your lives. So we are here to help you break free from the darkness and find your way back to your light.

Before you stand three strong goddesses. Yet, you wonder why you have not seen us until now. Our reputation is varied, but our mission is one: to guide those who are lost back to a healed state.

My name is Hecate. Our mission tonight is to help you transition into your power by taking you through The Valley of Reconciliation. Its purpose is to reunite us once more with the sovereign power of the sacred feminine. This journey is long, and it is testing. Trust that you are here because you are worthy and you are ready." She looked at them all peacefully before turning towards her comrades to her right. Next to me are Goddess Freya and Goddess Brigid. The three of us have been summoned to help you heal, remember, and realign to knowledge, magic, and power. We have a long way ahead, so let's start walking.

The three goddesses began crossing the field, and the women made haste to keep up with their quick pace. All three of them were wearing flowy dresses and capes that were flowing in the wind as they marched. Their unleashed hair echoed the power of their free spirits. They were both fierce and strong, embracing their force as they made their way through the fields. The women were struggling, trodding along behind them in every attempt to keep the pace without them noticing their physical weaknesses. After quite some time, they finally reached a tall gate. At this point, they were all out of breath and clasping their waists to discreetly attend to muscle cramps and conceal the fact that they were out of tune with Hecate, Freya, and Brigid.

But they eventually turned their attention towards the gate and looked up. It was standing several meters tall, nestled between two mountains. Ayla tried to make out the symbol at the top. It was three interlinked circles. "The trinity of the divine feminine: Mother, daughter, spirit," Meira whispered. The gate opened, and any curiosity about what was on the other side immediately left their bodies. Before them, there was a thick black smog. The twelve women stood firmly in their tracks, looking at each other with a slight terror in their eyes while trying to find comfort in Brigid's healing light. But eventually, it was Freya who spoke. "Come on, we haven't got all night." Her long blonde hair swept across her shoulders and nestled into the fur on her cloak, and her blue gown billowed in the wind.

Ayla took the hands of Meira and Jiya and formed a long train with the other women, holding on to each other for comfort and support as they walked the narrow passage that serpentined between the two mountains. The smog eradicated any trace of the landscape around them, but they could glimpse the violet bushes of the heather and thyme, and that helped them navigate their way through the valley. As it turned out, the thick smog was just a protective shield, and as they passed through to the other side, the entirety of the valley revealed itself amongst the vast magnitude of the tall mountains.

The valley of mild purple floral bushes was now accompanied with a blanket of black roses that guided the rest of the way and unraveled a round stone building with a dome-shaped roof in the distance. The roses ushered them along down the valley until they found themselves at the bottom of its stairs.

Hecate spoke. "Before we enter this space of holiness, it is important for you to remember the purity of your heart. It is important for you to remember that your womb is still holding on to trauma. Trauma that still echoes the memories of your ancestors and the fight that women have found themselves in for thousands of years. This part of your journey is orchestrated for you to unlock the trauma and unleash your rebellious heart. For without it, you cannot find peace."

They all looked at each other, some had anticipated what was to come, but not all. Jiya finally dared to ask the question on everyone's mind: "But didn't we already clear the traumas of our wombs in our last dream with Green Tara?"

Freya answered this question. "You all did excellent progress with Green Tara, that is why you are here today. Allowing yourself to witness your wounds is the first step to forgiveness, acceptance, and self-love. But the womb is a sacred space that has been polluted for generations and essentially has been the emotional dumping ground for humanity for thousands of years. There are many layers to clear. We are here today to clear the energies that clog your memory of your own divinity and power. You must remember once more that darkness is not evil. Darkness is the key to open your heart to your own wisdom and abilities."

The women looked at each other and nodded along with every word she spoke. It all made sense very much. They looked up the stairs and nodded again. We are ready. The staircases were wide enough to hold all twelve of them, so they ascended in unison, but as they reached the top, they were instructed to enter the building one by one, in the order of their assigned chakras.

While the dark stone continued on the floors inside, a low white platform ascended in the middle of the room like a hovering round plate. The altar was made of white selenite, and in the middle of it was a large symbol of an eight-pointed star, created in onyx stone. There was a small circle in the middle and a large circle around it. They all formed a circle around it, and Ayla studied it for a second as she waited for instructions. Freya, Brigid, and Hecate had taken their places at three points, standing in a half-moon behind the twelve women.

"Wow, that is marvellous," Evelyn exclaimed. "Such a beautiful masterpiece. The

whole room, actually, but the altar with its star is incredible." "Do you know what it means?" Ayla asked.

"It's the 8-pointed star," Evelyn answered. I've seen it in many places, but I don't actually know what it means.

Danica answered, "It's the Star of Ishtar."

"I don't know what that means, either," Akira said, shaking her head. A few others joined her sentiment.

Danica continued, "Well, it's the Star of Inanna, does that help?"

The others shook their heads again, and Danica didn't know how else to say it or how to describe it, but she didn't have to. Soon her frustration was interrupted. A woman dressed in a dark purple gown with a black mantle appeared in the doorway.

She immediately answered the question for her.

"The Star of Ishtar is the most important symbol for you to know. It is the very reason why you are here." She quickly made her way through the group and stepped onto the platform. She paced the platform as she continued, her dark hair flowing softly in the wind as she did so.

"This star represents the teachings of Venus that many goddesses, deities, and ascended masters have tried to initiate into Earth at various times. The wisdom of the Divine Feminine. Many of us succeeded in our times but failed to anchor it into the feminine blueprint. Over history, we became known as goddesses and deities to fear, and so our knowledge has therefore been lost. The narrative changed, and our voices disappeared. But you stand before us because you are next in line to carry the torch. You have agreed to restore feminine power to Earth. And this time, we will not fail. This time, so many of you have incarnated onto Earth at the same time that darkness cannot win. Dear daughters, sisters, and mothers.

You are a lightworker, and everything you do with the power of yourself will shake the ground beneath you, challenge the system, and cause disruption.

We are with you tonight to clear your heart womb from low energies and release all that no longer serves you so that new, higher energies can spread for yourself, for the collective, and for Gaia."

She had now stopped in the middle of the street. She glanced over the room with a sovereign presence.

Jiya studied the silver embroidery in her purple velvet mantle. It was the spiral again, but this time in an intricate pattern forming a line on a cloak. Her purple dress was even more elaborate. It had two snakes slithering along the hem, meeting at her center, where they spiraled up and faced each other in her heart. She appreciated all the symbolism, but she could still not figure out who she was.

The woman continued, "I am not shocked by your confusion as to who I am. My name has been erased from history a long time ago, because of my rebellious spirit. The polarity of mankind is such that the masculine fears strong women, and therefore, we have been cast into the shadows and the greatness of our powers overshadowed with stories of virtue, sexuality, and witchcraft. My name is Lillith. But whether you have heard of me or not is unimportant at this point. Most of what you have heard is incorrect, as the truth has been concealed over the years. My assignment in this initiation is to open up your heart womb and enable you to release trauma that you hold with regards to religious programming, surrounding purity, morality, or virtue. For it is time to release all shame surrounding your sexuality, sensuality, and creative powers.

I invite you to place your hands on your womb. They all placed their hands on their wombs and prayed together.

"May you find your inner light

May you shine your world so bright

Until you doubt yourself no more

And bring your heart back to shore."

As they opened their eyes again, Lilith got off the platform and placed herself behind the circle, so the four deities stood at each right point and the twelve women could form a seamless circle around the star.

"Your assignment now is to reawaken the sacred feminine flame. That is done through the power of your voice. To remember the strength of your authentic expression once more. So, give us your best roar."

The twelve women roared together. At first, it was quite weak, but then they tried again and again. As their voices grew tired and became faint, Lilith instructed them to pause for a minute as she and the three goddesses united their power to raise the energy of the room. A fog formed between her and Hectate to her right, to Brigid, to Freya, and then back to Lilith. All of them placed their hands out to create a sacred space, which first appeared as a small grey fog but suddenly began to create sparks of light. The wind whirled around them, creating the sensation of a light storm that first rose to the ceiling before it settled and became quiet. "Now try again."

The twelve women thundered in a united effort to carry their power from their roots through their systems and create the rumbling sound that awoke their senses. The roar that eventually came out was both powerful and expansive, and as it left their throats, they felt the satisfaction of feeling free. Their newly found power of their lungs was tried again. For the third time, they managed to synchronize, whereupon a flame sprang to life at the center of the star on the platform. They repeated their efforts, and it grew bigger and more intense. Lilith looked into the fire for a few minutes. The powerful goddesses around her held the energy of the room to allow the fire to grow stronger, bigger, and brighter. Eventually, they were satisfied with their strength, so Lilith glanced at them with a satisfied look. "This is the beginning of something great. You have resurrected the feminine flame and can now start to heal the imbalance of your inner power. I need you to line up in front of me." Hecate, Freya, and Brigid walked up to stand next to Lilith, and the women formed a line, facing them. As the fire continued its fiery efforts, Lilith took out a collection of brass keys attached to hooped chains. She walked up to Nora, took out one of the keys, and held it in her hands as she said, "I hereby give you the key to remembrance and reconciliation". Then she placed it like a necklace over Nora's head. She continued to Danica and repeated her words as she placed a key around her neck. She took a step to the right and continued down the line to Akira, Ming, Phoebe, Ayla, Elena, Jiya, Meira, Esther, Evelyn, and finally Hanwi. When they all had a key around their neck, she said. "You are now ready to continue your journey to the next part." She stood to the side. They all issued "thank you" before stepping out of the building again, down the steps, and into the valley as they walked into the night.

They hadn't gotten far when their path was suddenly blocked by a large mirror. Ayla looked around at the bare rock glimmering in the moonlight and shallow shrubs swirling in the wind. The moon was more visible now, creating a ghostlike glow on the silver frame of the mirror. They looked at the three Goddesses with questioning eyes. "Your task right now is to shatter your old image of yourself," Hecatate said, standing next to the mirror and scanning the group of women. Freya continued. "Stand in a line again, next to each other. Then take out the dagger in your belt." Brigid intervened. "I think you need to come a little closer, or else the throw will not have an impact. All of you need to hit the mirror with your dagger." She joined the other goddesses at the sidelines.

Hecate took the word again. "The best way to do this is if you all apply as much force as you can into one strong throw. Take a stance, arms back." The women adjusted their bodies, looked around to make sure that everyone was getting into the correct position. "On the count of three. One, two, three." Twelve daggers swung into the air and touched the surface of the mirror with a piercing sound of metal before falling down to the ground. A crack formed and spread across its surface. "Very good," Freya said, "One more time." The women went to pick up their dagger and regained their position, took a stance to enforce strength in their movement. Freya continued, "Everyone ready? One, two, three." The daggers flung in the air again and hit the mirror, this time with a much greater force, which shattered it entirely. Everyone felt relieved, but Evelyn asked boldly, "Doesn't this give us seven years of bad luck?" Hecate had waited for that question and quickly said, "Superstition is for those who are afraid of magic. We are not afraid of magic." She urged them on. They picked up their daggers and placed them in their belts before they continued on the path ahead. They walked down the valley, with the two protruding mountains that framed their pathway revealing their vast nature. The small bushes of thyme and heather remained loyal on both sides, and by now, they were a sliver of comfort in a grim landscape. The wind was picking up, and they suddenly heard a rumble in the distance. Freya told them to hurry up, and they picked up their pace. The thunder rumbled again in the distance, but was gaining on them. Not before long, the heavens opened up above them and drenched them in rain. As the water sipped down their faces and glued their clothes to their backs, they kept marching on, determined to reach their destination. But their hopes soon tarnished as they reached the wood line of a towering forest. Freya took the lead in front of them. She let them take refuge under the crowns of the trees before she spoke.

"We have entered the Forest of Shadows. And it is exactly how it sounds. Trust that we are here to guide you and protect your energy, but you have to use the courage of your own heart to navigate through the darkness. We will be waiting for you on the other side. Good Luck."

Hecate, Brigid, and Freya left, leaving the twelve of them stranded and wondering what to do.

They looked at each other. Eventually, Hanwi was the one who took the lead.

"I guess there is only one way to go, the good thing is that we are not alone this time." The forest was truly unwelcoming. It was dark and damp, and the rain compromised their vision even further. They took a deep breath and marched on together.

After walking for just a few minutes, however, the pathway disappeared. It was almost completely black, and they had to succumb to their senses to find their way. They remained confident in energy for the first few steps, but soon enough, the sounds of the wind and rain became sources of fear. They kept marching on, trying to remain calm, but eventually, Evelyn tripped over a root, and Meira walked into a thorny bush.

Ayla made them all stop.

"Ok, this isn't working. I think we need to find a better way to navigate the forest. I can hardly even see you and you are right in front of me, how are we supposed to make it to the other side?" she said.

"Maybe we need to see with something other than our eyes?" said Phoebe.

"Yes, good idea," said Elena. "But how do we do that?"

Hanwi turned out to be the wisest of them all in this area. "To be honest, I don't know what you're complaining about. I can see just fine."

Danica got annoyed by that comment, "But that's because you're Native American. It's in your blood to know how to navigate. The rest of us don't have that knowledge."

"Ok, that settles it, Hanwi will guide us," said Jiya.

"Hang on, I don't want to guide. It's really scary to be the first to walk into the dark forest." Hanwi protested.

"But someone has to walk first, we can't just walk next to each other, then all of us will take a trip," said Nora.

"Ok, then you go first. You're the stellar gateway chakra. So naturally, you go first," said Ming.

"No, I'm terrified of the dark," replied Nora.

Elena got slightly annoyed with them all and said, "Ok, you know what. I will just go first. I'm not afraid of the dark, so."

The others clapped and cheered in relief at her sacrifice.

"Great, that's just great," said Phoebe, "Now the question just remains how to navigate."

"Well, you're the third eye," said Evelyn, "the third eye is the eye of the soul. So, you should actually be able to take the lead here."

At this point, Esther got really irritated by everyone's indecisiveness. It was dark, it was cold, and it was raining. Nobody could see a thing, and everyone just wanted out. "Oh, for God's sake, step aside. We can't stand here and freeze all night." She said and pushed everyone aside and took the lead. They formed a chain again and started walking into the dark. But they didn't make it more than a few meters before Danica tripped.

"Seriously?" She said, "It sounded like you had everything under control?" Elena volunteered again. "After all, I have been assigned the heart chakra, and everyone knows that you should follow your heart, so somehow I should be able to guide us." They tried another try, but this time it was Ayla who walked into a stone and bruised her leg.

"Ok, maybe we actually need to use our heads instead of our legs," Ayla exclaimed. She was not used to speaking up like this at all, but now she got annoyed with how badly they were agreeing to one thing.

Evelyn said with compassion in her voice. "We are all scared, and the fear is getting in our way." Her silver hair shone in the silver moonlight. "Why don't we all just take a few deep breaths?" They all followed her order and breathed as they tried to come up with another strategy. Hanwi was the first to speak,

"Ok, fine. I will guide you. But I don't feel happy about it." She took Danica's hand, who took Jiya's, who took Evelyn's, and soon they formed a chain again. Hanwi started using her knowledge to find her way through the darkness, slowly taking them through the forest. They still almost didn't see anything. The trees were just dark silhouettes, the rain distorted them even further, there was a shiver of light coming from the moon above, but not enough to outline any details or the ground below.

After a while, Evelyn was having a hard time keeping up with the pace, and even Meira struggled at the back. She kept tripping because they were moving too quickly.

"Please, slow down or I won't make it to the other side in one piece," she said.

"But I'm walking as slowly as I can. I thought I was considerate." said Hanwi. "Well, not considerate enough," complained Meira while catching her breath. Hanwi took offence. "Well, you do it then if you think it's so easy."

"Ok, fine, I will." Meira took the lead and tried to make sure to lead them on a route that involved no slippery stones and no bushes. She mastered it quite skillfully until they reached a climb. "Ok, everyone. It looks like we need to let go and climb this hill to the top. Please say your name when you've made it all the way up, so we know. Or, actually, it's good to know if you're stuck, too." She reached out to feel her way up. It seemed like a small hillside filled with rocks; apparently, some moss . She eventually put her hand on a root, so there was definitely a tree somewhere. She tried to make out if it was close to them or not. It seemed fine. The others were right behind them, trying to navigate the space in the dark.

"Sorry, sorry Ayla" laughed Phoebe as she accidentally bumped her head into Ayla's butt. They both chuckled and tried to refrain from laughing too hard as they needed to stay focused on the stones and roots that they were holding onto. Eventually, Meira made it to the top of the hill and yelled at the others, "It's actually not that far, you are almost there. That was a ridiculously short climb."

"I wonder how this would all look if the lights were on." Laughed Jiya. "We would look ridiculous". Everyone started laughing at the thought of a seemingly big challenge being just a small mound, and their agonized faces trying to face the grand quest of nothingness. They all continued laughing. "Well, it's good to laugh. But it's also noteworthy that fear is real, and the challenge is the fact that we cannot see, so we have to use our other senses. Humour helps too, apparently," said Evelyn.

"Oh, so that's the challenge!" exclaimed Elena.

"What?" asked Danica.

"To see with our chakras when the eyes are blind," added Elena.

"Ooooh," echoed among the group.

"Cool," said Phoebe, "Does anyone have a clue how we do that?"

"You all saw superhero movies when you were kids," said Nora, "Of course, we are all different nationalities and generations, but they were all more or less the same."

"You don't really expect us to shout some power phrase and twirl in the sky, do you?" said Edith with a negative tone.

"Why not?" said Nora, "Look at where we are. It couldn't hurt to try." "Omg, this feels so ridiculous. But ok, what should we shout?" said Ming. "Go, team awesome," shouted Akira and laughed. All of them laughed at her. As they laughed, they noticed how their skin suddenly caught a case of shimmer. "What was that?" said Danica and looking at Akira's arm. But it all went dark just as quickly.

"Ok, someone says something funny," said Danica. "It went quiet. All of a sudden, no one could think of anything to say. "

"Okay, how about we all just laugh," said Elena. They all laughed. Their skin shimmered again slightly.

"I think it might need to be a heartfelt laugh, more genuine," said Jiya. They all started laughing again, trying to keep their spirits higher. Their skin gave off a shimmer again, they told another joke, and it shimmered again, and again. So, they kept going, trying to come up with funny and happy things to say to keep the laughter going and keep a happy mood. Soon, they were all laughing along, glowing a steady light for them to follow as they found their way out of the darkness. As they reached the edge of the forest, they were happily surprised to find a small fortress revealing itself amongst the shadows. It was built like a traditional cottage but much larger, with a small tower and wooden beams. The warm lights coming from within were inviting and made them hurry down the hillside. Freya greeted them as they approached and opened the heavy wooden door and held it up for everyone to enter. She closed it behind them. They were quite satisfied with the revelation that the first thing that greeted them upon entrance was a large open fire. The smell of wood was soothing. They were standing in a hallway with tall ceilings. A staircase to the right spiraled up to the second floor, but they were going to the room behind the fire. They entered a space that they could not make sense of at first glance. Its tall ceiling was made up of an intricate design of naked wooden beams, and a large chandelier took center stage in the room. At the opposite wall were two tall arched windows with tinted glass, and between them hung a black tapestry with delicately embroidered women, flowers, and apples.

Below the tapestry stood a long cypress table with just one object in its center. A golden chalice.

The other walls were adorned with weapons. Two swords, a silver shield with an embossed spiral, and a golden bow with five arrows in gold.

Between them and the chalice was just an empty room. Carved into the wood of the floor was a large rose with a circle around it.

Ayla looked at Phoebe, who looked back, and then at Jiya. Looking at the expression of the other women, they seemed both thrilled and puzzled. They were all clinging to the entrance, not sure what to do. But soon enough, Freya was inviting them in to stand around the rose. She took a place in the circle, next to the wall with the tapestry. The other goddesses were also standing in the circle along with the other women. Suddenly, a door opened to the left, making everyone jump. But it was just a warm elderly woman dressed in a tweed dress with a tartan pattern in dark red and white. She walked around the room with a large tray, handing everyone wooden cups filled with hot chocolate. They all happily accepted one. Ayla heated her hands around the comforting mug and breathed in the aroma. Honey and chamomile had been mixed into the drink. It was a soothing blend.

"I hope you are all feeling better in the warmth. We need to regain our strengths for the next part," said Freya as she closed her eyes to drink and enjoy the richness of the humble drink. The others did the same.

"The journey that you are on tonight is not easy. Clearing trauma and standing in your power when the world is chaotic is a test of your resilience and strength. I might be celebrating many things, but even I struggle with the tarnish of my name. So does Brigid, and so does Hecate, and so does Lillith. Throughout history, most women who step into their sovereignty have had their dignity and pride stolen from them by men of power, even the Goddesses. In our power resides the ability to respond, but we choose not to. In our sovereignty resides the determination to stand firm even when the ground shakes. In our free spirit resides the mission to carry on the sanctity of divine feminine love. But feminine love is the most powerful force on the planet. It is not in our interest to simply guard it and protect it. We must unleash it, let it run free. It is the only way to restore the balance we once lost."

The elder woman came back out with her tray to collect their cups.

Freya paused and looked around the room to allow the news to land amongst the women. There were so many questions, but none of them dared to speak. So, Freya continued,

"Who is the enemy you're fighting, you might ask? It is not the enemy you think. Look around you. Your biggest enemy is you."

She paused again and cleared her throat while they all looked at her in disbelief.

"For eons, the patriarch has made sure that any woman who stepped out of line would be punished. What did that do to your love for yourself? What did that do to your trust in fellow women?"

They all looked around, finally understanding what she was saying, but also feeling the wound. It was deep. "Most of you have had your back stabbed by other women more times than you care to remember. Each time, the wound will stay with you for a lifetime and beyond. By now, you may be carrying dozens of backstabbing wounds. These types of wounds are so painful that it is easier to hide from them than to attend to them. "Freya paused, giving them all a fierce look with her blue eyes, and then she continued. "To begin to restore that trust, we will now start with a ritual called the Golden Arrow. I tell you that it is now safe for you to remove the shields on your back." The women lifted up the leather straps that held the shield in its place, took it off, and leaned it towards the wall before resuming their position in the circle.

Freya started guiding them through some movements of martial arts movements. Slow at first, but with intensity that grew with each new stance. It was a slow but powerful dance between feminine sensuality and masculine warrior energy. They paused for a second, and Brigid walked around the room with golden coins, placing them on each and every point that was painful. Most of the women soon had their entire backs filled with golden coins while working hard to contain their tears. While a valuable lesson, the exercise brought forth wounds that were deeply buried underneath their inner shields of protection.

Brigid paused with each one and said in a comforting manner, "You are allowed to feel hurt. You are allowed to cry. You are allowed to show emotions. Do not hold back. Let it all out."

As Freya's lesson through the movements came to an end, Brigid took over and instructed them to stand in the circle again. "The next part will have each of you take turns sitting in the circle. Let's go in the order you are standing. You will sit in the middle, on your knees, and hold a bowl in your hands." The elder woman came back out and gave them all a metal bowl each. She then continued,

"Each of you will step forward to remove one coin until all of them are gone."

Danica sat down in the middle, sitting on her knees, holding her bowl. They all stepped in and took turns to remove a coin and put it in the bowl in her hands. When they were done,

Freya instructed them to step closer so that they all could touch the top of her head.

She then instructed them all to close their eyes and led a prayer,

"Blessed are there, we've come in spirit to liberate you from your pain. We see your wounds, we honour your scars, we heal your heart."

The words made them all emotional. Danica wept and stood up to join the circle, holding her bowl of golden stickers. They continued with Phoebe, who sat down in the same way, fighting to hold back her tears that were streaming down in effect of this teachable moment. They continued in turns until every woman had been relieved of her pain, and eventually they were all standing with small bowls of golden coins in their hands.

Now, Brigid has taken the word again.

"Now, let's place the bowls in a circle in the center of the rose."

She waited as they placed them on the floor and stood back up. She then took one long match and lit it on a black candle, as she said,

"I will now pass you a match. Light a fire in your bowl and pass the match on. As you do, concentrate your thoughts on the potential origin of these wounds." As the match was passed from woman to woman, the elder woman handed Brigid a carafe containing water.

The women were each concentrating their attention on their respective bowls. As the last fire was burning low, Brigid took center stage and stood in the middle of the circle, holding the carafe. She was waiting for the last fire to burn out before she started pouring water into each bowl, all the way to the brim. "I now cleanse you of all your pain and sorrows." She repeated twelve times as she went around the circle. "We have now done a crucial clearing of the wounds that broke your heart. The next step is to strengthen your self-confidence.

You are now picking up the bowl in your hands, and into the water, you say the first thing that comes to mind about yourself that makes you proud. You say it out loud, and then the person to your right says one nice thing, and so on. We start one by one, but I need you to keep up the pace; you don't have time to think. Anything at all and as quickly as you can."

The room soon started buzzing as they all were busy thinking of nice things to say about themselves, saying them out loud, and passing on the word.

"The next exercise is the same exercise, but this time you say it about the other people standing in the circle with you to you."

The room buzzed again, although at a slightly slower pace. Brigid stood in silence, watching them in their pursuit of the gentle expression, and waited until it waned out.

"Now you take a sip of the water in your cup. The ashes of your past traumas, coupled with the soft healing water, will strengthen your spirit and heal your heart. You have faced your fears, overcome your own criticism, and begun the healing process of your sister's wound. "For millennia, the world around us has been working hard to keep us apart, to make us think that we are alone, and to silently judge and outdo each other. They wanted to keep us apart because together we are strong. But once we see past our conditioning, we know that our collective force is fierce."

Brigid started humming an etheric tune, and Freya took the word for a moment. "Now stand closer together and put your arms out, put your left hand upwards and your right hand downwards towards your neighbours and hold each other's hands.

As they completed their circle, Brigid continued. "Your love matters, your strength matters, your vulnerability matters, your peace matters. In the midst of healing, one can easily lose track, and amongst daily life, one can easily forget. War is not only about bloodshed. It's about the fight that goes on inside of you every day."

Brigid continued humming and transitioned into a soft whispering song as the suspension in the room grew; her singing grew louder. She had brought out celestial drums and increased the vibe with a rhythmic beat. Freya swayed from side to side while joining the singing, reaching her arms out as they felt the energy and the rhythm of the tune. The women closed their eyes but kept holding hands as they softly danced to the music. Hecate also joined in chanting as Brigid's voice rose to the ceiling on a high note. She left it afloat until the room was alight in a bright light. The women opened their eyes and watched in wonder at the miraculously enchanting glow that engulfed them all before it settled as Brigid's voice lowered and eventually stopped. She looked around and beamed brightly. "Now, my friends. It is time for your next lesson. Hecate will take the lead."

Hecate had already prepared and stood by the open hallway, and as the women came out, she gave each one a torch. "Place your torch in the fire. You will carry it with you to the next place." She held up the door as they exited the grand building and resumed her position in front as soon as everyone was outside. She took a left and had just about passed the building before she stopped at a wooden door in the stone wall that surrounded the grounds. She opened it and revealed a stone passageway that started as a terrace lodged to the facade of the cottage castle, but although the building was vast, the pathway continued in its absence, clinging onto a mountain behind it like an extensive balcony between two different worlds. They stopped for a second to encompass the echo of the grand valley beyond their feet. All the fog had lifted at this point, allowing the extravagant performance of the night sky. The moon was bright, and the stars twinkled their light. But that was not what caused the wondrous sight. Over the black and blue hues swept auroras in green and magenta, enchanting them all with their transformative dance. They walked beside the mountain in a dreamy state as they strolled on the safety of the balcony to the other side of the mountain. There, they were met by another castle, nestled into the mountain and stretching down towards its foot. They entered the grounds through an archway in its outer wall and crossed a small courtyard, bare of any ornaments beside the stone path leading up to the door. Hecate knocked three times, and it opened without a trace of force or anyone to greet them on the other side. They entered one by one and spread out inside with their torches still in hand. As Freya crossed the threshold, they were all inside, and Hecate closed the door behind them. The room they were in was not grand. It was a simple hallway with a Persian rug on the floor and a black Chesterfield chair at the center. Hecate took the lead again, and they followed her towards an opening to the left that turned out to be a flight of stairs to the story below. The space here was a lot more grand. Gothic features in wood and stone embellished the walls, and a decorative painting in the ceiling. Two circles are linked together with a third emphasizing its middle. Each withholding scenery and lush landscapes where powerful women dressed in black and holding enchanted objects of swords, wands, and glass bottles. A few black cats were included, too, as was a serenade of roses in black, red, and silver. The women had paused for a second to admire the artwork but were soon ushered on by Freya. This room was just a corridor, despite its grand size. But its greatest impact was not from the tall ceiling of three stories, but the grand mandala window that covered the entirety of the greeting wall. The moonlight paired with the window to create an enchanting shadow on the wooden floor that aligned perfectly with a circular fireplace made of shadow stone and placed in the center of the room. Hecate took a strong position underneath the window and told them to light the fire with their torches and then place them in the handles on the opposing walls, six on each side. Brigid and Freya held the energy of the space outside the circle and started gesturing with their hands, gently swaying their arms up and down to grow the fire. As its flame grew taller, footsteps echoed through the corridor and revealed their final member. Lilith. She made a gesture with her hands and took a strong position by the door as she simply said, "It is time to reclaim your dark feminine power and allow your bewildered energies."

The women had been compliant up until now, but uneasy energies arose from the group as they tried to level with that request. All their lives, they had been told to embrace the soft, feminine, and although they could grasp the purpose of unleashing their wilder sides, it felt unfamiliar and scary.

Freya spoke, "Good. This is exactly the energy we need to bring to the surface. You are afraid. You are carrying an ancestral wound where women had to display only the light, and any feminine who stood confident in her dark power was portrayed as a sorcerer, an enchantress, or a demon. Something to fear and punish. But it is learned behaviour. Behaviour that taught you that you were only lovable if you were submissive, easy, and sweet. But light cannot exist without darkness. You must walk through your inner shadows to become the warrior you were always meant to be."

Hecate added, "You have been conditioned by the system to fear your power, because that was the only way they could control the fire within. But we are here to unleash the storm." "You are afraid to lose control over your lives, how you are perceived by men and women alike. You are afraid of being inadequate. When you dare to step into your powerful energies, you are afraid of being an impostor, you are afraid to fail, you are afraid to become an outcast. Lift your insecurities to the surface; this is a safe space. Form a circle like you did before, holding each other's hands with one palm facing up and the other down." Brigid completed the speech before she and the other three goddesses began another ritual to unleash the power held in the room. The women stood in a circle, first looking around them to see what was happening and then closing their eyes as the energies sparked. The goddesses began chanting in light language, creating an etheric swirl surrounding the group.

"Now, sing and chant with us. Whichever you prefer. Do it in your native tongue, in light language if you can, or make something up. Just sing." Freya screamed to be heard over the soaring of the wind and the rising energies. As the women joined the song, the energies rose to the ceiling, creating a strong forceful wind that stormed around them, slowly attuning itself to a purple tone. As it became dark purple, Hecate put her arms up in a powerful stance and quickly threw them out towards her sides, causing the purple storm to violently blow in every direction before it vanished.

The divine feminines in the circle touched their hearts in awe, in an expression to cope with a powerful experience. The energy in the room had shifted. From fearful and anxious to peaceful and supreme, and they all felt it. "Now that we have cleared the fears that blocked your path, we will share our wisdom," Lilith said as she placed both hands on her heart. She then approached the circle with aligned timing with Brigid, Freya, and Hecate to join the divine feminines. Brigid instructed them all to close their eyes as they allowed the energy to pass through their hands as they joined forces in the sacred circle. Hecate initiated a small spherical light shining dimly in orange that she passed on to the woman next to her. The light touched their left hand, then travelled to their heart where it initiated a light that remained alit as it passed through the right hand to the next person, lighting up the heart of everyone in the room. As it made its way to Hecate, it began pulsating in the rhythm of their beating hearts, creating a seamless circle of light. They watched the fire in front of them as they felt the warmth spread from their chest. They closed their eyes again as Hecate, Freya, Brigid, and Lilith started mumbling a verse in light language. The sacred fire started flickering, increasingly tall flames until it eventually transformed into a pillar of light that shone brightly at the group's center. Hecate whispered loudly at this point in words the women couldn't understand, but it caused an intensity in the light and a brightness that touched them all. "We lift our spirits, our courage, and our belief in ourselves. We allow entry to wisdom, knowledge, and love." Freya said and repeated it over and over until the pillar returned back to its original state as a small fire. "We have now sparked the fire within you that you can carry with you in your journey and grow at the pace of your comfort," Brigid said and urged everyone to place their hands on their hearts to hold the light within. Lilith looked at everyone with compassion before she spoke. "I am excited about the progress we have made here today. Together we have reunited the dark feminine power to its authentic divine form and sprung to life a motion that will ripple out to the collective. You are now ready to unite within." She took the lead, and, with steady steps, she walked towards the back of the building where she took them down a flight of stairs, then through the ground floor of the castle and the grand terrace on the outside. They followed her down another set of stairs, where the stone-paved grounds of the castle led out to a bridge that took their journey to the other side of the valley. They kept a steady pace with Lilith as they marched over the treetops, but slowed down at the sight of a gate. The railing of the stone bridge was already quite high and decorated with Gothic piers. The frame of the gate was made of the same limestone and elaborately decorated with carvings of roses and thorns. The gate itself was oak and sparsely decorated except for twelve rose-shaped locks spread across its body. "At our first encounter, I gave you a key each. That key unlocks this gate, so all of you step into position and find your lock." Lilith watched as the divine feminines found their place in the line and entered their key to the lock it belonged to. As soon as they were all in position, they looked at each other, nodded, and turned.

The gate sprang open and revealed that they were greeted with a white fog. They walked through with the goddesses behind them. For a few steps, they walked on the bridge in the whiteness that revealed little orientation or information about what was waiting on the other side. As they emerged, a soft morning sun greeted them, enhancing the transformation from their red jump suit armors into red floor-length dresses. Their braids were undone to bewilder their hair and decorated with golden forehead tiaras holding a large stone of crystal quartz secure at their third eye. They admired each other and their new attire as they kept up their pace and crossed the bridge. On the other side, they were faced with yet another task of climbing stairs, but it was only a few steps until they reached the platform above. They glanced towards the rising sun over the mountains as they walked the stone paved avenue, trying to make sense of where they were. Pillars of climbing roses held up statues of doves, mirroring each other on each side of the avenue. The first two pillars were red roses, the next were white, then pink, and then blue. The last set of pillars was mixed in all four colours and climbed up towards an arched half dome in the shape of a seashell. Under it a woman waited for them to make their way all the way up towards her. The twelve divine feminines formed a line again to face her. Lilith stood alone behind them, and Hecate, Freya, and Brigid stood next to each other at the back.

She looked at them all with compassion in her eyes. Wearing a similar red dress and a red rose in her hair, she answered Elena's quiet wave before she spoke, "I am Mary Magdalene, and I am proud of you all for courageously walking the path of the rose." She said. "You are true champions. We have waited thousands of years for this moment in history when women can reconcile the shattered feminine power and bring the fragmented pieces back together for one united force. We have been working in the darkness and behind the scenes, keeping the codes of the flame alive, awaiting the right moment for it to be revived. You are the keepers of the flame, finally ready to pass on the light. Divine is within every part of you, and protected is your journey towards true love. Blessed is your soul." She stepped forward to hand a red rose to each of the divine feminines before her. As she stepped back, she watched the crowd. The divine feminines, Hecate, Freya, and Brigid, before her gaze landed on Lilith. "Come, dear sister," she said as she proceeded to approach a pedestal that was standing at the center of the stage, raising a golden chalice towards the sky. She cupped her hands around it and looked at Lilith again before she raised it towards the sky. "From this moment on, we cannot be divided into superstitious prejudice, fear, and fractured souls. We are united in wisdom, united in power, and united in love." She drank from it and handed it to Lilith, who also drank before raising it into the air, "We forgive the perpetrators, reconcile the fracture, heal the pain, and open our hearts to divine love once more." She then placed it back on the pedestal, and as Mary Magdalene and Lilith stepped aside, and invited the divine feminines to walk through the portal behind them, stopping to have their heart touched by united feminine power before continuing on.

On the other side lay land in glistening light. They first looked over the hills in the far distance before recollecting that they were in the present, standing in an expansive apple orchard. The orchard extended in the distance, rolling over the hills like a scroll, whispering wisdom across the land. The sweet flowers attracted the mightiest of servants and filled the air with a sweet sound of reminiscence. The frequency of bees filled the air as their wings glimmered in the golden sunlight. They strolled through the pathway that was nestled between two rows of trees, admiring the variety of apples in red, green, and gold. In the air lingered a tune of gratitude and relief. They embraced a dreamy state, allowing their mind to wander and their hearts to be sprinkled with joy. The fulfillment of achieving peace was very welcome and well-received. The stroll through the landscape seemed quite long, but eventually, they did reach a meticulously groomed garden and stopped at the edge of the carefully manicured lawn. The grand white English mansion behind it made no attempt to hide. Its grand architecture and a large arched entrance gave an exquisite touch to a rustique building. The lady of the house was already waiting for them in front and waved cheerfully as they approached. Looking around at the powerful group of women, they couldn't help but wonder who she could be. Who could possibly be missing? Their thoughts of curiosity and wonder stayed in the air as they came closer. They looked at her feminine dress and silky brown hair. Who was she? They stopped before her and quieted their minds.

"Welcome, everyone!" she said, beaming a friendly smile. She had strong charisma and a soft glow. She was delicate with pale skin and dark brown, silky hair flowing effortlessly over her narrow shoulders. She was wearing a long beige tulle dress with off-the-shoulder sleeves and small florals sewn into it like they were swirling around her. "You have had a long night with many trials. Rest assured, you have arrived at the good part. I want nothing from you, I expect nothing from you, I only want to give." The woman paused to look over the crowd, clasping her hands merrily as she continued joyfully,

"You have entered my etheric kingdom because you are ready to embody what I craved for and could not resist. Wisdom. Within me, as with you, lies the key to sacred wisdom. All we have to do is unleash it."

"There is so much wisdom and knowledge, and most of it has sadly been forgotten. But it is not lost. It will be revived again, and there is no better way to do that than to share it. By now, I gather that all of you have guessed my identity, but for those in doubt, I am Eve, and you are very welcome to my home."

She said as she spread her arms, gesturing with her warmth for everyone to step inside her modest mansion. As she started walking towards the grand front door, it was easy to see that her elegance was just as gracious when she walked. Feeling the effect of her warm hospitality, they followed her inside. The modest mansion did not fail to impress once inside. They had to savour the moment of being in the presence of such a simple yet effective composition of a happy space. It was all built like a conservatory with a grand space in the middle surrounded by an artwork of glass and wood. There was a snug right by the entrance with a white sofa and armchairs, and what appeared to be an enclosed area at the back with a kitchen and bedroom, but otherwise it looked like a gardener's dream with an open-spaced stone floor hosting a long wooden table. It had been festively decorated with napkins in white and tablets in gold, coupled with the finest porcelain and cutlery. Big bouquets with pink peonies, roses, and dahlias were spread across the centerpiece. "Please, take a seat. You are here to enjoy yourselves, to receive the gift of compassion and love through a friendly social celebration marking the defeat of your quest. You are worthy to savour the moment and feel the happiness within. So please, be my guests."

Eve sat down, as did Lilith at the other end of the table. Mary Magdalene took a place in the middle, next to Freya, with Hecate and Brigid on the opposite side of the table. The divine feminines spread out in between. The table was big enough to seat all 18 of them quite comfortably. As they were seated, they glanced at the feast before their eyes. Apple pies, crumbles, salads, and savoury delights. Freya looked at it all and joked, "You do know there are other fruits, don't you?" "Yes, but only one champion," Eve responded in a loud voice. She had gone to the kitchen and came back out carrying a large basket and walked around the table, handing out golden apples to each of her guests. She then sat down and said, "Within each golden apple lies the truth to divine knowledge. Let's all hold them up and toast to the reunion of sisterhood, our free spirit, and our right to wisdom. Cheers." They all took a bite to open the ceremony and placed it to the side. A carafe of apple cider made its way around the table as joy filled the air and merry tunes bounced off the acoustics of the room. The energies rose as they ate merrily and conversed with the goddesses as equals. Ayla made eye contact with Elena and Phoebe and smiled as she gathered courage to raise her glass. "I just want to briefly say thank you for the powerful guidance today and for the extraordinary experience to dine with the divine. May it be the first of many." The other divine feminines joined her and raised their glasses in gratitude and respect.

CHAPTER 14

The Sun

*P*hoebe woke up the next morning feeling much better. The shaman ceremony from the day before did wonders, as Gabriel's unexpected show did. She got up and knocked on his door, but he wasn't there. Instead, she found him downstairs in the living room, watching TV.

"Good morning. Did you sleep well?" She walked over and gave him a kiss.

"It was alright. I woke up at 5 am and have been watching TV ever since. How about you? That ceremony yesterday was really something else."

"Yes, very effective. I feel so much lighter today. Have you had anything to eat yet? Coffee?" she asked and walked towards the kitchen.

"I just had a little bit of coffee and some juice." He said.

"I'll go and see what I can find." She said and went to the kitchen. Catalina came in shortly after.

"Good morning, I heard you two were up, so I thought I would help you fix breakfast. Let's make a brunch." She said and got her apron out. "What do you want to do today?" Phoebe asked Gabriel as he sat down to eat.

"I actually don't have any preferences. I'll go where you want to go."

"Ok, because I really want to see the Mayan temples."

"Yeah, that sounds like fun. Is that far?" said Gabriel

"Actually, all of them are quite far away. If you want to see them, you will have to travel," said Emiliano, who was just walking down the stairs.

"Ok, then maybe not. You just got here." Phoebe said, trying to come up with something else to do.

"I don't mind. Really, it's fine. I'm happy as long as I'm with you."

"Aw, that's so sweet," Catalina said in an impressed tone. "The closest one is a few hours away. You can take the bus, I think.

Emiliano added, "But there are a few other types of monuments around here that might work just as well?"

"Thank you for the ideas. We'll see what we do." Phoebe fell into silence as she contemplated her options.

After breakfast was over, she turned to Gabriel and said, "I think I need to tell you something." She took him up to her room. He sat down on the bed as she sat by the desk, flipping through her notes, trying to figure out where to start.

"Do you remember the weird dreams I had a few weeks ago?"

"No, not really," he answered as he shook his shoulders.

"Well, I had a few weird dreams where I visited temples and palaces filled with strong lights and codes. Then, I wanted us to stay at Fatima on our way to my father's, remember?"

"Yes, that I remember." He said he looked suspicious.

"I never told you any of this because I thought you would think I was crazy. But Mother Mary has come to me on several occasions, trying to instruct me to follow a soul purpose. I still don't quite understand what she is saying. But it is part of the reason why I am here."

"Ok?" He said while raising his eyebrow and looking increasingly skeptical. She was afraid to continue. "Go on." He eventually said.

"Anyway. Mother Mary told me last night that I need to find my roots, but I struggle to figure out what she means. I have been to all sorts of places in the region now, except for the Mayan Temples. So, I'm thinking that is what she meant. But currently, I don't know how to read the signs."

"May I ask a question?"

"Go ahead."

"What are the signs you are referring to, and why would Mother Mary, who is Christian, want you to visit Mayan Temples that were built long before her time?" She looked at him in relief and put her hand to her heart, "I am so happy that you believe me enough to ask me a proper question instead of dismissing the events in my life." Then she opened her bag and took out the crystal blue rose. "The day I was in Fatima, Mother Mary gave me this. It is supposed to help guide me back to my heart. But I don't get what she means."

Gabriel took it in his hands and studied it. He looked at the little bubbles inside and studied the embossed trinity symbol at the bottom.

"I can't figure it out either. But let's find out then. We will go to the temple that is closest to see if we get any more clues." He gave it back to her and said excitedly, "It's like an invisible treasure map that we need to figure out how to read. I like that."

"I can't believe you accepted everything I just said, just like that. I thought I was going to sound crazy to you," she said, astonished.

He just looked at her, surprised, "You have known me for three years and you didn't know I was religious?"

They gathered their things and headed over to the bus station to wait for the next bus. The trip was over five hours and not a very comfortable one. The bus was a little bit bumpy and travelled across the countryside on roads that needed a lot more maintenance. But they eventually got there in one piece. The sun had begun to reverse to afternoon, but it was scorching hot, and the deep forest added an unwelcome humidity. They bought some water and snacks at the shop before they began their walk. Phoebe was now so happy, not only that Gabriel was here, but that she had dared open up to him about everything. It was a game changer, and she was happy not to have to go through it all alone.

After a gruesome walk, the temples finally emerged over the canopies. They walked all the way up to them, making their way through the different constructions, reading, learning, and exploring. Phoebe touched the stone wherever she could think of to get a sense of energy. When they stood in the center of the square, they agreed to sit down to rest and think about their next move.

"I don't think there is a logical way to think about this. But from what I gather, I think you must be the one to decide what we should do," he said. Phoebe looked around at the different constructions, sizing them and trying to remember their different functions, and determining which one would be most significant. She eventually went up to the one that was considered the astrological observatory. "I believe this is the one. Let's climb it and see what happens." He followed her and they started ascending the pyramid together. When they reached the top they stopped for a while, admiring the view seated at the staircase. Phoebe eventually took out the blue rose and held it in her hands. The small bubbles inside shimmered slightly in the sunlight.

"Was that the sunlight or something else?" asked Gabriel, who got caught off guard.

"It has done that before; I think it's just the sunlight that reflects into it," Phoebe answered, holding it up for them both to see clearly. But this time, it turned out that there was a slight glow to the shimmer.

"I actually don't think it is only the sunlight. I think it's reacting to something else." Gabriel said.

She looked at him, then looked deep into the blue rose, as if it were a crystal ball, to try to determine what it wanted her to do. She eventually followed her intuition and placed it on the stone at the top of the building. The silver metal leveled to the smooth stone, and just a few seconds later, the shimmer began flickering like bubbles in the sea. She looked at him again. His attention was directed towards the rose, but he was looking at her for answers. He seemed both confused and excited about this quest that he had embarked on with her. The flickering light twinkled in the sunlight, and the gleaming glow grew into a magnificent aura surrounding it. After a few mesmerizing minutes, a stream of light shot out from it and up to the heavens, creating a pillar. Phoebe got startled and almost lost her grip, but managed to stay focused. Gabriel laughed and got really excited and placed his hand in it to determine that it was, in fact, there.

"Wow, this is incredible!" He exclaimed, "What do you reckon this is?" "The word liquid light is popping up in my mind because the rose looks like water, and then there is a pillar of light. Did we just activate a portal?"

"Did we? That would be really cool."

"Maybe you shouldn't put your hand in it until we figure out what it does exactly." But just a few seconds later, the light dimmed itself and the rose returned to its original state. Phoebe looked at the rose in awe. Gabriel was equally amazed. "Ok, that was one of the coolest experiences of my life," She said, "but what do you reckon happened exactly?"

"I totally agree, that was incredible," he said and then continued, "I suppose the answer needs to come to you.

Why don't you write down everything you are feeling at the moment and all the things you think it might be, and then I will try to do the same. That way, we can memorize this experience and figure it out later." "Good idea." She took out her journal and scribbled everything she could think of. They then made their way down and tried the same experience on another pyramid, but nothing happened. So, they decided to walk around a bit before heading back to the tourist center, to then take a taxi to the hotel they had booked. Gabriel stayed quiet the whole way back, deep in thought as he was trying to figure things out. "Honey, I think I might be the one who needs to figure this out," Phoebe said. "It seems rooted in my purpose, and why it was given to me out of all people." "That's true. I will drop it for now and wait for you. But I think you need to write down a list of places that you are connected to, so we know where to go next," he said. "What? But that's too hard. My ancestors are scattered across the globe. Even I have ties to so many different countries. How would we be able to determine which one it is?" She felt devastated for a second.

"You are right, we don't. But it's a start," he said.

"What are we even looking for?" she asked, "After today, I'm not sure of anything. My whole sense of reality has shifted."

He looked at her and tried to come up with something to say, but he could not. "You are right. I'm sorry; I got carried away. You must be feeling overwhelmed. I'm sure the answer will come to you when you are thinking of other things. Let's go eat and continue tomorrow."

As the dawn broke, both of them were ready to get out of there and head back to San Cristobal de las Casas. But they had found a place in their tourist searches that piqued their curiosity, so they had decided to stop there on the way. So instead of the bus, they went to the tourist office to join a group trip around the area. As they waited for the tour guide, they found some proper breakfast at a small stall, sat down by a fountain to eat. They finished just in time. The tour guide arrived, and they got into his van with four other people. The first stop was a walk through a national park to see the great waterfalls in Misol-Ha. It was a challenging terrain amongst towering trees and lush bushes. The landscape was impressive and incredibly beautiful, with the green hills and nature's forces. Phoebe felt small and intimidated by the great waterfall, but to her surprise immediately felt an intuitive push to go into the pool of water at its feet. They changed quickly to swimming suits and jumped into the water. The water was cold, but it felt both refreshing and purifying to submerge into its stillness. They swam for a little while, enjoying the moment. But as she got used to the presence of the waterfall, Phoebe got a sudden urge to take the rose with her into the cave. Being afraid of both water and dark spaces, it was not an action that felt natural to her. Gabriel tried to go with her, but she told him that she needed to be alone, so he stayed in the lake instead, enjoying himself in the water as he waited for her instructions. Phoebe had brought the whole bag so that no one would see her hidden treasure. She took it out and placed it carefully on the wet rock. Mother Mary appeared, if only as a transparent and discreet figure. She answered Phoebe's question without delay.

"The rose transcends time. Its role is to purify places and merge your soul with your distant memories."

"Is that what the pillar of light was for?" Phoebe asked,

"In part, yes. You are searching for answers that are already within you, and the rose activates your memory and everyone else's memory to that place. It has now been brought out here to heal your memory of water. Your soul holds a trauma with water that is linked to your mother wound."

Phoebe felt stunned. Why would she need a waterfall in Mexico to heal her mother's wound? But then she realized that the waterfall was linked to her mother. "So, is that why I'm in Mexico in the first place?"

"You have opened the door to the memories you tried to forget; now you must open the door to the memories you wish to have. How deep is your ocean?" She vanished into thin air, and Phoebe looked at the rock she had been standing on. Phoebe felt utterly befuddled at what she had just said.

She put her hand out and waved for Gabriel to join her. He jumped out of the water and hurried along the shoreline to join her in the cave. She told him what Mother Mary had just said. "How deep is your ocean?" The words spun in his head, and he tried to twist and turn the phrase, but he couldn't think of anything to say that would add value. Unfortunately, they ran out of time, as the tour group was moving on to the next stop. They changed back into their clothes and headed back to the van. They were now going to the next stop of their trip. They were feeling tired from the last place, but this was a much shorter walk. As they approached the site, they could hear the sound of the swarming waterfalls before they saw them. The blue lagoons and turquoise swirling water were not only a refreshing welcome, but they were also a feast for the eye. They changed into their bathing suits again and went into the cool water. This time, Phoebe thought to try something that she hadn't thought of last time. She and Gabriel walked to a secluded part of the waterfalls. She took out the

blue rose and submerged it in water. It was as she expected. The rose created a ray of sunlight in the water. It didn't ascend towards the sky like a pillar this time but instead created a ball of radiant yellow light around it. Phoebe looked at Gabriel and said. "I think we need to go to the ocean."

They had gotten back to her aunt's house late the night before. After a wonderful day of swimming in waterfalls and crystal-clear waters, they had gone to bed on a high vibe and slept through the night like two babies. Phoebe woke up feeling rested and happy. She glanced over at the blue rose that was sitting on the desk. She studied it from afar, trying to piece together the various clues and occurrences that had been scattered like breadcrumbs during the past few days. It suddenly came to her attention that there might be more to the inscriptions than she had first thought. She had focused so much of her energy on the rose and its light. But the silver triangle and the trinity braid at the bottom must be equally important. Could they mean something more? Maybe that was what she was asked to focus her attention on. She went down to the kitchen to get something to drink. No one else was up, even though the sun was shining bright outside. She went back upstairs to wake up Gabriel. But he was difficult to wake up, as always. She tried to kiss him, tap his skin, and run her fingers through his hair. But he didn't wake up. So instead, she lay down beside him, gently holding onto him and remaining still, trying to go back to sleep herself. There was no point in stressing to figure things out. She eventually fell asleep and woke up again when he turned around. He looked at her gently and kissed her good morning.

"How long have you been lying there?" he asked.

"I came in a bit over an hour ago when I myself couldn't sleep. I tried to wake you up, but you are an impossibly sound sleeper. So instead, I fell asleep as well." He drew her closer and hugged her while still half asleep.

"I just came to realize that the trinity symbol at the bottom might mean something other than what we think. Maybe it's a clue to something else? I was eager to talk to you about it, but then I realized it could wait a few hours," she explained. "I'm listening." He mumbled while still keeping his eyes closed.

"I searched the internet and realized that I had a misconception of the symbol. It's not a trinity symbol as in Father, Son, and holy spirit. It's a triquetra because of the circle behind it."

"Ok, what does that mean?" He asked, still mumbling into his arm. "I am not sure. I think it could mean a variety of things. I couldn't find an answer that stood out. But because of how it reacted to the pyramids and the waterfall, I'm leaning towards the elements."

"Unity on Earth." He said and rubbed his eyes and sat up. "The symbol represents unity, and if we are talking about elements, that must mean the elements of life, meaning water, air, and earth." He yawned and tried to wake himself up.

She was sitting up too and looked at him in awe. "How do you know all that in your sleep?"

He just shook his shoulders, and she continued. "But if it means the elements, what happened to fire?"

"Fire is within Earth. It is what created the planet," he said, as he rubbed his eyes. She became silent, trying to think. "Is there a place that embodies everything that this symbol stands for?"

"Don't ask me, you're the historian. I'm better at symbolism. Can we go downstairs and get coffee to help us think?" He said as he put on some clothes. They walked downstairs and continued talking as they made their coffee and sat down on the lounge chairs. But once the sun's rays warmed their faces, they took a short break from it all. Their heads were hurting, and they needed the caffeine to kick in before they could use any more energy to think. Catalina came down and greeted them. She made herself a coffee and sat down next to them.

"What are you two talking about? You sound like two parrots," she said while looking at the two of them with a curious expression.

Phoebe looked at Gabriel and thought briefly about how to describe it. "I don't know how to summarize this," she started as she tried to think of how to explain. "We are trying to figure out the symbolism behind a blue crystal rose that was given to me by, ehm, Mother Mary." Phoebe looked at her aunt with widened eyes, trying to read her reaction before she continued.

"The thing is, she appeared to me shortly before I came on this trip, and she gave me a rose. I believe it is meant to lead me to something, but we can't figure out what." Phoebe looked at

Gabriel, not really knowing how to behave, having shared too much. But Catalina just cleared her throat and said, "I knew you were here for a reason. I could feel it. Am I allowed to see it?" Phoebe went up to her room and came back with it. She placed it on the side table next to Catalina, who picked it up to study it.

"Mother Mary never gives maps. She gives knowledge." She said in a low voice as she turned the figurine. "Are you sure you are interpreting it correctly?" "Yes, we definitely are. It lit up both at the pyramids and at Agua Azul. That must mean something."

"There is a Celtic trinity knot at the bottom and some sailors' knots at the sides. Are you sure you will come to the right place?"

Phoebe looked at Gabriel with a slight panic in her eyes, but then she remembered what Mother Mary had said.

"Yes. I had to find my roots and heal my mother wound first so that I could then properly follow my heart. That's what she said." Phoebe answered with certainty. "Follow your heart?" Catalina echoed. "So, what does your heart tell you?" "I don't know," Phoebe said in an irritated manner. "My mind is spinning about this, and I just can't wrap my head around it. Gabriel thought that maybe the trinity knot was not the Christian interpretation, but more spiritual or connected to the elements. But the internet gives other possible meanings to it."

Catalina looked at her as she rambled on about their different theories. "If you are the one who was given this, then you are the one who holds the knowledge. Never mind the internet.

What does your heart tell you?" she repeated. Gabriel looked at her with raised eyebrows, impressed at her intuition. "Well, I think it's all of them," Phoebe said. "That's why it is so difficult. Then we have the blue rose on top of that, which has like air bubbles inside that trap lights." Catalina held it up to the light to see how it danced inside the glass, trying to think of something to say that would be helpful.

"If you think about it, the rose is blue, it's made out of glass, which is basically sand melted by fire, and the bubbles that trap light look like air bubbles under water or at the brim of the ocean wave."

Phoebe sat in shock, looking at Gabriel with extremely widened eyes. "That's basically what I said, but I didn't know that's how you make glass. But we had already reached the conclusion of going to the ocean, the question is which one?"

"I can only think of one place that encapsulates all of these clues," said Catalina.

"Which is?" said Gabriel.

"Hawaii. It's the only place that embodies all the symbolic meanings of the trinity knot, and all the elements: ocean, earth, fire, and air. And it's a land that could possibly hold knowledge that you need to tap into."

"Hawaii is far, though. We can't go there based on just a hunch." Phoebe looked at Gabriel. "How much time did you take off, anyway?"

"I took two weeks, so we're good. Going to a paradise island is never a bad idea, even if our hunch turns out to be wrong."

"True. But it is far. You have come all this way just to have to travel even further." Phoebe said.

"Oh, quit placing your excuses onto me. I am fine. It looks pretty close on the map, look." He zoomed in on his phone and gave it to her. It's probably just a couple of hours away. Let's book a flight for tomorrow and spend the rest of the day with your family. I want to see the town."

Phoebe took his phone to look at the map. It was actually just off the coast. She looked at Catalina, who seemed thrilled about the idea, and she looked at Gabriel, who seemed to be undisturbed by the idea of leaving Mexico after just having arrived. She closed her eyes for a few seconds to try to read her heart and determine if she felt comfortable with this twist. She thought she had come to Mexico for a slow vacation, not an action-filled quest. But her heartbeat said yes, so as she opened her eyes again, she turned to Gabriel, "Ok, let's do it. Let's see if we are right."

As the train approached the final destination, Ayla felt both excited and anxious. After having pondered on her decision during the entire train ride, she had finally woken up to the conclusion that she deserved more adventure, so she had called him from the train to tell him that she would indeed be joining him in Hawaii. He was, of course, beyond thrilled, while she was also nervous. She had not been to the tropics in many years and had not packed anything that would be suitable for warm weather. Her duffle bag was filled with the essentials only.

As soon as she got off, she found him waiting for her at the end of the platform. To her objections, he insisted on taking both her bags. She had agreed to stay at his place for convenience only, so they took a short detour to leave her bags before continuing on an excursion through the city to find her some summer essentials in stores that were still carrying the winter collections. She enjoyed having him take her through the city, showing her the main tourist attractions as she browsed the stores. He was surprisingly helpful and good at keeping his spirits high. She found it weird how they had only just met, yet it felt like they had known each other for ages. It was also so easy to talk to a kindred spirit for once.

She was grateful for that as she hadn't been in a relationship in a long time and was way out of her comfort zone. But she was also excited that she finally had someone whom she could open up to about everything that had happened in her life in the past few weeks. Despite her attempts with Cassandra and her mom and dad, it felt like no one really understood. But being able to talk about it without a filter helped her to see things from a different perspective.

As they walked along the pedestrian street in the heart of the city, the cold air grew stronger and created roses on their cheeks. He put his arm around her to comfort her in the cold, and she felt the warmth seep through all the layers. The awkward feeling slowly started slipping away to make room for a much more pleasant gut feeling that this could be something great.

The afternoon gradually transformed into evening, and he insisted on taking her to one of his favourite restaurants in the city for dinner. It was a warm welcome to escape the cold. It was a cute little bistro with a modern interior and a young vibe. As she sat down, she admired the big chandeliers and bold prints. They received the menus and ordered them in a beat. They shared a cheese platter and then chose the same vegetarian burger. She felt unnervingly calm and relaxed in his presence. But as she was trying to figure herself out, she realized that she was overanalyzing. She looked at him, silently taking in his calm aura.

"How do you do that?" she asked.

"What do I do?" he asked, looking surprised.

"You seem to carry a very grounded and calm aura," she said.

"Years of practice," he joked as he put down his burger. He drank some water and thought a little. "Actually, it is years of practice. I used to be really anxious about everything. But then, like you, I had a sort of awakening, and that changed my life and also my mindset towards everything."

She nodded to what he said. "It does change everything once you see the grand scheme of everything. But I haven't gotten to the part where I am able to keep that level of grounded energy, yet."

"There is no need to rush it. You have opened other areas of knowledge that I haven't tapped into yet. So, it evens out." He beamed at her with warm green eyes. She felt that he was right. It was all about that balance.

After dinner, they strolled through the city as they made their way back to his place. The cold had grown more intense, so luckily it wasn't far to walk. Upon arrival, he went straight to the kitchen to put on a pot of tea.

"Would you like black tea or chai?" He asked over his shoulder.

"Chai sounds lovely, thank you." She started looking through his books on his bookshelves. His whole living room was like a library, very old-fashioned in that sense. There were a couple of old records too. "I didn't have you pinned down as a retro guy," she said.

He laughed, "I thought everything about me made that quite obvious. But as you see, I like other things too." He said as he popped his head over her shoulder and gave her a cup.

She took it and sat down on the couch. His living room was quite masculine with dark wood and a dark brown sofa, but he had decorated beautifully with accents of burnt orange and green. She sat down and sipped her tea. He had gone back to the kitchen to get his own cup and came back with a bowl of chocolate-covered almonds and put them on the table before he sat down respectfully at the other end of the couch.

"So, what do you like, then?"

"I think I might be a little bit classic in my taste. But I can be bold too. Like my sofa is red, but then most other things are either white or blue. My home is very much reflecting my love for the ocean, so there are also lots of pictures of boats and stuff." She started laughing at herself. "I am just as much a cliché as you are."

She noticed his modest gaze and put down her tea to adjust herself to sit closer to him, before casually picking up some almonds while looking around the room and nervously commenting on different things.

It turned out that her cue wasn't as discreet as she had thought because he noticed it right away. He graciously took her hand in his and pulled her closer, discreetly pulled her hair from her face, and cupped his hand at the back of her neck to kiss her. At first softly and tenderly, but it felt so comforting that she could hardly let go. So, they succumbed to each other's presence for a few moments. She opened her eyes slowly and looked deep into his eyes before leaning towards his chest in a warm embrace. They stayed like that for a while. As the darkness was falling outside and the evening was coming to an end, he stood up and took their cups and empty bowls to the kitchen before going into the other room. He came back carrying a duvet and pillow. "While the couch is really comfy, I thought you would have a much better sleep in bed. If you just give me a second, I will fix that for you.

"Thank you, that is very considerate." She just said with mixed feelings but amazed at his gentlemanly gesture. She sat on the couch, unsure about what to do. But he eventually came back out and said sarcastically.

"My lady, your bed is ready." as he gave a small bow and gestured towards the door. She chuckled and got off the couch to get ready for the night.

The next day began at the break of dawn. Within just a few minutes after walking, they were out the door, hurrying down the street to get to the station in time to catch the first train to the airport. As they arrived, they checked in their luggage as quickly as possible so as to get through security and to the nearest café. Ayla had never before gone that long without coffee in the morning and was craving it more than food. She was unusually alert, though, for being that early in the morning. Everything had run really smoothly, and she felt ready for the adventure ahead. They managed to get seats in the armchairs and sat down to relax for a few moments as they enjoyed their breakfast. Waiting for the gate to open, they did their best to stay alert and maintain an upbeat conversation. They had managed to get on the same plane but were nowhere near each other, so they headed in different directions. Ayla sat down next to a mother and a child. She had gotten the window seat, though, which made her happy. She loved looking out over the clouds. She brought out her journal and headphones and listened to music as she processed the events of the last few days. Eventually, however, her fatigue took over and she fell asleep. A few hours later, she was abruptly woken up by the announcements of the pilot. Her head was still in a foggy dream state as she looked around to orient herself. The music had been playing in her ears this whole time, so she turned it off to save battery. She checked her seatbelt; it was still on, so she just put her seat in the upright position and looked out the window to follow the landing. Palm trees and sandy beaches. She felt the excitement rising to her face, and soon she was grinning from ear to ear. She had definitely made the right decision.

Samuel made his way over as soon as they were off the plane. He was apparently a very considerate man. She didn't mind, but she also felt like it was unnecessary. As they made their way to the baggage claim, he went through some of the details for the day. After just an hour, they were finally able to leave the cool air conditioning and step out into the humid heat outside the airport. She was thrilled with the warmth that hugged her body but instantly regretted the purchase of her t-shirt. What had seemed like a summer top in Canada was way too warm for Hawaii. She managed to cope until they got to the hotel, but as he left to set up for the retreat, she went to the city center to find some proper clothes. She found a few nice tops and a pretty dress. But hurried back to the hotel as soon as she could. She needed to shower after the trip and wanted to relax by the beach in her new bikini. Her luggage was waiting for her behind the reception, and she checked in and texted Samuel about her whereabouts as she went up to her room. She opened the door to her room, inside, and breathed in relief. It was a beautiful room that was very pleasing with light blue walls, white accessories, and light wood. It was very soothing to the senses, as was the stunning view over the ocean. She opened the door to the balcony and let the wind play with her hair as she looked down on the complex and the surroundings around the hotel. There was a gorgeous white sandy beach just a short walk from the hotel.

She went back inside, took a quick shower, and changed to go to the beach. Samuel was already finished with his errands and was waiting for her by the bar. He got up as soon as he saw her and greeted her with a kiss. They walked down towards the beach and spread out their towels in the sand. Everything had felt so incredibly comfortable over the past few days with him. It was almost unsettling how easy it was. Ayla felt that she was not used to someone being so sensitive and considerate. She was used to the guys who left without a word or broke her heart at the first chance. So, her guard was still up, but as she was adjusting to the idea that there might be genuinely nice men in the world, she also needed time to remind her heart that it was safe to open up. But she enjoyed watching his movements, studying his facial expressions, and learning how his brown hair swirled down his forehead. She leaned over and kissed him tenderly. "You might be one of the best things that has happened to me in a long time," she finally managed to utter in half a whisper. She flinched at what she had just said. She had never said anything like that before and was just not used to being romantic in that way. It felt strange and awkward, and she expected him to brush it off or pretend he hadn't heard.

But he didn't budge, like she thought he would. He just leaned a little bit closer and said, "I feel the same way." He kissed her forehead and hugged her, squeezing her hair affectionately as he did so. She felt so safe and so loved. As the afternoon sun tanned their skin, they lay there on their towels, joyfully playing with each other's fingers. It took them nearly an hour to realize that they still hadn't touched the water, so they hopped down to the soft waves, playing like children as they ran and swam. As they walked back up to their things, Ayla remembered that she had brought the compass to try it in the sand. She took it out of a safety compartment in her bag and looked up at the sky to determine the direction of the light before placing it in the sand. Samuel watched with high anticipation. He looked like an excited child. After just a few seconds, the pink flower came to life. This time, it wasn't just the center, but the whole web lit up and created a soft glow as it traced the lines in different hues of pink.

Ayla got really excited and exclaimed, "This is incredible! I can't believe it!" "Have you received any new information about what it could mean?" He asked. "Still none. I mean, I know it's the flower of Venus, but I still can't figure out what it's doing on a compass or what it means when it lights up when it touches sand like this. Do you have any guesses?"

But he shook his shoulders and said, "I don't know. I think some things are meant to take time to figure out. You need to be patient. The answer will come to you." She looked at him. He always knew what to say. She put it back in her bag, ready to keep on looking for clues tomorrow.

The shades in the sky were slowly shifting, so they hurried up to the restaurant to get a good table. Ayla brushed off the sand and put on her new beach dress, and Samuel put on his shirt over his beach shorts. They had lost track of time, getting lost in their emotions at the beach, and now I didn't have time to go up to the rooms to change before sunset. But the restaurant was welcoming nonetheless, and they managed to get a good table on the terrace. The front view and a spectacular show that filled the sky with brilliant shades of orange, red, and pink. Ayla always got goosebumps whenever she got to experience a spectacular sunset and today was no exception. Samuel noticed and placed his chair closer to hers so that he could put his arm around her. They watched in silence as the sun slipped away in the distance and ordered as soon as the lights had settled. The romance bathed the aura around their table as they chatted to the moonlight. Ayla was quite happy how the day had turned out and even more grateful that she tagged along, so she got to experience it. She felt completely ready to experience his retreat and learn more about herself, the island, and him.

Elena didn't even get the chance to finish breakfast and take the kids to school before Lucy knocked on the door.

"Pack your bags." She put a magazine in her arms and continued to help herself with some coffee. "Hi, kids. How are you today? Have you had fun at Grandma's in the last weeks?"

"Yeah!" All of them screamed in joy because grandma gave them cookies and ice cream every time they visited, no matter what day it was, especially these days. She then turned to Elena. "We need to leave for Hawaii right now. Like today. "Why, what's such a hurry?"

"Apparently, Zenith Power is going to go to Hawaii to try to convince the local government to give the necessary permits to mine. Given that this is not a precious gemstone, they might as well succeed, but we know that it is precious enough not to be messed with."

"How do you know this?" Elena asked as she flipped through the magazine, looking for clues.

"I have my sources."

"Let me take the kids to school, and then I can call my mom. At this point, she has been doing so much, I'm not sure I can ask her again."

"Well, it's already done. I called her myself on my way over."

"What?" Elena looked shocked. "Ok, what do we do now, then?" "I take the kids to school. You go back upstairs to pack." Lucy flicked her hair and tried to raise the energy in the room, and most importantly, Elena's, "We're going to Hawaii, baby!"

Lucy said and put her hands up in the air and clapped as she hurried out, somehow thinking that she would walk the kids to school in heels. But she confidently took their hands, helped them with their shoes, and walked down the street. Thirty minutes later, she was back and entered the house, still in a high-vibe mood and with her phone in her hand.

"The next flight leaves in less than four hours. Are you finished packing?" She leaned over the railing to yell up towards the second floor. She heard the sound of Elena's footsteps running back and forth, panicking and yelling swear words here and there. She chuckled to herself, thinking how fun it was to put pressure on her friend, but more importantly, to go on a trip together. They hadn't done that since university. She looked at herself in the mirror, adjusted her ponytail as her black silky hair kept falling down. She had a small mascara smear on her lower eyelid and cleared it off with some saliva. She took out lip balm and put some on while admiring her reflection and dancing to a tune in her head.

"Ok, now we really need to go. I'm bored down here!" She yelled again. "Coming! I'm ready, I just need to close it." Elena hurried down the stairs, double-checked her bag to make sure she had her passport, and ticked off items in her head. "Let's go." She laughed, feeling invigorated.

They got into Lucy's car and drove to the airport. They had plenty of time to spare and could check in without any stress. "I didn't know you already had tickets. I thought we were just winging it."

"I didn't. I asked my assistant to buy them while I was waiting for you." She smiled a carefree smile. "Here you go."

"First class? Oh my, I'm taking you are charging the company?"

"I'm not charging the company; I'm putting it on the client's bill." Lucy jokingly did a bit with an evil laugh.

"Sneaky. How are you going to manage that when we're going there to ruin his business?"

"I'll figure out a way. Besides, he doesn't need to know that." Lucy said with confidence.

They went straight to the gate and had the time to amuse themselves in the first-class lounge before it was time to board. Elena eventually got the chance to adjust to the sudden turn her day had taken and felt quite grateful to have such a resourceful and generous friend. They got on the plane and eased into the comfort of their seats. They had quite a fun time on the plane, adding a spark to their friendship with champagne and good movies. A warm welcome after having been out of touch for a whole week. They eventually arrived at the international airport, feeling rested despite the long flight. They were a bit sore from having sat down for so long, but all of their uneasy feelings completely vanished as they stepped outside in the sunny weather. Lucy put her phone on.

"Hey, did you know that we just went back in time? It's Thursday morning again." "Wow, that's cool, I never thought of that before," Elena said, feeling quite happy about that level of productivity.

They looked around and quickly found their chauffeur. Lucy greeted him and gave him their details.

"Your assistant is amazing. I need to remember to thank her later." Elena exclaimed happily. So much luxury in one day.

"Yes, I know. She's the best. I looked this hotel up. I promise you will not be disappointed. It has a gorgeous pool area, a spa, a world-class restaurant, and the rooms look amazing."

"Thank you. I really needed this." Elena said as if she gave Lucy a warm smile. The hotel was just a short drive away. As she got out of the car, she looked up at the grand complex. It was a modern luxury hotel with an authentic design. Very tastefully done. The reception was open air, and any trace of windows and terrace doors was hidden in the walls. It was like a breeze in white and turquoise. The two of them walked up to the reception on the right. There was an ornament with orchids, and they were greeted with the traditional plumeria necklace and a coconut drink.

Very exotic, Elena enjoyed the tropical vibe and went to explore the bar and terrace that were taking center stage, merging with the lounge.

"Let's take a day just resting at the beach, and we will attend to what we came here to do tomorrow." Elena said, looking around in excitement.

"Good idea. We can start by researching this rock and try to locate it tomorrow." Lucy said.

"I love how you are taking care of everything for me, even the things I should be in charge of. Thank you, that is a good plan."

They planted themselves in a lounge chair each and enjoyed the view of the beach and ocean as they sipped on their coconut drinks. Elena thought of how her week had started in such a mess and felt scattered in every direction, and then all of a sudden, everything came together in such a wholesome way, and she was soaking in luxury in paradise. She felt truly grateful. She looked over at her friend and smiled. As they went to their rooms to change, Elena took the opportunity to read up on the rock. Lucy had given her the magazine she had found. Elena flipped through that one and skimmed through an article. It started to sink in that her role here must be bigger than she could imagine. Why would she, of all people, be the one who could heal the rock? She had no apparent connection to this land. She still didn't quite understand what she was meant to be doing. But she was there, and she was ready to surrender to whatever it was that she had to do.

After a full day relaxing in the sun, Elena had gone to bed feeling quite happy with life and woke up in a contented spirit. Lucy knocked on her door as she was getting dressed, and the two went down to the restaurant for a slow, slow brunch in the morning light. The terrace was particularly delightful at this time of day, with the breeze coming through the palm trees and the gentle sound of waves crashing. While enjoying the sun, they looked through the bits of information that they had on the stone.

Elena had found that there was a beach in the south that was covered in stone, so that should be the obvious first stop. They had hired a local guide to help them with their search. He arrived in a small white SUV, wearing a fancy Hawaiian shirt and khaki shorts, looking a lot more suave than the two of them who were in hiking clothes.

"I hope you are up for the day we have in store for you," Elena said in a cheerful Australian accent as she took out her books. "We are on the lookout for this one." She also took out the stone that was in her bag to show him.

"The peridot. We have lots of it. What do you want to do? Where do you want to go?" He asked with an expression that could not hide his wonder. "Well, what's the most important site? I thought that perhaps Papakōlea Green Sand Beach would be a good place to start." Elena said, pointing to one of her brochures. He wanted to ask more, but instead he just said, "Yes. That could work. Let's go there."

"Well, what else is an important place?" Lucy asked

He thought for a moment. "Do you want to buy it or just look at it?" "I want to see where it comes from, look at it and touch it," she said with a firm voice, but could hear herself how odd that sounded.

"Ok." He scratched his head. "I know where to go." He started driving down the coast. It was a beautiful day with a warm breeze coming in from the ocean. Lucy and Elena both sat in silence, resting their eyes and charging their energy for the day ahead. They eventually got to the green beach. The driver stopped the car, and the two women got out. They walked down the hillside to get to the beach. Although their pulse was high, displaying their eagerness to follow their quest, the steep hill meant it took them a while to get down. Eventually, they reached the smooth rock, looking out towards the lime-green grains of sand. They looked like tiny apple candies in the sunlight, and the water from the ocean had a beautiful effect on their smooth, crystal hue. Elena walked down towards the water, sat down, and put her hands in the green gems. She studied how the rocks interacted with her hands. Nothing particular happened; they were just normal. She stood up and looked out towards the ocean. Lucy came up next to her and looked over towards her friend, "What do you think we are supposed to do?"

"I don't know. Nothing is happening. Did we just come all this way to be disappointed?" she asked.

"No, no, we did not. There must be a reason for it. We are probably looking in the wrong place." Lucy looked around to find some other explanation. "Maybe we mistook it for a peridot when it's really something else?" Lucy tried.

"But it's the only rock on the island that is in enough supply could attract an investment of that size," Elena said, feeling puzzled and ready to cry out of disappointment.

"We might have missed some other detail. Let's go back up and find more clues." Lucy tried to console but was herself feeling slightly confused and frustrated. They walked back up to the guide.

"Is there any other site where the stone is exposed like this? Maybe a volcanic site or something like that?"

"I don't know. I don't think so. But we could try the Volcanic Park." He said. They agreed to go there instead. It was not far away, but he drove them there and waited near his car while Lucy and Elena went on a short hike in the park, walking through the caves and trying to experience the various parts of both stone and soil. It was a magnificent experience to be close to such a force of nature. But no matter what they did, nothing seemed quite right. They took a few photos of themselves before they went back, feeling satisfied with the experience but disappointed about the lack of success.

Elena showed it to the guide again. "Are there any likewise men or women who would know about the origin of the stone?" Where it comes from and how it got to the beach. Where is the volcano that made it?"

He looked at her in awe, "The volcano that made it is still active. I'm not sure I can take you there. And, unfortunately, I do not know of any wise men and women who can give you advice. Sorry."

Elena started to feel frustrated. "What are we going to do, Lucy?" she said. "Let's go for lunch and figure out our next move," Lucy said.

They went to a cozy wooden restaurant in the area, ordered a poké bowl each, and sat down on the open-air wooden terrace while looking out towards the horizon over the ocean. It was a pleasant lunch, but both were silent, deep in their own thoughts. Elena eventually spoke. "You know, we really are quite stupid."

Lucy's almond eyes lifted upward in a warm laugh at Elena's honest but funny comment.

"I'm pretty sure we are. Why?"

"Because we went to the place where the rocks are already cleansed and purified by the water. Happy rocks. Then we went to a place where they are nowhere near the surface. Still in the womb of the volcano."

Lucy pondered Elena's statement, took a bite of a mango, and chewed before she answered.

"So, we need to go to the wound. Where it is being taken by force. Do we know where that is?"

"You would know that better than me. Do you know where he is getting the stone from?"

"No, unfortunately, I do not. Let's just head back to the hotel and take the rest of the day to figure out our next move." Lucy said. Elena agreed, so they went back to the guide, who had been waiting further away, and took them back to the hotel to resume the search the next day.

As they walked through the lobby, they noticed that a roll-up had been put on display. Elena went to the reception desk to ask about it.

"It's a retreat that will be held here next week." The receptionist informed. "What kind of a retreat?" she asked.

"I don't know, actually. I think it was something about opening the heart, but I'm not sure. We are just hosting the space. The facilitator is somewhere around here, setting things up."

Lucy had had enough of the quest for one day and had gone to the bar, but Elena had an inner curiosity stirring that needed to be calmed first. She looked around the place and eventually found a tall athletic man with dark brown hair, wearing a light turquoise piké shirt with a logo on it. She walked straight up to him. "Hi, my name is Elena. Sorry to bother you. Are you the initiator of the retreat that is being held here next week?"

"Yes, I am. My name is Samuel." He put his hand out to shake hers before he continued. "The retreat starts on Sunday if you're interested."

"Not really. I am actually here on a bit of a quest. I went to a retreat last weekend, so I wasn't really planning on another. But it looks interesting, so I would like to hear more," she said, pointing towards the roll-up.

"Yeah, it will be great. People are coming from all over the world, so it's going to be a big group, but there is room for more. We will start in the big conference room at the hotel and then move around the island to different sites over the course of four days." He explained.

"That sounds interesting. Is there any particular theme or just general yoga and stuff?"

He laughed, "Not really, no. There will be no yoga at this retreat. We are celebrating Mother Earth and awakening the remembrance of Lemuria. That's why we're visiting different sites around the island."

She looked at him in shock and didn't know what to say at first. "What? That's basically the reason for our trip, too. Except I don't know what Lemuria is, but it sounds interesting." She looked at him, trying to think quickly if she should ask him or not, but eventually she interrupted him again. "Actually, can I perhaps ask for your help with something?" She took the stone out of her bag. "This may sound weird, but the reason why I'm here is to help this rock. I need to find its place of origin so I can help it heal." She heard how crazy that sounded and wrinkled her nose and glanced over at Lucy, who was sitting further away with a piña colada in her hand.

He took it from her hand and held it up to the light.

"It looks like an untreated peridot. But it's the kind that hasn't gone through the stages of purification. It's still in its volcanic crust. While it is a stone that there are plenty of stones on this island, one should never extract them directly from the core. You'll get cursed. Where did you get it?"

"It's a long story. The important part is that I saved it, but I think I need help to figure out what to do next. I thought it would help to go to the site it's from. Do you know where that could be?"

"They are called Pele's tears for a reason," he said. "She cries when they are taken by force. I take it you heard it, too?"

"Yes! Omg, everyone else thought I was crazy." She looked over at Lucy and brimmed with excitement.

Samuel gave it back to her. "I would say you need to go to the Halemaʻumaʻu Crater, which is Pele's home."

"Thank you so so much! I am ever grateful! My friend and I will definitely join your retreat. See you on Sunday!" She hurried back to Lucy, holding up her hands in a victorious dance.

"Wow, that was amazing. I now know where to go."

"Ok, but can we wait for tomorrow, at least? I really want to just sit here and relax for the rest of the afternoon.

"We are so worth it, too. We'll go tomorrow." Elena said as she picked up the drink Lucy had gotten for her and raised her glass.

The morning was fresh when they went down for breakfast the next day. They were both a bit sore from all the walking the day before and even more sore from the drinks. But they were determined to get to the Halemaʻumaʻu Crater before all the tourists got there. This was the type of work that needed a secluded spot and calm energy. They had agreed with the same driver to pick them up after breakfast, and he was waiting for them at the lobby, just as promised. He took them to a market first to get some fruits and flowers to offer to Goddess Pele. One wasn't allowed to visit her home without a gift. They arrived at the site feeling tired but full of anticipation. It was not far to walk, but the ground was uneven, and it was hot. They walked the path that led them around the crater in a circle before taking them close enough for them to feel its raw energy. They placed their offerings and bowed. Elena knelt down to touch the ground beneath her feet. It felt warm and welcoming, and lots of energy streamed up her arms. She stood up and took out the stone from her bag, bowed again as she held it close to her heart, and closed her eyes. She prayed a silent prayer. She actually didn't have any wise words to say, but she tried to get her emotions and intentions to come through. Lucy stood next to her, waiting patiently for Elena to finish whatever it was that she was doing. Elena finally kneeled down again and placed the stone next to her feet, and both her hands next to it. She closed her eyes again and whispered. "We're sorry, we love you" three times. She opened her eyes. Small flickers of green glimmers shimmered under her hands. She kept them steady in place and watched in amazement as it first grew around her hands and then spread out like green veins across the crater. Lucy watched in amazement and knelt down too to try to get a closer encounter of the green shimmering in the ground. Elena started laughing heartily as she looked at Lucy's reaction. It was quite an amazing experience. Soon, the green light had spread across the entire crater and was beating like a heart, creating a mesmerizing shimmer that reminded her of the aurora lights.

The wind was picking up and blowing their hair out of their ponytails. Both turned emotional but couldn't find the right words to express their emotions. But they understood each other and laughed in excitement. It wasn't long until a low-pitched rumble was both felt and heard across the land, and an etheric song echoed in the valley. It wasn't sad, it was joyful.

She had heard it before, and it wasn't frightening. It was enchanting. The etheric voice felt embedded in her memory, like it was the song of her soul. Elena felt an inner peace spread, sensing that she had done something good, even though it was hard to say what she had done exactly at the moment.

For now, she was satisfied with the knowledge that part of their mission was now complete. There was still more to be done, but she could leave the stone here, knowing that her small act of kindness to unite it with its mother would create a ripple effect that was a step along the way to heal Gaia's broken heart.

CHAPTER 15

The Plumeria

They opened their eyes at the same time and were immediately relieved that they were all together. The twelve of them were seated comfortably in armchairs cushioned in exquisite red satin in a room without walls. In its place, tall stone pillars lined the four walls elaborately painted in blue, red, and yellow. Sheer orange curtains danced around them, lending some comfort to the heat. Above them, a ceiling painted in royal blue with a golden sun in its middle, its rays swirling out to each side. The room was perfectly square, and the narrow space that connected the pillars to the roof was painted with sacred symbols and Egyptian deities. "I guess we are in Egypt," Phoebe said and looked at the others. Meira nodded and added, "We must have done a pretty good job if we are all seated together this time." "Quite divinely dressed, too." Jiya added as she admired her dress and jewellery. In the center of two pillars hung a tall mirror, so they all stood up to admire their attire, in awe. Crisp white floor-length gowns embellished with pure gold at the hem. A heavy belt of gold around the waist, decorated with a polished sun and a round necklace braided into a plate with a thousand threads of gold. Around their right arm, a golden spiral and forehead adorned with tiaras, two delicate wings on each side, and a ruby at its middle. "I think we made it." Elena exclaimed joyfully after taking in the view of herself. Her blonde hair had been put up into an elegant bun, but this time, they were not all alike. Each one of them had their natural hair individually expressed in its best light. As they all felt completely satisfied with their exploration of space and themselves, they looked at each other with a vague wonder. "What are we supposed to do now?" Ming asked. "There is no one here to guide us and no apparent path to take." They stepped outside to take in their surroundings. The area around them was lush with green tropical plants and palm trees as far as the eye could see. In the far distance, they noticed the pyramids rising above the landscape and figured that was where they were heading. But the path ahead was not very clear. There were a few steps down towards the white stone pavement that stretched out in every direction. They proceeded to cross the open space, nonetheless, shielded from the sun with a few scattered plantations of palm trees, papyrus, and stargazer lilies. The further they walked across the space, the more greenery surrounded them until they finally stood under the canopies of lush fig trees, forming a paved avenue that was easier for them to follow. They continued navigating towards the pyramids but were soon interrupted at a crossroad, and the sound of rippling water caught their attention. It came from raised rectangular basins stretching out into the distance. They watched the delicate blue lotus flowers dance in the swirls, accompanied by small goldfish. The path graciously revealed itself with every step becoming more beautifully decorated with plants and flowers as they came near an entrance marked by the end of the basin, which continued its path at the other side. But the twelve of them had stopped in the vast open in the avenue and gazed at the sight with amazement. The pavement continued into the distance and led up to a white gate as tall as the statues surrounding it. Two stone Hathors touched the sky in vast magnificence. The gate itself had one large golden sun stretched out over the upper half of it. As they advanced in its direction, they felt increasingly tiny in comparison to its size. Eventually, they stood before it and looked up, no longer in view of its top, but unequivocally sensing its significant essence. Although it was a solid white, it was embellished in gold all the way down to where they were standing. There was no handle, but instead a plate formed like a moon and a sun joined together as one. They all placed their hands on it, and the gate opened, leaving them stunned in their tracks. The courtyard inside was buzzing with feminine voices and figures adorning the space as proudly as the colourful pillars that surrounded them. Just as the last time, they were swiftly greeted by an angel dressed in gold, offering them refreshments after their long walk in the heat. They accepted the drink and placed themselves near a pillar, socialising with one another as they awaited further instructions. It wasn't long, for as the last drops of their drinks cleared, an etheric song echoed from above the stairs, sending a shiver down everyone's spines. "It is time," said an angel as she walked around gathering glasses. The large crowd of women began making their way up the stairs like a swarm of bees, completely covering its surface. Stella, Nora, Danica, Meira, Ming, Phoebe, Ayla, Elena, Jiya, Evelyn, Edith, and Hanwi stayed together and waited for their turn to ascend. It was steep, but not far. Although countless women were moving along with them, they still felt a strong connection amongst themselves. As they reached the top, they admired the architecture for a second before proceeding. A wide paved path lined with grand pillars led up to a tall building. The ground beneath their feet was no longer white but an azure blue that created a carpet continuing all the way up towards the building and up towards its top. Large golden symbols decorated its facade, and even the entrance was framed in gold. The temple stood erect like a tall tower with its top leaning outwards. Their curious eyes continued to study the symbols on the building and the pillars surrounding them as they followed the masses inside. As they made their way through the tall golden entrance, they instantly felt how the air shifted from the heat outside to a calm chill inside. The thick stone walls offered a stillness inside that was scarcely felt in other places. They all walked in silence, looking up at paintings, feeling the intimidating effect of the large blocks of dark stone that led them up a slight slope before the building could properly greet them with a vast corridor framed with blue pillars that were adorned with lapis lazuli. They continued to walk in silence until they reached a grand space, painted blue in its entirety and luxuriously decorated in lapis lazuli on all the walls. But the floor was decorated in a white selenite crystal and adorned in its middle by a large Venus rose in gold. Along the tall walls, the raised stone beds held up not only pillars but on each side were three large statues of Hathor, the seventh behind what appeared to be a raised altar or stage. The room was on a different scale of grandeur, big enough to host all of them comfortably. Voices rose to the ceiling again, and the bounce of sound emphasized the effect of their sheer number, causing most to feel chills and goosebumps. The experience was that of another world to be standing together with so many women in a place like this. As the group made their way to the stage, they noticed that three women were standing at the feet of Hathor, barely visible from afar but notably important. The two to the left were blonde. On the right side were two brunettes. All of them were wearing gowns of Egyptian design but in shades of yellow, and tall golden crowns. In the center, the fifth stood firm in the same attire but with a large headpiece depicting two golden horns cradling a radiant sun disk. She resembled the large Hathor that guarded the room, but her colourful wings gave her away as she spread them out in a gesture to greet them all. But they all stood in stillness as they waited for the crowd to settle. When she finally spoke, her voice was strong but compassionate.

"I am Isis. She of a thousand names. I am a multidimensional sovereign power. Some call me a mighty Goddess, but I accept the title you choose.

I have summoned you here to empower your divine light with codes from ancient times. The chosen temple for this conduct is called the Temple of Love. Next to me stand two powerful goddesses: Inanna, also known as Ishtar; and Aphrodite, to some known as Venus.

The three of us are aspects of the same divine force, carrying our own distinct codes of the divine feminine. I am the pillar of light that binds us together. You were all gathered to walk this journey at the same time for one specific purpose. To restore the frequency of divine love to Earth. Angel Sophia shared her wisdom in your first meeting, and now I will share mine, after which you will take on the role as warrior of light and love. It will not be the end of your journey, but it marks a new beginning. It is a vital steppingstone to reach your inner sacred self. All of you need to be ready for the journey ahead."

No longer will I feel unworthy of the love and aid of any God so wholly connected to me.

My voice will henceforth be free to express my authenticity without fear of judgment

I will not let my own mind fill me with anxiety that separates me from my own power.

I will no longer self-reject or shame myself for any part of my personal power.

I reclaim my sexuality as my own holiness and not a part to be shamed.

I redeem my power over my path as a human, my divinity, and my destiny.

I forgive myself for any limitations, blockages, and stagnations caused by my fears

I forgive myself for belittling my human experience with excuses and victimhood.

I forgive myself for any pain that my fears have caused me or others along my journey.

I allow my love and light to flow freely.

And so, it is. It is done.

As she opened her eyes, Aphrodite and Inanna did the same and looked across the room. Most had begun weeping with the words that she spoke in self-reflection and remembrance of the pain. Isis waited for everyone to feel lighter before she spoke again. The other two then took a step out to stand next to her as they all joined forces to lift the vibration of the room all the way towards the ceiling, where it transformed into light that drizzled down over the crowd, raining over them like drops of glitter. As they held the energy, the glitter continued until every woman was covered. As she slowly waved her colourful wings back and forth, she made an upward motion with both hands stretched out. Over each and every divine feminine, a small light appeared, hovering over her head. They all looked around at each other's lights and felt the kundalini shiver spread across the room like a wave on the ocean.

"You have been awarded the ankh symbol of life. It is sacred and your worthy reward from the divine for completing this part of your journey. Watch as it shines brightly in your soul star chakra. She then turned her palms to face downwards in a gesture that allowed the thousand ankhs to transition from the soul star chakra, down through their crown and rest comfortably in their hearts, where its crystalline light filled the room with a white glow.

I now hold the power of love within."

We are done for tonight, and I will set you free to go back to your consciousness. Use this gift wisely. We will see you again soon.

Elena woke up unexpectedly and suddenly. She looked at the time. It was 4 am. What a dream. She lay in bed for a while, trying to fall back to sleep. She got up and made herself some tea, but as the little teabag tried to spread some joy to her cup, she decided to get dressed instead and go down to the lobby. As a delightful surprise, the terrace was open. She had brought her tea along and sat herself down in one of the armchairs to enjoy the breeze in her face and the sound of the waves. It was soothing. She sat in silence for a while, but soon another woman came down and sat at the far end. "Jetlagged?" Elena said and peeked at her through the leaves of the plant on the floor. "Yes, I think so. Mind if I sit with you?" "Sure, come sit," Elena said and took herself out of her bubble to be able to socialize. The lady came over and sat down with her own cup of tea. She looked at Elena with curiosity, but with an expression as tired as hers. "Where are you from?" Elena asked. "I'm from England. I flew in for the retreat." "Oh, I signed up for that yesterday, too. It was nothing I had planned, though, so I don't know much about it. What made you travel across the world for this retreat?" "Oh, I don't know. I was looking for some place to go where I could reconnect with Mother Earth and ground myself. I looked at other places too, but there was something about the volcanoes and powerful landscape that drew me in."

"I can see that. The energies here are quite strong. Are you here with someone?"

"My husband, but he is asleep upstairs. He handled the jetlag better than me."

"Nice. I'm here with a friend." Elena sat in silence for a few moments and tried to think of more things to say, but her tired mind interrupted her thoughts. "The tea had an effect. I think I'll go back to my room and try to go back to sleep."

"Ok, I will see you later."

Elena went back upstairs, and after just a few tosses, she managed to fall asleep again. Three more hours of deep sleep did wonders, and she woke up feeling refreshed. But it was Lucy's knocking that had woken her up. "Are you ready?"

"Oh, sorry, I just woke up. I had a rough night. You can go down for breakfast. I'll be down in a minute," Elena said and closed her door again. She wanted to go back to bed, but got help from the shower instead of waking up. They had a full day ahead, so she did not have time for more sleep.

Lucy was sitting in the back today, as the breakfast was crowded with hungry tourists. Elena joined her and said as she sat down, "Let's start with the Cultural Center. I haven't heard back from the Environmental Center, but I will try to call them again. It's the weekend, so maybe we need to wait until Monday. Have you heard back from the Trade Office?" "They just answered my e-mail that they were not the right institution for this type of issue. I'm thinking we stick to those who can help us get the ball rolling so we can leave it with them." She took out her list and skimmed through it. "I think we have what we need."

They finished their breakfast in a hurry and hailed a cab to go into the city. An older Polynesian man greeted them at the Cultural Center, shook their hands politely, and invited them inside. Looking around, they immediately felt like they had gone to the wrong place. The building was modern but modest in its aesthetic, but the man was warm and charismatic.

"Now, tell me more about the issue, and I will see how I can help you." He said, sensing that they were out of place. Lucy took out her information, summarized her findings, and showed him some photos on her iPad. He looked troubled and scratched his head. "This is a big problem, indeed. Very disturbing. Thank you for alerting me." He leaned back on his chair and crossed his arms as he pondered the problem. "I think you need to do three things. First, you need to get hold of an environmental institution that has the power to stop this contract from happening. I have a connection there. I will give them a call and see what I can do. The second is to find a local environmental group that can help you continue with the fight. And third, is to get help from the kahunas, Hawaii's wise women." Elena was quick to answer, "I like that, let's start there. How do we get in touch with them?"

"We are the Cultural Center, after all, so I have their information." He got up and went into his office to find a phone number. "Call this woman. She will tell you what to do."

They thanked him and left. Lucy was multitasking, searching on her phone as she walked back to the street. "There are several, all of them sound plausible candidates for this task. I'll just contact them all. Did you get hold of the wise women?" She looked up towards Elena, who was on the phone. She hung up with a smile. "She said she wants to meet us now." A new cab pulled up and took them to a charming bungalow that was painted green. The kahuna greeted them at the door. Wearing a long white kapa dress with several large crystal necklaces and a few bangles, she lived up to the sanctity of her profession. They sat down in the lounge. She offered them some tea, which they gladly accepted. Lucy took out her information again and showed it to her. The woman put her hand to her heart in shock and immediately whispered something towards the sky. "That is dreadful news. One must never steal from Pele. Let's do a ceremony together to pray for it all to stop and that the stones can find their way home. She stood up to prepare some herbs and incense, then took them through to the big meditation room, a large space with more green walls and big windows facing the back garden. Elena and Lucy sat down in lotus position on the large straw mat, and the kahuna sat in front of them, gesturing in the air, creating a sacred flow with the incense. She took out a big green peridot crystal that had been purified and a big black piece of the raw material. She placed them next to each other, picked up a bowl of incense, and began gesturing over it with an ama'u leaf as she sang a powerful song. Elena felt the intense energies of the room and closed her eyes to take in the melody. She tried to the best of her ability to do her own prayer. She didn't know much about Pele, but she did the best she could to focus her mind on her. After the ceremony was over, they thanked her and walked out again, feeling how their own energies had clearly shifted. They felt more optimistic now, and rightfully so. Lucy looked at her phone and saw that both the Environmental Center and a few of the groups had already answered. But both she and Elena were too tired at this point. She wrote back to set up a meeting the following week, and the two of them decided to call it a day and go back to the hotel. They ended up spending most of the afternoon under a parasol on the beach, awaiting the time of the retreat.

Phoebe and Gabriel had gotten in late last night and slept through any trace of morning, waking up in full sunlight, both woke up squinting their eyes. Phoebe hurried to pull the curtains so they could get some more sleep. They had no proper plan for today, so they decided to sleep off their fatigue and went to breakfast just minutes before it closed.

They sat down on the terrace and enjoyed the sunlight and gentle morning breeze.

"Where do you want to go first?" Gabriel asked, "I don't know, actually. maybe we can do some sightseeing and then go to the beach."

"Shouldn't we focus on the quest? We're so close."

"But we also need to enjoy the moment. We are both so tired from all the travelling. Maybe if we stop chasing the answer, the answer will come to us," she said, feeling satisfied with her pineapple juice.

He looked at her as she drank, trying to make up his mind, "Alright, you win. It's your call, and we are not in a hurry, I guess. Where do you want to go, then?"

"I'm not sure, let's go to the reception after breakfast and ask them." After breakfast, they walked through the lobby as suggested to get ideas. Phoebe noticed a large sign promoting a retreat. she looked at the images of turtles, palm trees, and volcanoes as she tried to make out what it was exactly. She asked the receptionist instead, "What's this?" "Oh, it's just a retreat that is starting later today," the receptionist answered casually. "What is it about?"

"I'm not sure exactly, I believe it's some Hawaiian ceremonial thing to celebrate Mother Earth," the receptionist said, looking unsure about her answer, and getting back to Gabriel about his question.

"There are several things you can do in the area if you want to explore the culture. You can go to Hulihe'e Palace,

Kamehameha Statue, or perhaps the Pu'uhonua o Hōnaunau National Historical Park, or perhaps the Volcanic Park if you're up for a bit of adventure. We also have Lei Day coming up later this week. Here is a good brochure that lists everything you need to know." Gabriel thanked her, took the brochure, and walked over to Phoebe, who was still studying the promotional sign.

"Babe, we need to do this," she said assertively.

"Oh, come on. I don't want to meditate and stuff. Let's check these places out and pick one." He nodded his head slowly as he tried to convince her.

"You can do all that if you want, but I think I need to do this."

He sighed in defeat. "Fine, if it's important to you, I'll go. When does it start?" "Don't look so sad. It says that this is just a couple of hours a day, and it doesn't start until 4 pm, so we have time to do other things. Give me just a minute to try to get hold of the people hosting this thing." She sat down in an armchair in the lobby to call the number while he took out his phone and started searching for the tourist spots. She interrupted him shortly after with a big smile, "I have now booked us." He smiled back and looked back on his phone. "I think this place would be a good place to start understanding the culture," he said, and showed her his phone. She looked at the images of the large stone figures by the ocean. "Yes, that's a good place." They went back to their room to get their things. Phoebe put the blue rose in her purse, in case the energies felt right.

As they got out of the taxi at the site, Phoebe stopped to take a deep breath of the ocean air. It was a beautifully located site, pulsating with energy, but she closed her eyes and calibrated her inner peace before she started walking towards the shoreline lined with black volcanic rocks. The palm trees danced in the wind, and the ocean crashed against the rocks. The sounds of the elements were mesmerizing. Gabriel had stopped by a vendor to buy water while she had closed her eyes for a second to take it all in. They resumed the walk together, following the shoreline towards some buildings. They eventually reached the buildings, read up about their usage, and the cultural history of the place. As they walked around, Phoebe felt a growing connection to the site. Once she noticed the tall statues, she paused to look at them with all of her senses. She informed Gabriel that they needed to walk around a little bit to explore the whole park before returning to the site. So, they did and returned almost an hour later. It was midday, and the heat had caused a drop in tourists, so very few were close to them. She looked around before she took out the rose and placed it in the sand in the middle of the group of statues. It lit up, and sparks of light surrounded it for a moment. There was no big show with a light pillar, but it was grand, nonetheless. She let it stay in the sand for a while, Gabriel leaning over it to lower the risk of being seen. Phoebe studied the vibrancy of the light, and as it dimmed, she attempted to pick it up but ended up getting burned. She quickly reacted to the scorching heat and put her finger to her mouth to tend to the wound. She stared at Gabriel with a questioning look, but he looked just as puzzled. "What just happened exactly?" she said, "Did the sand cause the heat?" "No, that's not possible. The sand is cold." She let it stay put for now as she searched for clues. First by studying the lights, then by closing her eyes and listening to her heart. "Look, look," Gabriel shouted, causing Phoebe to open her eyes again. The blue rose had caught fire. He grabbed for his water bottle in his backpack, but Phoebe stopped him and shouted. "Don't put it out! It is meant to burn." She closed her eyes and added in a whisper, "Goddess Pele is reviving ancient knowledge about Lemuria and healing the timeline. Her fire purifies and strengthens. We should let it be until it burns out." He looked at her, impressed, and sat back down to watch the fire together with Phoebe. When Phoebe picked it up again, the metal was returned to a cool state, but edged in the rock underneath was the trinity knot and the triangle, leaving a permanent mark on the site. She felt bad about it at first, then realized that Pele had done it herself. She put the rose back in her bag and stood up, looking at Gabriel to help her figure out their next move. "I think our work here is done for now. Let's go back to the hotel and spend a few hours by the pool before the retreat starts." He agreed and stood up as well, kissed her softly on her forehead, and hugged her as he said, "You did good."

Ayla had struggled to fall back to sleep after the powerful dream. She remembered receiving a lot of information, the smell of myrrh, and all the palm trees. She wrote down everything that immediately came to her and figured she would be reminded during the day about all the details. She got dressed and went to knock on Samuel's door. He was ready, so they headed down to breakfast together.

"What do you want to do before the retreat starts? Is there something I can help you with, or do you possibly have time to go to the beach?"

"The other facilitators are arriving at 3 pm. All I have to do before then is pick up fresh lei necklaces. Everything else is set. So, we have a couple of hours to relax. I do need your help with checking off the list of participants, if that's ok?" "Sure, no problem."

As they sat down with their breakfast, she stared towards the horizon to gather her thoughts about the day. "I think I would like to do some sort of tourist attraction with dolphins today. It bothers me that I can't figure out the dolphin symbol on the back of the compass. I would like to have an encounter to see if something comes up.

"There is a place on the other side of the island that takes you by boat to a bay where you can swim with them in their true habitat. It takes just a couple of hours. If we eat quickly, we will have time to go without stress." He picked up his phone and booked the trip as he ate.

Stepping into the boat made her heart flutter. Its soft clucking sounds towards the dock unleashed a childhood memory, while the anticipation of seeing a dolphin in real life filled her emotions. She quickly picked a seat along the sides of the boat, and Samuel sat down beside her. The other tourists stepped aboard, and the guide walked them through the tour, procedures, and safety before taking the wheel. Ayla watched the movements of the water with excitement and put her hand out to drench it in the blue hues. A few dolphins appeared over the surface, swimming with the boat. She looked at Samuel with pure joy, and he smiled back and hugged her stomach in affection. The drive was sweet but short, and soon they reached the bay. She was quick to put on the snorkeling set that the guide handed out and flung herself into the sea. The dolphins had learned the routine of tourists and quickly joined them to socialize. There was no end to Ayla's excitement as she swam next to them and gently touched their fins. Then a few of them started talking and singing, and it immediately had a profound effect on her heart chakra. It felt like she had been hit with an intense stream of light codes, putting slight pressure on her heart chakra. The sensation echoed throughout her body, but while it was a wonderful feeling, it was also scary. She decided to get out of the water to rest on the boat for a few minutes. She watched Samuel as he snorkeled with the group, enjoying himself as much as Ayla. He eventually noticed she had gone up and approached the boat to ask her about it. "The songs of the dolphins had a scary effect on my heart chakra, so I'm just resting a little, but I will go back soon. Not to worry." She took a sip of water and glanced towards her backpack on the seat. 'Maybe it's the reason for the symbol,' she thought, and took the compass out. She placed it securely on her belly in her swimsuit and returned to the ocean. It wasn't long until one dolphin came up to her, nudging her gently with its nose. Another made a few twirls in the water, and the rest started swimming around her as they whistled, sang, and clicked at a high frequency. She reached out her hands to touch them as they swam past her. She felt amazed but a little scared at first, unsure how to handle this sort of interaction with wild animals. Samuel swam up to her to make sure that she was ok. She told him that she was fine but quickly came to the conclusion that the energies were too intense and that she needed to get out. Samuel got up on the boat and helped her up, too. She sat down on her seat again and fished out the compass from her swimsuit. The Venus rose was magenta pink, and the golden ball was now moving freely, going around and around as it traced the carved web. Samuel looked over his shoulder to get the status of the other tourists. Ayla turned it over, and almost as expected, the dolphin on its back was now glowing in magenta pink too. That was all they had time for before the guide and the other tourists climbed back onto the boat. Ayla quickly wiped it on her towel and put it back in her bag, keeping it out of sight until they reached the hotel, where she quickly took it out again and placed it on the desk. It had gone back to its original state, but she looked at it. Samuel sat on the bed, curious to learn more.

"This is not a compass to guide towards a destination in space. Its purpose is to guide towards a state of being, help me find and hold the frequency of sacred truth."

"Any idea of where to find the sacred truth?" he said, looking at her in astonishment.

"I have already received the codes in my dream last night. I think my mission now is to anchor them," she said as she looked him in the eye. He kissed her and said, "You, my love, are an extraordinary woman. Thank you for sharing this with me." He then left to get ready for the retreat. Ayla decided to take a bath and fantasize about her adventures and the beautiful man who had suddenly entered her life.

It was a beautiful round building in the middle of the hotel complex, standing alone near the ocean. Samuel had opened all the windows to allow the air and the sounds to rush through the site. The other facilitators were arriving and helped him to finish setting up the space, with all the drinks and snacks.

As they attuned their instruments, Ayla skimmed through the guest list. Some of the names sounded familiar. She went to ask Samuel, "Is this the complete list?" "Two people joined last minute this morning, so that should add up to twenty-eight even," he answered.

She clicked her pen. "Alright, are the last two already on the list, or should I print another one?"

"They should be there." He skimmed the list and pointed to their names. Ayla got a chill down her back that she couldn't quite explain. She grabbed herself some tea and sat down on a sunbed, looking out over the ocean. She wanted to give herself the space to recalibrate but noticed that some people were already walking towards the venue.

She stood up again and approached the door, holding her clipboard.

"Hi. Welcome to the retreat. Can I take your name?"

Lucy was the one who answered, as Elena just smiled and entered the building. They were greeted by one of the facilitators, who placed a Lei around their necks and offered them some refreshing drinks.

Ayla had sat herself down again as she waited for more people to arrive. She managed to regain her strength before a big group arrived, and she hurried to get everyone's names and check them off the list. She hardly had time to look up. Soon, the room was filled with people. She looked inside to see what was happening. Everyone seemed to have scattered and were standing in different corners of the room. Samuel was walking around the room, greeting them, trying to make them feel comfortable. He came out to check on her. "It was a bit stressful when they all arrived at once, but I'm ok. We're just waiting for the last two." "Ok, let's give them a few minutes. Maybe they had difficulty finding it."

Before long, two figures came running towards them, panting as they finally reached the entrance.

"So sorry we're late. I'm the one who called this morning. We thought it was at the other end of the complex." Phoebe was breathing heavily and coughed before she continued.

"There is no rush. Take your time to settle down. There are drinks inside," Samuel said.

Ayla looked at her and checked off their names. Phoebe followed her movements and studied her face with an odd sensation.

"Do we know each other? I feel like we have met before." Phoebe said, trying to recall where that could have been.

"I believe we might. I recognize you, too, but I can't figure out where." Ayla smiled at her and ushered them both inside and took her place amongst the others. All twenty-eight of them had managed to form one big circle and were now looking at each other while waiting for things to start. Ayla looked at the other men and women in the room. They had come from all over the world. Some had joined intentionally for this retreat, and others had joined at the last minute. She wondered silently what was so special about it, but she also felt the kundalini that was already taking a grip on her spine. There was something in the air.

A woman started the ceremony.

"Good afternoon, everyone."

I am so happy to see so many people here with us today. My name is Melissa, and I am one of the key facilitators of this retreat, together with Samuel over there. We're also joined by Healani, our lead vocalist and musician."

As she spoke, Elena made eye contact with one of the women. She had long grey hair and piercing blue eyes. She felt like she had seen her before. "Maybe she's an influencer?" She tried to convince herself. She looked at Lucy, who was standing next to her. She noticed her gaze and gave her a small shove with her hand. "Focus", she said jokingly.

Melissa stopped talking, and Healani took the stage. He began by blowing a Pu.

Elena had never heard that sound before. It really travelled to the core.

"Oh my, that sound is quite effective," Phoebe exclaimed and tried to shake it off discreetly. She didn't want to seem impolite and glanced at Gabriel to see his reaction.

But he just looked at her with a funny expression on his face.

Healani started chanting in a high pitch as Melissa played a rhythmic tune on the singing bowls. They switched, allowing Melissa to share her voice as Healani played on a wooden harmonica. The mood that spread throughout the room was quite enchanting. While Healani was still singing, Melissa began swaying from side to side, ushering the others to dance on the spot while joining in her chant to sing the words ho'oponopono a couple of times to ask for forgiveness, reconciliation, and gratitude. They all swayed to the sides, feeling the joy rise in the room. She added to her chant

I'm sorry.
Please forgive me
Thank you
I love you

and told them to repeat them with her as they continued to loosen up their bodies in a rhythmic dance. After a few minutes, they stopped the music and Melissa introduced herself. "We are here for this retreat to spend the next three days together in order to attune ourselves to our mind, body, and soul and pay tribute to Pele and Gaia.

So, I want to start the ceremony with a traditional honi. It's an ancient ritual where we share a breath with the person next to us to connect the circle and create one life force for everyone who is co-creating in this space. Melissa and Healani started the ritual by passing it on to each other, then sent the energy across the room, watching as each person pressed their forehead towards their neighbour, sharing a "ha" breath, turning to the next neighbour, allowing themselves to both give and receive the united energy. Healani was drumming his pahu the whole time, creating a grounding vibe that echoed throughout the space. Ayla was standing next to the last, and Samuel was last. But as the force reached full circle, the room went completely quiet. Healani stopped his drumming. The air was thick. They watched each other with the same horrified look as you would give a ghost. Eyes wide open, holding their breaths. Heavy in fear but thrilling to the senses. Their hearts were beating heavily, causing a throbbing pulse in their temples. The stillness of the inaudible tension made the others in the room highly uncomfortable, but they waited patiently to learn more about what was going on. Lucy glanced at Elena and tried to piece together what was happening. They were all there. Ayla looked at Phoebe, who looked at Elena, who looked at Evelyn, passing the terrorized gaze on to Meira, Jiya, Akira, Danica, Nora, Edith, Stella, and Ming. They were all there. All twelve of them were in the same room.

After a few minutes of silence, Ayla finally regained her voice and turned to Samuel,

"I think we need to take a break to understand what just happened."

www.ingramcontent.com/pod-product-compliance
Lightning Source LLC
Chambersburg PA
CBHW031202310726

48969CB00001B/184